CARRIER

Book Nine
ARCTIC FIRE

Keith Douglass

JOVE BOOKS, NEW YORK

CARRIER 9: ARCTIC FIRE

A Jove Book / published by arrangement with the author

PRINTING HISTORY
Jove edition / June 1997

All rights reserved.
Copyright © 1997 by Jove Publications, Inc.
Excerpt from *A Flash of Red* copyright © 1996 by Clay Harvey.
This book may not be reproduced in whole or in part,
by mimeograph or any other means, without permission.
For information address: The Berkley Publishing Group,
200 Madison Avenue, New York, New York 10016.

The Putnam Berkley World Wide Web site address is
http://www.berkley.com

ISBN: 0-515-12084-7

A JOVE BOOK®
Jove Books are published by The Berkley Publishing Group,
200 Madison Avenue, New York, New York 10016.
JOVE and the "J" design are trademarks
belonging to Jove Publications, Inc.

PRINTED IN THE UNITED STATES OF AMERICA

10 9 8 7 6 5 4 3 2 1

CHAPTER 1
Sunday, 25 December

Russian Colonel Kamir Rogov braced himself against the icy side of the Kilo diesel submarine's conning tower. Five hundred meters away, the snow and ice-covered island loomed forbiddingly. Forty-knot winds kicked up loose snow, at times reducing visibility to less than the distance of the island.

Even as he felt the cold cut through the wool scarf wrapped around his face, he welcomed the chance to escape the cold, dark confines of the submarine. After three weeks underway, submerged most of the time, the stench of cooking, diesel fuel, and too many humans packed in too small a space had grown almost unbearable.

"Almost ready, Comrade Colonel," the submarine's skipper said.

Rogov acknowledged the report with a sharp nod of his head and glanced down at the yellow inflatable raft slamming into the submarine's side. The weather was barely within minimum standards for attempting to launch the raft from the submarine, but there was no help for that.

1

Nothing could be permitted to delay this mission—
nothing.

A young sailor poked his head out from the small
igloo-shaped craft, which had a superstructure of domed
plastic to provide some protection from the wind. The
sailor looked pale and queasy after only five minutes
inside the bobbing boat. He waved to attract his captain's
attention, then nodded, making a thumbs-up gesture. The
captain turned back to Rogov.

"Now, sir?"

"*Da.*" Rogov turned and looked down the open hatchway behind him. He made a come-along motion with his
hand. The Spetsnaz commander smiled up at him, an
unholy look of glee under the circumstances, and started
up the ladder. The four other Russian Special Forces
soldiers were crowded around the base of the ladder,
chivying for their turn to escape the metal hull.

Russian Spetsnaz, trained and groomed for offensive
operations anywhere in the world. This cadre was a
select group, each member chosen not only for his
technical skills and aggressiveness, but because of one
other important characteristic: his Cossack blood.

Did the Russians even suspect? Rogov wondered. No,
they couldn't—wouldn't. It would not occur to them that
there could be loyalties stronger than to Mother Russia at
work within the military, especially not in the prestigious
Spetsnaz ranks. But the Cossacks had preserved their
ancient warrior ways, remembering their heritage from
Ukraine and gentler climates even during the centuries of
their forced resettlement to frigid Mongolia. While their
Russian masters grudgingly treasured those racial characteristics that had earned the Cossacks their fearsome
reputation for savagery, filling the ranks of their hard-

ened shock troops with members of the tribe, they'd never fully accepted the Cossacks. Nor returned the land stolen from them so long ago.

No matter, Rogov decided. If this mission succeeded, there would be no turning back. The Cossacks would earn—take by force, if necessary—their rightful place as masters of their continent.

Clad in heavy parkas and winter gear, carrying bulky packs on their backs, the Spetsnaz Cossacks barely made it through the narrow hatch. The conning tower was crowded now, and reeked of the submarine's stench.

"Your men are ready?" Rogov asked.

The Spetsnaz commander took in a deep breath of the fresh air, his smile deepening. "Spetsnaz is always ready, Comrade." He looked out at the distant island, then down at the bobbing raft. "A challenge—our specialty."

"Then no more delays. Let's get underway."

The submarine captain motioned to the young sailor. The man clambered out carefully, reaching for the steel-runged ladder attached to the side of the submarine. As his one hand closed over the first ice-covered rung, a wave slammed into the submarine, rolling it away from the man.

With his balance already committed to the move, he didn't have a chance. He teetered for a second on the edge of the raft, leaned forward, and almost caught himself on the rope that ran through on steel loops outside of the raft. His hand closed on it briefly.

The submarine captain slapped the man standing next to him on the back and shouted to be heard over the rising wind. The lookout nodded and started down the ladder to assist his shipmate.

Before he'd moved down two rungs, hypothermia

claimed the other sailor's consciousness. His hand clenched on the ice-coated rope, then relaxed. A wave washed over his head, and the suction from the submarine's seawater intake valves pulled him away from the raft.

The lookout stopped two rungs down and looked back up to his captain, stricken. The captain motioned him to return to the conning tower. Trying to retrieve the dead sailor's body would be an impossible task in the freezing waters of the North Pacific.

Rogov turned to the Spetsnaz commander. "A reminder."

"We know our job." The Spetsnaz reached for the first steel rung and pulled himself over the side of the submarine. He paused, his head just above the level of the conning tower. "Be careful, Comrade Colonel. There are things here more dangerous than the ocean."

Rogov grunted. "Such as?"

"Me." The Spetsnaz commander took one hand off the ladder to motion to his companions. "And them."

Rogov impaled him with a look colder than the frigid air swirling about them. "There are some things more powerful than muscle and bone," he said softly. "You would be wise not to forget that."

The Spetsnaz commander shrugged, then started down the ladder. As he entered the small raft, he looked back up at Rogov. "But where we're going, Comrade Colonel," he continued, pointing at the barren island behind him, "I think you'll find that that's what matters."

Tomcat 201
15,000 Feet
South of Attu Island, Aleutians

Lieutenant Curt "Bird Dog" Robinson scowled at the
ocean, the sky, and the clear hard plastic aircraft canopy
overhead. From this altitude, he should have been able to
see a fair stretch of the Aleutians stretched out beneath
him. The island chain, formed from volcanic activity
eons ago as the tectonic plates of the earth shifted in their
slow orbits, jutted up from the Pacific Ocean, stretching
from the southwestern tip of Alaska to the eastern edge
of Russia. Earlier today, during a rare moment when the
weather had cleared, he'd been able to see most of the
United States' westernmost territory.

But not now. He felt the aircraft rock under his butt,
and compensated for the turbulence automatically. The
F-14 Tomcat responded smoothly to his touch, the low
growl of its engines almost a satisfied purr. Despite his
foul mood, Bird Dog smiled with the sheer pleasure of
feeling 61,000 pounds of aircraft respond like an exten-
sion of his own body. The marriage between a fighter
pilot and his aircraft was the closest thing to heaven he'd
ever experienced with his clothes on. And, he had to
admit, it lasted a lot longer that most anything else that
came close. At least in a Tomcat you could always refuel
and stay airborne.

Not that he was all that certain he wanted to right now.
Fifteen minutes earlier, one of the infamous williwaws
had blown in. The wild northern storms, born out of the
interaction between the relatively warm Japanese current

and the frigid arctic waters it flowed into, generated fearsome brutal winds capable of reaching a hundred knots in minutes. The battle between the two masses of water also generated the thick, impenetrable fog already curling up the sides of the rocky islands. Now, only the highest cliffs peeked out of the white blankness below him.

The lousy weather wasn't the only reason for his foul mood. Even if he *did* prefer flying to almost anything else, there were some limits to his obsession. "Damn, Gator, why the hell did we get stuck pulling Alert Five on Christmas Day?" Bird Dog asked for the third time.

"You *ought* to be out here, shipmate," Lieutenant Commander Charlie "Gator" Cummings said wearily from the backseat. "Me—I'm senior to most of the other NFOs in the squadron. If I weren't stuck with such a junior pilot for a partner, I'd still be in my rack sleeping off that huge meal last night."

"Yeah, yeah, yeah, that line's getting real old," Bird Dog snapped. "You think it's fun being a lieutenant?"

"You think it's fun flying with one?"

Bird Dog sighed. There was no way he could win this argument. Gator was right—the junior members of the squadron *did* pull the worst duty on the ship.

"Whales," he said out loud. "I joined the Navy to fly against MiGs, not to stand by to buzz Greenpeace boats."

"Would have thought you'd gotten enough of that on our last cruise."

"That was something, wasn't it?" Bird Dog said reflectively. "MiG-29's, F-11 Chinese fighters—hell, that's the most fun I've ever had with my clothes on."

And it had been. On their last cruise, his first deployment on board a carrier as a full-fledged naval aviator, the USS *Jefferson* had intervened in a nasty eastern Asian squabble over oil rights to the Spratly Islands. The North Koreans and the Chinese had teamed up to conduct an impressive exercise in operational deception. The Chinese had attacked and destroyed several of their own base camps perched on the tiny rocks and shoals that made up the Spratly Islands, hoping to convince the rest of the Pacific Rim nations that the United States was behind the aggression. Fortunately, Rear Admiral Matthew Magruder, "Tombstone" to his fellow aviators, had figured it out, and managed to put together a coalition of fighter squadrons from the other nations to expose and repel the Chinese marauders.

"Bet Tombstone is freezing his ass off right about now, too," Bird Dog said. "ALASKCOM—colder'n hell up there, too, isn't it?"

"I've got a radar paint on the Greenpeace boats," Gator announced. "Should be about fifty miles ahead of us."

"Well, let's go give them their daily taste of naval aviation. Probably the most fun they have while they're out here in this godforsaken ocean."

Bird Dog yanked the F-14 into a sharp turn.

"Hey, was that really necessary?" Gator asked sharply, grunting as he performed the M-1 maneuver, designed to force blood into the extremities of an aviator during high-G operations. The sudden turn had caught him by surprise, and his vision had started to gray out at the edges.

"Sorry. Just trying to remind you what it's like to be tactical."

"Yeah, well, we're sure as hell not going to need it against a Greenpeace boat."

"That's what we thought about that tank in the Spratlys, isn't it?" Bird Dog reminded him. "Remember? That damned old Soviet tank, sitting all by itself out on that rock in the middle of the ocean. And those poor guys—whenever I think I have it rough on the carrier, I remember those two guys sittin' on top of the tank, about six feet above the waves."

"I remember the Stinger missiles," Gator responded. "Though it took me a while to convince you that you ought to be thinking about them, too."

"I've got a visual on them. Let's slow down a little, mark on top for a few minutes and take some pictures."

"'Kay. I'm ready," Gator said.

Bird Dog took manual control of the mechanism controlling the sweep-back wings on his aircraft. Normally, he would allow the computer to select the appropriate position—swept back along the fuselage for power and speed, or extended to provide maximum lift for getting airborne. The awkward configuration of the extended wing structure was what gave the Tomcat its affectionate nickname of "Turkey."

"Two hundred knots—that's about as slow as I want to go," Bird Dog said. "Stall speed is only a hundred and forty knots at this weight."

"You sure as hell better keep us airborne, shipmate, because that water ain't that inviting. Survival time is about fifteen seconds."

Bird Dog put the Tomcat into a gentle arc, two hundred feet above the ship ahead of them. "Now, don't you go worryin', Gator. I got you back last time, didn't I?"

Gator muttered something incomprehensible under his breath.

"Besides, there's no way those Greenpeace boats are carrying Stingers," Bird Dog continued. "I mean, what the hell—what would that do for their image as peaceful ecologists?"

"They care about endangered bobcats, not Tomcats."

Bird Dog sighed. "Let's just take the pictures and get out of here. I want to do a few barrel rolls and some acrobatics on the way back to the ship."

"Just stay away from that damned cruiser this time, okay? I put up with that all last cruise, and I'm not going to do that again. Gets old, standing tall in front of CAG and explaining why I let the junior lieutenant driving my bird pretend to be an incoming missile for an Aegis cruiser."

"Sure got their attention, though, didn't it?" Bird Dog chuckled. "You RIOs have no idea of how to have fun."

Bird Dog put the Tomcat into a lazy port turn, increasing the angle of bank so he could get a good look at the ship below them. The converted fishing trawler was skirting the edge of the fog bank, plowing heavily through the rough seas. While the churning yaw and pitch looked damned dangerous, the SS *Serenity*'s deep draft let her bite through confused swells that would have capsized a much larger vessel.

The boat looked well-maintained and neat, from what he could see. There was no debris littering the deck, where lines and rope lay neatly coiled. A thin coating of ice over the superstructure and weather decks reflected the sun, occasionally generating a bright, painful flash of light. Its hull was green, its railing and fixtures painted white. A rainbow graced the starboard bow. From one mast a Greenpeace ecological flag flapped briskly in the wind. No one was visible on deck—not surprising,

considering the weather. Bird Dog dropped the aircraft
down to 150 feet and peered at the glass-enclosed bridge.
He thought he could pick out two figures moving inside.

"You finished?" he asked Gator.

"One more shot. There, I've got it. Let's head for
home."

"Your wish is my command," Bird Dog answered. He
let the Tomcat roll around the final arc of the circle, then
broke off the turn to vector back toward the aircraft
carrier, now out of sight. "I'll let Mother know we're
headed home." He keyed the tactical circuit. "Homeplate, this is Tomcat Two-oh-one, inbound."

"Roger, Tomcat Two-oh-one. Say state?" The operations specialist, or OS, on the other end asked.

Bird Dog glanced down at the fuel gauge. "We're fine,
homeplate. Six thousand pounds."

"Roger, Two-oh-one. Tanker airborne in ten mikes,"
the operator replied. "I hold you on radar now."

Bird Dog switched off the tactical circuit and keyed
the ICS, the interior communications switch. "Nice to
know they have such confidence in my ability to get back
on board," he said to Gator.

"Don't take it personal," the RIO replied. "The last
thing we want to happen is to get low on gas out here.
Not much place to bingo."

"Yeah, but I've got plenty of fuel for two passes at the
boat. What, they don't think my track record's so hot?"

He heard his RIO sigh. "They've launched a tanker for
every returning flight in the last two days, asshole. If you
think you're such hot shit, maybe I'd better find me
another pilot. Nothing kills air crews faster than over-
confidence."

"Well, when was the last time I did anything except

get on board first time and catch the three-wire?" Bird Dog argued.

"I'm just saying, it's a normal—wait, what's that?" Gator said.

"What?"

"Radar contact—way down to the south, maybe a hundred miles. It wasn't there before," Gator said, a note of excitement coloring his usual professional monotone.

"Probably another fishing boat. What's the big deal?"

"I'm telling you, it wasn't there before. Now it's solid. You know what that means."

"A submarine? You're calling a pop-up contact a submarine up here? Jesus, Gator, you sure as hell must be bored. What the hell would a submarine be doing surfaced out here?"

"That's the whole point, Bird Dog. It shouldn't be. Snorkeling, maybe, if it's a diesel recharging its batteries, but no submariner in his right mind would surface out here. For what? To get a good look at an iceberg?"

Just then the voice of the operations specialist on the *Jefferson* came over the circuit. "Tomcat Two-oh-one, we're holding your contact approximately two hundred to the east of us, one hundred miles from your position. Request you vector back to *Jefferson*, take on fuel, and investigate."

Bird Dog sighed. No point in complaining that it was Christmas Day, that he really would prefer to be asleep in his rack instead of chasing sea ghosts, or that he was now desperately wishing he hadn't had those two cups of coffee before they launched. He toggled the tactical switch. "Okay, okay, we're on our way in."

"Better than buzzing Greenpeace, isn't it?" Gator asked.

"Would be if I didn't have to pee so bad. But as cold as it is out there, I'm afraid I'm gonna get stuck in a real embarrassing, personal sort of way if I use the relief tube."

Gator laughed. "Come on, Bird Dog, those are just old sea stories. It's not like touching your tongue to an ice cube tray."

"Yeah, well, you try it with *yours* first," Bird Dog snapped. He gazed down at the relief tube, conveniently mounted and accessible to the pilot. While most of the time he appreciated the convenience, since he despised the piddle-packs the Hornet drivers had to use, he was damned uncomfortable at the thought now. Holding the Tomcat in level flight with one hand, he stripped off a glove and touched the relief tube. It was icy cold, just as he'd feared.

"Not much better than a Coke bottle," he grumbled.

"I told you to go before we left home," Gator said solemnly, in a tone he normally reserved for his three-year-old daughter. He gave a short bark of laughter. "That's what I always say when we drive up to the gas station in the car."

"Funny guy." Bird Dog touched the relief tube again, and wondered if he could manage to wait.

Kilo 31

Rogov waited until the last Spetsnaz commando entered the raft before reaching out for the ladder himself.

"Comrade Colonel, do you really think it's such a good idea—?" the submarine captain began.

Rogov cut him off. "You don't need to think. I'm

going ashore with the detachment to survey the site," the Cossack snapped. "Your orders, Captain, are to deliver me here, and to maintain radio contact should I need assistance. I will return to this ship in six hours, and you are to be here waiting for me. Are we clear on that?"

The submarine captain nodded, relieved that the colonel would be leaving. The Mongolian Cossack's cold, menacing presence had become almost unbearable in the close confines of the submarine. If only he didn't look so different, he thought, he might be almost tolerable. But the slanting, almond-shaped eyes, high cheekbones, and ruddy brown-red color marked Colonel Rogov as a descendant of the barbarian hordes that swept across so much of the continent during earlier centuries. If the stories told about the Cossacks were true, then the blood of merciless conquerors and masters of torture ran through Rogov's veins. He studied the massive man descending the ladder below him, noting how much he looked like the Spetsnaz. It was some quality of the way they moved, smoothly yet gracelessly, power imbuing every motion. It was a clear, cold menace that every man of European descent recognized—and feared.

He shook his head, dispelling the beginnings of a shudder. What mattered was not the man's bloodlines, but the mission he was on now. While he had no need to know the details, the little he had learned made his blood run cold.

As Rogov stepped onto the raft, the submarine captain saluted, then cast off the last line holding the small craft moored to the submarine. He looked up and stared back out at the island. Despite his misgivings about Rogov, he would not willingly have sent any man out onto the bleak, barren island so close to them. Especially not in this weather.

He watched the raft pull away, the steady thrum of its outboard motor echoing eerily in the fog. Godspeed, he said silently, as he felt the weight left off his shoulders. He turned back to his submarine, and descended down into the command center. The sooner they were submerged and back below the surface of the sea, the safer the submarine would be from any prying eyes.

Tomcat 201

Bird Dog eased the Tomcat forward slowly, concentrating on the plastic basket streaming aft of the KA-6 tanker. Landing on a carrier deck at night was by far the most stressful part of carrier aviation, but refueling ran a close second. He resisted a temptation to look down at the icy water.

"Looking good, Bird Dog," Gator said encouragingly. "A few more inches, a few more inches there, you've got it."

Bird Dog felt the Tomcat shudder as the retractable refueling probe located on the right side of the fuselage near the front seat slid home.

"Good connection. How much ya want, Bird Dog?" the KA-6 pilot asked.

"Let's get her topped off," Bird Dog said. "Going to take a run out west to check up on one of Gator's ghosts."

"Roger—commencing transfer now."

The Tomcat and the KA-6 flew like a strangely mated pair of bumblebees for six minutes, the KA-6 pouring fuel into the Tomcat. When both wing tanks were topped up, Bird Dog said, "That'll do it."

"Roger. Have fun chasin' ghosts."

"Maybe it's Santa Claus on his way home," Bird Dog answered.

"Sounds good to me. You been a good Bird Dog all cruise?" the other pilot asked.

"Good enough."

"What are you gonna ask him for?"

"The only thing that comes to mind right now is a nice warm land-based urinal, but I'll give it some thought on the way out there." Bird Dog heard the other pilot chuckle in response.

Bird Dog eased back on the power slowly, carefully disengaging from the KA-6. As soon as an adequate degree of separation had been achieved, he rolled the Tomcat gracefully to starboard and headed out to the west.

Attu Island

As the raft bumped up against the island's southern shore, the Spetsnaz in the forward part of the boat leaped out, skidded on the ice, and then tugged on the mooring line. The bow of the small craft slipped up out of the water and onto the ice. The rest of the Spetsnaz piled out quickly, moving easily even after twenty minutes of sitting on the cold, hard boards that ringed the interior of the raft. Rogov followed more slowly, trying to conceal the stiffness already setting into his muscles.

He stepped out onto the ice, felt it shiver slightly under the weight of the men on it. Two Spetsnaz were hauling the boat completely out of the water. Rogov walked cautiously to the edge and peered down.

No gradual sloping of land into sea as there would be on a continent, he thought. Just a sheer, dark plunge into the depths. He could see the ice go straight down for perhaps six feet, and then it was lost in the inky blackness of the Pacific Ocean. He stepped away from the edge, suddenly conscious of how very tenuously a layer of solidified water overlay the volcanic base of the island, separating them from its more liquid counterpart. A few degrees warmer, and half of the island would melt back into its original state.

"Sir, come on," the Spetsnaz leader insisted. He grabbed Rogov's arm just above the elbow and pulled the colonel away from the edge of the ice. "The camp's just up ahead. This cold—it's deceptive, Comrade Colonel. You don't know you're freezing to death until it's too late."

Rogov ignored the man for a moment, long enough to make a point. Then he turned and followed the five figures, almost invisible against the island in their white Arctic suits. It was easier to track the yellow raft they hauled behind them than to focus on the commandos directly.

His feet crunched a small layer of fresh snow that skittered across the hard-packed ice. Ice crystals stung his eyes, driven at him by the winds now reaching gale force. He reached into one pocket of his parka with a glove-covered hand and withdrew a set of goggles. If the Spetsnaz commander hadn't suggested he put them on earlier, he would have, but it was imperative that he show no sign of weakness in front of these men. If they knew what was planned . . . he let his thoughts slide away from that and focused on the island of yellow ahead of him.

Ten minutes later, they reached a towering mass of ice. A wooden frame was set into it, a blank wall of timber hauled at impossible-to-estimate cost to this deserted spot. A steel door was centered in the dark wood wall.

He saw the Spetsnaz commander watching him carefully. He strode forward, put one gloved hand on the wooden bar set crosswise in the two U-shaped supports, and lifted it out. The door unbarred, he tugged it open. The interior of the structure was pitch-black.

Rogov turned to the Spetsnaz commander. "Get some light in there."

The man nodded, looking faintly disappointed, as though he had expected Rogov to show some signs of fear now that they were alone on the forsaken island. He motioned sharply to one of his subordinates, who produced a flashlight. "We'll get this generator started immediately, Comrade Colonel. The batteries are probably completely drained, especially in this weather. We need to run the generator for three hours a day to keep the batteries charged. Unless we make some extraordinary energy expenditures, that will be enough to keep the life support functioning."

Rogov stepped inside the structure, following the man with the flashlight. He gazed upward. A thick continuous sheet of heavy plastic was bolted to the overhead, a thin layer of insulation between the occupants of the cavern and the massive mountain of ice overhead. "Ingenious," he murmured. He'd studied the pictures, the mission briefings, but the actuality of this impressive engineering accomplishment could hardly be conveyed in the dry technical words of the science teams who had been there before them. The world's best insulation against cold—ice.

The Spetsnaz commander said, "It warms up some once we get the heater started, but not very much. We can't risk too high a temperature. The plastic keeps the overhead from dripping on us, but if too much of it melts, it will cool down on the deck and start refreezing around our feet."

"Comfort is the least of our concerns while we're here," Rogov said. "There are supplies for how many days stored here?"

"Two weeks." For the first time, the Spetsnaz commander looked at him uncertainly. "Will it be much longer than that, do you think?"

"When you need to know, Comrade Commander, I will tell you," Rogov snapped. "I suggest you concentrate on getting this camp fully operational as quickly as possible. Perhaps the memory of two weeks of rations will add speed to your preparations."

The Spetsnaz commander barked orders to his compatriots, his air of braggadocio considerably diminished at the thought of being stranded in the camp with no rations. Rogov smiled to himself, pleased. How long they would be here would depend on the Americans. And it was Rogov's job to ensure that the United States found very little to interest them on this westernmost Aleutian island.

At least, not right away.

CHAPTER 2
Sunday, 25 December

Rear Admiral Matthew Magruder forced himself to relax the tight grip he had on the seat's armrest. The worn upholstery on the C-130 transport plane was testimony to the years that it had been in service in the United States Navy.

How many times had it made this trip? he wondered. Five hundred? Two thousand? He glanced around the cabin, trying to distract himself from the tricky approach onto the Adak Island airfield, wondering how many other admirals and other dignitaries had made this same flight during the last five decades. Not many in recent years, he would be willing to bet. And this would be one of the last ones, since he was en route to Adak to preside over the decommissioning of the last P-3C Orion squadron assigned there.

He looked down and saw his fingers had curled around the armrest again. The nubby, well-worn fabric was rough and slightly oily under his hands. He grimaced and shook his head. Like most naval aviators, Rear Admiral Magruder despised being a passenger.

An F-14 Tomcat pilot himself, he found it particularly unsettling to be strapped into a seat thirty feet away from primary flight controls. He felt the plane shift slightly, and his left foot pressed down automatically, trying to compensate for the aircraft's slight wobble.

"Please remain in your seats," a terse voice said over the speaker. "We're getting some strong crosswinds. Normal for this part of the Aleutian Islands, but it makes for a tricky landing." A slight chuckle echoed in the speaker. "Don't worry, folks, I've done this about eight hundred times myself." The speaker went dead with a sharp pop.

Eight hundred times, Magruder thought, and tried to relax. I had that many traps on an aircraft carrier by the time I was a lieutenant commander. Now, with over three thousand arrested carrier landings, Magruder was one of the most experienced pilots in the Navy. He would have gladly foregone the promotions that went along with that.

Three months ago, he'd been commanding the carrier battle group on board USS *Thomas Jefferson*, responsible for the safety and well-being of over five thousand crew members and aviators, as well as close to one billion dollars in equipment. *Jefferson* had been on the pointy end of the spear, intervening in a conflict between China and the southeastern Asian nations over the oil-rich seafloor around the Spratly Islands.

And this is my reward. His uncle, Vice Admiral Thomas Magruder, had warned him at his change of command that he was up for an exciting new assignment. Tombstone had spent two months at the Naval War College for a quick refresher in intelligence and satellite capabilities, along with an update on Special Forces capabilities. It had been difficult to put the information in context, since his ultimate duty station was still classified top secret.

Alaska. When the word had finally come, learning that he was to be commander of Alaskan forces with sole operational responsibility for everything from Alaska across the Pacific Ocean, it had been a letdown.

They might as well have told me I ought to go ahead and retire. ALASKCOM might have been a big deal back during the days of the Cold War, when Russian submarines routinely plied the straights between the Aleutian Islands, but it was a backwater post these days. The Soviet forces lay rusting and decaying alongside their piers, with the exception of some long-range ballistic missile submarines that still deployed under the ice cap. The SOSUS station and most of the P-3 squadrons that had been stationed at Adak during the Cold War had either been decommissioned or pulled back to CONUS—the continental U.S. The Aleutian Islands, along with the frigid Bering Sea to the north of it, were a tactical wasteland.

Still, his uncle had promised him that it would be a good deal more exciting than he thought. He sighed, staring out the window at the thick white clouds now racing past the double-paned plastic. Surely his uncle had something in mind besides a touchy landing in strong crosswinds on a remote island.

Not only was this assignment operationally uninteresting, but it also put a crimp in his personal life. During his time on *Jefferson*, he'd finally broken off his long-term engagement to ACN reporter Pamela Drake. It had been partly due to the realization that neither one was willing to give and take enough with their career priorities to make it work. Additionally, Pamela had been increasingly uncomfortable with the more dangerous aspects of his chosen career. It was all right for *her* to go flitting off to the most dangerous combat areas of the world to report her stories, but the idea of Tombstone launching off the carrier to take on adversary air over the Spratly Islands was more than she could take. They'd ended it just as Tombstone was realizing his attraction to one of the hottest female aviators in the Navy.

He felt his mouth curl up in a smile, an expression that would have surprised most of the officers who'd worked with him in the last twenty years. Lieutenant Commander Joyce Flynn, "Tomboy" to the rest of the squadron. The name suited her, although it didn't adequately describe the more delicious aspects of the petite, redheaded female naval flight officer.

While they had both been assigned to the *Jefferson*, a relationship had been impossible. Tombstone had been in command of Carrier Battle Group 14, while Tomboy was a RIO (radar intercept officer) in VF-95, a Tomcat squadron on board. Faced with the possibility that his tactical decisions would put her in danger, and knowing the Navy's strict policy against fraternization, they had finally come to an agreement to put everything on hold until they'd both transferred off the ship. The possibility of Washington, D.C., tours for both of them had been exciting.

But now Tombstone took a deep breath. A lousy operational assignment and separation from Tomboy seemed to be in his future.

Last month, Tomboy had received notification that she had been selected for the test pilot program in Patuxent, Maryland. Pax River—the big brass ring for every naval aviator, flying the latest in tactical and surveillance aircraft, getting to see the future of naval aviation up close and personal. As much as it hurt, he knew he couldn't have asked Tomboy to pass up that opportunity. He wouldn't have himself, had it been offered.

Knowing it was the right thing to do didn't make it any easier, though. They'd carved out two weeks together, and spent them in Puerto Vallarta, on the Pacific coast of southern Mexico. He smirked, thinking about the comments his colleagues had made when he'd come back from vacation with hardly a sunburn. If they only knew how much of their lovemaking had been at Tomboy's instigation!

The speaker crackled to life again. "If you look out the port window, you might be able to see that we've got company," the pilot's voice said, a determined casualness masking what must be mounting tension in the cockpit. "It doesn't happen often anymore, but the Soviets— excuse me, the Russians—still decide to send their Bears out to play with us from time to time. One joined on us about twenty miles back. He's edging in a little closer than I'd like under the circumstances, but there's not a whole helluva lot we can do about it right now. I'll keep you posted."

Tombstone craned his neck and stared out into the thick cotton-candy cloud cover. Slightly behind the C-130, he could make out an occasional silvery flash of light, behind them and above them. The Bear, solidly in place behind the C-130 in a perfect killing position.

Why would a Russian Bear aircraft find tracking a C-130 transport down to an almost deserted naval base of such critical interest? Tombstone felt his gut tighten and the hair on the back of his neck stand up, his instinctive reaction to the possibility of airborne danger. Something

wasn't right. What, he couldn't say just yet, but every
tactical instinct in his body was screaming warnings.

Most variants of the long-range turboprop aircraft
were reconnaissance aircraft, configured for antisubmarine warfare (ASW) or electronic surveillance, with their
only offensive weaponry three pairs of 23mm NR-23
guns in remotely activated dorsal and ventral turrets.
While the guns were generally thought to be primarily
for defense, even those weapons could pose a deadly
danger to the unarmed aircraft he was in. Additionally,
and far more worrisome, both the Bear-H and -G
versions carried long-range air-to-surface cruise missiles.

He unbuckled his seat belt, raised one hand at the
flight engineer who stood up to order him back to his
seat, and went forward. He identified himself through the
closed door, and stepped into the small cockpit.

"What kind of Bear?" he asked immediately.

The pilot glanced at the copilot, who was staring back
aft, searching for the contact. "He's not certain, but he
thinks he caught a glimpse of a large ventral pod. If he's
right, that makes it a Bear-J."

The copilot looked away from his binoculars for a
moment. "I'm pretty sure I saw it, Admiral."

"A Bear-J. Now what the hell would it be doing out
here?" Tombstone said, puzzled.

The Bear-J was the Russians' version of the U.S.
Navy's EA-6A and EC-130Q TACAMO aircraft. It
possessed VLF—very low frequency—communications
gear that enabled it to stay in contact with national
command authorities and missile submarines from almost anywhere in the world. The ventral pod housed the
kilometers-long trailing wire communications antenna.
The aircraft was slightly over 162 feet long, with a

wingspan several feet larger than that. In addition to its guns, the Bear-J could also carry the largest air-launched missiles in the CIS inventory, and sported outsize, extremely fine resolution radars.

"Have you told anyone about this?" Tombstone asked.

"Your people already know. And *Jefferson*—she's on station for the Greenpeace monitoring mission." The pilot couldn't entirely keep an offended note out of his voice. "Admiral, we're five minutes out from Adak." The pilot motioned toward the extra fold-down seat in the cockpit. "If you'd like to stay, we'd be pleased to have you in the cockpit for the landing."

As long as I park my butt before you have to order me to and I quit second-guessing you, Tombstone thought, a sliver of wry humor cutting through his concern over the Bear. *The only thing worse would be if you had to explain how I got smashed up when the landing got rough.* He took the hint and strapped in, turning sideways and craning his head around to look forward. He might be three grades senior to the pilot, but as long as they were in the air the pilot had command of the aircraft and was responsible for the safety of the passengers. And that included keeping senior officers from getting themselves hurt.

The copilot reported that the Bear was now maintaining position two miles behind them. He then abandoned his binoculars and resumed the prelanding checklist that the Bear had interrupted.

Flying this close together in marginal weather was a foolishness Tombstone would have never permitted in his own air wing. Not unless the tactical situation were critical.

Maybe this tour would be as interesting as his uncle
had promised, after all.

1625 Local
Tomcat 201

Ten minutes later, the fighter was orbiting above the
radar contact's position, barely two thousand yards above
the ocean. Bird Dog could see the rough chop of the
waves, the massive shape of a whale moving below
them, the clear sky—and nothing else.

"Where the hell did it go?" Bird Dog asked.

"Damned if I know. But it was there before."

Bird Dog heard the frustration in Gator's voice. "Well,
maybe it was a submarine," he said skeptically. "I
suppose it's possible. But I'd bet on the fellow down
there." He watched the whale surface, flip a tail at the
aircraft, then dive.

Gator snorted. "About time you started believing me
on radar contacts, Bird Dog. A biologic doesn't give that
solid of a return, if you see it at all. After the Spratly
Islands, I would think you'd be a little bit more cautious
about sea ghosts."

"Just because you were right *that* time doesn't mean
you're right *every* time."

During the Spratly Islands, the first clue that China
was behind the aggressions had come from Gator's
sighting of two intermittent contacts on radar. At the
time, Bird Dog had voiced his opinion loudly that Gator
had been drinking too much coffee, and was making
radar contacts out of sea clutter. When an island five
thousand feet below them had disintegrated into a

massive cloud of tank fragments, bodies, and bamboo building materials, Bird Dog had been forced to admit that his RIO was right.

"Let's circle this area for a while, see if we pick anything else up," Gator said, his voice holding no trace of animosity. "I know what you think about sea ghosts, but this wasn't one of them."

"Okay, let me call Mother and tell her what we're up to. Damnit, Gator, we're going to end up tanking again if we stay out here much longer."

"You might want to consider doing it earlier than you need to," Gator said, tension creeping into his voice.

"Why? You holding out on me?"

"No. It's just that I don't want to be running short on fuel if something unexpected comes up. You know the old saying—better safe than sorry?"

"Okay, okay, you don't have to rub it in."

Bird Dog made the call to the carrier and told the operations specialist on the other end what they'd seen. Or rather, what they'd *not* seen. The OS sounded dubious, and dropped off-line for a moment to confer with the tactical action officer (TAO).

While Bird Dog was waiting for an answer, Gator gave off a sharp yelp from the backseat. "Look! And you talk about sea clutter!"

Bird Dog put the Tomcat into a tight left-hand turn and studied the ocean below. A glossy black shape was lurking just below the surface, a huge man-made leviathan. "Holy shit," he said softly. "Jesus, Gator, what is it with you and submarines? There are probably no more than two or three Russian submarines deployed in this whole ocean, and you get me marking on top of the only one within two thousand miles."

He could hear the smugness in Gator's voice as the RIO replied, "Guess I'm just good."

"Or lucky."

The tactical channel was now chattering with demands for information, directions to maintain contact, and anxious queries about their fuel status from the OS. Finally, a familiar voice cut through the chatter.

"Tomcat Two-oh-one, say identity and classification of submarine." The slight Texas twang was all Bird Dog needed to hear.

"I don't know, Admiral—wait, let me drop down a little." Bird Dog shoved the control yoke forward, and started down toward the surface of the ocean. He arrested their descent at two thousand feet above the ocean, continuing to circle over the contact to get a better look at it.

"An Oscar," Gator said softly. "That's the only thing of that size that would be out here."

"You sure? It could be a Typhoon at that size."

"No." Gator's voice held a note of finality. "I can see enough of the sail structure from here to make the call. That's an Oscar, no doubt about it."

Bird Dog relayed the information back to Mother, and then felt a slight chill as the implications started to settle in.

The Oscar was the latest cruise missile ship in the Russian inventory. It had one, and only one, primary mission in life—killing American aircraft carriers. The building program had begun at Shipyard Number 402, located at Severodyinsk, in 1982, during the height of the Cold War. The Oscar I and the later Oscar II were the largest submarines to be built by any nation, except for the Soviet Typhoon ballistic missile boat and the U.S. Trident SSBN.

The Oscar carried the SS-N-19 Shipwreck antiship missile, with either a conventional or nuclear warhead. With a range of greater than three hundred nautical miles and a speed of Mach 2.5, the five-thousand-kilogram missile was a deadly threat to any surface ship. The Oscar could receive targeting information from most Soviet tactical aircraft, as well as satellite downlink positioning. Both of those assets permitted it to fire at surface ships well outside its own sensor range. In addition to the Shipwreck, the Oscar carried the SS-N-15 and 6–16 torpedoes. Although hard data was scarce, her 533mm torpedoes were reputed to be capable of speeds up to forty-five knots, transporting a high-explosive or nuclear warhead of 1,250 pounds on a straight run, or in acoustic homing mode. Supposedly, one of those torpedoes exploding under the keel of a carrier would be sufficient to break the carrier's back.

"How far away from the carrier is she?" Bird Dog asked. He winced, hearing the slight tremor in his voice.

Gator's voice was dark and somber. "Four hundred miles, right now. But with her speeds, there's nothing to say she couldn't close that to within Shipwreck range within one day."

"You'd better tell the Admiral. I think he's going to be real interested in this."

Rear Admiral Edward Everett Wayne, "Batman" to his
fellow aviators, swore quietly as he listened to the RIO's
report. An Oscar. Great. Just when every asset in the
United States Navy had been lulled into a peaceful sense
of security because of the demise of the Soviet Union, an
Oscar turns up. What the hell were the Intelligence
people thinking? And why hadn't he had any warning at
all about this possibility?

He stared at the large blue video screen that dominated
the forward bulkhead of Tactical Flag Command Center
(TFCC). Judging from the relative geometry, the carrier
battle group would be safe from the Oscar for at least
another day, maybe more, depending on what course she
followed.

"Get some Vikings in the air. Now," he snapped. "It's
time we got some work out of them."

"I imagine they'll be happy about that," his chief of
staff, Captain Jim Craig, remarked. "Their CO was
telling me he's getting damned tired of ferrying mail
back and forth for us. To have a real submarine problem,
as nasty as it may be, that's meat and potatoes for the S-3
Viking ASW aircraft."

Batman nodded sharply. "It's the kind of opportunity I
don't want to have on this cruise. I told Tombstone I'd
keep his people safe."

The TAO, seated at his console two feet in front of
Batman, swiveled his chair around and looked at the
admiral. "Sir, we need to get that Tomcat some more gas

if she's going to mark on top while we prep the S-3's. He's got enough gas to stay on station for another hour and still make it back safely, but—"

Batman cut him off. "Good thinking. Better to have too much gas than too little. The first situation you can fix—the second you can't. Make it happen."

The TAO turned back to his console and talked with his counterpart located in the Combat Direction Center (CDC), fifty feet forward on the ship. After a hurried conversation, he toggled the circuit off and turned to the OS manning the plastic status board located on the right side of the TFCC. "Put down Seven-oh-one and Seven-oh-two for the next two events. Seven-oh-three and Seven-eleven will be in Alert Fifteen. And we're launching another tanker now, now, now." Without waiting to see if the OS had caught it all, he turned back to his console.

"An Oscar. What does that suggest to you?" Batman asked his COS.

Captain Craig looked thoughtful. With thirty years as surface ship officer in the Navy, four at-sea commands under his belt, and an advanced degree in ASW systems from the Naval Postgraduate School in Monterey, he had forgotten more about submarines than Batman had ever known. "Nothing good. She could make us real unhappy characters by just staying within weapons release range."

"And that Bear-J up around Adak doesn't make me breathe any easier. Based on that, I think we have to assume that the Oscar has detailed targeting information on the entire battle group." Batman turned back to the screen. "And is in contact with Russia's military command. The question is, *why*? Is this just another one of those political statements, or something worse?"

Captain Craig shook his head, a weary expression crossing his face. "And I thought we'd seen the last of these games. Figured I'd make one last deployment, then think about retiring. It's starting to sound like I might want to put that off some."

Batman clapped him on the shoulder. "Better now than ten years from now," he said. "The Navy needs us Cold Warriors—after all we saw, we're the only ones with the right suspiciously paranoid mind-set to detect the first signs of trouble."

The COS shot him an amused look. "Do I detect a lack of confidence on the admiral's part in our superb intelligence network?"

Batman snorted. "Hell, they couldn't even tell us when the Wall in Germany was going to come down, and every last one of them missed the breakup of the Soviet Union. Given that, what do you think the odds are that they detect a reunited commonwealth on the move again?"

"I wish to God I didn't agree with you, Admiral. But I do." The chief of staff stared forward at the screen, watching the arcane symbology that represented the battle group, her aircraft and escorts, steaming west just south of the Aleutian chain. "And I hope to hell both of us are wrong."

Tomcat 201

"You think she knows we're here?" Bird Dog asked.

"Probably," Gator answered. "At this low of an altitude, we're putting a helluva lot of noise into the ocean. I thought I saw an ESM antenna pop up there a little while ago. Either way, I think we can count on her knowing we're here."

"Well, there's not much she can do about that, is there?"

"I don't think so." Bird Dog's voice sounded doubtful. "But after the Spratlys, with those surface-to-air missiles on that submarine, I'm not feeling so safe and secure orbiting over a submarine anymore."

Bird Dog swore quietly to himself, wishing he'd paid more attention to the last intelligence brief. Did the Oscar carry a surface-to-air missile? And if so, what was the range? "How about we move on up to four thousand feet?" he asked. "Just give us a little safety room."

"No objection from back here. I think I'll still be able to follow her from that altitude. I'll let you know."

Bird Dog tapped the throttles forward slightly and put the Tomcat into a slow, graceful spiral upward. He glanced overhead and saw the heavy, thick bottoms of the clouds looming above him. "Three thousand, maybe," he said, hazarding a guess. "I'll throttle back so you can keep a visual on her."

At 2,800 feet, just below the bottom of the clouds, Bird Dog leveled the Tomcat out. Gator informed him that he still had a clear, if slightly fuzzy, visual on the massive black hull sliding through the water.

"Who would've thought we would have been able to see her?" Bird Dog said. "That doesn't make any sense. I mean, the whole purpose of a submarine is to remain hidden. Doesn't she know that the water is so clear up here that we can see down thirty or forty feet?"

"That's what worries me," Gator said soberly. "The Oscar can fire her Shipwreck missiles while submerged, and there's absolutely no reason for her to stay at shallow depths for any period of time, not unless she's coming up for a communications break. And if this were a com break, she would have already stuck an antenna up, squirted out her traffic, and been back down at depth. There's only one reason for her to stay shallow like this."

"She *wants* us to see her? Why?"

"I'm flattered to think that you believe I can read the mind of a Russian submarine commander," Gator said sarcastically. "But for what it's worth, I can think of only one reason that she would stay this shallow. She wants us to see her."

"Why?"

"That, my friend, is the *real* question."

1650 Local
Adak Island

The C-130 shuddered to a halt, using up most of the runway as it gently braked. The Bear aircraft had broken off when they'd started their final approach to the small island airstrip, and now circled overhead at fifteen thousand feet.

Tombstone paused at the C-130 hatch and stared out at the cold, barren island before him. The hard arctic wind buffeted him, and the movable metal steps now rolling up to the aircraft swayed gently. He sucked in a deep breath and felt the frigid air sear the delicate tissues of his lungs.

In the distance, he could see a forlorn line of P-3 ASW aircraft parked on the tarmac. Just as few years ago, there would have been two complete squadrons of the Orion aircraft permanently stationed here, ready to pounce on the first sniff of any Soviet submarine that ventured into these waters. Now, due to downsizing, or right-sizing, as some called it, he thought bitterly, most of the United States Navy assets were being pulled back to the mainland. Only these five aircraft remained on this isolated base, the forward edge of the American continental security envelope. He looked over in the other direction and saw the squat gray concrete building that housed the SOSUS station, now silent and cold. Adak had been a challenging duty station for generations of ocean systems technicians, but the bean-counters in the Pentagon had decided this forward-deployed ASW capability was no longer needed.

The peace dividend. He snorted. What they never seemed to realize was that peace was a temporary state of affairs between conflicts. By stripping herself of so much fighting capability, America simply guaranteed that a long, economically painful, and manpower intensive buildup would be required the next time. And there would be a next time, he thought, surveying the westernmost base under his command. Regardless of how much the politicians claimed they'd achieved it, and how much the everyday citizen wanted it, he couldn't convince himself that this peace would last. It was merely a matter of time before it crumbled.

The rickety steps finally reached the aircraft, and two technicians hurried to decouple the frail structure from the small yellow tractor towing it. By hand, they pushed it over against the aircraft. Its forward lip clanged against the scarred and battered surface of the C-130.

Tombstone wrapped his parka around himself more tightly, grateful that his supply clerk back in ALASKCOM headquarters had insisted he take it, along with the thick, fur-lined gloves now snuggled in his pockets. He reached for the metal railing, intending to make the short dash down the ladder and to the waiting van without the gloves.

A technician grabbed his hand as he reached for the railing. "Sorry, sir, but you'll want to put those gloves on first. You touch that metal, we'll have to bring the hot water out to unfreeze your hand from it."

Tombstone nodded his thanks and pulled the gloves on before stepping out of the aircraft and onto the metal platform. He touched the metal railing and felt the bitter cold seeping through the thick leather and fur. The man who had grabbed him had been right. He walked down the steps, feeling the structure shudder and sway in the forty-knot gale. By the time he reached the van, only twenty feet away, the cold was already seeping through the parka and his face was numb.

As he climbed into the front seat of the van and looked across at the young female petty officer driver, a memory flashed into his mind. Brilliant sun, the gentle pounding of Mexican waves against a clean, white sandy beach. And Tomboy, nestled under his arm, pressing gentle curves into the hard, lean lines of his own body. He smiled, wondering what she would think if she could see him now, decked out like an Eskimo.

"Welcome to Adak, sir," the driver said. "I understand this is your first trip here?"

"Sure is." He glanced at the front of her uniform, wondering what her name was, but her stenciled nameplate was covered up by the bulky cold-weather gear. "And you are?"

"Petty Officer Monk," she said, the hard edges of a New England accent clipping her words off. "I'll be your driver while you're here, Admiral," she added, candidly assessing him.

"I don't imagine we'll need to go a lot of places," Tombstone said. "After all, the base isn't that big, is it?"

"No, Admiral, but you'll want a driver even to get between most of the buildings. This cold," she said, shaking her head, "I thought I'd be used to it, but this takes even me by surprise."

"Maine?" Tombstone asked, hazarding a guess.

Her face brightened. "You've been there?"

"Several times. Did a lot of skiing up at Sugarloaf years ago."

She nodded vigorously. "Only about forty miles from my hometown," she said happily. "Gets cold up there, but nothing compared to Adak."

Something about the young sailor reminded Tombstone of Tomboy. It wasn't just the physical similarity, he was sure, although Petty Officer Monk was about the same size as his lover. No, it was something in the set of the eyes, the bright gleam of mischief that not even naval courtesy and custom could entirely dim.

"Oh, by the way, Admiral," Petty Officer Monk said suddenly, breaking into his reverie. "A few members of the press arrived yesterday on the last C-130 for the decommissioning ceremony. There're only three reporters, though," she added hastily, seeing the expression of dismay cross his face. "Just one from a major network."

As the last passenger climbed into the van, Petty Officer Monk started to pull away from the aircraft. She'd left the engine running while sitting there.

"And just who might that be?" Tombstone asked, already feeling a curious, pleasant fluttering in his stomach. If it were—

"Miss Pamela Drake," Monk said cheerfully. "She's staying at the Bachelor Officers' Quarters—BOQ—but most of us have gotten a look at her. She's from ACN."

Pamela Drake. Why wasn't he surprised? Tombstone shook his head. During the last ten years, Pamela had managed to turn up on every major press pool covering United States Navy operations, particularly those that involved a certain Matthew Magruder. At first he'd thought it was coincidence, but on his last cruise, Pamela had finally admitted that she never passed up an opportunity to cover anything involving Tombstone. When they'd finally broken their engagement, he thought those days would be over.

Evidently not. A new thought struck him, and he grimaced. Now just what would Tomboy have to say if she found out that Pamela Drake was on the same isolated island as her lover? He shook his head, quite sure that it wouldn't be pleasant.

1710 Local
Tomcat 201

"Okay, we got it," the voice said over Tactical. "Solid visual on the COI—contact of interest."

"About time you guys showed up," Bird Dog grumbled. "This is a fighter, not a babysitter."

"We do our best, but our max speed is four hundred and forty knots," the other pilot retorted. "You might be able to get here faster, but you can't do a damned thing about her while she's submerged. We can," he concluded smugly.

Bird Dog stared out the windscreen at the squat,

blunt-nosed S-3 Viking ASW aircraft. She was less than half the size of the Tomcat, he figured, but her long fuel endurance and highly efficient engines enabled her to remain on station far longer than the Tomcat could have dreamed of without tanking. Two Harpoon antiship missiles hung slung on either side of her fuselage, with two torpedoes on each wing occupying the outer weapons stations. Evidently, the carrier took this business seriously, sending out the S-3's fully armed.

While the Tomcat could carry a wide range of antiair missiles and bombs, there was damned little it had against a submarine. Rockeyes, ground-attack missiles that carried a payload of bomblets, could be effective against a submarine on the surface, but the Tomcat had no antisurface or torpedo capability whatsoever. Indeed, on this flight, which was intended to be a simple quick look-see at the Greenpeace ship, Tomcat 201 carried only a minimal weapons load-out, more for training than for any other purpose. Sidewinders graced the outer weapons stations, with two Sparrows occupying the ones closer to the fuselage. They'd elected to forego the longer-range Phoenix missiles, whose massive weight significantly reduced the Tomcat's on-station time.

"Okay, we're out of here. You guys take this bitch out if she even so much as moves like she's going to take out my stereo," Bird Dog said.

"Don't worry about it," the S-3 pilot said dryly. "You might have noticed that you and I live in the same apartment building."

CHAPTER 3
Monday, 26 December

Colonel Rogov returned to the submarine after the initial camp setup, leaving the Spetsnaz commandos huddled inside their sleeping bags inside the creaking, groaning cave carved out of the cliff. The small raft had barely made the trip back to the submarine safely, taking two waves completely over it and being turned into a miniature version of its mother ship several times.

He watched the men move around the submarine's control center, noting with disdain the black circles under their eyes and the fatigue in their every movement. Europeans, all of them. The strong Slavic stock of their ancestors bred out of them and diluted by the effete blood of inbred royalty. None of them would have lasted long under his command. And none of them could have endured the conditions ashore in the ice cavern.

Not that the submarine's crew would have seen it that way. They saw themselves, he knew, as vastly superior to the Western Europeans that inhabit France, Germany, and England. He snorted. If they only knew.

Approximately half of the crew was Russian, the last

41

remnants of a grand race that had done its best to extinguish everything noble and superior in its blood-lines in the coups that destroyed the czars' line. The remaining crew members were primarily Ukrainian, with a few mongrel Georgians, Azerbaijanis and Armenians thrown in. All in the latter group were at least half Polish, some even with strong German stock mixed in with the historic blood that had first flourished in the fertile steppes of the Ukraine and in the high, craggy mountain regions of Azerbaijan, Georgia, and Armenia. Had they but seen what they would become, he doubted that any one of them would have chosen to consort with the invading hordes that swept east from Europe from century to century. Instead, they would have preferred to fight to the last man and woman, chosen defeat over the hybridization and bastardization of their blood.

Not so with his ancestors. The Cossacks, driven out of their homeland surrounding the Black Sea and on the Crimean Peninsula, had remained a closed, insular nation without a country, warlike and incapable of being de-feated. The best the Russians could manage was to drive them out into the vast desolation of its most eastern areas, consigning them to Mongolia, Siberia, and the rugged alien terrain of the eastern Soviet Union. Yet even centuries of forced relocation had failed to extinguish their strong tribal instincts, their sense of *who* and *what* they were. Primary among those attributes was their identity as Cossacks.

He watched the men again, noting the pale faces, the languid, almost feminine movements as they carefully monitored the complex array of sensors, weapons, and electronics installed on the small submarine. Such a powerful submarine, even for its small size. The Kilo

combined ham-handed Russian design with frighteningly
advanced electronics and computers obtained from
Japan, Korea, and yes, even the United States. A powerful ship, one that deserved better than the masters she
now had.

That would change.

He felt the submarine captain watching him uneasily.
He turned and faced the man full on, letting him see the
disdain flicker at the edges of his normally impassive
expression. This man most of all would have to go. His
hesitation when one of his crew members had been swept
into the icy sea was just further evidence of his unfitness
for command. While he might possess the requisite technical and tactical knowledge required of a commander, he
lacked the single most important ingredient—the iron will
so necessary for transforming a collection of equipment and
machinery and men into a potent, irresistible fighting force.

The present situation illustrated that point perfectly.
The Kilo submarine lingered ten miles away from the
island, barely making steerageway through the silent
ocean. Hours ago, the sharp pops and groans of the ice
floe had subsided as the sun sank back down below the
horizon. Now, the ocean was a silent, dark cloak of
invisibility.

Had Rogov been the skipper, the submarine would
have been snorkeling, topping off the last bit of charge
on its batteries in preparation for any immediate tactical
need to stay submerged for hours. True, the bank of
batteries was currently charged to ninety percent, but one
never knew when that additional ten percent of capacity
would spell the difference between life and death for a
submarine and its crew.

This skipper, however, after a brief communications

foray to the surface to monitor the group ashore's progress, had decided that the weather was too bad, the seas too rough, to inflict the nausea-inducing pitch and roll of a submarine near the surface on its crew. He fled the surface and returned to the depths, where the motion of the storm above them was imperceptible. The crew had all looked relieved at that decision.

Pah! The men ashore would hardly have it so easy. Even safe inside the ice cavern, the scream and howl of the winds alone would have been daunting. The winds had built steadily throughout the night until sixty-knot gales, at times growing to hurricane force, now scoured the desolate island.

"Captain," a young lieutenant said suddenly. His quiet voice echoed in the tomblike control center. "The other submarine—I think—yes, it's her."

The skipper stepped away from his normal post in the center of the small room, and stationed himself behind the sonar operator. "Where?"

The younger man pointed at the waterfall display. "It's barely distinguishable from the background noise yet, Skipper, but this appears to be a line from her main propulsion equipment." He pointed to a series of dots that looked to Rogov's untrained eyes to be merely part of the noise.

Rogov allowed a trace of satisfaction to tug at the corner of his mouth. So far, all was going according to plan, although neither the Russians on this boat nor their larger counterpart knew it. The Oscar-class nuclear cruise missile submarine was one of the most potent ship-killers in the Russian inventory today. Equipped with SS-N-19 Shipwreck missiles, it had a tactical launch range of over three hundred nautical miles. It could obtain targeting data from any other platform, including the Tupelov Bear aircraft or the Ilyushin May-76 reconnaissance plane. When properly aligned, it could also download targeting data from Russian surveillance satellites, relieving it of the necessity of obtaining enemy positioning data from its own organic sensors.

The Oscar's deployment had been suspended in the first few years following the breakup of the Soviet Union, but had resumed in 1995. It roamed with impunity the vast reaches of the Pacific Ocean, occasionally making forays into the smaller Atlantic. Her torpedoes, twenty-eight feet long and over five feet in diameter, could crack the keel of an aircraft carrier with one well-placed shot.

As it would soon, if necessary. He smiled, wondering what his Cossack ancestors would have thought of him, riding this massive underwater seahorse into battle again. A far cry from the days when his ancestors had swept out of the mountains and across the plains, decimating Ukrainian and Russian troops with their bloody sabers. While today's Cossack might depend on invisible electrons and satellite data instead of a finely honed blade, the principles remained the same—attack, attack, attack.

The Americans would remember that soon.

0800 Local
VF-95 Ready Room, USS *Jefferson* CVN-74

The Ready Room was one of the larger single compartments on the aircraft carrier, and served as both a duty post and a central point of coordination for the VF-95 squadron. Ten rows of high-backed chairs took up the forward starboard portion of the room, arrayed in front of

a chalkboard and overhead projector. The port side was a
general congregating area, and its bulkheads were ringed
with hard plastic couches and the all-important squadron
popcorn machine. A battered gray table protruded from
one bulkhead. Bird Dog, Gator, and their squadron
commanding officer were gathered around it.

Bird Dog glared down at the chart spread out before
him. A series of standard Navy symbols was penciled in
on it, connected with a faint line representing the track of
the contact. The Greenpeace ship had been meandering
around the area south of Attu for two weeks now, and
there was still no discernible pattern to her movements.

"I still don't see what the hell is so damned important
about flying out to take a look at that ship," Bird Dog
grumbled. "Why not send an S-3B out instead? That way
she can look for that Oscar at the same time."

Commander Frank Richey fixed him with a pointed
glare. "Lieutenants aren't asked to decide what's important, mister," he snapped. "If the United States wants to
make sure her citizens can count beluga whales in the
North Pacific in peace and quiet, then we're gonna make
sure that happens. You got it?"

Bird Dog heard Gator, seated next to him, sigh and
move away imperceptibly. Bird Dog nodded, acknowl-
edging the rebuke with bare courtesy. When he was the
commanding officer of a squadron—*if* that day ever
came, which was looking more and more unlikely these
days—he would remember what it was like to be a
frustrated junior pilot, blooded on one cruise but still not
considered an important enough member of the team to
be fully briefed on the mission.

Fully briefed. He snorted. The skipper thought it was
enough that he understood his flight profile, knew what

his weapons load-out was, and was able to make the F-14 Tomcat dance around the sky like a ballerina. But no one ever bothered to talk about the bigger issues—why the United States was here in the first place, and just what the hell babysitting a group of peaceniks and longhairs on a Greenpeace boat had to do with national security.

Although, he had to admit, the powers that be had proved right about Spratly Islands. There, their routine surveillance of the rocky outpost in the South China Sea had been the first step in building stronger ties with the small nations that rimmed that body of water.

Still, would it have cost the skipper anything to give him a better explanation? He sighed. Maybe he'd wander down to the spook spaces later today, see if any of the professional paranoids that lived in the Carrier Intelligence Center, or CVIC were willing to discuss the mission with him. Somehow, he had the feeling that if he just knew more, he might be a whole hell of a lot more interested in the mission than he was at this point. If it hadn't involved flying, it would have been a complete waste.

"So, I take it you've got the big picture now?" his skipper said, distracting him from his thoughts.

"Yes, sir, Skipper," Bird Dog replied. "We'll fly a routine surveillance mission over this area," he said, tracing out a large square on the chart in front of him. "I'm to report the location of the Greenpeace ship, drop down to one thousand feet for a quick pass over her for rigging, then we're to take a quick look at all the islands. Make sure none of them have moved." Bird Dog winced as he heard the sarcasm in his voice. Damn it, when was he going to learn to keep his mouth under control?

"There's islands bear close watching sometimes," Gator said softly. "Remember?"

"Hell, yes," Bird Dog said in the same tones. "But that was Asia. The Aleutian Islands are part of Alaska—American property! Do you really think that they're going to be blowing up like the Spratly rocks were?"

Gator shook his head sadly. "That's what they pay us for, shipmate—to make sure that they don't."

1200 Local
SS Serenity

Tim Holden, first mate on board the third and largest ship in the Greenpeace inventory, kept his hands firmly wrapped around the overhead stabilizer bar. The line-covered steel rod ran from port to starboard near the ceiling of the bridge on board the ship. In rough seas like today's, crew members virtually hung from it, suspended like bats in order to keep their balance.

The former fishing boat had a deep draft, its keel extending some thirty feet below the thrashing waves around it. Even with that, though, the ship bobbed and twisted in the waves, her powerful diesel engines straining to keep her bow pointed into the long line of heavy swells that extended out to the horizon. Holden watched the helmsman make minor adjustments to their course. The man had good sense, far more than most of his counterparts, and could be trusted to take immediate action without Holden giving rudder orders for every small course change. It relieved the strain of standing watch in heavy seas.

Although just why he was out here in the first place

was something of a mystery. He knew what the Green-peace people said. He'd paid attention during all the briefs, had been impressed by their starry-eyed inno-cence and fanatic dedication to their cause, but it still didn't make much sense to him. Spending months watching for the occasional appearance of a pod of whales and trying to develop a complete census of the creatures didn't strike him as doing much for world peace and endangered species. It'd be a hell of a lot more effective if the Navy put a couple of torpedoes up the ass of Russian fishing vessels that harvested them. Well, at least the wages made up for part of the misery of bobbing around like a cork in this storm.

He paused, squinting at Attu. From this distance, the twenty-mile-long island was only a smidgen on the horizon, a bleak white outcropping of ice and rock. While the uninhabited island had played a major role in World War II, today it served mostly as a landmark for fishing vessels and ecologists searching for schools of fish and pods of endangered whales.

Like his current passengers. A nice enough herd, if a bit single-minded. After four weeks of listening to their unflagging enthusiasm, their nightly dinner speculations about the state of whales in the northern Pacific were starting to take on a wistfully plaintive note. As much as he begrudged it, he'd found himself eager to find something to cheer them up. One whale—that would do for starters.

Holden scanned the horizon again. He'd pit his expe-rienced seagoing eyes against their array of techno-toys and sonar monitors any day.

Finally, he saw what had caught his attention. There was something between the *Serenity* and Attu, a trace of darker color against the roiling blue-black, whitecapped ocean. He took two quick steps forward to the front of the bridge, grasped the railing there with one hand, and lifted binoculars to his eyes. The picture came into sharper focus.

Yes, something definitely was there. He reached for the ship's telephone to call the scientists, already grinning with anticipation at the childish cries of glee that would shortly be filling the bridge.

1210 Local
Kilo 31

"She's surfacing, sir," the sonar technician said.

"What the hell—?" the Kilo's skipper muttered. He leaned over the sonar console, his face almost next to his technician's. "Any indication she's having trouble?"

"Could be, sir," the technician replied. "I thought I saw some instability in her electrical sources."

Rogov watched the Kilo's commander analyze the possibilities in his mind. A reactor failure, a casualty of some sort, or, worse yet, every submariner's nightmare—a fire. He waited for a few minutes, then decided to intervene, and shoved himself through a mass of technicians and sailors to the sonar console.

"It is not our business," he said neutrally. "We have our mission—nothing must interfere with that."

"There are one hundred and seventy-eight men on that submarine," the skipper said. "If they have to abandon ship, we have to be there to pick them up immediately. Otherwise, even with the protective life rafts, they have no hope of survival."

Rogov shook his head from side to side almost imperceptibly. "The mission," he reminded the skipper.

For the first time, the man showed some signs of fighting spirit. "May God rot your soul," the normally passive submariner snapped. "You saw what that sea does—ten minutes, at the most. We must—"

"And just where will you put all these men, Captain?" Rogov asked. "Have them standing in line in your tiny passageways? Will you jettison your torpedoes to make room for them in those tubes? No," he concluded, "even if you were to reach them, you have no room for them on board. If they have problems, they must solve them themselves. I'm sure their captain is a resourceful man."

"They could get to shore. Your camp there—at least they'd have a chance!"

Rogov stiffened. The breach of operational security was unforgivable. While every sailor on the submarine knew that the boat had surfaced, had noted the absence of the forbidden figures that had boarded it in Petropavlovsk, few knew any details of the larger mission. The captain himself had been ordered to ensure that his crew remained absolutely silent on the matter, and to crush any speculation immediately. To blurt it out now, within earshot of every junior sailor in the control room, was completely unacceptable.

"A word privately?" Rogov said, moderating his tone to a respectful murmur. "Perhaps there are options—" Rogov stepped back to allow the submarine captain to move away from the console. He followed the other man aft down a small passageway to the captain's stateroom.

The two men squeezed themselves into the tiny compartment and stood face-to-face. "These options you mentioned—what—"

Rogov's hand slammed into the captain's neck, cutting off the questions. He pinned the man against the steel closet set into one side of the cabin, increasing the pressure on the man's neck. The submarine captain's eyes bulged, fright and indignation warring in his face. He reached up and tried to pull Rogov's hands away from his neck, but the Tartar's massive fingers were now interlaced behind his neck, his thumbs pressing against the captain's throat. Panic flooded the man's features as he realized the Tartar had no intention of easing up. With one massive thrust, Rogov crushed the man's windpipe, ending the contest. He let the skipper fall to the deck, and watched the life fade out of his eyes as his brain ran out of oxygen. Just before the man died, Rogov kicked him in the crotch. No reaction. The foul smell of human waste flooded the tiny compartment as the captain's dying brain gave up control over its autonomic functions.

When he was sure the man was dead, Rogov lifted the captain up by the back of his collar and positioned him carefully on the bed. He tossed a blanket over him, then turned the man's face toward the wall, cushioning it on a pillow. He felt several tiny vertebrae snap as he forced the man's head into position.

Although he was certain the ruse wouldn't last for long, it was always handy to give men an excuse to do what their fear compelled them to. If they thought the captain had suddenly taken ill, and might eventually retake command of the boat, there might be less initial resistance. And by the time they were completely certain the captain was dead, it would be too late.

Rogov left the compartment and returned to the control center to take command of the submarine.

"There," Holden said, pointing to the northeast. "Do you see it?"

"Yes!"

Holden could see a broad smile spreading below the binoculars, and shook his head. Why seeing one whale made up for the misery of being at sea in the North Pacific for these people, he would never understand.

"Can you get closer to it?" the scientist asked eagerly. "It's huge; it could be one of the largest of the species ever seen."

"We'll try, sir, but the seas are a bit touchy right now." Holden walked back to the navigator's table and studied the position plotted for the whale on the paper overlay. Maybe, just barely, they could run northeast for a while without getting broadside to the waves. It would take some careful tacking and maneuvering, but it could be done. He looked up and met the navigator's eyes, exchanging a brief look of disbelief.

"Yes, sir, I think we can do it," he said finally, straightening up. "Helmsman, come right to course zero-one-five."

The sickening yaw of the small boat increased, but was still within the limits of safety. Holden felt the boat shudder as the waves caught her more solidly on the beam.

"Oh, man, oh, man," the scientist said happily, sounding like a child in a candy store. "If this just—"

"What?" Holden asked sharply.

The scientist's smile had disappeared. He lowered the

binoculars slowly. His face was pale. "It's not a whale," he said shakily. "I think we'd better—"

Whatever the man had intended to say was lost forever. The fishing boat's bow shot up out of the waves like a seesaw, standing her almost completely on her stern. Holden, along with the rest of the men on the bridge, smashed into the aft bulkhead, which now seemed like a floor beneath them. Holden was vaguely aware of the unnatural motion of the ship as it gyrated around on its stern, now truly resembling the cork it had been imitating earlier.

Someone landed on his back, the impact forcing the breath out of his lungs. Holden felt two ribs crack. The deck—no, the bulkhead—careened crazily underneath him.

Finally, after what seemed an eternity suspended in the air, the bow of the ship headed down toward the ocean. Holden was flung forward again, this time hitting the glass window in the forward part of the bridge. He felt it crack, quiver underneath him, the steel safety mesh embedded in it preventing it from shattering completely.

But steel mesh couldn't keep water out. The bow and forecastle plunged down, water washing over the bridge and covering most of the forward part of the ship. It quickly filled the bridge, prying Holden off the shattered window and tossing him around on its roiling surface along with the other flotsam and jetsam on the bridge. Holden flailed, barely conscious, trying to lift his head far enough out of the water to try to breath. It was cold, so cold. Thirty-four degrees, he remembered from yesterday's meteorological report. Survival time—well, in these waters, it was measured in seconds rather than in minutes. No danger of living long enough to ever see a shark or any other leviathan of the deep approaching.

Holden struggled bitterly to hold on to consciousness, knowing he had only seconds left to live. He had just managed to suck in a deep breath when the last bit of his consciousness faded.

SS *Serenity* twisted and rolled in the waves for two minutes longer. The water was already lapping over her bow and washing around the decks. Suddenly, she gave one last shudder and rolled to port, dumping her superstructure into the water. Her starboard side remained visible for a few minutes longer, until one particularly large wave washed over her and shoved her down into the depths. By that time, the core body temperature of the crew and scientists on the ship had already slipped well below the levels needed to maintain consciousness. They all drowned, not a single one of them aware that they were breathing seawater instead of air.

1237 Local
Kilo 31

Rogov stood now in the middle of the control room, occupying the same position the captain had just hours earlier. The stilled, troubled looks on the crew members' faces told him he had not yet solidified his command of the boat. But he would, and it would be sooner than these young men ever suspected. His Cossack ancestors had learned long ago that fear was a more potent motivator than any pretentious ideals of friendship or mutual respect. These men would understand that soon.

He stared at the sonar screen, examining what he saw

there with the rudimentary amounts of knowledge he had. While he was a quick learner, his time on board the submarine had been too limited to allow him to develop much expertise in interpreting the arcane lines and symbols that streaked across the screen.

"What is that?" he demanded, pointing at a jagged-looking cluster of lines on the screen.

The technician swallowed nervously. "An—an explosion, sir," he said nervously. "Some distance away from us."

"The cause?" Rogov demanded.

"I thought—I thought I heard a torpedo just before that. Maybe. I can't be sure."

Rogov slammed his beefy hand into the side of the technician's head, knocking him out of the chair. The technician sprawled on the deck, looking up at the Cossack. Fear glazed his eyes.

Rogov regarded him levelly. "Next time, you will not be so slow to bring significant matters to my attention," he suggested. "You are not indispensable—none of us are. If you ever lie to me or tell me less than the complete truth—or, as in this instance, neglect to bring some matter to my attention—I will kill you."

The technician nodded, a bare twitch of his head. Rogov pointed at the chair. "Resume your duties." He turned to the rest of the control room crew, letting his cold gaze wander over them, impaling each one where they stood. "You have observed. It is up to you what you have learned. Learn quickly and you will live longer." He turned back to the technician. "Tell me about this explosion."

"It— it was far from us, maybe thirty kilometers," the technician babbled, profound relief at still being alive making his voice shaky and uneven. "The Oscar—she fired, I think. Maybe a torpedo—I don't know, I couldn't hear it all, but—"

"The target," Rogov demanded. "Was it the carrier?"

The technician shook his head. "No, Comrade, the carrier was too far away. It was another surface vessel, I think. There was a fishing boat—at least I think it was a fishing boat. It sounded like one, although it did not act like it. The diesel engine, yes, but no indication of trolling nets or any of the other activities I expect from a fishing boat." His voice ceased abruptly, as though he realized he was babbling. "There is nothing else I can add, Comrade."

Rogov seized the back of the man's neck, clamping his viselike fingers down hard. He felt the man's pulse beat under his fingers, fluttering now like a bird's. "Do not call me Comrade," he said quietly, menace in his voice. "You may call me sir, you may call me Colonel, but never Comrade. You and I—we have no blood in common. You will remember that, along with your other duties."

"Yes, Colonel," the man squeaked, barely able to force his voice past the cruel pressure on his throat. "I will remember."

"And so will the rest of you," Rogov said, raising his voice slightly. "Your people have forgotten much, but I will ensure that you remember this much. A Cossack is no comrade to any of you," he said, pronouncing the hated word with disgust dripping in his voice. "We remember what you have forgotten. You will learn, during the next weeks, how much that is." He turned back to the navigational chart, pretending to examine their position relative to the Oscar, buying himself some time to think at the expense of the crew's nerves.

It must have been the Oscar, he decided. Her orders were to stay in the deep waters that were her natural abode, using her speed and nuclear propulsion to interdict any vessels that approached too close to Attu or threatened to compromise the mission. For now, at least. Later, she'd have other missions, ones that made better use of her potent ship-killing capabilities.

But why surface to fire? He puzzled over that for a moment, trying to peer into the mind of the other submarine commander's mind. Maybe to get a visual on the contact, to better weigh the delicate considerations that went into deciding to fire. With the American carrier in the area, the Oscar's commander would have wanted to make sure he was not attacking within clear view of any warship. Unexplained losses in the North Pacific were common since the poorly equipped fishing vessels plied unforgiving waters and treacherous, unpredictable seas, but killing one of them within sonar range of the battle group would have been idiotic.

That must have been it, he decided, and felt a sense of relief as the unexplained explosion slipped neatly into an understandable tactical pattern. The Oscar's commander was also a Cossack, as reliable and implacably determined as Rogov himself. And, as with Rogov, the Russian submarine force's chain of command had never suspected either man's higher loyalties.

The engineering problems the sonarman mentioned—was it possible? He shrugged. There were contingency plans for just such an occasion. There always were. But before he could alter his own plans, he had to find out whether or not the Oscar was out of commission.

Rogov turned to the conning officer. "I wish to observe this boat that the Oscar has attacked."

The conning officer nodded and gave the commands preparatory to surfacing the submarine. Facing the churning ocean above was far less dangerous than remaining submerged below.

**1500 Local
Adak**

Tombstone Magruder strode briskly to the front of the room. He paused behind the podium and surveyed the faces arrayed before him. The assembled media and camera crews had that eager, slightly slavering look he'd come to expect from the press. He had even seen that expression on Pamela's face at times, and flinched away from it.

Where was—there she was, seated in the middle of the pack. He suppressed a smile, wondering what sort of mistaken maneuvering had earned her that chair. Pamela Drake, star correspondent for ACN, had never been pack—never in her entire life. Her normal seat at any press conference was in the front row, directly in front of the speaker, where her astute questions and bulldog glare could rarely be avoided. She must have arrived late, he mused, and wondered what had been the cause of that.

"Thank you all for being here today," Tombstone began, shuffling the papers in front of him. "As you know, this is a sad but historic occasion for the Navy. Decommissioning a command that has served this nation so honorably is never a pleasant task, but in these days of downsizing—right-sizing, as some of you have chosen to call it—most of our forward deployed units are being pulled back to CONUS—Continental United States, for you civilians," he added, noting a few puzzled looks. "Now, I'll start with a brief—"

"Admiral Magruder," he heard someone say. He turned away from the slide presentation he had been about to begin, covering the illustrious history of the P-3 squadron's service in Adak, his eyes going immediately to the slim, all-too-familiar figure. Pamela's voice still could cut through him to some warm, secret place deep inside. Memories of the last time he had seen her aboard USS *Jefferson* surfaced.

Now, seeing her again after more than six months, the strength of his reaction surprised him. Memories of Tomboy should have erased every trace of Pamela Drake from his soul. Yet there was still something compellingly attractive about the strong, smooth curves of her body, the emerald eyes framed by dark hair now touched with gray, the easy athletic balance of her stance. He sighed. Pamela Drake had quit haunting his dreams five months ago. He supposed seeing her in reality was the payback for that. "Miss Drake," he began coolly, "if you could just hold your questions, there will be plenty of time for them after the presentation. I think you'll find that most of the information you need is already contained in this brief."

Pamela regarded him bluntly, a slight tinge of amazement creeping into her expression. "Evidently you haven't heard, yet, Admiral," she remarked. "If you had, you would know that the decommissioning ranks a poor second against this current story."

"And what would that be, Miss Drake?" Tombstone asked. The conviction in her voice gave rise to an uneasiness in his stomach. Whatever else she might have been, Pamela Drake was one hell of a reporter. If she was hot on the trail of another story, then there was probably something to it.

"About thirty minutes ago," Pamela said, reading from a slip of paper in her hand, "the Greenpeace vessel SS *Serenity* disappeared fifty miles north of here. Immediately prior to that, an F-14 Tomcat was observed circling overhead. Did the crew of that Tomcat see anything that might explain the disappearance of this peaceful research vessel? And what is the squadron here doing as far as SAR goes—sea-air rescue?"

Tombstone rocked back slightly on his heels, stunned at her claim. He locked eyes with her for a moment and saw the determination burning in her eyes. "This brief will be postponed indefinitely," he said abruptly. A protesting murmur arose from the crowd, quickly growing to a clamorous racket. "Miss Drake—please accompany my people immediately to my briefing room."

Tombstone turned and strode away from the podium, aware of Captain Craig and two master-at-arms approaching Pamela. Tombstone heard her high heels clattering on the worn linoleum behind him.

Three minutes later, they were alone in the briefing room. "What is this about?" Tombstone demanded.

"No time for hi, how are you?" she said sarcastically.

"Not when lives may be at stake. Damn it, Pamela, what are you talking about?"

She met his gaze levelly. "Fifteen minutes ago, a fishing boat just south of the Aleutian Islands reported seeing a large explosion. The fishing boat was departing the area. The Greenpeace ship had been interfering with their operations, and their captain had finally given up trying to fish those waters. The captain claims to have seen a large fireball, and then the Greenpeace ship disappeared off the radar scope. Now what does that sound like to you?"

Tombstone swore silently, then turned to his operations officer. "Get everything we have airborne," he ordered.

The operations officer said, "Admiral, there's not much chance—"

"I know, I know," Tombstone said. "With survival times in the North Pacific, there's probably not much we can do. But I'll be damned if I'll sit here and hold a briefing while there's a chance we can save someone. Go on, get moving!"

The operations officer had just reached the door when Tombstone thought of something else. "Captain Craig," he said. "That squadron—they're supposed to fly out for CONUS tomorrow morning, right?"

The chief of staff nodded. "The support staff will be here for another week, but the aircraft are leaving."

"Hold back two of those P-3's and enough maintenance personnel to keep them up and ready to fly. And get a full load of sonobuoys and torpedoes on them."

The operations officer turned back to him, and looked at him uncertainly. "You think that—"

"That the boat might have suffered a massive engineering casualty," Tombstone said. "But based on my experience, the most common explanation for a surface ship sinking unexpectedly is a submarine. And if there's one out there . . ."

He let the thought trail off. If the Soviets were deploying their submarines again—excuse me, the *Russians*, he thought bitterly—then it was the height of foolishness to pull this squadron back to CONUS. Now, more than ever, they might be needed at the westernmost point of America's strategic envelope. He turned back to Pamela Drake. "Thank you for the information, Miss Drake," he said. "We won't be needing you here any longer."

"Oh, but I think you will, Stoney," she said softly. "Unless you want me to break the story of how ACN is now briefing Navy commanders on their operational responsibilities, I suggest you let me stay. And I'll want full access to the crews of those P-3's when they return. Otherwise, you're not gonna like my report when I file it."

Tombstone groaned. In the span of ten minutes, Pamela Drake had gone from fond memory to nemesis.

CHAPTER 4
Monday, 26 December

1530 Local
Kilo 31

Two hours later, moving west at an undetectable eight knots, the Kilo approached the area where the explosion had occurred. Except for the chirping clicks of snapping shrimp and the low, plaintive calls of a pod of whales, the ocean around them was silent. The lack of noise told him what he needed to know. Had the Oscar truly suffered an engineering casualty, she would not have been so quiet.

"Colonel, sir!" The sonar technician swiveled around in his chair to face the center of the control room. "American surveillance aircraft in the area." He pointed at a line on his waterfall display.

Rogov darted across the control room, a surprisingly quick movement for one so solidly built. "Classification?"

"A P-3 Orion—one of their ASW air-surface surveillance aircraft."

"I know what a P-3 is, you fool." Rogov laid one hand on the man's shoulder and pressed in gently, finding the sensitive nerve endings embedded in the trapezius. "Tell me something useful."

"Sir, it's not very close," the technician said rapidly. "Five miles, maybe more. So far I have detected no noise of sonobuoys entering the water."

"No indication of helicopters? Or active sonobuoys?"

"No. All I can hear is the aircraft."

"Circling?"

The technician pressed his hands over his ears, crushing the earphones down to eliminate every last vestige of noise inside the control center. He listened carefully, all too aware of how much his safety hung in balance. Finally, he shook his head. "No, Comra—Colonel, sir," he said carefully. "They are maneuvering in the area, but they do not appear to be circling over a sonobuoy field or making MAD runs in the area." That was all the technician knew, and he hoped it would be enough.

Rogov released his grasp on the man's shoulder, and patted gently the very spot he'd been probing with his fingers just moments earlier. "Very good," he said soothingly. "See—you can learn how to operate as I wish. In the future, pattern your reports on the questions I just asked."

The sonar technician nodded nervously, wondering just how likely it was that he would survive the cruise after all.

"Set quiet ship," Rogov ordered to the conning officer. The word was passed in whispers throughout the submarine. Unnecessary machinery was turned off, and the few crew members still wearing shoes slipped out of them, treading silently on the steel decks in thin cotton socks. Aft, in engineering, the engineers reset all of the machinery to its optimum quieting configuration, relying on the extensive shock mounting and sound isolation systems built into the propulsion plant to prevent any noise from radiating out through the hull into the sea. In the galley, the cooks quickly secured every bit of gear within reach, padding the edges of the braces holding large pots and utensils to ensure that no sudden shift inside the boat would cause noise to come out of their compartment. Based on the rumors that they'd heard floating back from the control room, disobeying one of their new commander's orders would bring swift and serious consequences.

"The antiair missiles?" Rogov said, turning to the submarine's executive officer. "When were they last tested?"

"Six months ago, Colonel," the man said quickly. "We've detected some minor operating deficiencies in their performance. Whether or not they would work now, after having been—"

"Colonel! Colonel, sir," the sonar technician said suddenly. "The antiair missiles and CODEYE radar were tested just three weeks ago, right before we deployed on this mission. The captain said," the man paused and swallowed, then continued doggedly, "the captain said it performed within specifications." The technician shuddered slightly, and leaned back against his chair, wondering whether or not he had just done a good job of following orders or had committed treason. The line seemed so very unclear anymore.

"Very well," Rogov said quietly. He turned back to the executive officer. "You were perhaps not on board during that workup operation?"

The executive officer stood silent. Rogov leaned forward, and in a motion so quick that the executive officer barely had time to flinch, reached out and slapped the man across the face. "I need an answer," Rogov said, in the same quiet tones. "I must know now whether or

not I shall need to be constantly watching my back,
or whether you will perform your duties. Make your
choice."

The executive officer took in the faces of the men
standing behind Rogov, saw the pale, pleading eyes, the
fearful yet supportive expressions. What he decided
would make a difference in their lives—whether they
lived, whether they died, and whether anyone with
sufficient technical knowledge of the submarine remained on board to ensure their safe return home. The
executive officer swallowed hard, then said, "My memory
seems to have failed, Colonel. The technician is right. I had
forgotten about that test."

Rogov slipped behind the executive officer and thrust
one meaty forearm around the man's throat from behind.
Pulling the XO's head back, Rogov extracted his pistol
from its holster. He placed the snub nose of the 9mm
against the executive officer's temple and said quietly, "It
may be that I will need to kill you very soon, but it will
be your decision, not mine. As I said—make your choice
now. Will you follow my orders? On your word as a
naval officer."

The executive officer could barely breathe as the arm
tightened down over his windpipe. He managed a hoarse
gasp. "Yes." The pressure ceased abruptly, and he felt the
cold, hard barrel move away from his head.

As his vision cleared, he saw that the aura of fear in
the crew's face had turned to sheer terror. If Rogov had
fired the pistol inside the submarine, there was a good
chance it would have penetrated the hull, sending a
fire-hose-hard stream of water into the most sensitive
electronic gear on the submarine. Even if they'd been
able to patch it, too much of their war-fighting capability

might have been permanently damaged. Moreover, the ricochet might have killed someone else in the control room on its way to penetrating the hull.

"Get the system ready, then," Rogov ordered. "We won't use it unless they force us to."

"Colonel, if we use the system, we've just given away our biggest tactical advantage—our invisibility. Seconds after we fire, every aircraft in the area will be dumping torpedoes into the water. And they'll have our exact location based on the trajectory of the missile."

Rogov turned to him and almost smiled. He raised one finger and waggled it at the executive officer in one of his sudden changes of mood that so unnerved the crew. "You're making two assumptions, both of which are wrong. First, that there will be more than one aircraft in the area. As of now, we have indications of only one. And second, if there is only one aircraft, you're assuming that the shot will miss."

"But with a new system, op-tested only once and still in prototype stage—" the executive officer began.

Rogov cut him off with a sharp laugh. "Then do not miss."

Tuesday, 27 December
0600 Local
Attu

The Spetsnaz commander pushed the door open. Finally, the vicious storm had started to break. Wind speed had dropped to less than thirty knots, and visibility had increased to at least two kilometers. Not ideal weather, but certainly not the paralyzing arctic blast that it had been two hours ago.

Even foul weather was better than having Rogov with them. He sighed, wondering if there was any way to convince the senior Cossack to stay on board the submarine. There was nothing in this part of the mission that he could help with, anyway.

Behind him, his men crowded toward the door, eager to escape the confines of the dripping cave. The commander made a small hand motion. No words were necessary when dealing with these highly trained special warfare commandos. He heard a few small noises behind him, and knew without turning to look that they were readying their gear. Finally, sensing that they were ready, he shoved the door open the rest of the way. Though the ice cave had never been warm, the frigid air that poured in was markedly colder than the interior temperature. If nothing else, he thought, ice was a good insulator. Five hours' worth of body heat had accumulated in the small cavern, although their breath still frosted on their full whiskers and the air still gnawed at exposed flesh.

He stepped out into the open and surveyed the land around him. It was just as he'd been briefed. A low, flat plain rose gently toward the cliff that contained their cave, ice covering tundra. Except for the wind still screaming across the craggy ridge behind him, it was silent. There were no signs of habitation or wildlife, and certainly not of vegetation. Nothing could have survived for long on this island—nothing.

He turned back and smiled at his companions. They moved out quietly, almost noiselessly, the fresh, wind-blown snow barely crunching under their arctic-wear boots. They fanned out in teams of two, their commander staying carefully out of the way by the ice cavern, watching. He was the safety observer for the operation, a role he took extremely seriously. He had to, given the nature of the explosives his men were handling.

Each man had shouldered a pack onto his back, something slightly larger than a knapsack. Each bag contained four specifically designed explosive devices, for which the outlaw gang of Cossacks had paid a small fortune to the Japanese. Microsecond timers, all slaved to a common signal, were nestled in a special titanium compartment at the end of each long, cylindrical wand. Packed in the rest of the two-foot shaft was a special formula of highly toxic plastic explosive formulated for use in subzero environments. According to the Japanese, each stick would blast a hole five feet straight down into the frozen ice and tundra. The charge was shaped to blow a stream of ice and water out of the hole. The melted sides of each cylinder would immediately refreeze, creating a smooth, slick interior surface to each shaft. The bottom of each hole might be a bit ragged, he mused, but that would hardly matter.

He watched the two teams measure carefully, setting the charges at the corners of a twenty-foot box. Each man then extracted an ice drill from the pack, and began the laborious process of creating a tamping hole for the charge.

Thirty minutes later, after each hole was complete, they measured again. Exactly on point, as the commander had known they would be. Behind the wool scarf that covered his mouth, the smile broadened once again. The four holes would hold the support structure for a small but potent antiair defense system. With the help of German engineers, experienced in the manufacture of Stinger missiles and their own superb brand of weaponry, they had built a modular, transportable system that had no equal in the world. One-tenth the size of an American Patriot battery, yet capable of being operated in either a local or remote mode, the system could track and target twenty incoming aircraft simultaneously. It was also effective against missiles operating at less than Mach 5, a limitation that put most other nations' armament well within its capabilities.

Once in place, the system would be virtually automatic, requiring operator input only to disable it from incoming friendly flights.

He watched as the men carefully set their charges into the holes, then returned to join him at his side. The commander reached into his own backpack and extracted the firing control box. After ensuring that everyone was safely out of harm's way and had covered their ears and turned away from the holes, he clamped a large set of earphones over his ears and turned away. Holding the remote control at an angle away from his body, he punched the detonation switch.

The reaction was immediate and impressive. The explosion shook the ground under their feet, setting off a series of groans and creaks, not only from the ice underneath them but from the sculptured cliffs around their cave. For a moment, he wondered whether the island, essentially ice covering an old volcanic flume, could withstand the shock. Even at a distance of fifty feet from the explosions, ice rained down on them.

Thirty seconds later, the ominous rumbling and creaking under his feet subsided. He removed his earphones and checked his comrades, pleased to note that not a one of them showed the slightest bit of concern. He motioned again, and the four men set out to check their holes.

For the first time since he'd started the evolution, his

thoughts wandered. He stared out at the icy, dark gray sea, wondering where the transport was. According to his information, a Ropuchka amphibious transport ship was en route to the area at that very moment, following carefully in the wake of a Russian icebreaker. In the Ropuchka were antiair batteries that would be erected over these holes, as well as a support crew of technicians, engineers, and guards.

Not that there was anything to guard against. He glanced around the landscape, still uneasy for some reason he couldn't exactly define. Not a single survey had ever turned up a trace of life on the island, and he saw no indications now that those estimates had been wrong. Still—

Well, it never hurt to be too careful. After they'd finished inspecting the blast holes, he'd send two men out on a quick area survey, just to make absolutely sure that the island was completely uninhabited. He looked behind him, assessing the difficulty of climbing the jutting spires carved into the ice. What might be impossible for most men would simply be the first challenge his team had had all week.

**0642 Local
USS *Jefferson***

"What did your SAR find?" the familiar voice said. Batman smiled, despite the seriousness of the situation. Tombstone had been his wingman for too many years for his voice to be anything except immediately recognizable.

"The same thing your P-3's found—nothing," Batman

answered. "One of the S-3 pilots thought he saw an oil slick, but it's hard to tell in this weather. The wave action would have dispersed anything floating on the surface by now."

"No debris?"

Rear Admiral Edward Everett "Batman" Wayne shook his head glumly. "Admiral, I wish I had better news for you, but I just don't. You know how hard it is to find wreckage from a boat in this weather."

Tombstone's frustrated sigh carried clearly over the radio circuits. "Yeah, yeah, I know, but that can't stop us from trying. You wouldn't believe the news media I have breathing down my neck out here."

Batman thought he detected something besides true professional annoyance in his old squadron mate's voice. "One of those news media people wouldn't happen to be the lovely Miss Pamela Drake, now, would it?" he asked shrewdly.

If swearing on a Navy radio circuit weren't prohibited, he could have sworn he heard Tombstone mutter a curse. But then again, the private circuit rigged up between the two admirals was hardly a normal channel.

"Of course it is! It just wouldn't seem right, with things going to hell in a handbasket, if she weren't around, now, would it?"

"And how is that working out?" Batman pressed.

Silence descended on the circuit. Finally, Batman heard Tombstone sigh. "I'd be lying if I told you it was easy," Tombstone said finally.

"Does Tomboy know she's out there?"

"No. And I'll thank you not to tell her. I'll get around to it in my own time, in my own way. The separation hasn't been easy on either of us."

"At least she gets to fly every day," Batman said, a note of longing in his voice. "I'm tempted to put myself on the schedule for one of those reconnaissance flights."

"That was one of the hardest parts of that job, Batman," Tombstone's voice said soberly, "realizing that it wasn't my turn anymore—that I could do more good for the battle group by staying where I was supposed to be, in TFCC and in command, than I could trying to outdo some youngster with faster reflexes and better eyesight."

Batman chuckled. "Am I going to be following you around for the rest of my career, Stoney?" he asked, "Learning every lesson two years after you've learned it?"

"Up to you, shipmate. You're going to make mistakes. We all do. I recommend you avoid mine, and make your own."

Batman felt the ship shudder as another Tomcat on the cat spooled up to full military power. "You hear that, Stoney?" he asked.

"The sound of freedom."

"Yep, and for all that I get tired of following in your footsteps, I'd sure as hell rather be out here than stuck ashore like you are right now."

"Don't rub it in, asshole. You'll get your turn ashore. In the meantime, why don't you see if you can't rustle up some evidence of what happened to that Greenpeace boat? Out there, you can always have a convenient communications failure. Back here, I can't seem to get away from these people. Give me something I can use." Tombstone's voice took on an ominous, pleading quality.

"Roger that. I'll see what we can come up with."

Batman replaced the receiver thoughtfully and stared

at it for a moment. In the twenty years that he had known
Tombstone, he had never known the hotshot Tomcat pilot
to sound so beleaguered. Even in the midst of the
Spratlys conflict, or engaged in a dogfight over the
Norwegian coast, Tombstone had had the ability to
maintain an absolutely unflappable demeanor that had
earned him his nickname. If shore duty had the ability to
make his friend sound like a pussy-whipped lieutenant,
then Batman wasn't sure he wanted any part of it.

Batman walked out of his cabin, through the Flag
Mess, and toward the far entrance to the mess. His chief
of staff's combination stateroom and office was located
immediately inside the door to the mess. Batman rapped
lightly once on the doorjamb. The chief of staff glanced
up from a two-foot sack of paperwork, then immediately
stood. "Yes, Admiral?"

"Let's get everybody assembled in the briefing room at
fifteen hundred, COS," Batman said. "We need to do
some serious thinking about this Greenpeace boat."

COS regarded him soberly. "Admiral, you know
there's no chance that those men are still alive. Even if
they made it into the rafts, the cold would have killed
them by now." COS shook his head. "A damned shame,
but I don't know what we can do about it at this point."

"That's not what worries me, COS. Sure, we need to
make every effort we can to find any survivors. People
survive under the damnedest conditions, and if those men
and women have the guts to hold out in a life raft, I'll do
my damnedest to find them. But what worries me even
more is why they sank in the first place."

COS shrugged. "Sounds like a massive engineering
casualty to me."

Batman looked at him thoughtfully. "Maybe. Or they

could have even struck a submerged iceberg. All of those are possible explanations. But we don't get paid the big bucks to think of the easy solutions. I want to make sure we're all thinking on the same wavelength."

"You think they were attacked? By who, a coalition of angry fishermen who want to kill whales?"

Batman shook his head. "I don't know, COS. And that's what worries me. Until we have some evidence of what happened to them, I'm going to assume they wandered into harm's way. And I want everybody on this ship thinking the same way."

0800 Local
Adak

Tombstone heard a light rap at his door. He looked up and saw Pamela Drake framed by the doorway.

"Do you have a moment for me, Admiral?" she asked politely.

"Only if you're not going to rake me over the coals," Tombstone answered. "After yesterday, I'm not up to any more surprises."

She walked across the room and settled into the chair in front of his desk with that too-familiar combination of easy grace and sensuality. She crossed her legs, not bothering to yank her skirt down when it rode up over her thighs. "Off the record, Stoney—can I still call you that?"

He nodded. "There's a lot of history between us, Pamela. I wouldn't change a bit of it."

"Not even the way it ended?"

He shook his head. "Neither of us was willing to

compromise. I won't quit flying; you won't quit hop-scotching around the world in search of the hottest story. It was inevitable. That doesn't mean I have to like it."

She sighed. "I suppose you're right. Still, it's good to see you again."

"And you as well. Now," he continued briskly, "what's on your mind? Still off the record."

She looked troubled. "This Greenpeace boat. It's a tragedy, of course. There are several million of my colleagues out interviewing family members as we speak." She grimaced, as though disgusted with the inevitable state of how-does-it-feel-to-lose-your-husband questions that were sure to be posed to the surviving families. "And as bad as it is for the men and women who were on that boat, I'm not sure why you're mobilizing the entire ALASKCOM and a U.S. carrier battle group to look for survivors. As your operations officer said, there's little chance that the men are alive."

"Men and women," Tombstone corrected. "Two years ago, you would have chided me for making that mistake."

"Okay, men and women. But still—"

"Why are we mobilizing a full-scale SAR exercise when we're fairly certain that no one survived?" He let his eyes rest on hers, and studied the sea-green eyes flecked with gold. There had been a time when just looking at her brought a thrill of anticipation to him, a tightening and hardening he'd never been able to control. Now, seeing her here, he was surprised to find he still had the same reaction. Muted, perhaps, the edges smoothed away by his fascination with Tomboy, but the echoes of their long relationship still sang in his body. Suddenly, he wanted nothing more than to pull her toward him, run his hand over the smooth curves and sleek skin, feel her body warm to his touch and respond to him. He shook his head and tried to push the image of Pamela naked on the bed beside him out of his head. "A short lesson on governmental politics is in order," he said, aware that his voice had softened and become more intimate.

Pamela caught the change. "It's still there, isn't it?" she said softly. "Me, too, Stoney."

He sighed. "And the more senior each of us gets, the less likely we'll do anything about it. For now, let me see if I can bore us both for a few minutes."

She regarded him speculatively. "Maybe that's better for now."

"You know about NGOs—nongovernmental organizations," he began. "They're always a factor in policy decisions, regardless of whether the government wants to admit it or not. These groups have more power than many of the strongest lobbies in the United States. Things like the American Red Cross, the Ralph Nader groups, the nonprofit corporations—"

"And Greenpeace," she finished. "I understand that part, but why is it important now?"

Tombstone pointed to a large map on the wall behind him. "The Aleutian Islands, that's why. They stretch from the tip of Alaska in a long, south-curving arc over to Russia. At the closest point, the last Aleutian Island is only eleven miles from Russian soil. For centuries, the people who lived there wandered back and forth between the two countries, ignoring all the political boundaries that we set up from five thousand miles away. But during the Cold War, that changed."

"Because they're so close to Russia?"

He nodded. "During the days when we were con-

cerned about Russian submarines, the Aleutian Islands
contained some of the most advanced listening posts and
tracking stations in the world. In addition to that, here on
Adak, four P-3C Orion squadrons were stationed in case
we ever escalated into full-out war. Up to the north of the
Aleutian Islands, in the Bering Sea, the Soviets used to
conduct regular ballistic missile patrols. With the long-
range missiles on the Delta-IV and the Typhoon ballistic
missile submarines, those boats damn near don't have to
leave port to strike any place in the continental United
States. But they deployed them to the North Sea, under
the ice, to make them harder to find." He shook his head.
"You wouldn't believe what a tactical nightmare it is,
trying to track a submarine under the ice. Sonar echoes
off the ice overhead as well as off the ocean bottom. The
water is so cold that there's virtually no temperature
gradient. Sound energy travels straight to the bottom and,
if you're lucky, might reflect back up to be detected. Add
to that the noise caused by ice floes, icebergs calving,
and hordes of snapping shrimp, and you've got a
virtually sonar-proof environment."

"So that's the reason for the Aleutian Island stations.
But how does that fit in with Greenpeace?"

"Downsizing. We can't afford to maintain all these
stations, so it's essential that we convince the American
people that they're not really needed anymore."

"And you're saying that's not true?" She reached
almost reflectively for her tape recorder, and then forced
herself to stillness.

"I'm not saying anything. We're off the record, remember? And as to how Greenpeace fits into this—well,
they're a very powerful organization. In the last fifteen
years, they've developed an array of international con-

tacts and supporters. Most of the time, we've been at loggerheads with them. If we do anything except make a full-out push on the search for survivors, the Greenpeace advocates who haunt the halls of Congress will claim that the United States military left them out to die. No one will ever question why they were up there in the first place in a boat not well suited for those waters, or whether some fault on their part led to this tragedy. Instead, it will become all our fault. The military is the favorite punching bag for every problem in the world these days. Someday soon, I expect to see the Navy blamed for crime in the streets and welfare problems."

"That's not fair," Pamela said sharply. "Many of the things I've reported on were the United States Navy's fault. The problems with women on ships, the death of that aviator—don't tell me that some of these weren't caused by the Navy pushing through unqualified people."

"We've had our problems, true," Tombstone acknowledged. "But no more than any large organization. You're talking about somewhere around half a million people— the United States Navy is a huge organization, Pamela. You're gong to get some bad apples in it. There's no way to screen them all out."

"So you're saying this search for survivors is primarily politically motivated?" She shook her head. "The Tombstone I knew ten years ago wouldn't have seen it that way."

"And the Pamela I knew ten years ago wouldn't have blindsided me in a press conference like you did yesterday," he shot back angrily.

She stood. "I guess this concludes this off-the-record interview, doesn't it? And it's still the same old thing. You and the Navy, that's all you ever think about."

He gazed at her, feeling the sense of familiarity and longing wash out of him. "I guess it is, Miss Drake," he said softly. "But just remember—you're the one who said it first."

The Spetsnaz stuffed the four holes bored into the ice with plastic to keep out the blowing ice and snow. That accomplished, the commander ordered them out into a surveillance patrol. The men split up into their two-man teams and began a careful survey of their temporary home.

The island itself was twenty miles long and five miles wide, and was one of the smaller outcroppings of the Aleutian chain. Two men headed west, examining the first plain that led down to the water. The other two headed east, climbing gear in hand, and set out to explore the ragged crust of ice that formed the upper boundary of the island.

The first half mile was relatively easy going, and they needed no more equipment than their hands to ascend the steadily increasing slope. After that, however, their progress was broken up by the need to set pitons in the jagged surface and relay up the slopes one after the other. While climbing it freestyle without the aid of ropes and climbing gear was well within their capabilities, their commander had cautioned them that they were to take no chances. With only five men on the island until reinforcements arrived, casualties were completely unacceptable.

After a brief discussion, the two Spetsnaz commandos

headed for the highest peak they could find, a promontory that jutted nine hundred feet above sea level. They spent the better part of an hour climbing it, checking along each stage of the way to make sure their tie-off points and ropes were set securely in the ice. Another time of year, any slight warming might have rendered the surface prone to crumbling, but in December the surface was as hard as rock.

"You see anything?" the lead climber asked his companion.

The second man shook his head. "No. Not a damned thing could survive out here, not without the kind of gear we carry."

The other man nodded agreement. "Always better to check, though," he remarked.

"Well, we've done that." He shivered slightly as the wind picked up, gusting and keening between the sharp crags. "Let's get back down and report."

Suddenly, the other man shook his head and pointed out at the ocean. Since the wind had died down, the swells and breakers pounding against the island had dropped down to four to five feet each. Marching across the ocean in sets of seven, each breaker was flecked with white and capped with a thin froth of foam, the twenty-knot wind still kicking up whitecaps. "Look over there."

The second man raised his binoculars and trained them in the direction his companion pointed. He swore quietly. "If I hadn't seen it—"

The first man grunted. "Commander isn't going to like this." He trained his own binoculars in that direction.

Perhaps two miles offshore, a small boat plowed through the waves, obviously bound for their island. "Where the hell did they come from?"

The other man shrugged. "One of the other islands, I guess. Though why the hell they'd bother to come here, I don't know. Nothing to eat."

"Maybe they're just fishing."

His companion shook his head. "I don't think so. They've got some gear on board, but they're not maneuvering like a fishing boat would. Look, they're headed straight for us."

The other man sighed. "We wait for them to come ashore and take them out, or we go back and report?"

"Let's radio back for instructions. I think I know what the boss is going to want, but let's double-check. You know what he told us."

The other man grinned wolfishly. "Yes. No survivors."

1338 Local
Kilo 31

"What do you mean, natives?" Rogov demanded.

"Just what I said. My men have detected a small boat with approximately six people on board, inbound this location. Unless directed otherwise, I intend to eliminate these complications. Your orders?" The Spetsnaz commander's voice was harsh and broken over the speaker. The Kilo was moving at steerageway just barely below the surface of the ocean, her antenna poking up above the surface for a scheduled communications break with the team ashore.

Rogov paused, staring at the microphone, then swore quietly. The key to executing this mission successfully required no interference from outside sources. At the very least, if the natives landed, they would be witnesses.

They must be Inuits or Aleuts, or one of the many other bands of native Alaskans that roamed the waters between the islands, foraging from the sea and living as they had for centuries on the desolate islands. Since the Oscar had eliminated the prying Greenpeace intruders, that was the only possible explanation. From what the Spetsnaz commander had said, the boat was too small to attempt trans-Pacific voyages. Therefore, it had to have come from one of the other islands.

He paused and considered his options. Sinking the Greenpeace boat had been accomplished silently and stealthily with a submarine, and there was no evidence left behind to betray the mission. But Inuits—somebody might miss them, and one of the other isolated islands might have contact with the mainland. Finally, he reached a decision. "Avoid them if possible. If you are observed or if they come ashore, take them hostage. We'll consider other options at a later time."

"Very well."

"And I will be joining you ashore tomorrow morning." He glanced over at the Kilo's executive officer, who was watching him with a faintly hopeful look on his face. "The Kilo will remain offshore to provide assistance as needed."

He hung up the microphone abruptly, knowing that the Spetsnaz commander understood exactly what the phrase "other options" meant.

The executive officer didn't. If he had, he would have known that no Cossack ever left an untrustworthy officer at his back.

CHAPTER 5
Wednesday, 28 December

Commander Busby frowned and stared at the technician standing in front of him. "You're sure about this?"

The technician nodded. "No doubt in my military mind, sir." The younger man pointed at a series of lines stretching across the printout. "Look at those frequencies. Those aren't from military communications. Not ours, anyway."

"What *are* they from, then?" Busby asked. The three lines on the paper that the technician pointed to were cryptic strings of numbers, indicating frequencies and times of detection. To anyone else, it could just as well have been a report from a Supply logistics computer. He smiled for a second, wondering how many top-secret reports looked just as mundane.

"What's your best classification?" he asked finally, tapping his pencil on one column of numbers. "These frequencies—this isn't a long-range system."

"You're right about that. I'd call it some sort of short-range tactical system—maybe even handheld. Look how the signal strengths vary so widely. Could be caused by geography—somebody walks behind a rock and the antenna's not fully extended, you get that sort of dip."

"Did you check with our SEALs? Maybe they were playing with some of their toys."

The technician smirked. "Thought you might ask about that. And no, it's not our SEALs. The frequencies don't match up at all."

Commander Busby sighed and tossed the paper on his desk. The last thing he needed right now was evidence of unknown short-range tactical communications in their vicinity. He closed his eyes for a moment, visualizing a chart of the area. Nowhere those signals could have come from but the islands to the north. He opened his eyes and saw that the technician had come to the same conclusion.

"This is impossible, you know. Just how am I supposed to explain to the Admiral that we're detecting radio signals from the godforsaken rocks called the Aleutians? Nobody lives there, and we're certainly not ashore. If we're wrong about this, we're going to stir up a hell of a lot of trouble for nothing. Every intelligence group on board and back home is going to get their shorts twisted in a knot over this."

The technician nodded. "Yeah, but if everybody was where they were supposed to be all the time, they wouldn't need us, would they?"

Busby motioned to a chair sitting next to his desk. He reached for his coffee cup, curling his fingers gratefully around the warm, rough ceramic mug. The temperatures in CVIC—Carrier Intelligence Center—consistently hovered around the sixty-degree mark. Maintaining a stable, cool temperature inside the most sensitive spaces on board the carrier was one of his continual headaches, and no one had ever been able to come up with a compromise between the needs of the sophisticated equipment jammed into these small spaces and the human beings who operated it. As usual, operational requirements won out over human comfort.

"Okay, we need a game plan," Busby said finally. "Make me look smart here, Jackson."

The technician scooted his chair over next to Busby's and picked up the printout. "You can read it yourself, Commander; I know you can. Maybe some of those fellows believe you don't know everything that goes on back there, but not me."

"Pretend I'm dumb for a minute. Chances are, you'll explain something I would have forgotten to ask about."

The technician shot him a sardonic look. "Okay. See, here's the first detection," he said, pointing his pencil at the fifth line from the top. "Short duration—only two minutes. High frequency—you see, right here in this column?"

"Yeah, I've got that. But tell me how we know it's tactical communications."

"The signal breaks up. If this were a large transmitter, one drawing a hell of a lot of power, it would blast right around some of the obstructions. Instead, we get these changes in signal strength that indicate somebody's moving around. Or maybe walking around a rock, or something like that. Not something you see, except on mobile field communications."

"You ever seen these frequencies before?"

The technician shook his head, paused, and a thoughtful look crossed his face. "Something like it, but not this one exactly. Way back in A School, when we were studying the old Russian Bear. You remember, back

when we had an enemy? Hearing about the Bear-J that's
been in the area reminded me of it."

"So what does it look like?"

"I'm not certain, sir, but I remember one day they
played back for us some short-range Spetsnaz communications. Looked a little bit like this." The technician
shrugged. "Course, no telling who's using all that gear
these days. They could've farmed half of it out to the
border guards. And, like I was saying, there's nothing
really unique about this, except for the frequency. In the
range of short-range tactical communications, and not
one of ours. That's about all I can tell you for certain."

Busby thought for a minute, then hauled himself out of
his chair. "Guess I'm about as smart as I'm going to get,
then. Thanks for the briefing, Jackson. I'll let the admiral
know what's happening."

The technician took the hint, and rose to walk out of
the office. He turned right at the doorway, heading back
to the even chillier operating spaces within CVIC. At the
heavy steel cipher lock that shut his spaces off from the
rest of the intelligence center, he paused, then turned
back to watch Commander Busby's figure disappear
around the far corner.

Lab Rat. The technician chuckled a moment, wondering who had first hung that moniker on the diminutive
Commander Busby. Good call, whoever had done it,
although he thought the commander might have wished
for a more impressive nickname. But with his pale,
almost colorless hair, bright blue eyes magnified behind
thick Coke-bottle glasses, and generally frail, nervous
appearance, Commander Busby hadn't had a chance in
the world of avoiding that one.

Wish all officers were more like him, the technician

mused, punching in the numbers that would open the cipher lock to his outer door. Professionally demanding, tough to work for, but he took good care of his troops. And no pussyfooting around when it came to threat signals. The commander had said he'd take this straight to the admiral, and he would, carefully shielding his technicians from the myriad political considerations that would arise once the report went out.

The heavy door swung open, and a slight puff of air caressed his face, the result of the positive pressure gradient between the sensitive crypto spaces and the rest of CVIC. Jackson stepped over the shin-high knee-knocker and shoved the door closed behind him, waiting to make sure he heard the ominous click announcing the door was secure.

Well, it would be up to the admiral to decide what they did now.

1015 Local
Admiral's Cabin, USS *Jefferson*

"You think this is really something?" Batman asked Commander Busby.

"Define 'something,'" Busby said. "If you mean, do I think it's a valid detection, the answer is yes. But what it means—that I don't know, Admiral."

Batman sighed. "And you can't tell me what was said on the circuit, just that somebody was transmitting?"

"That's about it. It was all encrypted. With enough time, enough resources, NSA might be able to make something of it, but we can't here. And I'm not even sure that NSA could break it that fast—there are too many

good commercial encrypters on the market these days."
Busby shook his head. "I know the U.S. has tried to keep
control of digital encryption technology, but other nations aren't quite so vigorous."

"So for all we know, this could be that Greenpeace
boat communicating with their people back in the States?"

Busby shook his head. "Not at that frequency. You'd
see a high frequency—HF—for that. One thing we're
relatively sure of, this was a short-range signal."

"Satellite?"

"Not enough power. No, Admiral, I was hoping that
would be the case, but this signal has no other reasonable
explanation. None that I can come up with, anyway."

"Damn it. And we can't ignore it." Batman handed the
commander the printout sheet and stood up. "Well, I'll
have our people check it out. You'll want to debrief them
as soon as they return, I imagine."

"The SEALs?" Busby asked.

Batman smiled grimly. "They've spent the last three
months running laps in the hangar bays, taking up hours
on the Stairmaster machines, and generally chafing at the
bit. I imagine their commander is going to be more than
eager to jump on this one. And what better way to check
out a spurious radio signal from an island than to send in
the SEALs?"

1532 Local
Kilo 31

The ocean was peculiarly calm, cloaked in an uneasy,
expectant hush Rogov had come to associate with the
quiet before a williwaw. The covered lifeboat, pressed

once again into service as a shuttle between the submarine and the shore, bobbed gently against the hull.

Rogov set one foot on the first rung of the ladder, paused, and turned back to the executive officer, now in command of the boat. "You understand your orders?"

The executive officer nodded. "We remain surfaced until you signal that you are ashore, then maintain the original communications schedule for the next two weeks. If you fail to make four consecutive scheduled contacts, I am to return to base immediately and report the lack of contact to the man you have designated."

"And?"

"And to no one else," he added quickly. "My word as an officer, it will be done."

Rogov studied him for a moment, then let a grim smile of approval cross his face. "Very well. On your word. That will mean as much to you as it does to us."

"You may depend on it."

Rogov put his other foot on the first rung and started descending the ladder to the boat. Halfway down, the expression that had lulled the executive officer so easily melted into something that would not have calmed the most junior sailor on board that boat.

Rogov fingered the transmitter in his pocket. Cossacks never left enemies at their back. In this situation, four pounds of high-explosive plastic compound cemented to the wall of their dead skipper's stateroom would ensure it.

Two thousand meters later, he pressed the button. The Kilo shivered, then the ocean around her fountained up in a gout of metal, machinery, and men.

"Goddamned carrier jocks," Lieutenant Commander Bill "Ramrod" McAllister grumbled. "Be nice if they could learn to tell the difference between a civilian craft and a tanker." He put the P-3 into a gentle, left-hand bank, circling the large commercial vessel located below. "Even at this altitude, I can tell what it is."

"We going in for a closer look?" Lieutenant Commander Frank "Eel" Burns asked.

"Not unless you really think it's necessary. I can tell what it is from here," the pilot replied.

"Yeah, well, if we drop down and rig it out, it might be good practice. Not damned much else to play with out here," Eel replied.

"All right, all right," the pilot snapped. "If it'll keep you guys in the backseat from playing with yourselves, we'll go take a look." He nosed the P-3 Lockheed Orion over and headed toward the ocean below them.

Eel glanced uneasily at the antisubmarine warfare technician sitting next to him. AW1 Kiley Maroney, an experienced technician with five cruises under his belt, shrugged. He made a small movement with his hand, signifying a continuation of a discussion they'd dropped before boarding the aircraft. Pilots had their moods, and all a decent backseater could do was put up with it. When it came down to tactical command, they both knew that the man sitting in front of them would do what they needed.

"How 'bout we take a look at the island at the same time?" Eel suggested. "*Jefferson* claimed she got some strange signals coming off that island last night. Wouldn't hurt us to take a look."

"I tell ya, it comes from too many arrested carrier landings," the pilot said, continuing the diatribe he'd started earlier that day. "Scrambles their brains, it does. Just look at that," he finished, standing the P-3 on one wing to circle around the massive foreign-flagged tanker below them. "That's exactly where they reported that Greenpeace ship at. Does that look like a converted fishing vessel to you?"

"No, it certainly doesn't," Eel said slowly. "And I don't think even an F-14 jock could get the two confused."

"Well, if that's not what they reported, where the hell is the Greenpeace ship?" the pilot demanded. "I tell you, slamming into the deck that many times a day just rattles their brains. Ain't a damned one of them that's got a bit of sense."

"Let's go back to your first question," Eel suggested. "Where the hell *is* the Greenpeace ship? We know she's out here—too many people besides that Tomcat jock have seen it."

"Oh, it's out here, all right; I don't doubt that," the pilot answered. "But we try to work these things out so the carrier turns over some decent locating data to us. Some hotshot just made a bad report, and now we're going to have to re-search the whole area. And it's not like they'll get tasked to do that themselves—nothin' on the carrier's got long enough legs to pull the shifts that we pull."

"The S-3 might—" the technician started.

The pilot cut him off with a sharp laugh. "Yeah, like we can get them to agree to do surface surveillance," he said angrily. "If it doesn't involve dropping sonobuoys, they try to snivel out of the mission. People, we're gettin' screwed on this one."

Ten minutes later, after completing a detailed report on the superstructure of the tanker as well as a close scrutiny of the flag flying from her stern, the P-3 climbed back up to altitude.

"The island?" Eel suggested again.

"Give me a fly-to point," the pilot replied.

Eel busied himself on his console, laying in course and speed vectors to take them directly over the last island in the desolate Aleutian chain. Finally satisfied with his plan, he punched the button that would pop it up on the pilot's fly-to display.

"Got it," the pilot announced. The P-3 immediately leaned into a sharp right-hand turn. "Looks like about twenty minutes from here."

Eel flipped the communications switch over to the circuit occupied only by himself and the enlisted technician. "What you thinking?" he said quietly. "Me, I don't like the sound of this."

"Me neither, sir," the technician said uneasily. "Too many ghosts. That same F-14 jock reported a disappearing radar contact right before his Greenpeace locating data. Me, I'd want to check that out a lot more carefully."

"I'm inclined to agree with you. Especially with these EW—electronic warfare—signals that keep cropping up. Too many unexplained oddities in this tactical world."

"I'm staying heads up on the ESM gear, sir," the technician replied. "And the frequency they reported is

well within our capabilities. If somebody's talking down
there, we'll know it."

"They landed, cleaned the fish they'd caught, ate, then
left," the commando reported.

"And your men weren't seen?" Rogov demanded.

The Spetsnaz officer shook his head. "There was no
sign of it. The men were well hidden in the cliffs, and the
natives left immediately after they'd eaten."

"Then why did they come ashore at all?"

The commando shrugged. "Who knows why these
people do anything? Maybe their gods told them to;
maybe one of them had to take a crap. All I can tell you
is that they came, they left. I've left two men on watch
there, but we won't be able to keep that up forever. The
hike across the cliffs takes too long."

"Keep me advised."

Rogov stared up at the clear sky, which was already
starting to darken as the short day ended. At this latitude,
there were no more than a few hours of daylight out of
every twenty-four. Dismal living conditions, especially
when the frequent winter storms obscured even those
few hours of sunlight. He shook his head, marveling at
the strength of his ancestors who survived the long
march across this land bridge to enter the North American continent.

He snugged the cold weather parka more closely
around his face and readjusted the wool scarf covering
his mouth and nose. After only a few hours ashore, his

goggles were already slightly pitted from the blowing ice crystals. A thin tracery of ice had taken hold around the edge of one lens. He considered taking the goggles off long enough to clean them, but the memory of the sharp cold that had bitten into his face last time he tried that dissuaded him.

The Spetsnaz commander had been absolutely insistent on the importance of maintaining an outside watch, and rightly so. Rogov was tempted to remove himself from the watch rotation, but in the end decided that he would take his turn in order to assert his equal standing among the small band of trained killers he commanded. He shook his head as he turned around, scanning the horizon and air above him. Two days ago, he hadn't known he'd be worried about that.

Living under Attu conditions was already proving more harshly draining than he ever dreamed possible. Subsisting on field rations, trying to catch a few shivering hours of sleep in the dank cave, and pushing the men to complete the foundations for the weapons systems had taken more out of him than he thought possible. Was it possible, he wondered, that he'd been a fool to insist on supervising this mission personally? At forty-eight years of age, he was a good fifteen years older than the most senior Spetsnaz here. How significant that was hadn't shown up until he'd come ashore.

Somehow, the Spetsnaz seemed to thrive under the hostile, alien conditions. The danger, cold, and deprivation just seemed to bring a gleefully unholy look to their eyes. Nothing bothered them, not even the small section of ice cave crumbling in on them last night, almost landing on Rogov. He'd cried out, he remembered, when the first slabs of ice had hit his sleeping bag. The disdain in the other men's eyes had been evident.

Off on the horizon, the thin traces of color were already deepening, evidence of the approaching dark. A flicker of movement caught his eye. He squinted. Had he seen something or was it just—no, there it was again, barely visible against the gloom.

He raised the radio to his lips, then paused. If it were a military aircraft, he ran the risk of its detecting the radio transmission. Better to be safe, he decided, and tucked the radio back into the oversize pocket on his parka. He turned and moved quickly toward the entrance to the ice cave.

The Spetsnaz were assembled and standing together as he entered the cavern. That was another spooky thing about them—their instantaneous reaction to any change in their surroundings. Between the time the first icy draft from outside had penetrated the cave and the time that Rogov had stepped across the threshold, they'd all piled out of their sleeping bags and grabbed their weapons. Now, looking at them, he could not tell that seconds earlier they had all been asleep.

"An aircraft," he said. "The radio—it occurs to me that maintaining tactical communications with it is a dangerous idea."

The Spetsnaz commander nodded. "As we discussed. However, I recall you were not quite so ready to listen to that suggestion earlier."

"Assemble your team," Rogov ordered unnecessarily, ignoring the intended rebuke. "I do not like the thought that the aircraft is headed directly for us."

The Spetsnaz commander spread his hands out, palms

up, as if to say, what preparations? Clearly, the men around him were already ready for action.

"Then take your posts," Rogov snapped, annoyed—and, he admitted to himself, the tiniest bit afraid—that they'd readied themselves so quickly. But then, that was to be expected, wasn't it? These were, after all, the finest unconventional warfare experts in the world.

The men slipped out of the ice cave quietly, each one heading directly for a previously scouted position. They would be, Rogov knew, even now snuggling down into the concealment they had either discovered or created. The odds of their being detected by the overflying aircraft were zero.

Almost zero, he corrected himself. He glanced over at the Spetsnaz commander, who was waiting.

"You will take the Stinger," Rogov ordered. The Spetsnaz commander's smile deepened.

1615 Local
Pathfinder 731

"You see anything?" the pilot asked.

The copilot shook his head in the negative. "Not a damned thing except ice and water. Too damned much of both."

Toggling on the ICS switch, the pilot said, "You happy now?"

Eel glanced over at the technician, who shook his head wordlessly. "We're not detecting anything," Eel admitted reluctantly. "One more circuit, just to make sure. Then we'll head home."

"That's all it will be, then," the pilot said. "Flying this

low—I'm not doing anything that gets me below a real
healthy reserve on fuel. Not over this water."

"Understood. If someone's down there, they ain't
talking now."

As the aircraft started its final circuit over the island,
cruising at barely three thousand feet above the land and
water, Eel stared out the small side window at the
rugged, desolate terrain, wondering what it was that
made him so uneasy.

1620 Local
Attu

From his concealed position in the scree located at the
base of the cliff, Rogov watched the black speck grow
larger. Within minutes, he could distinguish the stubby-
nosed profile of a P-3 Orion.

He nudged the Spetsnaz commander at his side, who
looked over at him, annoyed. "You see?" Rogov pointed
out. "Had we used the radios, they could have undoubtedly triangulated on our position."

The Spetsnaz commander shrugged. "That will not
make any difference in a few moments." He shrugged
himself up off the ground and raised the Stinger missile
tube to his shoulder.

1625 Local
Pathfinder 731

"Look! Over to the right!"

Eel moved over to a starboard window, trying to see
what had excited the two pilots.

"I saw movement—I know I did," the copilot's excited voice said. "Just near the base of that cliff. In the rubble."

Eel brought the binoculars up to his eyes and trained them on the area. Nothing, nothing, nothing—wait. He tweaked the binoculars into sharper focus. Against the shades of white and gray that made up the arctic landscape, an odd shadow protruded at an awkward angle. He looked at the ice above it, trying to decide what escarpment would cast such a—damn it!

He snatched up the nearest microphone and shouted, "Get us the hell out of here! There's someone with a Stinger missile down there."

"How can you be so sure?" the copilot's surly voice came over the circuit.

Eel felt the P-3 jerk sharply upward as the pilot ignored his fellow aviator's question. The pilot had been around long enough to know that if the TACCO wanted the aircraft out of the area, it was better to just do it and ask questions later. Explanations took time, and sometimes a few seconds made the difference between life and death.

"Altitude, now!" Eel insisted. "Just shut the fuck up and—"

The black cylinder nestled among the chunks of ice moved, shortening in length as the deadly firing end pointed directly at them. He stared at it with horrified fascination. The heat-seeking warhead carried enough explosive power to knock the wing off a P-3, or to seriously damage an engine. Even if the aircraft managed to stay airborne, what might be a minor mechanical problem or minor battle damage in these climates could soon turn deadly. He stared at the missile launcher, trying not to think of the barely liquid water beneath them. If they went in—no, he couldn't think about that. They were as good as dead if they had to ditch the aircraft. In these waters, they wouldn't even stay conscious long enough to escape the sinking airplane. They would be unconscious and drowning before they could reach the hatch.

"Flares!" he shouted. "Flares, chaff, and altitude—now," he ordered.

The angle on the deck steepened as the P-3 fought for altitude. The range on the Stinger missile was only three miles. Three miles, and Pathfinder 731 was well within those parameters.

**1628 Local
Attu**

"He's seen us!" The Spetsnaz commander stood, hefting the missile easily on his shoulder. "No other choice, now."

"Stop it!" Rogov struggled to his feet, wondering when the ability to move so quickly had left him. "Didn't you see the tail markings? That's an American aircraft." He put one hand on the rugged missile barrel.

"So?" The Spetsnaz commander bore-sighted the aircraft, trapping its tail end easily in the crosshairs of the simple scope. "If she gets a report back to her base, our mission is blown."

"No! If you shoot down that aircraft, there's no chance. Do you think the Americans would let that go unavenged?"

The Spetsnaz commander shrugged, barely moving

the missile off its target. "It is already compromised beyond recovery if they've seen us. You failed to follow my advice in this matter."

"You agreed with posting the sentries. You insisted on it," Rogov shouted.

"Yes, but I also said that they should return to the cave if contact were gained. You ignored that. No, this is all your fault."

Rogov saw the man's finger curl around the firing trigger as he braced himself for the recoil. "No!" he shouted. As the Spetsnaz's finger tightened, Rogov slammed his fist down on the top of the tube.

The Spetsnaz commander was quick, but not as quick as the missile. As the tube started its downward arc, the missile left out, quickly gaining speed. Before it could recover from its initial firing vector, and begin seeking out the heat source that had called to it so sweetly just moments before, it impacted the barren ice and snow below. The fireball explosion blasted both men.

"You fool!" The Spetsnaz commander tossed the empty tube away, murder in his eyes. "The rest of the missiles are in the cavern. There is no time—" His voice broke off suddenly as he saw the pistol in Rogov's hand.

"There are many chances, Comrade," Rogov said sarcastically. "You had yours—now, I'm afraid, we'll have to do things my way."

The Spetsnaz commander moved swiftly, almost blurring in Rogov's vision. But he'd been prepared for that. At the first movement, he fired, aiming not for the head but taking the more certain gut shot.

The Spetsnaz commander howled as the 9mm bullet gouged out a bloody path through skin, muscle, and vital organs. The impact spun him around, and he finally fell to the ice, on his back, leaving a trail of spattered blood behind him.

His guts steamed, and blood pooled quickly over the parka, freezing almost immediately. Rogov watched the color drain from the man's face. He was tough, he would give him that. The Spetsnaz commander, even with half of his midsection in shredded tatters, was trying to climb to his feet, reaching for his weapon, still fighting despite the soon-to-be-fatal shot.

Rogov watched him, unwilling to get too near the man while even a trace of life remained in the body. He saw the man fumble in his pocket for his pistol, and ventured close enough to him to kick his hand away.

Rogov crouched down in the snow, still well out of reach of the Spetsnaz, and aimed the pistol at the man's temple. "You don't understand everything—not at all," he said softly, pitching his voice low. He glanced around him briefly, wondering if the other men had heard the shot. Probably not, not with the silencer still affixed, although there was no telling how long it would be effective in this climate. Even now, he suspected, the cold had frozen the extended cylinder permanently to the barrel.

"They will kill you for this," the Spetsnaz managed to gasp. "Kill you."

Rogov smiled. "Did you really believe that was our mission?" he asked. Rogov shook his head. "And I was worried about you," he admitted.

He could see the Spetsnaz commander's face turning pale as blood flowed away from the brain, struggling to replace the frozen, pulsing mass in the man's midsection. "Since you're dead, I'll tell you," Rogov said. "In memory of your bravery, however foolhardy. There are no missiles on the way, Comrade Spetsnaz. None at all.

There never have been, there never will be. Do you really think that we would be so foolish as to provoke an international incident by planting our own guns and missiles on American soil?" He shook his head again, wondering about the inflexible military mentality that made such lies plausible to men like this. "No, it is a much deeper plan than that," he finished.

The Spetsnaz commander gave one final gasp, and then grew still. Within moments, Rogov could see ice starting to rim the delicate tissues exposed to the elements.

Now what? he wondered. This possibility had been discussed, that he would have to eliminate one or more of the Spetsnaz commandos. It had seemed a far easier— and safer—plan back in Russia, but now the difficulties seemed to have increased logarithmically. If it had been anyone except the commander, he thought, and shook his head again. No, this is the way it would have to be. Tension between the men had already been running too high. With the commander eliminated, there was at least a fifty-fifty chance the rest of the men would obey him unquestioningly, yielding with that peculiarly Slavic resignation to authority. And perhaps this would increase his stature within the group.

He debated for a moment trying to hide the body, and then decided against it. The Spetsnaz would, he was certain, send out patrols to try to locate the missing commando. Better that they know where it was now, and that Rogov admitted responsibility.

He stood and watched the speck that was the P-3 Orion dwindle in the distance. Now it was time for the next phase of the plan to unfold. He trudged down the slope to the cavern to await his new subordinates.

"Jesus, did you see that?" Eel yelped.

"You betcha." The pilot's voice was grim. "And I don't care what Intelligence says, there damn well is somebody down there. Radio emissions, ghost contacts—hell, it's entirely different when somebody starts shooting missiles at you."

"Better lucky than good," Eel said automatically. He stared back aft at the frozen landscape fading in the distance behind them.

Had they been lucky? one part of his mind wondered. They had to be—what else could explain the missile impacting with the ground instead of clawing up the ass of the Orion? A misfire, perhaps? Or something wrong with the guidance system on the Stinger? He shook his head, wondering at the possibilities. The Stinger was among the most simple weapons to operate, a feature that made it popular with every insurgent nation around the world. Simple, easily transportable, and almost unbearably deadly. It had been the advent of Stinger missiles on the ground in Afghanistan that had driven back the potent Soviet air force, and forced the Russians to a virtual defeat there.

As the adrenaline started to fade away, he felt his hands quiver. One Stinger missile versus one P-3 Orion aircraft—no contest, he decided. A Stinger would do fatal damage to the aircraft too quickly, and the lumbering Orion had too few tricks up its sleeves to evade it. The flares might have worked, but at that point, Eel was unwilling to bet his life on it. And glad he hadn't been required to.

"You mind giving me a fly-to point for home?" the pilot said harshly. "I think there are some folks on the ground who are going to be mighty interested in talking to us."

Eel returned to his console, automatically running the configuration of speeds and distance vectors necessary to take them back to their home base in Adak. That done, he punched in the communications circuit of their home base and began trying to raise the operations officer. After a few seconds, he broke off, and called up the USS *Thomas Jefferson*, asking them to come up on the same circuit. He had a feeling that the carrier battle group to the south would be at least as interested, if not more so, in what he had to tell his boss.

**1658 Local
East Side, Attu**

White Wolf crouched behind the ice and rock, hugging up close to it. He felt the vibrations from the explosion radiate through his bearskin parka, felt the intricate crystalline structure of ice and rock tremble beneath his sensitive fingers. Some small part of him reached out to the surrounding cliffs and rocks, searching for any sign of instability. Long experience with avalanches and earthquakes had bred into the native Inuit population an uncanny ability to sense the movement of the earth around them.

White Wolf glanced at his grandson, Morning Eagle. While the younger man had less time treading the frozen

tundra of their homeland, four years of service in the
United States Army Special Forces had brought his earth
skills up to par with his grandfather's.

Their eyes met, and agreement passed between them.
No, there was no immediate danger—at least not from
this explosion. The earth around them would stay secure
and stable, but neither was certain that the same could be
said for the people crawling around Mother Earth's
surface. White Wolf made a small motion with his hand,
barely a movement. The other man nodded. They moved
out silently, wraiths against the barren arctic landscape.
Forty paces down the path, a bare trail that no one except
an Inuit could have spotted, White Wolf paused. Morning
Eagle stopped five paces behind him, far enough away
that they would not both be immediately caught up in
any break in the thin crust of ice ahead. Then the younger
man heard it, too.

They moved to the edge of the path, climbed two small
shelves, and peered down at the campsite below them.
The sharp glare of light was almost painful to their eyes,
accustomed as they were to the gentle days and long
nights of the arctic winter. Fire ringed a crater in the ice,
the center of which was burning a hellish red-gold in the
midst of the blackened, crusted circle.

White Wolf pointed at the men assembled below. Four
of them—five counting the dead body they'd seen
further down the trail.

After watching the intruders for ten minutes, the Inuits
slipped silently away, back to the other side of their
island and to their boat. The noise of the outboard motors
couldn't be avoided, but they decided that the safety
distance from the island would bring was worth the risk.
Even so, White Wolf surmised, the white men arguing on

the ice on the other side of the small island would
probably not even understand what had happened. But
the Inuits did—oh, yes, they certainly understood this
latest skirmish in the ongoing battle between two giant
nations laying claim to the Inuit territory.

And, given half a chance, the Inuits would have a say
in their own destiny. That they would.

CHAPTER 6
Wednesday, 28 December

Tombstone Magruder held the radio receiver away from his ear. The voice screaming on the other end of the encrypted circuit was clearly audible to everyone in the room. He watched his chief of staff frown, his junior officers struggle to maintain their composure.

Finally, when the voice paused for breath, Tombstone put the receiver back to his mouth. "Yes, Admiral," he said mildly. "I understand your position. But I'm not certain that there's anything—" Tombstone stopped talking as the voice on the other end of the speaker resumed its tirade.

Finally, when he'd had enough, Tombstone interrupted. "I appreciate your call, Admiral Carmichael, but I'm a bit confused by your orders. The last time I studied our chain of command structure, ALASKCOM reported to commander, Pacific Fleet, not to Third Fleet. I called to discuss your tactical situation in *my* geographic area, not give you rudder order. Perhaps I didn't make that clear." This time, he kept the receiver at his ear, sacrificing the safety of his eardrums for a little privacy. He

waved his hand dismissively at his staff as he listened to
the tirade resume.

"Damn it, Admiral Magruder, you don't have the
faintest idea how delicate these matters are. The whole
world is watching how we handle the Greenpeace matter,
and your precious aircraft carrier can't seem to find its
ass with both hands. How the hell do you explain that?"
Admiral Carmichael demanded. "That's what comes of
putting someone with no experience in D.C. in command of
such a sensitive region. You have no idea, no concept—"

Tombstone's temper finally ignited. "With all due
respect, I've had just about enough. If you wish to
discuss ALASKCOM with me, I would welcome your
advice and thoughts. However, no one has seen fit to
place me under your command, and I'll be goddamned if
I'll take any more of your abuse. Is that clear? Sir?"
Tombstone snapped.

Silence. Then, a faint chuckle. "I've heard you had a
mind of your own, Magruder," the voice said thoughtfully, all trace of his prior anger gone. "Now, prove it to
me. Show me you're something besides a hotshot jet jock
who will never get beyond the one-star rank."

"If we had a few more operational commanders in
charge of policy in D.C., Admiral Carmichael, we might
end up with a more cohesive national strategy," Tombstone said tartly. "You may see this as a sensitive political
situation. I see something worse. I've got a missing
civilian vessel, someone shooting at one of my P-3C
aircraft, Bear-H's in the area, and Admiral Wayne's got
indications of activity on a supposedly deserted island.
Call me crazy, but I don't think it's all a coincidence.
Now balance that against your precious island geek tern
and tell me what you'd be worried about—some stupid

bird or your air crews?" And that, Tombstone added silently, will go a long way toward telling me exactly who you are.

Static crackled over the circuit as Tombstone waited for the other man to answer. Relationships between admirals could be tricky at best, as those in the highest rarefied circles of naval command and control fought the battle for their own political survival. Tombstone had no desire to join that fray, and if it meant he would retire with one star instead of more, that was fine with him.

"Tombstone—can I call you that?—let's put our cards on the table," Admiral Carmichael said finally. "I understand about aviation, and how you folks have your own way of doing business. Believe me, sir, I've got no intention of asking your boys to go into harm's way without adequate backup. But from here, it looks like a civilian vessel that's got a history of doing sneak attacks on us has gone missing and some asshole Inuit lighting off fireworks. And maybe playing around with a walkie-talkie while your P-3C pilot is thinking Stingers instead of sparklers. I'm willing to be persuaded, though. So start talking."

A rare smile cracked its way across Tombstone's face. He'd heard that Admiral Carmichael was a screamer, a flag officer that pushed those junior to him as far as he could with his reputation for an abusive temper. Rumor control also had it that the admiral would back down if confronted, and that half of the purpose of his screaming fits was to test the temperament of those junior to him. "Admiral, I don't believe in coincidence," Tombstone said slowly. He considered bringing up the issue of chain of command, and then abandoned it. Admiral Carmichael certainly knew where he stood in the pecking order, as well as whom Tombstone reported to. There was no formal need for Tombstone to tell Admiral Carmichael anything other than what the minimum requirements of courtesy dictated, but something about the man's reputation and in his voice intrigued the aviator. He would, he decided, make his own judgments about Admiral Carmichael.

"Coincidences are unlikely," Admiral Carmichael agreed. "What else have you got?"

"You may not have seen the reports yet," Tombstone said carefully, aware that Admiral Carmichael's staff may have dropped the ball in getting the information to him, "but *Jefferson* detected some spurious radio transmissions from the island yesterday. I was willing to buy the vessel-off-course-and-firecrackers theory until I heard that. I called the battle group myself, and asked the staff to relay the pilot reports to me. Regardless of what you've been told, sir, there's no way that was simply some firecrackers. First, the island is largely uninhabited, although Intelligence indicates it's occasionally visited by Inuits from neighboring islands. Second, the TACCO on that P-3 was an experienced aviator, and he damn well knows what a Stinger aimed at him looks like. No," Tombstone continued, shaking his head even though the admiral on the other end couldn't see the gesture, "there's something going on out around that island, Admiral. I don't know what, but it falls within the scope of my duties to find out."

"And within mine to make sure that *Jefferson* is safe," Admiral Carmichael said gruffly. "Listen, Tombstone, I don't know what you've heard about me, but I'm damn well not going to endanger one of my ships if I can help it. You and I are going to have to work together on this matter, and the sooner we get to know each other, the better. Care to come on board for a short skull session with my staff?"

"On board *Coronado*?" Tombstone asked. "Sir, I didn't realize you were coming this far north."

"I hadn't planned on it, no. We're doing operations off the coast of San Francisco right now in preparation for *Lincoln*'s deployment. However, despite what you may think, I'm more than a little concerned about the situation out there. I'll ask the captain to steam north, commencing immediately, and we should be within COD range by tomorrow. What do you think?"

"COD?" Involuntarily, Tombstone shuddered. As bad as flying on the C-130 out to Adak had been, he hated the workhorse personnel transports more. Suddenly, what should have occurred to him earlier dawned. "Wait. You can't land a COD on the *Coronado*."

"Ah. I see you haven't gotten the word on something," Admiral Carmichael said pleasantly. "On the *Coronado*, a two-seater training Harrier jump jet is considered a COD. The Marines own twenty-eight of the training version, and they're damned generous about loaning me one. I can arrange for tanking support out of the Air Force in California, and have that Harrier in Juneau in a matter of hours. What do you think?"

"Yes, sir!" An odd tingle of excitement ran down his back. Despite his years of aviation, Tombstone had managed to miss the opportunity to take a check ride in the Marine Corps' vertical takeoff and landing jet, the AV-8B Harrier. One of the mainstays of an amphibious assault ship air wing, along with the tactical helicopters the Marines used, the Harrier was built in close partnership by McDonnell-Douglas and British Aerospace.

Since its introduction into both nations' fleets in 1986, it had seen action in Desert Storm, flying missions both from airfields and from U.S. amphibious ships. In one mission alone, four of the AV-8B's were credited with destroying twenty-five Iraqi tanks. All totaled, the Harriers had dropped over three thousand tons of ordnance during the short conflict.

What made the Harrier seem so alluring to most aviators was its ability to both hover like a helicopter and fly like a jet, with its single Rolls-Royce Pegasus turbofan jet engine providing both lift and thrust. Two large air intakes on either side of the fuselage fed into the upgraded engine, and the swiveling exhaust nozzle replaced conventional systems. Outboard weapons stations could carry a wide range of bombs, air-to-air and air-to-surface missiles, as well as rockets or fuel pods.

"Okay, I'll have my guys pick you up tomorrow. Our operations people will talk later today to determine the exact flight schedule," Admiral Carmichael said.

"Aye, aye, Admiral." A small smile tugged at the corners of Tombstone's lips for the second time in the last ten minutes. "I'll be there, sir."

"Oh, and Tombstone," Admiral Carmichael said before breaking the connection, "since we're going to be working together, why don't you drop the 'sir' and 'Admiral' business when we're in private? My friends call me Ben. Big Ben, if you want the whole nickname," he added unnecessarily.

"Thank you, sir—Ben," Tombstone said carefully. "I'll see you tomorrow." Two clicks on his circuit were his only reply. Tombstone turned away from the patch panel in the communications center, all traces of amusement gone from his face as he carefully resettled his public facade. He turned toward the doorway and saw Pamela Drake standing there, an amused smile on her face.

"Can't ever miss the chance to go flying, can you?" she asked, a trace of bitterness in her voice. "It's still the boys and their toys, isn't it?"

"I don't deserve that, Miss Drake," Tombstone said formally. "And just what the hell are you doing in communications, anyway?"

She held out a single sheet of typed paper. "Your memo granting us access to certain areas to transmit our releases. Or did you forget?"

"It damned well doesn't include eavesdropping on my private conversations," he snapped. "As of this moment, you're barred from any further access here."

She walked over to him slowly, an insolent sway in her hips. "Oh, really?" she asked archly. "You seem to forget that we're still on U.S. soil, Admiral, and I have an absolute right to return to the mainland anytime I wish. And isn't it going to be a fascinating story that I file from Juneau that ALASKCOM and Third Fleet are pulling a blanket of secrecy over problems in the Aleutian Islands. That they're holding secret meetings on a ship to decide what to do, and that nobody is bothering to tell the American public what is going on in their own territory. And that civilian ships in the vicinity of USS *Jefferson* seem to keep disappearing suddenly, with no explanation in sight. Now what kind of lead story do you think that will make?" She smiled.

"Damn it, Pamela, you can't do this." His face took on a look of icy rage. "Push me too far, and I'll have you jailed for espionage," he said, regretting the words the moment they left his mouth.

"Oh, really?" Her smile broadened. "And the rest of my fellow journalists as well? Or don't you think they'd notice if I disappeared suddenly, and was held incommunicado."

Tombstone sighed. Whatever lingering fantasies he'd had about Pamela were fast disappearing. "Okay, tell me," he said finally. "What will it take to keep you quiet?"

Pamela strolled around the small room, carefully observing the equipment. She glanced up at the overhead, then wrapped her arms around herself. "Claustrophobic, isn't it?" she said, apropos of nothing in particular. "Being on land too long always makes me feel that way. Not like being on an aircraft carrier, or an amphibious ship." She looked at him meaningfully.

"You can't be serious. It's not even my ship, Pamela. Not that I'd take you on board if it were, but *USS Coronado* is under Admiral Carmichael's command, not mine. I have no say in who goes on board, and how. What you're asking is impossible, never mind that it's entirely unreasonable."

She walked forward, stopping only one pace in front of him. She was so close he could smell the unique mixture of sharp, spicy perfume and female that had always driven him insane with desire. Involuntarily, one hand wanted to reach out and touch her shoulder, caress the taut line of her jaw, trace its way down her neck to—*Stop it,* he told himself sharply. Whatever Pamela had been to him before, it was evident that more had changed than he'd thought with their broken engagement.

"I suggest you see what you can do, then, Admiral," she said harshly, something ugly in her voice. "Because whatever you're up to, you and Admiral Carmichael, I damn well don't intend to be left out of it."

"Bird Dog, you stupid idiot, do you have the slightest notion of what the concept 'airspace' implies?" Gator asked. "Because if you don't, now would be a very good time to listen to your RIO."

"Airspace? You want airspace? Then how about this." Bird Dog slammed the throttles forward and hauled back on the control yield, wrenching the Tomcat into a steep climb. "Just exactly how much airspace do you want, my friend?" he asked sarcastically, straining to force the words out against the G-forces. "Just tell me when there's enough."

"Asshole," Gator said. "I suppose you thought one hundred feet off the deck was good enough for government work?"

"Skipper said to get a good look at the island, didn't he? And I wouldn't want to miss that precious little Greenpeace boat, would I?" Bird Dog shot back angrily. "How the hell am I supposed to see anything if we don't get up close and personal with the ground and the water?"

"Skipper knows damned well that you don't have terrain-following radar in this bird," Gator said, his voice tart. "At one hundred feet, you have absolutely no room for error. If we hit a flameout, a bad drink of fuel, you've got no room to recover."

"Then you ought to be real happy about now," Bird Dog said. He let the aircraft continue on through 38,000 feet, finally pulling out of the steep climb as the Tomcat started to complain about the attack angle. The aircraft shivered slightly as she fought against gravity, shedding airspeed and approaching the edge of her stall envelope. As the very first tremors that indicated approaching stall speed shook the aircraft, Bird Dog dropped his rate of climb and slowly resumed level flight.

"Hell, can't you ever compromise?" Gator asked bitterly. "You forget who's on your side, Bird Dog. Me. The guy who stuck with you through the Spratlys, the guy who climbs into the backseat of this goddamned Tomcat every day with you, and the one who has to keep answering questions from CAG and the admiral about why I can't keep you under control. You want a new RIO? Fine, you got it. As soon as we get back to the boat, I'll ask for a crew swap."

Bird Dog considered his RIO's words. Gator sure sounded pissed off. True, he played smart ass with the balls to the wall climb, and he had to admit, one hundred feet was a little outside the envelope. Still, he'd been flying safe, hadn't he? They were both still alive, weren't they? And just what exactly was the point of being a fighter pilot if you couldn't have a little fun?

"Gator?" Bird Dog said hesitantly. "Listen, okay— you're right. Don't put in for a crew swap, okay?"

There was no answer.

"Aw, come on," Bird Dog wheedled. "I promise I'll cut it out, okay? Don't make me take another RIO."

Gator sighed. "Damn it, Bird Dog, when are you going to buy off on the concept that there are two of us in this aircraft? You treat me like I'm some sort of idiot backseat scope dope, somebody who doesn't matter a damned bit until you've got a MiG on your ass. Then you start screaming for vectors and angles, all at once wanting to know where the bad guys are. How do you think that is for me?"

It was Bird Dog's turn to fall silent. Even after eighteen months of flying with Gator, he'd never really stopped to consider how his actions affected the RIO. Gator was just—Gator, he guessed. His RIO, his back-seater, the man he depended on for information that kept his ass out of the sling. When there was combat, that is. Other times, he had to admit, he didn't stop to think about what his RIO was doing in the backseat.

What a lousy way to make a living, he thought, considering the plight of the RIO. Strapping into a Tomcat, but not getting to do any of the fun parts. Jamming your face up on the radar hood around the scope, twiddling with knobs and buttons instead of experiencing what was probably the closest thing to heaven on earth—flying the all-powerful, awesome, MiG-beating Tomcat.

"You're right, Gator," he admitted finally. "You've kept me from getting killed a couple of times so far, and I still haven't treated you right. Sir," he added belatedly, suddenly remembering just how senior Gator was. The latest results from the Commanders' Selection Board had just come out, and Gator had been advised that he'd been selected for promotion to commander, as well as for an executive officer tour in a Tomcat squadron. Bird Dog, still two years away from even a deep look at the lieutenant commander's board, was just a barely ripened nugget compared to the man in his backseat.

"Don't start with the 'sir' shit," Gator said wearily. "I

won't put it on for another year. But truthfully, Bird Dog,
I'm getting tired of this crap. Every other week, you've
got me standing tall in front of CAG. Enough's enough."

Bird Dog nosed the Tomcat over and began an orderly
descent back to a reasonable altitude. He leveled off at
six thousand feet and put the Tomcat into a gentle orbit
over the island. He recognized the tone in Gator's voice
too well. Words were not likely to convince him not to
request a crew swap at this point. Only some good,
orderly flying, something that demonstrated the teamwork that was supposed to exist between a pilot and a
RIO.

"Hold it, I—Bird Dog, take us back around the other
direction," Gator ordered suddenly.

Without questioning his backseater's directions, Bird
Dog snapped the Tomcat sharply around. He waited.

"Those radio transmissions Intel briefed—I thought I
caught a sniff of them. Can we get down and take a
closer look?"

Bird Dog resisted the temptation to note that only
minutes earlier Gator had been complaining about low-
altitude flights. Instead, he began executing a search
pattern over the small chunk of ice and rock below.

"There it is again," Gator said. He flipped his microphone over to Tactical and began an earnest conversation
with the operations specialist on board *Jefferson*. Finally,
after a few moments, he asked Bird Dog to move back
into a higher orbit.

After they leveled off at ten thousand feet, Bird Dog
said, "Could you tell me what that was about?"

Gator smiled at the unusually meek tone of voice. "I
told you, I got a sniff of that radio frequency they've
been talking about. And if you will recall, my dear

fellow, just yesterday there was a P-3 screaming bloody murder about seeing someone launch a Stinger from this very island. You do remember Stingers, I hope?"

Bird Dog snorted. "How could I not?"

"Well, unless you want to insist on trying to take out one with a Sparrow, I suggest we stay at ten thousand feet. And you keep your old Mark I MOD 0 eyeballs peeled up there. The first sniff we're gonna have will probably be visual—if we get that much warning."

Bird Dog shivered, then settled down into a tactical mind set. If there were Stingers in the area, then the last thing he needed to do was be surprised. It would only happen once.

1700 Local
Kiska, Aleutian Islands

White Wolf pulled the boat up close to Kiska, wincing as he felt the keel scrape along the bottom. The island was just as inhospitable as its western brother. Kiska jutted out of the sea, and its coastline, for the most part, consisted of a sheer plunge down into the black, freezing water. Only a few feet of hard, barren rock survived under water, but it was enough to hold the old boat off from the island.

He motioned to Morning Eagle, who nodded, then leaped from the bow of the ship onto the land, the mooring line trailing behind him. He tossed the circle at the end of the line over a wooden pole, then raised his hands to show White Wolf the task was done.

White Wolf locked the cabin behind him and disembarked, making the leap from boat to shore easily.

Should have used the pier, he thought, then dismissed the idea. The only functional pier was almost three miles away, located on the other side of the island. Between the time it would take to moor, fire up his ancient cold-weather Jeep, and motor back over to his home, too much time would have passed. What they'd seen on the island was important—so important that a few minutes might make a difference.

White Wolf tugged on the line once, making sure it was still solid and secure, then settled into a brisk walk toward the structure fifty feet away. At one time, it might have been a simple Quonset hut, but years and the necessity of surviving in the frigid climate had worked modification on it. Now, packed over with ice and snow, the best insulator available, it looked more like an igloo than a conventional structure. The two smaller buildings, housing a generator and some spare parts, were similarly encrusted with snow and ice.

He walked up to the front door, tugged it open, and pulled it shut behind him immediately. Morning Eagle walked off in the direction of the small outbuilding that housed their generator. A few moments later, White Eagle heard the steady rumble of the generator kick in. He flipped a light switch, and the overheads came on. He waited a few minutes, to make sure the power was stable.

Finally, when it appeared that there were going to be none of the unexpected current fluctuations that wreaked havoc on electronic circuitry, he walked over to the far side of the small hut and flipped on a master power switch. Two gray metal cases crackled to life. He patted one of them thoughtfully and smiled. Army equipment, built to last and survive in even these spaces. He ran his finger lightly over the metal equipment property tag riveted to one side. It had been years since he'd last fired this equipment up, too many years.

Or maybe not enough, depending on how you looked at it. He wasn't even sure if the old frequencies, call signs, and circuit designations that he'd memorized so long ago would still work.

As he waited for the circuits to warm up, he heard the front door open, then slam shut, and felt the brief blast of frigid air circulate in the small space. Morning Eagle walked over to the gear and stood beside him.

"I didn't think we'd need this again," Morning Eagle said finally. "But under the circumstances—"

"There are not many choices," White Eagle said mildly. "We both know they would want to know. Whether or not they've had the foresight to continue to monitor this net is up to them. We can only do our part." He stared at the row of green idiot lights, all brightly assuring him that the gear was still operational. "We won't know until we try."

Morning Eagle nodded. "That's all we can ever do."

1705 Local
CVIC, USS Jefferson

"Sir!" The enlisted technician looked up. "I think you might want to come back here."

"Can it wait?" Commander Busby asked. He glanced over at the aircrew he was debriefing and shrugged apologetically. He already knew that it couldn't from the tone in the technician's voice.

"No, sir," the enlisted man said grimly. "I think this has probably waited too long," he added cryptically.

"Which circuit?" Commander Busby asked.

"I think you'd better see for yourself, sir. I'm not sure I believe it myself."

Lab Rat made his excuses, and moved quickly back toward the top-secret EW surveillance vault. The technician waited at the heavy steel door, holding it open for him.

Lab Rat stepped inside the space, noting the small cluster of EW technicians located near one particular piece of gear. He snapped his head back to stare at the senior enlisted man who'd called to him. "You must be joking."

The technician shook his head. "Wish I were, sir. But it's for real. They're broadcasting in the clear. They tried coming up on the last code they had, but it was so old we can't even break it. Then they just went into the clear, without even asking permission."

"Damned civilians," Lab Rat muttered. He walked over to the circuit and picked up the microphone. "What have they told you so far?" he asked before depressing the transmit key.

The intelligence specialist looked up. "They've given us two code names, which I'm having verified by Third Fleet. I think they may have to go higher up than that—doesn't sound like something they'd have access to immediately."

"What do you mean?"

"I can't really say, sir, but there's a system for assigning these code names—or at least there was, years ago. These two I think I recognize. But it's been years," he said, almost to himself. "They can't still be in place, not after that many years."

"What are you talking about?" Busby said sharply. "If it has to do with CVIC, I'm cleared for it."

The intelligence specialist glanced at the other technicians in the room, and then made a small movement with his head. Lab Rat took the hint. "Everyone else out for a few minutes, okay? We'll get you back in here as soon as we can."

The other technicians dispersed reluctantly, intrigued as they were by the voice coming over the ancient equipment that hadn't operated in years. Sure, they'd done periodic maintenance checks on it, and even maintained it in readiness as part of their watch, but none of them had ever seen it used.

When the last of them filed out, the intelligence specialist checked the door behind them. Satisfied that it was shut, he turned back to Commander Busby. "CIA. Many years ago, during the Cold War. I've seen those two names a couple of times on intelligence reports, back when I was with DIS—Defense Intelligence Service. But that was ten, maybe fifteen years ago."

"The CIA? You're sure?" Busby asked.

The technician nodded. "As sure as I can be after all these years, Commander," he said. "You remember how it was back then. The Soviets had nuclear ballistic submarines deployed north of the Aleutians in the Bering Sea. As part of our surveillance program—paranoia, we'd call it now—the CIA had a number of agents in place, scattered around the islands. Their orders were simply to observe and report back. You may remember, there was a time when the CIA was afraid Russia was going to invade via the Aleutian Islands. At the very least, having tactical control of the passages between the islands put them in a better position if they ever had to

sortie their submarines for an attack on the continental
U.S. So we had people there." The technician shrugged.
"I'm sure it seemed like a reasonable precaution at the
time."

"But they're still in place?" Busby asked. "After all
these years?"

The technician nodded. "Evidently so. Or at least,
someone who's pretending to be them. There's no way I
can authenticate these transmissions, since these stations
were supposedly deactivated years ago."

"What are they transmitting on?"

The technician reeled off a series of numbers and
nomenclature, none of which answered the real question
pounding in Busby's head. "Okay, so maybe some of
them kept an HF radio after the CIA withdrew support.
Gear like that would be useful. Hell, they could always
tell the Company it was lost."

"I think you'd better talk to them, sir," the technician
said quietly. He handed Lab Rat the microphone. "Because if what they're saying is true, we've got a real
problem here."

CHAPTER 7
Thursday, 29 December

0800 Local
Adak

Twenty knots was considered calm on Adak Island. Given that, and with unlimited visibility and a relatively stable air mass to the north, Tombstone's takeoff from Adak Island was uneventful.

As it had on their inbound flight, a Russian Bear-J aircraft joined on them shortly after takeoff, once they were clear of U.S. airspace and over international waters. The electrical problems that had plagued the aircraft had been fixed, and the flight to Seattle was uneventful.

As the C-130 taxied in, a contingent of U.S. Marines rushed out to meet the aircraft. The pilot quickly brought her to a halt and waited for the metal boarding stairs. Tombstone was the first one off the plane.

"Come on, sir," a Marine major said loudly, struggling to be heard over the still turning engines. "Your aircraft is ready for you."

"Flight gear?" Tombstone shouted.

"Waiting for you in the Operations Center." The Marine Corps major paused, waiting for Tombstone to do exactly what he'd asked.

Tombstone shrugged and followed the sharply dressed major across the tarmac. The noise level dropped appreciably. "Where is she?" Tombstone asked.

"Over there." The Marine pointed toward the far end of the airstrip. A Harrier was making its gently eerie approach, coasting through the air at a speed too low to believe. If it had not been for the turbofans on her undercarriage angled downward, she would have crashed—her forward speed was insufficient to maintain stable flight.

Tombstone paused and watched the aircraft settle gently on the ground. He could see from the movement of the grass surrounding the tarmac the force of the downdraft. It had to be, to keep that much metal airborne, he thought, but somehow, reading about downdraft in manuals never compared to seeing the actual thing. Anyone underneath the fighter would have been seriously injured or killed by the hurricane-force winds it generated downward.

"She's a real beauty, isn't she, sir?" the Major asked appreciatively. "Just look at her. The finest fighting aircraft ever built for a Marine." He glanced at Tombstone's insignia. "Not that the Navy doesn't have some real fine aircraft itself," he continued generously. However, it was obvious from the expression on his face that the Tomcat or Hornet ran a distant second to his treasured Harrier.

"I thought you said this bird was ready," Tombstone commented. "Doesn't look too ready to me, since it's not even on the ground."

"Oh, that's not the one we're flying. Ours is parked next to Flight Ops." The Marine grinned broadly.

"Ours?" Tombstone asked.

"Yes, Admiral." The Marine saluted sharply again. "Major Joe Killington, at your service, Admiral. Always glad to help out a fellow aviator when we can. Especially in getting onto a boat your aircraft can't reach."

Tombstone groaned. Surely, he thought, there must be some right granted to an admiral by Congress not to be harassed by the Marine Corps. The prospect of spending hours airborne fielding such comments by the major irked him.

A trace of his thoughts evidently showed in his face. The Marine major snapped to attention. "Whenever the Admiral is ready, sir," he said politely. "And we are happy to be of service, Admiral. All one fighting force—that's the way we see it."

Tombstone nodded abruptly. "Get me to my gear, Major," he said. "I imagine we'll have plenty of time to discuss the relative merits of your service and the Navy." He looked pointedly at the insignia on the Marine major's collar. "Not that it will be much of a contest."

The Marine major braced, eyes pointed directly forward and locked on the horizon. "I'm certain the admiral can enlighten me if my views are out of order."

Finally, Tombstone relented. After all, this was one argument the major could never win. And it had nothing to do with Tomcats, Hornets, or Harriers—it had to do with the quick collar count that had just occurred. Stars won out over gold oak leaves, no matter what the service.

Tombstone turned toward Flight Operations and slapped the Marine Corps major on the shoulder. "Come on, son," he said mildly. "I think you've got some flying to do. I've never been up in one of your birds—it'll be a pleasure to get a look at it."

"Yes, *sir*." The major took off at a trot toward his aircraft.

"How far can this thing go?" Pamela Drake asked. She pointed to the battered commercial helicopter sitting out on the tarmac.

The pilot shrugged. "Far enough, if I put on the additional fuel tanks. We could get you to Juneau, no problem, ma'am."

"Juneau, huh?" She looked him over carefully. "Were you in the Navy?"

A look of disgust crossed the pilot's face. "No, ma'am, not hardly. The Marines." He pointed at the battered helicopter. "Taught me my trade, they did, flying helicopters off of amphibious assault ships. After a couple of tours, I got out, joined the Reserves, and bought this puppy with the money I'd saved up. Slap a couple of missiles on her and she'd be just as good as anything they're flying in the Corps today."

"Amphibious assault ships, huh?" Pamela looked thoughtful. "You're not in the Reserves or anything right now, are you?"

"No, ma'am." The pilot grinned. "Not many Reserve units drilling out this far. I do mostly scouting for commercial fishing vessels, some medical emergencies—that sort of thing."

"Well, sir, I believe we might just have a job for you." Pamela grinned broadly. "Just how much do you remember about shipboard landings?"

"Welcome aboard, Admiral." Ben Carmichael held out his hand to the officer standing in front of him. They'd met several times socially, but their professional paths had never crossed. Not that it mattered, he supposed. He'd heard enough about Tombstone Magruder to think he knew what he was dealing with.

Admiral Carmichael studied the younger admiral carefully. The same dark hair, clipped close to his head now, and dark, almost black eyes. No, he decided on reflection, they were brown, but only by a hair. He repressed a smile, remembering how Tombstone had gotten his nickname. Not for the famous shoot-out in Tombstone at the OK Corral, but for the invariably solemn expression on his face. He'd heard rumors that someone on Admiral Magruder's staff had once seen him smile, but Carmichael wouldn't be betting on it. Especially not under the circumstances.

"Thank you for having us, Admiral," Magruder said politely. "And I appreciate the opportunity for a famfly in one of your Harriers."

"Don't be saying that too loudly, now," Carmichael said, finally chuckling. "That they're my aircraft, I mean. Marines take that mighty personal, they do."

"As rightfully they should." Tombstone shot a pointed look at Major Killington, no trace of amusement in his face. "Major Killington has gone to some length to point that out to me on the flight out."

Admiral Carmichael turned to survey the young Marine Corps major. "He has, has he?"

"Major Killington was quite informative."

Admiral Carmichael looked sharply at Tombstone, then smiled. The stories about the man's impassive face might be true, but nothing else could account for the slight twitch of the wrinkles around Tombstone Magruder's legendary basilisk eyes. Obviously, he'd enjoyed the flight out—as well as maybe a little harassment of the young Marine Corps officer.

"Thank you, Major," Tombstone said. "Perhaps we'll have another chance to fly that Harrier of yours. I wouldn't mind taking the controls myself sometime."

The Marine Corps officer stiffened, turned slightly pale. "My pleasure, Admiral," he answered, neatly side-stepping the issue of Tombstone flying his aircraft. The major executed a smart about-face and exited the Ready Room. After he'd left, Admiral Carmichael turned back to Tombstone.

"I take it the young man has a sense of pride in his service?"

Tombstone nodded. "Always encouraging to see in a young officer." His tone was noncommittal.

"Well, I think you may know the rest of the people here. Hold on, I'll have the chief of staff hunt them down." Admiral Carmichael picked up the telephone, dialed a number from memory, and spoke briefly into the receiver. As he put it back down, he turned to Tombstone and said, "The rest of the team is just getting on board."

"The rest?" Tombstone asked.

"How about some coffee, Admiral?" Carmichael offered him a guest mug, and motioned toward the coffee mess. "Make yourself at home. You want something to eat, just ask the mess cook. I'll be right back." With that, he strode toward the hatch, jerked it open, and disappeared into the immaculate passageway beyond.

Tombstone filled the coffee mug and set it down on the table. He stretched his hands up over him, feeling the muscles and bones in his back complain. The Harrier had managed to come up with a lumbar support system even more uncomfortable than that in the Tomcat, a feat he had not thought possible. Still, he had to admit the flight over to USS *Coronado* had been worthwhile—educational in many ways, not the least of which had been the opportunity to talk tactics with a Marine officer. Despite the initial impression he'd made on Tombstone, Major Killington had proved to be an exceptionally knowledgeable aviator, one as skilled in the tenets of ground warfare as he was in the air. Tombstone had found himself liking the young major, despite the irritating undercurrent of Marine Corps pride that underlay almost every comment.

The door to the compartment opened, and Admiral Carmichael stepped back through. Two figures trailed him, both carrying flight helmets.

"I believe you already know these two," Admiral Carmichael boomed.

Tombstone stared at the lead figure, and a smile finally did cross his face. "Batman! How the hell are you?" He put down his coffee cup again and crossed the room quickly. His old wingman grinned back at him and held out a hand. The warm, strong, two-handed handshake, held a moment longer than politeness absolutely required, was evidence of the strong friendship between the two men.

He's aged some, Tombstone thought, studying his old friend. But commanding a battle group does that. Dark circles ringed Batman's eyes, and the laugh lines at the corners of them were deeper than Tombstone remembered. Since relieving Tombstone nine months earlier, Batman appeared to have lost weight. Tombstone noted new hollows carved out of the cheekbones, a bagginess in the flight suit around Batman's waist that had not been there before. "How's the tour going?" Tombstone asked, certain he already knew the answer.

"It's super," Batman responded immediately. "More work than I ever thought possible, but you left me a sharp team. The stuff that makes it past COS isn't easy, though."

"It never was." Tombstone shook his head from side to side. "He's pulled that line on you before, I bet—that if it was easy, you wouldn't be seeing it?"

Batman laughed. "You bet."

"And you've brought—" Tombstone's throat suddenly went dry. The smaller figure that had been hidden behind Batman now stepped forward, a polite expression of interest on her face.

Her face. Tombstone stared, trying not to let his excitement show. "Lieutenant Commander Flynn," he said formally, holding out his hand. "Good to see you again."

"And you, Admiral," she said, shaking his hand briefly. The smooth, warm feel of her fingers seemed to linger on his palm. Tombstone turned back to Batman, praying his friend had not noticed the color he could feel creeping up his neck. "And how did you manage that?"

Batman grinned. "Pax River was pretty eager to get some more operational time on those JAST birds," he said. "You remember, the one I flew out to *Jefferson* in the Spratlys?"

"How could I forget?"

"I thought you'd remember. Anyway, Tomboy did such a good job as my RIO against the Chinese that Pax River picked her up as a test pilot for the next version of JAST. They're at that same point again—too much data, not enough information. The program manager asked me if I would take two birds on board for a couple of months, see how they worked under field conditions. When I found out Tomboy was one of the aircrew, I couldn't resist."

"And what brings you out to *Coronado*, Lieutenant Commander Flynn?" Tombstone said, turning his attention to the diminutive RIO.

"Sounded like there might be some action here, sir," she said immediately. "Pax River is something else, but nothing beats the real thing. If we're going to buy these birds, we need to see how they perform in an operational environment. Just like the Spratlys." She smiled happily.

"When Batman—Admiral Wayne, I mean—" she amended hastily, seeing clouds gather in Tombstone's face, "offered me the opportunity to come over to *Coronado* with him, I jumped at the chance. Sound operational experience. Besides, if the JAST birds were going to be flying any missions, I thought it best if I got the inside scoop. Sir." Her voice trailed off as she saw the expression on Tombstone's face.

Tombstone turned back to Admiral Carmichael. "I should have warned you about Admiral Wayne," Tombstone said neutrally.

"No harm done, Admiral," Carmichael said heartily, deliberately misunderstanding. He'd heard the rumors, as had all the flag community, about the youngest admiral, Magruder, and his attractive RIO. Gossip Central held that both were stand-up officers, and that nothing improper had occurred on board USS *Jefferson*. It also noted with some malicious glee that both officers had disappeared for several weeks shortly after Tombstone's arrival in D.C. While there were no hard data points, it was a foregone conclusion that the two had taken the opportunity of their overlapping transfers to escape from Navy life for a while. Looking at the two of them, Carmichael hoped they'd made it worthwhile. "There's always room for another good officer at the briefing. You won't be staying on board, will you, Commander?" he concluded pointedly, looking back at Tomboy.

"Of course not, Admiral," Batman said hastily. "Commander Flynn and I will be returning to *Jefferson* later this afternoon. I wouldn't feel comfortable being away much longer than that, not under the circumstances."

Admiral Carmichael nodded sharply. Message sent, message received. "Well, speaking of tactical situations, let's get this brief started."

1350 Local
Adak

"No moving around back here," the helicopter pilot said sternly. "This bitch is going to be damned heavy for a while until I burn off some fuel. I don't want you shifting my center of gravity around."

Pamela nodded, resisting the impulse to point out to the man that she'd been on more than one helicopter flight in her life. Although, she had to admit, never one exactly like this. Up close, the helicopter had proved to be somewhat dinged and battered, and the interior spaces were in no better shape. Still, all the moving parts seemed to be well-oiled and clean, and she suspected that the mechanics and avionics got a good deal more attention from the technicians than the creature comforts. "When are you ready to go?" she asked.

"Anytime. You say the word, we'll be airborne five minutes later."

"And you understand what we're going to do?" she asked again.

The pilot grinned. "You just leave it all up to me, ma'am."

Five minutes later, as the helicopter careened away from the ground and settled into level flight, Pamela had her first doubts about the mission.

1425 Local
USS *Jefferson*

Ninety feet above Lieutenant Commander Brandon Sikes's head, the outward curving mass of USS *Jefferson*'s concave hull hung over his head like a massive gray cliff. The storm had abated, and the seas were ominously placid. *Jefferson*'s bow was pointed into the light swell, her two outboard engines turning just enough to keep her on course. In contrast, the docking platform lowered from her starboard elevator pitched and rolled markedly. The flat-bottomed floating structure drew only two feet of water and rode the swells heavily, the forward edge trying to bury itself in oncoming swells while the trailing edge lifted free of the trough between the swells.

Sikes planted his feet firmly apart, riding the pitching motion easily. Compared to what he'd be doing in a few minutes, this was a piece of cake.

The boat moored to the starboard side of the ship was just slightly more than thirty feet long. Twin inboard engines, heavily muffled for silence, drove it through the water at speeds in excess of seventy knots. Fifty-caliber guns mounted fore and aft provided additional protection, but her speed was her main tactical advantage. It was the ideal platform for getting the SEAL team in and out of places they weren't supposed to be quickly and covertly.

And that was exactly what this mission called for. Sikes turned his back on the boat and studied the men arrayed behind him. Four other men, each with his own particular deadly specialty. His eyes lingered for a moment on Petty Officer Carter, the newest member of the team. The young SEAL had graduated from BUDS only one year before, and followed that with a series of technical schools in the deadly arts that were the SEALs' calling cards. Carter was a good-natured, rawboned twenty-year-old from Iowa. Sikes shook his head. What was it about naval service that drew these men from their landlocked childhoods to the water? And why did they make such damned fine sailors? Carter was already showing the potential to be a superb SEAL.

"Let's get them moving, Senior," he said, pointing toward the horizon. "The sooner we get going, the sooner we're back. All your men understand what the mission is?"

Senior Chief Manuel Huerta nodded. "Yes, sir, we briefed again this morning. Just a quick sneak and peek, nothin' fancy. No heroics, no toys." The senior chief, a veteran of twenty-two years in the SEAL forces, looked faintly disappointed.

"As long as everyone understands that," Sikes replied.

"Depending on what we turn up, we may be going back."

He turned back to the boat, confident that the chief had done his job. If the truth be known, he admitted to himself, the men didn't really need him on this mission. They were more than capable of handling every aspect of it alone. Still, it was a matter of pride for the SEAL officer corps to be able to get down and dirty with the best of their enlisted men. Since Sikes's cold-weather experience was limited, he'd made it a point to come along on this mission to watch the chief in action. Nothing beat firsthand experience, and what he learned on this relatively simple expedition might save his life later. You never knew, he thought, shaking his head, just what bit of arcane, novel or trivial fact made the difference between success and failure. And for the SEAL team, the latter outcome was completely unacceptable.

And to be working with Admiral Wayne again on board *Jefferson* made his current assignment as Officer in Charge of the *Jefferson*'s SEAL detachment all the more satisfying. The admiral understood Special Forces, Sikes reflected, watching the senior chief move easily around the bobbing platform. And, as a matter of fact, Sikes took credit for that.

Four years earlier, one of then-Commander Wayne's squadron mates, Lieutenant Commander Willie "Coyote" Grant, had been shot down on a mission over Korea. Captured and tortured by the North Korean forces, only the intervention of a SEAL team made his escape possible. And although he'd been a boot lieutenant at the time, Sikes had been part of it. Senior Chief Huerta had personally snatched Coyote out of the firing zone.

Not that Coyote hadn't done a damned fine job of working his way over to the extraction point, he remembered. He might even have made it the entire way alone. They'd never know for sure, and as far as Sikes was concerned, Admiral Wayne would never have to worry about *this* SEAL team. The day he'd checked on board, Admiral Wayne had made it damned clear that he remembered the SEALs that had pulled Coyote's butt out of the fire.

So if Admiral Wayne wanted to know who the Radio Shack junkies were on some piece of rock and ice in the middle of the ocean, Sikes was damned happy to go find out.

1500 Local
Kiska

"Another one," Morning Eagle announced.

White Wolf looked up from the radio, concern furrowing his broad, smooth face. "Two days, two sets of invaders." He shook his head, straining to catch the high-pitched squeal of a powerful outboard motor in the distance.

"More Russians?" Morning Eagle asked.

"Does it matter?"

The younger man nodded his agreement. The alien mainlanders, with their hurried, strange ways and their lack of understanding of the islands, were as foreign to the Inuits as the Russians were. It made little difference to the natives of the island chain which set of masters claimed dominion over their territory. The harsh environment was their first taskmaster, the scrabble to remain alive in these hostile surroundings a more constant threat than the political ambitions of those from warmer climates. Voting in the white man's political system or bowing to the peremptory dictates of a Russian comrade had little effect on that.

"The Americans will come. I'm certain of it," White Wolf said finally. "And if they don't—" He shrugged, indicating that no matter what, the tribe would continue.

"You called them." The younger man looked questioningly at his elder. "Why?"

The older man stared at the horizon, listening as the sound of the quickly approaching engine deepened to a fierce growl. "Many years ago, there was a man," he said reflectively. "The mainlanders—you know what I've said about them." He cast a sidelong glance at the younger man to make sure he was paying attention.

The young man nodded. "Not to trust them. That we were no more than enslaved tribes to them."

White Wolf nodded. "Yes, that's true for most of them. But I made a promise to one man—a man I found I could trust—so many years ago. A promise, it's a sacred thing. You give your word, that's the most that you have to give any other man. Do you understand?"

Morning Eagle looked doubtful. "I suppose so. Even to a white man, a man's word counts for something. But what did you promise?"

"He came to my house, he ate my food. He was polite, respectful," the older man said, not evading the question but laying the foundation for its answer. "He asked me to keep watch. I told him I would."

The bare bones of the story did not satisfy the younger man. "But who was he? And why did you give him your word?"

"He was a lieutenant commander then," the man said, rolling the English words for rank around in his mouth as though they were not entirely comfortable to pronounce.

"It was so many years ago, but I remember him. His name was Magruder."

1555 Local
Tomcat 201

Bird Dog turned the aircraft north, heading on the outbound leg of the chainsaw defense pattern. To the east and west, other aircraft provided surveillance in those areas. South of all three, near the battle group, an E-2C Hawkeye radar surveillance aircraft coordinated the CAP pattern.

"Where the hell is he?" Bird Dog muttered. "For the last five days, that modified Bear has been overhead at just about this time."

"Hold your horses," Gator said. "He'll be here when he gets here. Besides, I don't know that's something to be wishing for."

"And why the hell not?" Bird Dog said angrily. "All these damned surveillance patrols, no one ever did a damned thing to him. Then for no reason at all, he decides to take a shot at a P-3. Well, if he wants to play rough, just let him try it with us. I'm loaded for Bear, that's for certain." He touched the weapons selector switch on the stick. "Though I'd give up those Phoenix birds any day for a couple more Sidewinders, especially against a Bear."

The Phoenix missile was the Tomcat's most potent long-range standoff weapon. Capable of intercept speeds of up to Mach 5, the Phoenix had an independent seeker head that could lock on and track a target at ranges of up to one hundred and twenty-five miles. Its major weakness was that it required continuing illumination of the target from the Tomcat, putting serious constraints on Bird Dog's maneuverability and ability to evade. However, even with its history of guidance problems, the Phoenix had one strong point—it forced the enemy onto the defensive immediately, disrupting any tactical formations and allowing the American aircraft to take the offensive. A Phoenix missile graced the outboard weapons station on either side.

Just inboard of that, Sparrow and Sidewinder missiles were nestled up onto the hard points of the Tomcat undercarriage. Both were fire-and-forget weapons, the Sparrow relying on radar designation from the Tomcat and the Sidewinder using a heat-seeking sensor head to guide it to the hot exhaust streams from a fighter. Both were short-range, knife-fight weapons, and were preferred by most pilots over the more cumbersome Phoenix.

"He's gonna get a Sidewinder up his ass," Bird Dog said. "First sniff you get of him, he's dead meat."

Gator sighed. "Why are you such an idiot? You know damned well we're not authorized weapons free. If that P-3 had gone down, maybe. But since he didn't, we need clearance from *Jefferson* to fire unless it's self-defense."

"I'm feeling mighty self-defensive about now."

"You'll feel it even more when you're standing in front of that long green table trying to explain why you shot down a reconnaissance aircraft," Gator pointed out.

"Like they don't have to explain why they shot at our P-3, but I have to explain shooting at them?" Bird Dog demanded.

"You got it, shipmate. You take a shot without my concurrence and I'm not backing you up. Not this time."

Bird Dog heard the real annoyance in the RIO's voice. "Okay, okay," he said finally. "I'm a big boy—I understand the rules."

As the Tomcat reached the end of its northern leg, Bird Dog used a hard rudder to pull her into a sharp, ascending turn. "On station," he said.

"Fine. Listen, Bird Dog, I know you think I'm some sort of wimp," the RIO continued, his tone softer. "But out here on the pointy end of the spear, we're not just a couple of hotshot fighter jocks spoiling for a fight. We're a continuation of diplomacy by other means."

"Your War College shit makes a lot more sense when we're on the deck," Bird Dog responded. "A lot of good philosophy does to me. I'd rather have a solid radar contact. Speaking of which—anything in the area?"

"I think I probably would have mentioned it to you if there were," Gator responded tartly. "What, you think I'm back here as some sort of a *zampolit*? I got news for you, Bird Dog. Some time at the War College is just what you need to get some perspective on things."

"Yeah, yeah, yeah. Thanks, but if it's all the same to you, I'll take an extra year on the bombing range over War College any day."

"Looks like you might have your chance." Gator's voice had gone hard and cold. "Radar contact, bearing zero one zero, range forty miles, speed four hundred knots."

"You got IFF?" Bird Dog asked, inquiring about the status of the international friend or foe transponder carried on most military aircraft as he broke out of the turn and headed along the vector Gator had reported.

"Negative. No ESM, either. At four hundred knots, this could be our friendly neighborhood Bear. Or—"

"Or one of his hotshot little buddies," Bird Dog said. "A MiG."

"Keep your finger off the weapon button until we know for sure," Gator warned. "I'm still in tracking mode. I'm not going to light him up until he's closer."

"If it is a MiG, when are we within weapons range?"

"Another twenty miles. Less than that, if he doesn't have the latest ESM warning modifications on him."

"Well, let's just go see, shall we?" Bird Dog said softly. He shoved the throttle forward, increasing airspeed to just over five hundred knots. "I'm staying at altitude for now—might need the gas later. You let Mother know what's going on, and I'll get us over there."

Bird Dog heard Gator switch over to tactical and begin briefing the watch team in CDC on board *Jefferson*. Although the TAO there would already have their contact information, since it was transmitted automatically via LINK 11 to the ship's central target processing unit, Gator was making sure that no one else was holding any contacts in the area. The other Tomcats were holding nothing but blue sky, *Jefferson* reported, a note of excitement already creeping into the TAO's voice. He heard the TAO say, "Roger, Tomcat Two-oh-one, come right to course zero-one-zero and investigate—oh." The voice trailed off as the TAO evidently noticed from the speed leader on his large screen display that Bird Dog was already doing exactly that.

Attu

"The pilot reports he will be overhead in twenty minutes," the senior Spetsnaz reported. He glanced over at Rogov, whose face was an impassive, unreadable mask.

"Very well." Rogov ignored the man. Whether or not he believed the story that it was merely a surveillance aircraft checking up on the detachment made little difference now. Twenty minutes from now—nineteen, he thought, glancing at his watch—forty Special Forces paratroopers would be spilling out the back end of the transport aircraft and parachuting down to the island. Unlike the Spetsnaz team with him now, these men were carefully selected. Each one of them was a Cossack, born and bred in the harsh outer reaches of the former Soviet Union, owing allegiance primarily to their tribe rather than any political subdivision. Rogov smiled. As skilled and deadly as the Spetsnaz on the initial team, each one of the paratroopers had sworn undying loyalty to his hetman, holder of the traditional Cossack mace. If the Spetsnaz could have seen him during their last ceremony, clad in his ancient Cossack regalia, they would not have doubted his prowess at the beginning of this mission and they would have known what he knew now: The Cossacks were coming.

CHAPTER 8
Thursday, 29 December

The fast craft skimmed over the top of the waves, acting almost like a hovercraft as it shot over the surface of the water. Sea state 2 consisted of mild swells without white tops, and Carter had the throttle slammed full forward. But even small swells act like a roller coaster at eighty knots.

"No sign of activity," Sikes shouted, struggling to be heard over the noise of the sea and the wind in the boat. "May be a false alarm."

The chief shook his head. "Doubtful. I don't know, sir, but there usually aren't too many of those. Not if they're sending us in."

Sikes nodded and gave up. It was all he could do to hold on to his lunch in the boat, and a lengthy political discussion was out of the question.

Ahead, the island jutted out of the sea like a fortress. The west end was relatively flat, climbing sharply into jagged peaks and spires. He studied the landscape, wondering if they'd brought enough pitons and line. Climbing up that icy moonscape would challenge every

149

bit of their physical reserves. And the danger . . . he considered it grimly. Intruders—if indeed there were any on the island—could be hiding behind any spire, waiting silently for the SEALs to make their approach. The tactical advantage would be theirs. The only way to achieve any degree of tactical surprise would be to airlift in with a helicopter, and even that would be problematic. First, the noise of the helicopter would alert their prey, and second, even the most reliable aircraft developed odd quirks and problems in the frigid environment. No, he decided, on balance it was better that they go in by boat, even with the problems that patrolling the jagged cliffs presented.

Fifty feet off the coast, now blindingly reflective under the afternoon sun, Carter slowed the boat to twenty knots. He turned broadside to the island, carefully making his way toward the westernmost tip. The plan was to begin their sweep there, working slowly toward the cliffs, postponing the decision to climb until they were closer in. If nothing else, it would give them time to adjust to the realities of arctic patrolling.

Five minutes later, the fast boat edged up to the ice, the SEAL stationed in the bow carefully surveying the water beneath her hull for obstructions. When the bow bumped gently against the shore, he jumped out, pulling the bowline behind him. Two other SEALs followed. As the first order of business, they drove a piton into the hard-packed ice to provide a mooring point for the boat. One of them would stay behind and stand guard while the other four executed the patrol in pairs of two.

Sikes was the last one out of the boat. After the gale-force winds that traveling at eighty knots generated, the almost calm air felt warmer. An illusion, he knew.

Unprotected, skin and tissue would freeze within a matter of seconds. He checked the lookout SEAL carefully, making sure his gear was in order, then pirouetted 360 degrees while the other man returned the favor. Satisfied that they were as well equipped against the environment as they could be, Sikes made a sharp hand motion. Without a word, one SEAL joined on him, while the fifth SEAL and Huerta stepped away together. With one last sharp nod to the lookout, Sikes pointed northeast. They took off at a steady, energy-conserving walk.

The ice under his feet was rough, the surface edged in tiny nooks and crannies from the ever-constant wind. A light dusting of snow blew along the surface, swirling around their ankles and obscuring the uneven surface. Still, he reflected, it was better than winter ice in the States, where intermittent warming and refreezing turned the surface slick as glass. Here, at least there was enough traction to walk. Just as well, since he couldn't see the ice beneath his feet for the blowing snow. His partner moved forward and took point. Sikes followed five yards behind, carefully surveying the landscape. After a few moments, it became apparent there was not much to see. The land was featureless, except for the jagged peaks ahead of them, and any traces of human habitation had been swept away by the wind. He glanced to the north, where he could barely make out the figures of the other two SEALs.

The wind picked up slightly, and he noticed the difference. It crept around the edges of his face mask, trying to find some purchase in the lining or some overlooked gap in his clothing. He could feel the heat rising off his skin as he walked, felt the air sucking at it.

The point man stopped suddenly. He pointed and made

a motion to Sikes. Sikes moved forward until he was standing by the man. "What was it?"

"Don't know for sure—something dark green, blowing in the wind. In this wind, it was gone before I could get a good look at it. Man-made, though—definitely."

Sikes lifted the radio to his mouth and quickly briefed the other group and the lookout on the sighting. Even after a few moments of standing still, he could feel his muscles start to tighten as the cold seeped in.

Every sense heightened, adrenaline pounding through his veins and further exacerbating the heat loss, he motioned for the other man to begin again. There was no more chance that this was a false alarm. Whatever the man had seen—and he had no doubt that the man had seen something—this patrol was now tactical instead of practice.

1710 Local
USS _Jefferson_

"Sikes just radioed in that they've seen something," Batman said into the receiver. "Whoever's taken up residence there and decided to start shooting at our aircraft isn't so hot of a housekeeper. Still, the island's supposed to be deserted. If they hadn't taken a shot at our aircraft, we probably never would have known they were there."

"Don't be so sure about that," Admiral Magruder's voice responded. "There's that radio report from the Inuits."

"And who would have suspected it?" Batman mused. "Some Aleutian Islander with a radio sees something strange and decides to call in the Navy."

"Not so strange as you might think," Tombstone responded. His voice took on a reflective note. "I wonder if it's the same—no, couldn't be. He'd have to be pushing seventy years old by now."

"Who?" Batman asked, confused by Tombstone's apparent change of subjects.

"Probably nothing," Tombstone answered. "But years ago, when my uncle was still involved in Special Forces projects, he spent some time out on those islands. We were in the middle of the Cold War, and maintaining the integrity of our homeland was a lot bigger issue than it is today."

"Vice Admiral Magruder on a field trip to the Aleutians?" Batman snorted. "I'd like to see that."

"He wasn't always a vice admiral," Tombstone answered dryly. "At the time, I believe he was a lieutenant commander. He told me the story a couple of times, how he went out to the islands, met some of the native tribes, studied their survival techniques. At the time, we were still in our infancy on cold weather tactics. Some bright mind in the Pentagon decided that the best way to shorten the learning curve was to study people that have centuries of experience at it. My uncle's always been an avid skier and camper, so somebody figured he was perfect for the job."

"How long did he spend there?"

"Three months. He visited five major islands, including one of the largest ones near the end of the chain. And that's the odd thing—he met an old fellow there, an Inuit who was considered the leader of the tribe. At first, they weren't too interested in talking, but my uncle managed to make friends with him somehow. It had something to do with killing a polar bear, though I never got all the details. Anyway, this old fellow decided my uncle was okay. They came to some sort of understanding about the Russians, although I gather the Inuit wasn't nearly as concerned as my uncle was. He said he left the man some high-tech radio gear—high-tech for that era, anyway— along with a list of standard tactical frequencies. From what my uncle says, they've had a couple of reports from them over the years, although I doubt that there's been anything for the last decade or so."

"And this fella is still alive, you think? And the radio's still working?" Batman asked incredulously.

"You got the report, didn't you?" Tombstone pointed out. "Besides, this fellow might have handed on the responsibility to his son as well. Who knows? At this point, I'm just grateful we've got an asset in place."

Batman shook his head, wondering. With the very latest ESM equipment, radars, and other highly classified sensor systems on board the carrier, in the end, the first detection had been made the way it had been for centuries: by a man on the ground.

Adak

Tombstone hung up the receiver thoughtfully. Was it possible, he wondered, that the same man would still be in place after all these years? He shook his head, deciding that it didn't matter. Barring the outside chance that this was a deception operation in some way, he was inclined to trust the radio report. Though Batman had been doubtful, he'd agreed to send the SEAL team in to investigate. And now it looked like that had been the right move.

"Admiral," Captain Craig said, poking his head around the corner into Tombstone's cabin. "Problem, sir."

"How did you hear—?" Tombstone broke off suddenly. The chief of staff hadn't been present while Tombstone was talking to Batman. He couldn't know about the debris the SEALs had found blowing in the wind. It must be something else. "What is it?" he asked, motioning the man to come into the room. "Dinner reservations screwed up again?"

"I wish it were that simple," the chief of staff said. "No, Admiral, it's an air distress signal. We're getting seven-seven-seven-seven blasting all over the place on IFF. Evidently it's a civilian helicopter experiencing mechanical problems about two miles from us."

"How serious?"

"Serious enough that they don't think that they can make it back to land. And there's no question of them ditching in these waters, of course. They're requesting permission to land on the ship."

"A civilian?" Tombstone frowned. What in hell's name would a civilian helicopter be doing in this area?

The chief of staff shook his head. "According to the transponder, it's a commercial craft. The pilot said they were out trying to do some spotting for a fishing boat when they started having problems. They're headed this way out of Juneau, they said." Captain Craig shot him a doubtful look. "The radar track doesn't jive with that, though. The only way it makes sense is if they're coming out of Adak."

"Adak? What the—" Tombstone cut the thought off abruptly. As soon as the chief of staff had announced the discrepancy in the flight's track, the conviction that

Pamela Drake was behind this had hit him. It had to
be—there was no other explanation.

Over the years, he'd watched Pamela's determination
to get in the middle of every fast-breaking story, marveling sometimes at the lengths to which she would go to
ferret out the smallest bit of information. As a more
junior officer, he'd rarely been on the receiving end of
her drive to be the best reporter on any network, bar
none. However, since he'd added stars to his collar, the
issue of their relationship and Pamela's profession had
become increasingly problematic. Where does one draw
the line? he wondered. While he might not be entirely
certain of the answer himself, there was one thing he was
sure of—with an ACN helicopter inbound, it was somewhere different than from where Pamela did.

"Admiral?" the chief of staff said, snapping him back
to reality.

"I take it the pilot's declared an emergency, then?"
Tombstone asked.

"Yes, sir—about five minutes ago." The chief of staff
sucked in his breath as he saw the cold fire settle over
Tombstone's face. He'd expected some reaction from his
boss, but not this one.

"Let them land," Tombstone said coldly. "As soon as
they're on deck, I want to see them all in my cabin.
Immediately."

The chief of staff turned to execute the orders, feeling
a fleeting pity for the civilians in the helicopter. They had
no idea of what they were in for.

"And COS? One other thing."

The chief of staff turned back to his boss. "Sir?"

"Get the senior JAG officer on board up here ASAP.
Let those civilian idiots cool their heels in the conference

room while I talk to him. And tell him to bring up his Dictaphone and any other recording equipment he might need. If this is what I think it is, I'm going to want criminal charges filed against every person on that helicopter."

As the chief of staff left the compartment, someone tapped softly on the door between his conference room and his cabin. "Come in," he said roughly, struggling to get his temper back under control.

The door opened quickly, and Tomboy's red-topped head peeked around the corner. "Good afternoon, Admiral," she said formally. "I was in TFCC, and I heard about the helo." She let the unspoken question hang in the air.

Inwardly, Tombstone groaned. The last thing he needed on top of the tactical situation and Pamela Drake's surreptitious arrival on his ship was Tomboy's questioning.

"You have a problem with that, Commander Flynn?" he asked coldly, immediately regretting the words. He saw Tomboy's face settle into an icy mask, not unlike the one he saw every morning in the mirror when shaving.

She drew herself up, seeming to add a few inches to her height. "None at all, Admiral," she responded in the same tone. "I just wanted to make sure you were properly briefed. With your permission—" she finished, drawing back as though ready to leave.

"Tomboy! Get in here," Tombstone said roughly.

She stopped in midstride. "Yes, Admiral?" she said.

"We have communications with this helicopter, right? Did you hear what they said?"

She regarded him gravely, a bland, professional look in her eyes. "Yes, Admiral, I did in fact hear the entire transmission. Would the admiral care for me to repeat it to him?"

Something in the back of Tombstone's mind started insisting that this was a very, very, very bad idea. "Yes," Tombstone said, ignoring it. "What is the nature of their problem?"

"Icing, Admiral. And there are specific requests for your assistance," she added thoughtfully, staring at a spot somewhere behind his head. "In fact, the actual request was, 'Ask Stoney if I can put this bird down on his precious boat,'" Tomboy said, her voice level. "The speaker identified herself as Miss Pamela Drake."

1740 Local
Attu

"Aircraft," Sikes snapped into the radio. "Everybody freeze." The phrase struck him as oddly absurd in this environment, but it was a fact that movement would draw the aircraft's attention faster than anything else. As long as they stood still, clad in their white arctic gear against a solid white background, there was a good chance they wouldn't be observed.

The lookout and the other patrol team rogered up, and Sikes watched the man in front of him hunker down on the ice. Sikes elected to remain standing, one hand reflexively going to the trigger of his weapon.

The deep-throated growl of a large aircraft was now clearly audible. Sikes schooled himself to keep his face down, not daring to risk exposing his tanned face to any observer overhead. He heard a change in the doppler effect, indicating the aircraft was turning, and waited. If the aircraft decided to orbit overhead, he was going to have to think of something fast. Under these conditions, remaining still could be deadly.

Three minutes later, he heard the sound of the engine shift downward, indicating that the aircraft had turned away from them. He let out a gasp of air, unaware that he'd been holding his breath. He gave it thirty seconds, then risked an upward glance.

The ass end of the Soviet transport aircraft disappeared over the line of the mountains. But far more worrisome was what it left in its wake. A cluster of parachutes was already visible in the overcast, and more were streaming out of the aircraft. He made the mental calculations swiftly. The nearest one would be only fifty yards away from them. Remaining where they were had become completely unacceptable. He raised the radio to his lips. "Move out."

Rogov wedged one heavily gloved hand into a crack in the ice and leaned forward against the belaying line. Perched near the top of a cliff, hidden from below by the jagged spikes, his position was somewhat precarious. The wind gusted harder at this altitude, and the surface of the ice was smooth, offering few footholds. Without the rappelling team, they could not have made it up to this site.

Yet, for all the difficulty in reaching it, it was perfect. He had a clear field of vision of the area below, including the prospective weapons station. Abandoning the ice cave as soon as they heard the boat approach, the Spetsnaz and Rogov had quickly availed themselves of their prearranged routes to the peaks. From their vantage points they saw the boat approach, do a careful survey of the western end of the island, and then moor to the far end. While the two teams had been difficult to see against the landscape, the night vision goggles made the job easier.

Rogov glanced up at the sky again, his heart swelling with pride. Arrayed against the overcast, all forty chutes had opened perfectly, and the men they carried were now drifting down to the ground. As their altitude decreased, their rate of descent began to seem impossibly fast. From this angle, it seemed inevitable that at least half of them would suffer broken legs or ankles upon landing.

Yet he'd watched them execute this similar maneuver many times before, always without casualties, and always precisely on time and on target.

He shifted his gaze back down to the Americans. At the first sound of the transport aircraft, they'd ceased all movement, making them a bit more difficult to spot, but he could still ascertain their location. He wondered what they were thinking, staring up at the parachutes. He saw one man look up, a break in patrol routine, flashing his tanned face against the white background and now easily visible. No matter, he thought. The men descending from the heavens had their ways of dealing with Americans. Oh, yes, indeed they did.

Sikes saw the first man touch down fifty yards away from him. He tightened his hand on his weapon and brought it up slowly, careful to make no sudden movements that might startle the other man into firing. He watched as the unidentified parachuter snapped his quick-release harness, the wind quickly catching the gusting folds of the parachute and blowing it away. In the same motion, the man brought the weapon he'd been carrying at port arms up, aiming it at Sikes.

For a few moments, it was a Mexican standoff, each of

them drawing down on the other with their weapons. Then, as ten more parachuters alighted behind them, the first man fired.

Sikes hit the deck the second he saw the man tighten his finger around the trigger, some instinct warning him he was in mortal danger. He brought his own weapon up and squeezed off a shot. He saw the first parachuter leap backward as though shoved in the middle of his chest with a heavy hand, and a bright red stain blossomed on his chest. Gunfire exploded around him, the rounds, every fifth one a tracer, exploding the ice into shards around him. The ricochets sang wildly with a distinctive high-pitched squeal as rounds left the ice at acute angles. He saw the SEAL beside him drop to the ground, falling face forward into the rough ice and blowing snow. The swirling particles partially hid the body.

Sikes returned fire, stopping only when the other side did. The odds were impossible, yet he'd be damned if he'd give up without a fight. As the gunfire from the other side ceased, he dropped to one knee, still holding his weapon at the ready. Not taking his eyes off the parachuters, he rolled his teammate over onto his back. He groaned.

Half of the man's face was missing, the bloody, seeping mass that had been its lower right quadrant already freezing in the arctic air. He'd taken another round in the gut, and on its way out, the round had evidently hit bone and ricocheted out the side of the man's body, blowing a massive, gaping wound in his right side. Irrelevantly, he noted the layers of clothing now exposed by the wound, layer upon layer carefully designed and donned to allow survival in this environment. For some reason, that struck him as particularly poignant.

He turned back toward the parachuters, rage fueling his movements. While he'd examined his friend, they'd moved imperceptibly closer, and he was now ringed by silent white shapes carrying arctic-prepped weapons. He snarled, hating to bow to the inevitable. A SEAL fought, and fought always, but there was nothing in their code of conduct that demanded suicide. For a brief moment, he wondered if he could somehow provoke them into firing and shooting each other, since their fields of fire were not limited by their formation, but decided against it. Slowly, he stood. He faced the man closest to him, and dropped his weapon to the ground.

In the distance, he could see the two members of the other team moving now, heading back toward the boat. Somehow, they'd managed to avoid the attention of the parachuters.

While the lead man fixed his gun on Sikes, he heard another man bark out rough commands. The group of parachuters quickly shed their gear and assembled themselves into five-man teams, looking very much like American SEALs in the way they moved and held themselves. He felt the chill bite deeper, wondering if these were the famous Spetsnaz he'd heard of so many times before but encountered only once.

He saw the men deploy in a standard search pattern. Off in the distance, his teammates were just reaching the boat. He heard a man cry out, and saw several start to run toward the boat, struggling to make headway against the wind in their heavy winter garments. The lead pair of parachuters stopped and raised their weapons. Gunfire cracked out again, oddly muted by the wind.

He saw his men reach the boat and leap into it, one step behind the lookout, who was already gunning the engine. The boat backed out, gaining speed at an incredible rate. As soon as it was clear of the land, it heeled sharply and pointed, bow out, to sea, quickly accelerating to its maximum speed of eighty knots. He breathed a sigh of relief and glanced down at his teammate. One dead, one captured, three alive. At least, if the boat could evade gunfire, the report would make it back to the carrier. As he stared at the grim face of the man approaching him, he realized that that was more than he could expect to do.

White Wolf stared at the action below, motionless, not even flinching at the harsh, chattering whine of the automatic weapon fire. Born and bred to this land, familiar with every nuance of its territory, he was truly invisible to the Spetsnaz infesting his terrain. He made a small motion to his grandson, who approached and put his ear close to the old man's mouth.

"See the mistakes they make?" the elder said quietly, his voice barely a whisper. "The positioning, the noise—they know nothing of this land."

The younger man swallowed nervously. "We are so close," he said in the same barely audible tones. "Your safety is important."

The old man made a small movement with his mouth. "If I cannot evade these men, then it is time for me to die," he said. "These things—you see how difficult it will be for the Americans when they come. These intruders are already scattered about our land, and dislodging them without killing the man they've taken will be impossible."

"Better them than us," the younger man said harshly. "And what exactly have they given us? Taken our land, given diseases to our people—why should we help the Americans?"

The old man gazed at him levelly, his eyes cold and proud. "My word."

The younger man sighed. "Yes, yes, there is that." He glanced back down at the land below, moving his head slowly so as to be undetectable. "What can we do? So many of them."

"And so inexperienced," the older man murmured. "They have many lessons left to learn—and this one will not be pleasant."

1800 Local
Tomcat 201

"A fucking invasion," Bird Dog breathed. "Oh, deep holy shit, Gator."

"Don't get happy with the weapons yet," Gator said tightly. "Mother's having a fit on the other end. A MiG they know what to do with. Same thing with a Bear. But an amphibious landing—or an airborne one—is a little outside of our marching orders. The admiral's on the circuit, yelling that if we so much as twitch wrong we could start an international incident."

"Like the Russians haven't?" Bird Dog asked. "Putting paratroopers on American soil seems to be a hell of an unneighborly thing to do. Not to mention shooting at our P-3 aircraft."

The Tomcat was circling at seven thousand feet, monitoring the progress of the paratroopers down to the ice. They blended quickly with the landscape, and were invisible after they landed to the aircraft above.

"Hell, I wish we had some Rockeyes," Bird Dog said, referring to the ground munitions missile that carried a payload of tiny bomblets that exploded on the ground.

They were the weapons of choice for use against enemy troops.

"You think you're gonna get permission to drop bombs on U.S. soil?" Gator demanded. "Think, man, think! For once in your life, just consider the consequences."

"We drop bombs on American soil at the range," Bird Dog argued. "What, you want us to sit up here and watch these bastards invade?"

"And just who the hell are they, do you think?" Gator snapped. "What insignia did you see on that aircraft they jumped out of?"

"You know who they are."

"When are you going to understand that your gut-level instinct isn't enough, not in today's world, Bird Dog. You've got no proof that that was a Russian aircraft— nothing at all. No transponder, no aircraft insignia, no Russian being spoken on International Air Distress— IAD. Just how do you think we're going to look?"

"*They shot at our aircraft.* What more do you want?" Bird Dog exploded. "Am I the only one in this battle group that's getting tired of every terrorist in the world taking a shot at American troops?"

Gator's voice turned colder than Bird Dog had ever heard it before. "If you can't get it through your thick skull that we follow orders first, then you'd best find some other way to make a living. This isn't about barrel rolls and Immelmanns, you asshole. This is about a very nasty situation and a world the rest of the country thinks is at peace. Hold it—" he said suddenly. "Mother's talking."

Bird Dog leaned forward against his ejection harness, feeling the straps cut into his shoulders. The pain gave him the feeling that he was doing something, which he desperately needed right now. The sight of invaders tromping across American soil—American soil, even if it was ice and frost and rime—touched some fundamental core of his being. It was one thing to watch the Chinese invade the Spratlys, the Russians take on the Norwegians, or any one of a number of nations attack a neighbor, but this was different. Different for him, at least. Along with the cool iciness and pounding adrenaline he had come to expect in battle, he felt an outrage so strong as to border on rage. Invaders, tromping across American soil—the battle group had to do something.

"Get a trail on that transport," Gator said finally. "High and behind, in position for a shot. But weapons tight right now—unless it's in self-defense, you don't even think about touching the weapons switch. You got that?"

"Yeah, yeah, I got it," Bird Dog snapped. He jerked the Tomcat back, standing her on her tail and screaming up to altitude. Over the ICS, he heard Gator gasp, and then the harsh grunt of the M-1 maneuver. Bird Dog's face twisted. Served his RIO right if he felt a little uncomfortable. Who the hell was he, anyway, taking an amphibious landing so casually? What did he think this was, the Spratlys?

"Cut this shit out," Gator finally grunted.

"Cut what out, shipmate?" Bird Dog snapped. "You told me to gain altitude—I gained altitude. And if you and the rest of the pussies on that carrier had any balls, you'd let me do something about this."

USS *Jefferson*

Batman stared at the tactical symbol on the large screen display, watching the hostile contact turn north and head away from the Aleutian chain. "That fighter jock is sure about this?" he asked. "Who's in Two-oh-one, anyway?"

"Yes, Admiral, they sounded certain. It's Gator and Bird Dog from VF-95," the TAO answered. He turned and gave the admiral a questioning look as he heard a sharp snort behind him.

"Bird Dog," Batman muttered. "I should've known. Anytime something starts happening, that youngster's in the middle of it. Damnedest luck."

He looked up and saw Captain Craig's face twitch. "You got something on your mind, COS?" Batman demanded.

"No, Admiral," the chief of staff said quietly. "You're right, that young pilot does seem to be in the middle of every tactical situation he's been near since he's been in the Navy." COS stopped and carefully assessed the man standing before him. "I was just thinking about someone else, that's all."

Batman stared at him. "Why, you old fart. Are you saying—?"

The chief of staff nodded.

Batman stared at the COS for a second, then turned back to the screen. "Maybe I won't court-martial his ass after all. TAO," he said, raising his voice, "get those Alert-Five Tomcats in the air. And move four Hornets and four more Tomcats to Alert Five. I want asses and cockpits on the deck and metal in the air. Now."

The TAO nodded, and picked up the white phone to call the CDC TAO. His counterpart twenty frames down the passageway would automatically add tankers and SAR support to his revised flight schedule.

Moments later, the full-throated growl of a Tomcat engine ramping up shook TFCC, which was located directly under the flight deck. Batman stared up at the overhead. "Damn, those bastards are getting faster every day."

1910 Local
Kiska

"How many of you are with me?" the old Inuit demanded. He gazed around at the circle of faces arrayed before him. To an outsider, the men would have seemed impassive, but he could read the subtle emotions as easily as he could distinguish between new-fallen snow and ice. He frowned. "There is a problem?"

One of the older men stirred. "This mission—we are not young men anymore," he began. He glanced around the circle, saw heads nodding in support.

"Not all of us are old," the elder argued.

"This is your war," a younger man piped up. "What have these men ever done for us? Let them kill themselves out there on the ice, for all I care."

"You forget your place," the older man said softly. "You are here at our tolerance only—you have no say in these matters."

"The old ways." The young man looked disgusted. "What have they gotten us?"

"You forget who you are at a price," the old man

responded sharply. "If you have no honor, then you are nothing—do you understand, nothing. You would no longer exist to me."

"All this talk about honor is a fine thing, but what have the mainlanders done to our people?"

"And you would rather live under the heels of these others? Have you not listened? Those men are Cossacks. *Cossacks*, I say." He saw a stir of uncertainty ripple across the faces. "Don't the stories mean anything to you?" he pressed.

An uneasy silence fell over the group. Men avoided each other's eyes. The women, standing in the back of the room, murmured quietly among themselves. Finally, the eldest woman spoke up. "Stories are kept safe for a reason," she said quietly. "The things I know—the things my mother taught me, and her mother before her, and on and on, are true. Above all, we must not let these invaders stay on our soil." Around her, the women moved closer in support.

The elder whirled on the circle of men. "Even the women remember," he said, disgusted. "And who would know better than they? Murder, rape, killing as the whim seizes them—this is what the Cossacks would bring to us." He made a motion as if to spit on the floor. "And you complain about the mainlanders? Pah! You know nothing."

Finally, one elder spoke into the silence. "Better mainlanders than Cossacks," he said, his conviction growing as he spoke. "Though it last happened centuries ago, that people has not changed. I would rather live with sickness and disease than under the Cossack hand. We should go."

The mood shifted in the room, as one by one the men

nodded assent. The women looked even graver than they, knowing that many of them would be widowed or would lose a son in the weeks to come.

"It is done, then." He turned to a younger man. "Your army experience—it will come in handy now. Begin assembling all the weapons that we have here, including all of the portable communications systems. Handheld radios, GPS—all here as soon as you can."

The younger man looked grim. "Be all that you can be," he said finally. A tight smile crossed his face.

2120 Local
USS *Jefferson*

"How many men?" Admiral Wayne asked again.

The young SEAL petty officer looked haggard and drawn. "At least thirty, maybe more. Maybe forty, I don't know for sure," he said. His fatigue was evident in his voice.

"Could you see whether your teammates were shot?" Lab Rat asked. He stared at the man before him, wondering at the combination of strength, training, and sheer courage that had brought the SEALs back alive.

"I don't know. We were too far away. I heard gunfire—a Kalishnikov, I'm certain of it. One burst from an M-16, that's all. I thought I saw a SEAL on the ground, but I couldn't be sure."

Batman turned to Lab Rat. "I suggest you start talking to the other SEALs, Commander," he said. "We're going to have to get them out."

"Let me go, sir," the SEAL they were interrogating said suddenly. A look of desperation crossed his face. "We don't leave our men behind—never."

Batman regarded him carefully. "This mission isn't going in the next five minutes, son," he said quietly. "You let the commander finish up with you, then you hit the rack for a good solid twelve hours. After that, we'll see what you and your shipmates look like. If you're up to it, there'll be a spot on the mission for you."

The younger man looked relieved. "Thank you, sir," he said.

"I think I'm done with him, Admiral," Lab Rat said. He turned to the SEAL. "Hit the rack, sailor. If you need something to help you sleep, see Doc. But if you want to be part of this mission, you'd better be asleep in the next fifteen minutes."

The young sailor left quickly, his eyes already half-lidded at the thought of sleep.

Lab Rat turned to the admiral. "This will be a bastard of a mission," he said quietly. "The SEALs will want to do their own planning, of course."

Batman nodded. "They always do. Anything they want—anything intelligencewise, or any other form of support, we get it for them."

USS *Coronado*

"She's on final, sir," the TAO said. Tombstone studied the plat camera mounted in one corner of TFCC.

"Doesn't look like she's having problems to me," he said shortly. "Airspeed good, hover is stable—no, I can't see a damned thing wrong with that bird." The helicopter gracefully settling onto the deck above him confirmed his suspicions. "Get them down here," he snapped at the chief of staff. Then he turned to the lawyer behind him.

"In my stateroom, Captain. You've got ten minutes to make me real smart on what my options are. Let's start with treason and work our way down from there."

Attu

The moment the weapon left his hands, something slammed into Sikes's back. The force sent him flying through the air like a linebacker, and he landed facedown on the hard ice, the grooves and ridges in it scraping the protective gear away from his face and smashing one lens of his protective goggles.

For a moment, he thought he'd been shot. He felt a deep ache starting in his back, and he wondered which would kill him first—bleeding from the wound or hypothermia from lying on the ground. A few moments later, he realized that he'd been body-blocked rather than shot. The familiar oozing of blood was absent, although the ache below his left shoulder blade remained. He lay on the ground motionless, not daring to move.

A harsh voice barked out a short pause, evidently a command of some sort. Sikes turned his head slowly, aware now of the ache in his neck, to look at the man who had spoken. Something about the phrase—he tried to remember if he had ever run across it in his language schools. No, but it was tantalizingly close to something he did know.

The man barked out another sentence, and two of the paratroopers approached him from either side. One pointed the barrel of his Kalishnikov along Sikes's head, while the other jerked his arms around him and bound his wrists with something rough, slipping it under his gloves

and white parka. Even with that brief exposure to the
frigid air, the skin on his wrists started to ache.

The man who'd bound his arms then yanked him to his
feet, pulling the arms almost out of his shoulder sockets.
Sikes repressed a groan. To show weakness this early—
that couldn't help.

A phalanx of men surrounded him, pressing close in.
The urge to strike back, to lash out with his legs, was
almost overpowering. He forced himself to stay calm and
think. To attack any one of them now would be fatal. He
might kill or seriously disable one, but the other multi-
tudes would kill him. Quickly, he hoped, although he
suspected that would not be the case after looking at their
faces.

From the little he could seer under the heavy-weather
gear, the men bore a striking resemblance to each other,
almost as though they were from the same family. High,
bronzed cheekbones, narrow, almond-shaped eyes, and
dark coarse hair peeking out from under their caps were
the common denominators. They were alike in physique
as well, broad in the shoulders, slightly shorter than the
average American, and giving the impression of being
heavily muscled.

Who the hell were these fellows? he wondered. He
studied them again, trying to find any identifying mark,
but each man wore the same solid white anonymous gear
that he had on himself. A few differences in the manu-
facturing, perhaps. He saw metal zippers poking out
along several pockets, a few ragged tears and rips that
would have been immediately repaired in American
forces, but evidently these men were not as careful with
their gear. For what it was worth, that was a mistake.

Above all things, SEALs are fanatical about their

equipment. Too often their lives hang in the balance, depending on the reliability of a boat engine, the tensile strength of a nylon rope, or on the comprehensive and completely updated information on a routine chart. Had Sikes seen similar signs of wear on his own men's gear, he would have had serious doubts about their qualifications to be a Navy SEAL.

He filed the fact away, along with the observation that there were no identifying marks of any kind on the clothing—not names, unit insignia, or even a country flag. Curious, but clearly indicative of the fact that these men were professionals. Wherever they came from, however they were trained, at least that much they had in common with the American forces.

A few of the men exchanged short phrases, but for the most part the group maintained tactical silence. Seeing that he did not understand, one motioned Sikes forward with his rifle, supplementing his instructions with another shove in the back. Sikes stumbled, then fell into a slow walk. A rifle butt prodded him in the ass, urging him to hurry. He feigned a stunned, disbelieving face, and stumbled slightly as he walked, hoping to convince them that he was in worse shape than he was. In reality, except for the now-fading ache under his shoulder blade, and the strength-sapping cold, he was in adequate shape.

The man who was in charge snapped out another set of orders, and three of the men traded a look universal to all military men—the look of disgust and disbelief when assigned some task they believe is below their capabilities. Without argument, they turned and walked back to SEAL 3's body. The tallest of the three men handed his own pack over to a comrade, then slung the SEAL's body over his shoulder. The ease with which he moved indicated massive upper body strength, a fact concealed by the heavy winter clothing. Another fact in the database, Sikes thought.

He walked for fifteen minutes toward the base of the cliffs he'd seen from sea. Just when he was actually beginning to feel the chill he'd been feigning for those minutes, they arrived at the base. Sikes studied the scree line at the base of the cliff, and then noticed the dark rectangle set into the base. He shook his head, wondering if he were in worse shape than he thought—that should have been the first thing that leaped out at him.

Sikes was hustled inside. After shoving him down to the far end of the room, one of the paratroopers kicked his feet out from under him. Sikes tried to twist in midair and land in a judo stance on his side, but he caught his shoulder wrong as he hit. He winced, showing no outward emotion.

He did not resist when two of the men came over and bound his feet with nylon rope.

The leader of the group walked over and studied him while he was lying on the ground. After a few moments, he motioned for a chair. One of the paratroopers provided it, then hauled Sikes to his feet and slammed him roughly into it.

"*Kak vas zavoot?*" the man said.

Russian. Memories of long hours spent at the Defense Language Institute in Monterey, California, came flooding back to him. An elementary phrase, one he'd learned his first day there—*What is your name?*

Sikes shook his head and let a bewildered look settle on his face. Whatever language they spoke among themselves, they also spoke Russian. Knowing that, he might be able to puzzle out a few phrases in the other language, and it was best not to let his captors know that he had any knowledge of either language.

The leader snorted in disgust. He turned and shouted something almost incomprehensible to another man, who stopped what he was doing and quickly approached. Sikes thought he recognized some corruption of the Russian phrase "Come here," but couldn't be certain.

A hurried conversation ensued between the two. The second man nodded several times, asked two questions, and then turned to face Sikes.

"What is your name?" the second man enunciated carefully. The heavy Slavic accent rendered the words harsh and guttural.

"Sikes." Better to give them no information unless they ask for it, he thought, glancing down at his foul-weather gear. Although there was not much chance of hiding what his true occupation was, given the nature and quality of his clothing. And the M-16—no point in even trying to pretend he was a civilian.

"You are SEAL?" the man asked.

Sikes shook his head in the negative. Under the Geneva Convention, he was required to provide only name, rank, service, and military I.D. number. While it might be obvious to both parties that he was a SEAL, the Code of Conduct required him to stick to just that information for as long as it was humanly possible. Under extreme torture—well, that was another matter entirely. Experience during Vietnam had taught the United States Navy that even the finest officer held his or her limits, a point beyond which the body overrode the mind's convictions in a form of self-preservation instinct. After reading the memoirs of many POWs, Sikes knew that the point came earlier for some, later for others, but for every man, there was some such breaking point.

And of course they knew what a SEAL was, he thought. Just as he knew what Spetsnaz were, and the names of the special forces of twenty other nations he could name immediately. They all knew of each other, the small, secret bands of men—and, in some countries, women as well—that fought the unconventional war, taking conflict deep into the heart of enemy territory by skill and deception, laying the groundwork for the arrival of conventional troops and gathering intelligence critical to the success of every mission. American soil, a man dressed like he was—there were only two possibilities. Russian or American. And since they hadn't even bothered to ask about the first, he had a sinking feeling he knew who they were.

The other man stepped forward and landed a solid punch on the left side of his face. The force knocked him out of the chair and sent him sprawling on the damp ice floor. He felt the skin scrape off the other side of his face, and his previously uninjured shoulder was now screaming in protest. As before, he lay motionless. The man walked up to him and kicked him solidly in the crotch.

While the layers of arctic clothing and padding must have cushioned the blow somewhat, Sikes could not believe the agony that coursed up his body, paralyzing his breathing and starting a gag reflex that threatened to turn into the real thing. The pain, oh, God, the pain. He tried to suppress a groan and couldn't as his body curled into a fetal shape. His consciousness dimmed out at its edges, his eyesight losing color and going gray. While he was still lying on the deck gasping for breath, the man walked around to his other side and kicked him solidly in the kidney. Sikes felt tissue rupture, the incredible pain radiating down his other leg, and the nausea now forcing him to vomit. He tried desperately to hold on to consciousness and failed.

Rogov stared down at the man on the ground. A SEAL, no doubt about it. He recognized the look in the man's eyes as easily as he saw it in his own troops. A field interrogation would be unlikely to yield anything of interest, he decided. No, not on this one.

"When is our next communication break with the submarine?" he asked.

The communications officer glanced at his watch. "Eighteen hours."

"Very well. Make the necessary arrangements. We will transport him back to the boat for further interrogation. The drugs, the other techniques—" Rogov glanced around the ice cave. "A nice outpost, but it lacks certain essential equipment. You understand?"

His communications officer nodded. "If the weather holds, we should be able to transport him in twenty-four hours. That will give them time to come to communications depth, receive our message, and make preparations for receiving this."

Rogov fixed him with a glare as cold as the weather outside. "Ensure that that happens. And as for the weather—after centuries of exile in Siberia, do you really think that we should worry about that?"

The communications officer nodded again.

Rogov turned and snapped out a command for his operations officer. A man detached himself from his comrades and walked over, still chewing on a high-protein, calorie-rich field ration he had taken from his pack.

"You understand, this is an American SEAL?" Rogov asked.

"Of course, sir," the operations officer said after swallowing the chewy mouthful. "Obvious from his gear, isn't it?"

"And what else is so very obvious?" Rogov sneered.

The operations officer looked uncertain. "That when there is one, there are more," he said tentatively. Seeing the expression on Rogov's face, his voice took on a more confident note. "And the SEALs do not leave their comrades behind. Never."

"Ah. Then you've already made preparations for an adequate defense of this entire area, have you not?"

"Indeed. But I will review them once again. It might be a wise idea to supplement certain positions."

The operations officer glanced over at the crumpled body of the SEAL, tossed carelessly in a far corner of the ice cave. He pointed to it. "You know the other thing we have learned about SEALs. They do not leave their dead behind."

Rogov sneered. "They have this time." But the expression on the operations officer's face made him add another phrase silently—*for now*.

2300 Local
Bicycle Alley, USS *Jefferson*

Sweat streamed down Bird Dog's face, stinging his eyes. He reached for the towel draped across the frame of the Stairmaster and glanced down at the LCD display. Fifty minutes elapsed, and two more steep hills coming up. Already his legs were burning, the lactic acid build-up turning them heavy and wooden. Still he pounded, increasing his stepping rate until he could no longer feel his feet.

"You can't kill us in the air, so you're trying to do it on land, is that it?" Gator gasped from the other machine.

"No pain, no gain," Bird Dog grunted. He reached out and touched the level display, increasing the difficulty from seven to nine. Immediately, he felt the added resistance of the stairs as he struggled to force each one down. Those next two hills—he groaned, then made himself work for it.

"I quit." Gator ground to a halt, then spent a few moments stepping gently on the machine to cool down. He picked up his towel and wiped his face off, then snapped it at Bird Dog. "And you would, too, if you had any sense."

"Ten more minutes," Bird Dog grunted.

Gator dismounted his machine and walked around to stand in front of Bird Dog. "Don't you think this is about enough?" he asked quietly. "I know it's frustrating, being up there and not being able to do anything, but pushing yourself to the point of exhaustion isn't going to help any. Hell, you end up all stiff and muscle-bound tomorrow, you're not going to be able to pull that turkey out of a tight turn if you want to."

Bird Dog didn't answer, keeping his eyes fixed on the numbers ticking off on the time clock. Finally, when the minutes display reached sixty, the machine started beeping at him. The queue of sailors waiting for the machine started protesting.

"Okay. That should do it," Bird Dog said finally,

stepping off the machine and grabbing his towel. "Maybe at least I can get some sleep tonight."

"You're not sleeping?" Gator shot him a worried look. "You okay, man?"

"Sure, I'm fine. Just needed to work off some energy, that's all."

But it wasn't, and Gator knew it. Bird Dog knew that his RIO knew him better than anyone else on the ship. The communications between the two men was almost psychic. And Gator knew that the idea of foreign soldiers tromping over American soil was eating at his pilot like nothing he'd ever seen before.

If pressed, Bird Dog admitted, he wouldn't have expected to have that strong a reaction. Sure, he'd taken numerous oaths since he'd joined the service, reciting gravely the words about protecting and defending the Constitution against all powers both foreign and domestic, swearing allegiance and obedience to his superiors. But in the last four years, even though he'd seen conflict over the Spratly Islands, he'd never really understood what a secret trust those words imposed on him. It bothered him, and it was even worse that no one else seemed as upset as he was. Hell, if he were the admiral, he would have nuked those sons of bitches to kingdom come by now rather than tolerate what amounted to an armed invasion on American soil. Even if it was just a rocky outcrop of ice and snow in the middle of the godforsaken North Pacific.

"A shower, maybe something to eat," Gator said. He glanced at his pilot appraisingly. "Sound good?"

Bird Dog tried to smirk. "Are you asking me on a date, Gator?"

"In your wildest dreams, asshole," the RIO said

promptly. "Even if you had boobs, you wouldn't be my type."

Bird Dog contemplated a sharp rejoinder, then thought better of it. To be arguing with his RIO over whether or not he would have made a good date was the height of idiocy. Besides, there were other things on his mind at this point.

Gator saw his change of mood. "Oh, come on, lighten up," he said, disgusted. "A hell of a lot of pilots go through a whole tour without seeing as much combat as we did over the Spratlys. You know that?"

Bird Dog shrugged. By now, they'd reached the corridor that housed the VF-95 pilots. Bird Dog paused at his door, his hand on the knob. He gazed at Gator for a moment, then said haltingly, "It just doesn't make much sense to me sometimes. You know that?"

Gator nodded. "I know that better than anyone else on this boat, shipmate," he said. "And I also know that there's not a damned thing we can do about it right now. You stick around this canoe club for a while, you start to understand it. You don't have to like it, but that's the way it is."

Bird Dog shoved his door open. "Ten minutes, I'll meet you down in the Dirty Shirt," he said by way of response.

Gator nodded. "The tactical scenario always improves on a full stomach, asshole," he said lightly. He snapped the towel again, catching Bird Dog on the butt.

2310 Local
Admiral's Cabin, USS *Coronado*

"Thank you, Commander," Tombstone said gravely. "I'd like for you to remain while I talk to them."

The lawyer nodded. He wondered how much the admiral had retained, since it felt like he'd dumped four years of law school and two years of postgraduate study into the man's lap in the last ten minutes.

"COS, send them in," Tombstone said.

The chief of staff walked over to the door to the conference room, opened it, and motioned to the four people seated around the large rectangular table. They filed into the admiral's cabin, not speaking.

Tombstone did not ask them to sit. Instead, he glared at them from a seated position behind his desk, assessing each one carefully.

"Your licenses are gone," he said finally, pointing at the pilot and the copilot of the helicopter. He turned his gaze on Pamela. "And if you had one, yours would be, too."

Pamela took one step forward. "The icing wasn't their fault, Admiral," she said quietly, her voice betraying no quaver of nervousness. "I admit, I pressed them hard to fly in this weather, even though they said they'd rather not." She shrugged. "Not a smart move, in retrospect. But there was certainly no attempt to—"

"Shut up," Tombstone said levelly. He turned his back on her to face the JAG officer. "Read them their rights before we proceed."

The lawyer stood and recited the Miranda warnings to

the four people. By then, the pilot and copilot were starting to turn pale. Yet nothing appeared to affect Pamela Drake, ace correspondent from ACN, Tombstone thought bitterly.

"Do you understand these rights as I've explained them to you?" the lawyer concluded. All four nodded.

"I can't hear you," Tombstone said neutrally, pointing at the recording equipment. One by one, the four people said yes.

"And, having these rights in mind, do you desire to speak to an attorney," the lawyer continued, "or do you wish to discuss this matter now?"

"As I was saying, Admiral," Pamela began.

Tombstone cut her off again. "I didn't ask for a narrative yet, Miss Drake," he said coldly. "This is the way this matter will proceed—I will ask questions, you will answer them. At the conclusion, I will permit you a brief—and I mean very brief—period in which to add any amplifying material that you might wish to. And, for the record, I'm not interested in your conclusions at this point."

Tombstone turned his gaze to the pilot. "There was no malfunction on your helicopter," he said bluntly. "That is true, is it not?"

The pilot cleared his throat and glanced uneasily about the room as though trying to find the answer to the question. He looked at his copilot, who shrugged. Finally, the pilot settled for staring at the deck. "No, there wasn't."

"Are you aware that it is a federal felony to falsely utilize the seven-seven-seven-seven emergency squawk?" Tombstone demanded.

The pilot nodded.

"I can't hear you," Tombstone said again.

"Yes."

"The next question will require a yes or no answer only. Did you falsely report an emergency condition in order to land on my ship, knowing that had you asked permission through normal channels I would've said no?"

"Yes, but I—"

"Thank you. That answers the question. Finally, did you take this action at the instigation of Miss Pamela Drake from ACN?"

The pilot, now thoroughly cowed, looked over at his former employer. Perhaps his last employer, he thought bitterly, trying to remember why in the world he'd ever been convinced this was a good idea. If he answered the admiral's question, no news organization would ever hire him for a charter flight again. But if he didn't, that would be the last time he was ever allowed landing rights or any other courtesy from any military installation. At this point, he wasn't even sure that he would have a license. "Yes." He continued staring at the deck, waiting for the explosion he was sure was coming.

"Admiral, I—"

"Miss Drake. One more outburst and I'll have you gagged. If you do not understand the full extent of my power on board this ship, then I suggest you consult with an attorney before disobeying any more of my orders. Is that perfectly clear to you?" And why should it be now, my dear? he wondered bitterly. It never was before. In all our years together, you never understood how absolutely compelling my power is over every bit of this ship. If I wanted to have you locked up overnight and held incommunicado, I could do it. There'd be hell to pay eventually, but until someone outside of my world heard of it, you'd be in jail. He stared at her face and noted with grim satisfaction she was starting to understand.

Tombstone directed his gaze to the copilot. "Do you agree with the answers your pilot has given?" he demanded.

"Yes." The copilot took less time to make up his mind.

Finally, Tombstone turned his gaze to Pamela. "And did you ask these men to commit this deed, knowing full well that I expressly said I did not want you on board this ship?"

"Me, in particular, or the news media in general?" Pamela snapped. "Honestly, Stoney, this has gone on long enough."

"My name," Tombstone said quietly, "is Admiral Magruder. Please bear that in mind from now on, Miss Drake. Do you desire to answer the question, or is it your wish to remain silent?"

"Of course I hired them to fly me out here," she stormed. "You can't cut the news media off from an event like this. It's not fair."

"Fairness has little or nothing to do with conflict, Miss Drake." Tombstone studied her carefully, watched the color rise in her cheeks. Pamela had never been particularly good at accepting no for an answer. Now it appeared that her insatiable desire to get the story at any cost had finally landed her in serious trouble. How serious, she would find out shortly. "I've spoken with our JAG attorney on board, and he advises me that you three have committed several serious felonies. As I said in the beginning, the least of the penalties will be the loss of your pilot's license." He smiled, a trace of bitterness at the corners of his mouth. "Not that that matters to you, Miss Drake. Even if you'd thought about the consequences to these two men before you decided on this course of action, I doubt it would have stopped you."

"Damn it, Stoney—all right, Admiral Magruder, if you wish—you can't do this," she stormed. "I demand—"

"Gag her," Tombstone said simply. He watched horror and shock chase each other around Pamela's face as two master-at-arms stepped up to her side.

CHAPTER 10
Thursday, 29 December

White Wolf pointed first to the north, then to the south, and eyed his grandson. The young army veteran nodded. He, too, had seen both armed patrols crisscrossing the island. Not very covert, given the fact that they were invading another country. But then again, they had no way of knowing any other ground forces were in the area.

The veteran made a motion as though hoisting something onto his shoulder. White Wolf looked puzzled for a moment, then comprehension dawned. He scanned the skies overhead and was relieved to note that there were no aircraft there.

The younger man moved closer. "Stingers," he said, automatically turning the *s*'s into a *th* sound with the reflexive caution of a foot soldier who knows how far sibilants carry in still air. "Very deadly against helicopters, easy to use."

White Wolf shrugged. If they'd been arriving airborne, he might have been concerned. But the small assault force with him had come across the ocean in craft built in keeping with their native traditions. Slow, but silent and virtually undetectable by modern technology, the boats were lightweight and easily transportable. They were already tucked in among the spires on the eastern side of the island, invisible unless a patrol happened to stumble right on top of them. And given the patrol patterns he'd seen, that wasn't likely. The two sets of guards remained on the flat western side of the island.

"They are ready?" White Wolf asked, gesturing to the men behind him.

"Yes." The veteran eyed him uncertainly. "As ready as we can be. You understand, I'm not certain what weapons they have here. There is a chance—"

White Wolf cut him off with a sharp gesture. "It is decided. We will not second-guess ourselves."

Morning Eagle sighed. Moving back away from the escarpment, he talked briefly with the men following them. They were broken into two teams of eight men each, and carried pistols and shotguns. Their strength, mused White Wolf, regarding the groups, would have to be in their ability to move undetected across the land. No mainlander—and that included Russians—could match that. Weapons were fine, but it was getting close enough to use them that was the real problem.

The young veteran returned to his side. "I still think you should stay here," he said, continuing an argument from the night before. "It will be dangerous."

That was exactly the wrong argument to make. White Wolf drew himself tall, feeling the old vertebrae creak and complain with the effort. "I gave my word," he said quietly. He held his hands out before him, spread them open. "Do you think I have a choice?"

His grandson sighed. "I suppose not. But for God's sake, don't take any chances."

White Wolf glanced at the seven other men clustering around him. Most of them were at least twenty years his junior, a few even younger, one almost as old. All in all, good men, made strong by the forces of nature they contended with daily.

He jerked to the north with his head, and set off across the rough terrain without waiting to see if they followed.

1015 Local
Tomcat 201

"I'd say hell would freeze over before they decide what to do, but that would be a bad choice of words in this case," Bird Dog said.

Gator sighed. "You think every problem can be solved with five-hundred-pound bombs?"

"No, of course not. Sometimes you want to use your two-thousand-pounder," Bird Dog snapped. "But there's not a damned air contact within five hundred miles of this place, according to E-2. And as close as *Jefferson* is to this island, we could be pulling Alert, sitting on the deck waiting for them to show up, instead of stuck in some miserable orbit overhead."

"What if the E-2 doesn't hold it until it's too late?"

"Like that will happen," Bird Dog snorted.

"Okay, how about this?" Gator asked, tired of the argument. "We drop down to five thousand feet, take a quick visual on the island. Then we come back up and do what CAG wants for a change. That make you happy?"

Bird Dog nodded, knowing his backseater could see

the gesture. "I'd feel more like I knew what was going on
if I could at least take a look at the island occasionally.
But with our cloud layer, it's gonna be more like three
thousand feet instead of five thousand. You up for that?"

"Just don't run me into a cliff, Bird Dog. That's all I
ask this trip."

1020 Local
Attu

Cover was scant as White Wolf led his men down to the
base of the cliffs. Twenty feet from the main cliff base,
it degenerated into little more than a series of rocky
protuberances from the ice, boulders barely waist-high.
He crept forward as far as he dared, then dropped to the
ground and waited. Behind him, he heard his men
moving into position.

Hours of observation had revealed the fact that the
northern patrol was a relatively predictable, if otherwise
diligent, watch-stander. His approach to maintaining
security consisted of walking east and west along the
northern half of the island, occasionally glancing around,
and making regular radio reports. It took him approximately thirty minutes to reach the end of the island,
surveil the sea, and then commence the return trip. As his
back was turned while he was heading west, White Wolf
took advantage of his relatively infrequent observances
to move the men into position.

The veteran would have the harder time of it, he
thought, feeling the cold start to creep into his belly. The
southern intruder patrol had appeared to be far more
unpredictable, varying the times at which he started his

rounds, and occasionally stopping to carefully surveil all 360 degrees around him. Twice in the last five hours he hadn't even continued on to the end of the island, but had instead unexpectedly doubled back on his path. For the veteran, that meant a shorter time period to get his men in position.

There was one constant in both men's routines, however. At some point during their circuit of their area, each one moved back to within assault range. With a little luck, White Wolf's man and the southern patrol would be near the rocks at the same time, another consistency in their patrol patterns they had not yet puzzled out. The two group leaders had agreed that the veteran would determine the time for the attack, based on when his more predictable prey was within range. At the first sign of difficulties on the southern area, White Wolf would order his men to attack.

He looked back over his shoulder and motioned the two men behind him to move forward. In addition to their shotguns, each one carried a bow and arrow, a relic of times long past. But despite modern technology, most of the men maintained at least some proficiency in the old way of the hunt, just in case. Who knew when the shipments of weaponry and ammunition from the mainland would suddenly cease, throwing the Inuit tribes back into their own way of life? Without the old knowledge, the ways of the hunt and the stalk, the secrets of silent killing, they could not have survived.

Their quarry was now reaching the westernmost point in his patrol area, and would shortly begin the return trip to the rocks. White Wolf saw the men flex their arms, keeping the muscles loose and the blood flowing. They had already drawn three arrows each out of their quiver and placed them in the snow alongside. No point in moving while the man was close and risk alerting him.

Just before the patrol turned back to the west, White Wolf risked a glance up over the rocks. He scanned the southern edge of the cliffs carefully, searching for any sign of the other group. He almost smiled. Wherever they were, it was beyond the ability of his old eyes to find them. How much more difficult for the Russians it would be.

1045 Local
Tomcat 201

"Watch for icing," Gator warned as the Tomcat passed through seven thousand feet. "When you hit that cloud bank, you're going to pick up some moisture on the wings."

"Already thinking about it," Bird Dog answered cheerfully. "Don't worry, we'll go through those clouds so fast you'll never even know we were there."

"And that worries me almost as much," Gator muttered darkly.

The Tomcat's nose dropped through fifty degrees, picking up airspeed as it did so. The dark night sky, speckled with stars and thin ribbons of the aurora borealis streaking across it, suddenly disappeared. As Bird Dog dove through the cloud layer, a dark nothingness surrounded the cockpit, pressing in on the two aviators. Gator fiddled nervously with the gain control on the radar, and could almost feel the icy crystals trying to creep through some small gap in the canopy and collect on the wings.

Five seconds later, they broke out of it. In the utter darkness of arctic night, it was more of a feeling of being free of the clouds than an actual change in visibility. With their regular navigational lights off, the F-14 was virtually invisible.

"Well, at least they can hear us," Bird Dog said. "We're at three thousand feet."

"The tallest of those cliffs is at two thousand," Gator reminded him. "Screaming through on the radar. Come left ten degrees to avoid them."

"Roger." Bird Dog made the course correction snappily, reveling in the quick response of the Tomcat. "Just testing the flight surfaces," he said hastily. "That would be the first sign, some sluggishness in how she handles on the turns."

"Yeah, right." Gator tried to remember if Bird Dog had ever avoided making a sharp turn when a gradual one would do. He bent over his radar, carefully watching the quickly approaching cliffs. It never hurt to be too careful. Sure, the altimeter said they were at least three thousand feet, but altimeters had been known to malfunction, so he kept his eyes glued to the highest peaks.

If it hadn't been for his paranoia, he might have missed the first sign. As it was, the short, quick blip on the highly capable look-down radar sent a jolt of alarm screaming up his back. The message transmitted itself to his mind and mouth before he had time to consciously process it. "Break right! Altitude—now!" he snapped, tactical reflexes taking over for considered thought.

Bird Dog obeyed instantly, wrenching the aircraft through a tight turn, slamming the throttles forward, and immediately climbing for altitude. "What—"

"Missile inbound," Gator said sharply, his eyes now

locked on the small, glowing blip on his radar screen. "At least that's what it looks like. We already know they have Stingers—I don't want to take any chances."

"Holy shit," Bird Dog breathed. "You mean—"

"Get us the fuck out of here, Bird Dog," Gator snarled, his temper barely under control. "You want to discuss the finer points of Stinger weaponry, let's do it at thirty thousand feet. Right now, I'm a little busy back here." The RIO's hands flew over the controls, ejecting flares and chaff into the wake behind them.

"And if they had any doubts about where we were, we just fixed that," Bird Dog said unhappily. "We just lit up that night sky like it was mid-June."

**1150 Local
Attu**

White Wolf gasped as the night exploded into fiery brilliance. The sun—no, five suns—no, wait. He shut his eyes as the light bombarded his painfully dilated pupils. Not suns at all, not some relic from an old legend, but flares.

The Americans. Pride and vindication coursed through his soul as his prediction of American aid proved to be true. It had to be them. The intruders would have shunned the light, and would not have left their patrols out wandering randomly had more forces been expected.

He focused on the man patrolling, now halfway between the western edge of the island and the cliff. He stood still, his head thrown back as he stared at the flares, his night vision completely destroyed. White Wolf debated with himself for just a moment, then concluded his southern counterpart would arrive at the same decision. "Shut your eyes," he said sharply, quietly. His men obeyed instantly. A few of them ducked their faces down in the crook of their elbows, understanding what White Wolf was trying to accomplish.

The flares would last no longer than five minutes, not nearly enough time for the patrol to reach their location. In addition, any man that exited the ice cavern would immediately be blinded as well. The Inuits, on the other hand, by shielding their faces, were preserving their night vision. The moment the flares went out, they would be well prepared to attack immediately, and could take advantage of the element of surprise.

But for the plan to work, one man had to watch and see when the flares disappeared. He sighed, resigning himself to being left out of the fight. Younger bodies, faster feet would do the fighting this time. He watched the man, keeping the flares in sight in his peripheral vision. He waited.

Tomcat 201

"It fell off," Gator reported, studying his radar screen. "If you know they're coming, if you catch them in time, those suckers aren't too bad to outrun. Nothing like a Sidewinder or Sparrow."

"But just as bad if it gets us." Bird Dog leveled off at eight thousand feet, just above the tops of the clouds. In the background, he could hear TAO on *Jefferson* demanding an explanation. Not only had Bird Dog left his assigned altitude, but the erratic movements and changes in altitude had caused alarm on board the carrier.

"You tell 'em what happened," Bird Dog said, his eyes still glued downward. "I have a feeling there's something else I'm supposed to see, and I'm not getting it."

Attu

"Now," White Wolf whispered urgently. The seven men around him sprang up as the last light from the flares faded. Opening their eyes, the landscape around them came into sharp focus.

To his left, White Wolf could see men pouring out of the ice cavern and fanning across the landscape. White Wolf's second in command took charge, leading the attack with several silent, deadly arrows into the throats of the men nearest to him. They fell, unnoticed by their comrades ahead of them.

Moments later, the inevitable happened. The man in the lead glanced back, noticed two men lying in the snow, and sounded the alarm. As he did so, the Inuits rose up from concealment and charged down the slope, firing their more modern weapons.

Two Inuit warriors fell, and rolled in crumpled balls along the rough ice. Brief anguish tore at White Wolf, to be replaced almost instantly by a sinking feeling. Instead of being blinded by the light, the men seemed to be as capable of functioning immediately after the flares went out as his men were. Spread out in a long line, armed with shotguns that had seen better days, the Inuits were no match for the Russian Spetsnaz. Kalishnikovs barked, and three more men fell.

The remaining two Inuits cast an uncertain look back up at the cliffs, then decided that retreat was the better part of valor. They turned their backs on the Russians and scrambled for the rocks, moving as fast as possible in that landscape. White Wolf watched them approach, anguish and hope warring in his heart. Ten more feet and they could—another man fell, rolled in the snow, and fetched up against the boulder that had been his destination. The remaining lone figure streaked across the landscape, finally reaching the safety of the rocks. From forty feet away, White Wolf could see the man crouch behind a hefty outcropping, his heaving chest detectable even under the heavy garments.

Looking to the south, White Wolf could see the bright spatter of gunfire marking the darkness, evidence of the southern battle mirroring his own. In the sudden light of one spate of weapon fire, he finally got a close look at the face of the Spetsnaz commando. Instead of seeing broad, Slavic features so like his own, he saw an insect face, complete with protruding eyeballs and jet-black shiny carapace. For the briefest second, old legends about giant insects flashed through his mind. Then he realized what he was seeing.

Night vision goggles. He groaned, now heedless of the noise. The men approaching would be half-deadened by the gunfire anyway, and there seemed no other way to let out the hard, cold feeling creeping through his body.

He heard sharp, guttural commands snapped, and the team of fifteen soldiers approached the cliffs warily, weapons at ready.

The sole survivor, crouched behind the rock, looked up at White Wolf. Their eyes locked, and something wordless passed between them.

The lead Spetsnaz raised his weapon, took careful aim, and fired. Instead of the sharp report of gunfire, White

Wolf heard only a muffled whoosh. Grenade-launcher, he thought despairingly. He hunkered down behind his own rock, knowing that the man below him was doomed.

Thirty minutes later, as the Spetsnaz patrol caught up with him among the icy spires, he put himself in the same category.

USS *Jefferson*

"How the hell can they be under fire?" Batman growled. "They're over American soil."

"That's what Bird Dog reported, Admiral," the TAO said. He shook his head, puzzled. "Unless it's Green-peace—they've been known to get militant at times."

"I refuse to believe that Greenpeace is taking on the United States Navy. Get me some other options." Batman stomped out and headed for CVIC. Maybe Lab Rat had some other ideas.

Attu

The Spetsnaz herded White Wolf roughly over to the far wall of the ice cave. They trussed his arms and legs, and shoved him over against Sikes.

The two prisoners regarded each other gravely. Old black eyes, shiny as obsidian, stared into pale blue ones. In that look, they each saw something they could respect in the other. Finally, Sikes nodded. "We wait for our chance," he murmured, his lips barely moving.

As careful as he'd been, one of the Spetsnaz overheard the exchange. He turned on them, and waved his Kalishnikov menacingly. The interpreter hurried over. "No talk, no talk," he said sternly.

Sikes shrugged and tried to look bored.

The Inuit moved closer to him, as though trying to pool his body warmth with Sikes's to fight off the cold. He twisted his hands behind him and touched the SEAL's arm. *Tap-tap-tap*. Sikes tried to maintain his bored expression as he considered the pattern of the taps. Was it—yes, indeed it was. Somehow, somewhere, this old native man had learned Morse code. And damned well; he had a feel for it. Now, if he could only recall his own training four years ago in BUDS.

The operations officer looked uneasy. "So what are we supposed to do with them?" he asked nervously. "One, maybe two people—sir, the submarine is small."

Rogov stared at him. "And there could be others still outside. A poor job of planning, and one that I will remember." The operations officer turned pale. Rogov reached out and slapped him across the face. "Remember that. Pray that is the worst you will receive."

The senior Cossack turned and strode over to the far end of the ice cave, stopping two feet before the two prisoners. He stared down at them accusingly, as though it had been their own fault they had been caught. Finally, the beginnings of an idea demanded to be considered. He almost dismissed it, then reconsidered. The beginnings of a cruel smile started on his face. It might work—it just might work at that. Abruptly, he turned and walked over to his operations officer. "There will be a change in plans."

"Sir?"

"I have something else in mind. Something more

valuable than whatever petty bits of international politics we can glean from these two prisoners. Who is our expert on American aircraft carriers?"

The operations officer started to ask a question, then apparently thought better of it. He pointed toward the man who'd been serving as interpreter. "Ilya. He has been on board several, in addition to studying their structure and characteristics in our military command school."

"Get him." Rogov waited impatiently for the interpreter to reach him.

The interpreter was among the youngest of the team members, barely three years in Spetsnaz. His nervousness was apparent on his face. He saluted respectfully and waited for Rogov to speak.

"How secure is an aircraft carrier?" Rogov demanded.

The interpreter looked startled. "At sea, sir?" he stuttered. "Virtually impregnable. There's no way to approach it—"

"Forget that part," Rogov instructed. "Once we are on board, how difficult would it be to move about the ship?"

"I was on board one once at sea, as part of an exchange program," the interpreter said. "Aside from the weapons storage areas and the engineering plant, most of the important spaces are located immediately below the flight deck. There are numerous passages down into that area, in addition to entries from the sponsons and walkways ringing the ship. But if I had to plan an operation, I would proceed directly from the flight deck down the ladder at the island. The combat direction center and the admiral's quarters are within easy reach then."

"Draw out a diagram. Have all the men study it. As

complete as you can remember." Rogov turned away, dismissing him.

The interpreter hurried back to join the rest of the team, relieved to be out of the presence of the stern hetman of the Cossacks. The aircraft carrier—he sucked in his breath, feeling his anxiety grow. Surely the *hetman* could not be planning to—no, he decided, it was out of the question. Not even a complete battalion of Spetsnaz would undertake an assault on an aircraft carrier.

Still, there was a reason that Rogov had been placed in charge of this operation. And if he wanted a map of an American aircraft carrier, that's what he would give him. He reached back into his rucksack, drew out a pad of paper, and began sketching.

Sikes found that Morse code came back to him quickly, even though it had been years since he last practiced. White Wolf slowed down and sketched in the essential details of the Inuits' attempted attack on the camp. Sikes carefully schooled his face to blankness, masking his surprise at the daring and ingenuity of the native island-ers.

"Wait, I listen," he began tapping out, interrupting the account of the assault.

Sikes listened carefully, trying to follow the corrupted Cossack dialect that was so similar to Russian. He caught a few words here and there, and then one phrase made his blood run cold. American aircraft carrier. He watched the younger officer take his leave from the man in charge and begin drawing something on a piece of paper. While he was watching, he tried to tap out a hasty explanation to his fellow prisoner, not certain how accurate his code was but hoping that the essential details were getting through. "And who taught you Morse code?" he ended.

"Magruder."

"Rear Admiral Magruder?" The SEAL considered this new fact carefully. How in the world—no, he decided, the explanation would undoubtedly be a long one. It could wait. Right now, they had more important priorities to discuss.

"We leave," he tapped out slowly. "Wait—wait for chance. Americans come."

The Inuit tapped out the short signal for affirmative, giving no sign on his dark, impassive face that anything was happening.

1150 Local
USS *Coronado*

"How close is the nearest island?" Tombstone asked. He stared at the speaker as though he saw Batman's face in it.

"About six miles away. There's a native settlement there, a small airstrip. That's where the radio signal came from." Batman's voice sounded tinny on the old speaker.

"And what are we doing about them? Batman, you're going to have to get them out of there. Plan a NEO—Naval Evacuation Operation. It's bad enough they're on one uninhabited island, but we've got to keep the situation contained. Get back to me within three hours with your plan."

"Aye, aye, Admiral," Batman said formally. Tombstone heard a note of chagrin in his old friend's voice. "I'm not sure I would have thought of it either, Batman," Tombstone continued. "Don't beat yourself up over it—just get it done."

"Roger, copy. I'll get the planners started on it as soon as we are done here."

"Top priority," Tombstone ordered. "The last thing I want during the first months of my tour is a hostage situation on American soil."

1200 Local
Tomcat 201

"I say we go back and take another look," Bird Dog argued. "It'll be easy."

"Nothing involving Stingers is easy," his RIO responded.

"The way I wanna do it, it will be. Listen, we go out thirty miles and drop down on the deck. We come in at the island at five hundred feet, so low they can't see us coming. We take a quick pass overland, on afterburners, and we're out of there before they have a chance to line up the shot. I say it'll work."

"And I say we don't do a damned thing until Mother gets back to us," the RIO retorted. "Jesus, Bird Dog, this is a fighter aircraft, not a surveillance one. Besides, you're too heavy with all that weaponry on the wings to get us the hell out of there if we need to move."

"So we dump it. Like this." Bird Dog reached out for the weapons jettison switch.

"You're out of your fucking mind," Gator shouted. "Do you know how much those missiles cost?"

"Yeah, I do. A hell of a lot less than the life of one SEAL on the ground and in trouble."

Attu

"It will be simplicity itself," Rogov concluded, glancing at the faces of the men around him. "Every man does his part, and within fifteen minutes we have the ultimate prize—possession of the nerve center of an American carrier."

He could tell they weren't convinced, although no trace of dissent showed on their faces. It was, he had to admit, a daring plan. But what were the options? Returning his two prisoners to the submarine was indeed a possibility, but his hold over the operational forces there was already tenuous. Besides, interrogating them was not essential to achieving their purpose. To truly demonstrate the might of a Cossack nation, to make the rest of the world take them seriously, what could be more effective than doing what no other force had done before—boarding and capturing an American warship. And not some small spy vessel, but the most potent force in America's arsenal. The aircraft carrier.

"You may ask questions," he said condescendingly.

"Sir, how will we keep control of the entire ship? With only forty men?" It was as near to criticism as Rogov was likely to get from any of the troops.

"I will explain again. One team will proceed immediately to the Wardroom Mess, enter the admiral's cabin through there, and from there go directly to TFCC. You understand, those doors that are locked when they're in port are most probably left open while at sea, just as they are on our own ships. The second team will move quickly up to the bridge, taking control of the people there. With those two areas secured, we will have enough leverage to do whatever we wish. Do you think the American troops would risk their admiral? Especially when we do no serious harm to their vessel or their crew."

"Yes, sir," the man said, not looking fully satisfied at the answer. "But as you said—getting on board an aircraft carrier is no easy matter. The flight deck stands thirty feet above the ocean, and even when they are lowered, the elevators are not much closer. How will we—?"

Rogov cut him off. "That is the simplest part of the entire matter. The Americans themselves will take us there."

CHAPTER 11
Thursday, 29 December

"And just how long am I supposed to stay here?" Pamela asked coldly. She made a short, curt motion to indicate the spartan stateroom. "It's bad enough you've got me held in here under armed guard—what's wrong, doesn't this ship have a brig on it? Run out of handcuffs?"

Tombstone studied her gravely. Anger had forced high color into her face, and it was obvious she sat motionless on the narrow single bed only through sheer force of will. Miss Pamela Drake, ACN star correspondent, was used to having her own way. And that most definitely did not include being placed under armed Marine guard in a tiny stateroom on board the ship while her colleagues covered a fast-breaking story.

What had he ever seen in her? he wondered, regret and nostalgia coloring his memories of her as strongly as the wild, passionate physical response they'd always had to each other. Back then, when he'd been a young lieutenant commander, she'd seemed the most glamorous, out-of-reach woman he'd ever seen in his life. During the years that followed, he learned that she possessed a drive and mind equal to his own. Somewhere along the line, he'd believed that would be enough to let them mold their two diverse lifestyles into one strong, satisfying life together.

But it hadn't been. Last cruise, when they'd finally agreed to break their engagement, he'd thought he'd never get over her. Now, on opposite sides of the room—and with battle lines clearly drawn—he wondered how he'd thought he could ever trust her. Her drive to succeed, to beat every correspondent on the glove in breaking the most sensational story, had pitted them against each other. He wondered if she'd given their relationship a single thought as she planned this daring—and he had to admit it had been that—assault on his amphibious ship. Had she thought at all about what her antics would cause, how difficult it would be for him? No, he saw, studying her carefully. She'd known what price he would pay, and she'd gone ahead with it anyway.

"Yes," he said finally, "there is a brig on the ship. Normally, however, an officer would be confined to his stateroom for something like this. I'm giving you the courtesy of treating you on the same terms, although I doubt you deserve it."

She shook her head angrily. "You don't get it, do you?"

"No," he said with finality. "And neither do you."

The SH-60F helicopter approached the island slowly. Five miles out, the pilot executed a turn to the west and began a slow circuit around it. The weather had cleared sufficiently to enable the pilot, ATO—Airborne Tactical Officer—and SO—Sensor Operator—to see the bare outlines of the island, but not much more.

"How are we supposed to see anything from here?" the copilot grumbled. "The whole landscape is one white blur. They could have a battalion of troops there in winter gear and we'd never know it."

"You fancy going in a little closer?" the pilot asked. "Weren't you paying attention at the brief? They've got Stingers on that damned island." He stopped talking and concentrated on maintaining level flight. Airflow over the land mass, probably from the rocky outcropping to the east, rocked the helicopter gently in the air. No cause for alarm, but after spending the last thirty minutes staring at the water below while it lapped at the frigid coast, he had no desire to let the normal develop into the unusual. Survival times were nil in the water, and land was too far away to reach if they had a problem.

"Well, let's sneak in another two thousand yards," the copilot suggested. "What are we supposed to be looking for, anyway?"

The pilot considered the request for a moment, then nodded. The range of a Stinger missile was no greater than two miles. Staying five miles away from the island provided an exceptional margin of safety, one that was tactically unnecessary. While he appreciated CAG's concern, there was no point in burning fuel if they couldn't bring back data.

"Just anything out of the ordinary," the pilot answered. "Something too small for a fast mover like an S-3 to see. And I agree with you—hanging around out here, we're not of any use. Just a little bit closer."

"Fine with me. It's damned cold out here, anyway. Maybe the pucker factor will warm me up some."

The pilot smiled grimly. "Oh, it will do just that," he said softly, remembering his days on patrol in Bosnia and the no-fly zone in Iran. Then, the mere hint of a Stinger missile was enough to raise the sweat level on any mission by a factor of ten. And rightfully so. "Let's just keep a heads-up on this. The first indication of a launch will probably be visual. I fly the aircraft, you keep up the visual scan. Got it?"

The copilot nodded.

1435 Local
Attu

"You hear that?" Sikes tapped out on White Wolf's hand. "Helicopter."

White Wolf tapped back the sign for interrogatory, and shot him a puzzled look.

Sikes closed his eyes and listened carefully. It was difficult to tell. The mass of ice surrounding the cavern was an effective sound-deadening barrier, but he thought he heard—yes, he was certain of it. He risked a slight nod, which White Wolf saw.

"U.S.?" White Wolf asked.

Sikes tipped his head slightly. It was, he was certain, a Seahawk. Barely audible, somewhere off in the distance, but he thought he could hear the distinctive *whop-whop* of the SAR helicopter at the edge of his perception.

But maybe not. Maybe it was just wishful thinking, an auditory hallucination born of desperate hope. He glanced around the ice cavern again. Ten armed Spetsnaz were scattered about the space, and another thirty were outside. He let his gaze rest on the leader of the group, the short, stocky man. For some reason, he didn't appear to fit with the other ones. Not that something was wrong with him—he was clearly in command of this cadre— but there was something that set him apart. There was a difference—not military, he realized suddenly, that's what it was. Though all the men were dressed alike, and possessed the same short haircut and broad features, there was something about their leader that was missing. Some difference in bearing, and the way that he spoke, that marked him as one whose life had not been shaped by the constant demands of doctrine.

Did it make a difference? He wasn't certain. At this point, it was just another fact, another data point in the hostile environment around him.

"We have to get out," he tapped quickly, feeling the determination run straight from his gut to his fingertips. As his fingers rested lightly on the old, wrinkled brown skin of the man next to him, he considered their odds. One man—no, two, he corrected himself—against the forty trained Special Forces men there. And their leader. He considered that fact again, wondering why it struck him as so important.

From fifteen hundred yards away, the island looked almost as featureless and impassive as it had from five miles. Except for a few additional contours and shadows in the cresting rocks, they might as well have stayed well outside of Stinger range. The pilot glanced at his companion. Their eyes met, and the copilot nodded. A grim smile spread across the face of the pilot. Whatever else he had to say about his copilot, it would never be that the man lacked balls. In that department, they were both light years ahead of their superiors.

The radio was squawking, as *Jefferson* demanded to know why the Seahawk was so close to the island. Every thirty seconds, the voice changed, as junior enlisted man was replaced by chief petty officer, and finally the tactical action officer. The next step, they both knew, would be someone on the admiral's staff.

"Easier to ask forgiveness than permission," the copilot said steadily. He reached over and flipped down the volume control on the radio.

The pilot brought the helicopter gently out of her orbit, turning her toward the island. Whatever there was to see would best be observed from directly overhead.

"They say the 'Never Exceed' speed on these babies is a hundred and eighty knots at sea level," the copilot said musingly. "What do you think?"

The pilot shoved the throttles forward to full military power. "I think in about five minutes we're going to try to break that record. And damned if I wouldn't kill for some afterburners about now."

**1436 Local
Attu**

"Hey," Sikes said loudly. "I need to go to the head—the can, the bathroom, whatever you guys call it."

The Spatsnaz, now clustered around the entrance to the ice cave, ignored him. The door opened, and two more came in, and the sound of the helicopter reached Sikes plainly. His hopes rose. If he could just signal—

"HEY!" he shouted. Finally, the man designated to serve as the interpreter walked over to him, annoyance plain on his face.

"Shut up."

"I have to go to the head," Sikes said, trying to work a pleading note into his voice. He crossed his legs, and crouched slightly. "Jesus, you guys have had us in here for hours. If I don't get some relief soon, I'm gonna piss all over your floor. Just think what it would be like, trying to sleep in here with that smell. I don't want that any more than you do. And it could get worse." He stopped, wondering if the interpreter would know the word for diarrhea.

Disgust spread across the other man's face. He studied Sikes carefully, then glanced down at White Wolf. "Him, too?" he said harshly.

White Wolf nodded.

The interpreter shot a frustrated look back toward the door, and then turned away abruptly. He walked over to the commander and said something too low for Sikes to understand. Finally, an unhappy look on his face, he came back over to them. "Later. As soon as—" his voice broke off as he glanced back at his superior.

"Okay, man," Sikes said. "You asked for it." He unzipped his parka, then reached for the zipper at the bottom of the front of his jumpsuit. "Don't say I didn't warn you."

The commander, Sikes saw, was now staring at them. Sikes thought he saw surprise and dismay flick across the man's face, then decided it might be as illusory as the first traces of the helicopter he heard. The commander snapped out a harsh, short sentence. Sikes recognized only the profanity.

"No," the interpreter said hastily. "Put that away." He pointed at Sikes's offending member. "We go outside," he concluded, then followed with a short string of obscenities in Russian regarding Sikes's ancestry and early toilet training habits. Four Spetsnaz commandos came over and joined them, circling them.

An honor guard, Sikes thought, almost amused. For a brief second, he wondered if he would be able to take a leak with so many strangers watching. Back in his early days of BUDS training, he found to his surprise that he suffered a mild degree of bladder shyness. The old native rose to his feet, his joints creaking audibly as he unfolded. He stepped toward Sikes, barely brushing past the first commando.

The small entourage moved toward the door. Sikes could hear the noise of the helicopter fading away, indicating that it had already made its closest point of approach. A feeling of desperation flooded him, increasing the pressure on his bladder. If they left too soon—no, don't think about it. He would just have to pray somebody was watching.

As they stepped back out into the frigid air, Sikes felt the blood drain away from his face. Cold, so cold—if the

Spetsnaz had any sense, they would have taken his arctic gear from him immediately, he decided. Trying to survive for even five minutes outside in this would be impossible.

The interpreter shoved him, directing him over to the right of the entrance and behind a large rock. Even in the frigid air, Sikes could smell the distinctive odor of a latrine. With two guards on either side, he and the old native stepped toward the rock, then took aim at the icy formation. Yellow stains and spatters already marred its surface, evidence of their predecessors, and an answer to the question of whether or not warm urine would melt arctic ice. Clearly, it wouldn't, freezing on contact instead.

Sikes tried to assume a nonchalant air as he prepared to pee. He gasped as he unzipped his jumpsuit and felt his balls shrivel up. Out of the corner of his eye, he saw White Wolf give a wry grin. Evidently, the older man knew what to expect.

The noise of the helicopter suddenly changed pitch, reaching up toward the higher spectrum of its octave. Sikes glanced up with his eyes, careful to keep his head straight forward and focused on the business at hand. Up doppler, an indication that the helicopter had changed course and was now approaching them once again.

The Spetsnaz heard it, also. One of them motioned sharply to the interpreter, who barked, "No! Enough— back inside." He grabbed Sikes by the shoulder and started to drag him toward the cave.

Sikes's right arm curled around and behind the other man's arm, coming up to brace his forearm under the interpreter's elbow. Sikes lifted up sharply and felt the joint crack. The interpreter screamed and fell to his knees.

As the sound of the helicopter deepened, obscuring every other noise in the area, he saw the Spetsnaz commander's lips move, but couldn't hear the order given. There were only a few seconds remaining. Desperately, he stared up at the helicopter, waved his hands, and then resorted to the only uniquely American gesture that came to mind.

As two Spetsnaz closed in on either side, weapons at the ready, Sikes raised one arm, his middle finger protruding from a clenched fist. If nothing else, at least they would know he was American. He was able to hold the gesture for only a few seconds. Suddenly, something hard crashed into the back of his skull. He blacked out immediately, and was unconscious before he hit the ice.

**1437 Local
Seahawk 601**

"Jesus," the copilot said. He started back at the figure, too astounded to feel the reflexive anger the gesture ordinarily invoked in him. "Hell, Brian," he said, aware that his voice sounded distant. "One of them damned invaders just flipped me off."

"What do you mean?" Brian replied, concentrating on maintaining safe altitude and level flight in the offshore burble of air. "You got the middle finger?"

"Yeah." The copilot frowned, trying to remember his college days' tour of Russia. "Only thing is, that gesture doesn't mean the same thing in Russia that it does in the U.S. Now why would—oh, hell!"

"Get on the horn to Mother," the pilot said, his voice hard. "Tell them that we just got a confirmation that our missing SEAL is alive."

"We have to get him out of there," Huerta said. The senior chief petty officer had no compunctions about standing up to anyone, including admirals, when it came to the safety of a fellow SEAL. "We don't leave our people behind. Not ever."

Batman rubbed a hand over his eyes wearily. How long had it been since he'd slept? "Of course we need to get him out," he said, trying to concentrate. "Now that we know he's alive."

The old, grizzled SEAL shook his head. "Doesn't matter to us either way, Admiral," he said neutrally. "Dead or alive, we never leave a shipmate behind. Never."

Batman looked up, saw the cold determination on the man's face, and felt the beginning of hope. "Tough odds. According to all the reports, there's thirty to fifty men on that island."

"You might be better off just leaving the planning to us, Admiral," the chief said, his demeanor defrosting slightly. "We've done this a time or two before."

"But the odds?" Batman persisted.

The SEAL smiled coldly. "Who cares if they're outnumbered?"

"You realize how stupid you were?" Batman glared at the two aviators.

The pilot met his stare defiantly. "We weren't doing any good where we were. And at fifteen hundred yards, I've got time to get away from a Stinger."

"But not at thirty yards. Which is exactly where you were, skimming over the surface of that island at ninety feet." Batman pointed at the copilot. "And you, young man—even if your pilot doesn't have any sense, have you forgotten that quickly what they taught you at OCS about obeying orders?"

The copilot blushed, glanced at his compadre, then faced forward. "No, Admiral," he said softly, "I haven't forgot at all. We spend a lot of time talking about getting the job done."

Batman sighed. As much as he'd like to continue chewing them out for their foolishness, they both had a point. More importantly, they'd been right. And that made up for a hell of a lot of disobedience. If I try to discipline them, he thought ruefully, I'm liable to wake up surrounded by the SEALs. These two are heroes to them. He continued to glare at the two aviators.

Finally, as the tension built to unbearable levels, he sighed. "You're going to be pulling every Alert Five your squadron has for the next three months, you realize that?" He tossed the two aviators' flight training folders on his desk. "And hell may freeze over before you ever get liberty."

Both men nodded.

"And for your little role in this escapade, I think you've just volunteered for another mission," Batman continued. "Seems like the information you brought back was important to a couple of fellows on this boat. To all of us, but to five others especially. You got any idea who that might be?"

"The SEALs?" the pilot asked.

Batman nodded. "Exactly. And they seem to think they can get in, grab their teammate, and get out. They have a little transportation problem, though. You men might be just the people to solve it for them."

"Yes, sir," the copilot said. He glanced at his pilot, suddenly aware that he'd usurped something that wasn't his privilege.

The older aviator looked pale. "We'd be honored to fly them in, Admiral," he said. "And out. If they're anything like the man I saw on the ground, the outcome's not in question."

Batman fixed the aviator with a steely look, trying to hide the note of concern in his voice. "The outcome's always in doubt, sir," he said coldly. "And don't you ever forget it."

Senior Chief Huerta looked doubtfully at the two men. "You ever flown Special Forces before?" he demanded.

"Only once. About half an hour ago, when we found out your man was still alive," the pilot retorted. "That good enough for you?"

"It will have to do." The chief's face softened slightly. "And don't think we're not damned grateful for that, too, sir."

"You just make sure we get out in one piece," the pilot said. He bent over the plotting table and studied the chart before him. "What's the plan?"

"A few details still to be worked out, sir," the chief responded. He pointed to a flat spot near the entrance to the ice cavern the pilots had seen. "We figure we'll want you to set down here. Our man may be injured." He glanced up sharply. "You said there was someone else with him?"

The pilot nodded. "I couldn't be certain, but it looked

like two of them were prisoners, from the way the guards were herding them around."

"Well, we might as well bring two out as one."

"Chief, that does look a mite risky, setting down right in the middle of them, don't you think?" the copilot said doubtfully. He looked up, and his eyes met the faded blue eyes of the chief.

"It would be, except they're not gonna be there," he said. He patted the copilot on the arm. "Don't you worry, youngster, we're a little bit smarter than that. Maybe in an armored helicopter we might come in closer, but as fragile as your bird is, we'll need every advantage we can get. We've got a little diversion planned."

"A diversion?" the pilot asked. "Like what?"

A lighter look lit the chief's face. "Let's just say we've got some allies we didn't know about before," he said carefully. "Up until now, they've been only voices on the radio. But one of the things we always try to do on a mission is to get indigenous forces to support us. Maybe not spearhead it—they're usually not trained enough for that—but for something like a diversion, or harassing action, they're damned fine."

"Indigenous?" the copilot wondered. "But there's nothing on that island—not apart from the intruders and your man."

The chief traced one finger east along the Aleutian chain, touching several larger islands briefly. "Maybe not on that rock, but there are on other ones. This whole chain is almost an island nation. Inuit tribes live on most of the larger ones, and travel back and forth to the smaller ones as needed." He reached across the table and pulled a brown folder toward him. "Did you guys get briefed on the native transmissions?"

Both aviators shook their heads in the negative.

"Didn't think so," the chief said. He handed the folder to the senior pilot. "You'll want to have a look at this, sir."

The pilot read rapidly, the copilot crowding in next to him to read over his shoulder. "Cold War trainees," he said finally. He closed the folder with a sharp snap. "And still in place. Who would've thought?"

"Nobody. And that's the point. If the U.S. Navy forgot about 'em, you can damn well bet the Russians did."

"But they barely have a radio," the pilot said. "What? You're gonna assault that island with shotguns?"

The chief shook his head. "No, we're not. Fortunately, we brought along a little extra armament." A grim smile cracked his face. "Plus a few fancy toys they've probably never seen before. Hell, we didn't get 'em till last year. But I'm betting those men will catch on pretty damned fast how they work."

The pilot shook his head doubtfully. "Aren't you depending an awful lot on an untrained mob?"

"Remember, they're only there as a diversion," the chief argued. "Here's what'll happen."

The chief spent the next ten minutes laying out the plan, covering all aspects of the diversion, the tactical pickup, and the successful exit from the area. When he'd finished, he said, "I don't care what the admiral told you, sir. Special Forces missions are always strictly a volunteer evolution. If you've got any doubts about this plan, we'll look for somebody else to fly it. We can't afford any weak links in this chain." He stared searchingly at the two aviators.

The pilot leaned back on his chair. A slow smile crept across his face. "I think if anybody can pull this off, you can. And as for your flight crew," he glanced at his copilot, who nodded, "I think you've already found your crew."

"You're sure this will work?" Batman asked.

"Yes, sir," Huerta said gravely. "We've torn this plan apart every way we can think of, and it's our best bet for getting Sikes out. But part of it depends on that fancy new aircraft of yours."

Batman leaned back in his chair and sighed. "The JAST bird. I notice it plays a heavy role in this."

The chief nodded. "You bet. We need that high resolution look-down, shoot-down capability. The regular Tomcat's a pretty impressive bird, but it's not enough for this mission."

Batman leaned forward and steepled his hands in front of him. "You probably don't know it, but we've got a serious problem here. The JAST pilot who flew the bird out was medevaced early this morning. Appendicitis." He paused, and surveyed the dismayed expressions on the three men's faces. "Any RIO can run the backseat on the JAST aircraft. The avionics are enough alike that it just takes a few hours of briefing. But the power plant, the flight controls, and the whole performance envelope are so different that it takes hours to get certified on it. Other than the man who drew it out, there's only one person on this boat qualified to fly it."

"Well, whoever it is, we need him," the chief said sharply.

Batman started to smile. "I think I can convince him to go along with this. You see, it's been a while since he's gotten to fly much, and he's pretty eager for a couple of extra hops."

"Just who the hell is this nonflying aviator?" the pilot said. "Everybody flies on this boat, everybody."

Batman's smile broadened slightly. "Me."

1700 Local
USS *Coronado*

"Come on, Tombstone, you know it's the right thing to do." Batman's voice held a pleading note. "That man on the ground deserves it."

"I'm not so sure," Tombstone said slowly. "One of the hardest lessons that I had to learn when I was in your shoes was that my flying days were quickly coming to an end. I hated it, but I finally admitted that I was of more use in TFCC than in the cockpit."

"This situation's a little bit different, don't you think?" Batman argued. "If it were a matter of just sending a Tomcat—hell, I've got plenty of men who'd volunteer. And women, too," he added hastily. "But the JAST bird is something else."

Tombstone sighed. As much as he hated to admit it, his old wingman was right. "And we can't get another pilot out from Pax River?" he asked one last time.

"No, Admiral." Batman's voice took on a formal note. "Too long of a time lag. Things are moving too fast—by the time we got someone else out here, that SEAL could be dead. The mission has to go ASAP."

Tombstone sighed. "All right," he finally capitulated. "What do you want me to do?"

"I could use your help, sir," Batman continued, the same grave tone still in his voice. "As you point out, the battle group needs an admiral in command of it. I

respectfully request that the admiral shift his flag to the
USS *Jefferson*, and relieve me of command. At least for
the duration of this mission," he concluded.

Tombstone sat bolt upright in his chair. "You want to
be relieved?"

"Well, I'd just as soon it weren't permanent," Batman
said wryly. "But things go wrong. In the event that
something happens, I don't want *Jefferson* left alone.
And since you've been admiral on board her before,
you're just the man to relieve me."

It made sense. Damn, but it made sense. "Okay,
Batman," he said, surprised at how eager he suddenly
was to feel the steel decks of *Jefferson* under his feet
again. "You realize there's going to be hell to pay for this
later?"

"There always is, isn't there, Stoney?" Batman chuckled slightly. "But we bring that SEAL home and all
screwups are forgiven. You know that."

Tombstone nodded, all too aware that what Batman
said was true. "Expect my COD flight in two hours,
then," he said, and broke the connection.

He stood up from his desk and started pacing the
room. The amphibious ship was a fine vessel, but it was
nothing compared to being on an aircraft carrier. To be in
command of one one more time, just one last time—he
sighed, thinking about how many lasts he was coming to
in his career these days. "One last time," he said aloud.
He smiled briefly. "A hell of a way to end a career."

Six hours and one Harrier flight later, Rear Admiral
Matthew Magruder took command of the aircraft carrier
USS *Jefferson*, relieving Rear Admiral Edward Wayne in
a short, hastily arranged ceremony. And, even though he

knew it was only for a short period of time, it felt damned good to be back.

Sikes regained consciousness slowly, driven out of the inky blackness by the sharp red flashes reverberating in his head. He groaned as the flashes turned into sharp pain. He moved feebly, trying to paw off the hand on his shoulder that was causing it.

"Go away," he mumbled. Damn, what was the matter—couldn't they let him sleep? Suddenly, he recalled where he was and what had happened. He forced his eyes open, almost blinded by the sparks that flew across his vision.

Slowly, the dark blur above him sharpened into the concerned face of White Wolf. How could I ever have thought him expressionless? Sikes wondered briefly, then was distracted by the pounding pain in his head. He groaned again, unable to suppress it.

"At least you're alive," White Wolf said softly. He glanced around at something in the distance. "They smashed you on the back of the head. I wasn't sure whether—"

Sikes tried to shake his head and winced at the effort. "Talking," he croaked, barely able to force the words past his throat.

"They don't seem to mind it right now, for some reason. Here they come."

Sikes heard the soft crunch of boots on ice, and two arctic pieces of footwear loomed into view. "Sit him up," a voice ordered harshly.

"I'm okay," Sikes protested weakly. He felt hands under his shoulders, grabbing his parka, pulling him into a sitting position.

"Drink," the voice continued. A hand thrust a mug in front of his face. Sikes reached for it, all too aware of the trembling in his hands.

To his surprise, he found that the outside of the mug was hot. A tantalizing aroma reached his nostrils. Coffee, he noted. Suddenly, that sounded like a very good idea.

"Well, we're still alive. For what that's worth," he said finally.

CHAPTER 12
Friday, 30 December

0900 Local
USS *Jefferson*

"You're sure about this?" Tombstone shouted, raising his voice to be heard over the cacophony on the flight deck.

Batman grinned. "As sure as I've ever been about anything, Stoney. This mission ain't got a chance in hell unless I fly lead on it. You know that. Besides, I've got that hotheaded Bird Dog up there to watch out for. He and Gator have more time circling this piece of ice than any other crew on the boat. I'll get them in, they'll dump some ordnance, and we'll all be back on board in time for midrats. Hell, I'd go it alone if my bird could carry enough two-thousand-pounders alone." He shook his head ruefully. "But in this weather, with a Bear-J in the vicinity, you gotta have some self-protection."

Outside the handler's compartment, the JAST bird and Tomcat 201 were waiting. Both aircraft carried two two-thousand-pound bombs, along with Sidewinders and Sparrows for air combat. According to the SEALs' mission plan, four bombs were necessary to ensure the desired kill factor on the mission.

"Well." Tombstone paused at the hatch leading out

onto the flight deck from the handler's compartment and stuck out his hand. "Luck. You'll need it, an old shit like you pulling this kind of stunt."

Batman grabbed his old wingman's hand in a strong, two-handed grip. "Luck always helps, but I'll settle for some damned fine avionics instead. That I *know* I've got. And the best damned RIO in the Navy." He jerked his chin toward the short naval flight officer behind him.

"Yes." Tombstone gazed down at Tomboy, once again aware of how petite she was. If he hadn't had first-hand experience with her ability as a RIO—and, he admitted, an even closer look at the strength in her body—he might have tried to talk Batman into taking another RIO along for this one. If, he added, he'd somehow found the courage to face the enraged Tomboy.

"Good hunting to you, too, Lieutenant Commander Flynn," he said formally. He let his eyes show the warmth he purposely kept out of his voice. "You kick ass up there, okay?"

"That and more, Admiral," she answered, her voice steady and her chin up. "I'll get Admiral Wayne back in one piece, I promise."

"See that you do. D.C. is going to be shitting bricks if they have to give me another at-sea command." Tombstone held out his hand, letting his fingers slide over hers as she did the same. He tugged gently, and she swayed almost imperceptibly toward him. "And hurry back," he said softly, pitching his voice so that only she could hear it.

She nodded briskly. "I intend to." She turned and followed Batman out to their aircraft.

And let the Handler try to make something out of that, Tombstone thought, watching the two of them walk away. As fast as rumor control worked on the ship, the story would have worked its way into a passionate orgy in the handler's office before the JAST bird returned from its mission, if he'd given it the slightest reason to.

0950 Local
East End, Attu

White Wolf's grandson studied the sky. The gods were cooperating, it appeared. Low, scudding clouds rolled in from the north, ominously low to the wind-lashed sea. At the horizon, the clouds and the sea were the same color, a dull, white-gray, featureless wall. Soon, he knew, the storm would blow in, driving visibility to barely two feet. They had to be off the cliffs by then, or the entire plan would have to be scuttled.

Or worse, he thought grimly. The small group had no way of communicating with the aircraft inbound from the American ship. If the fighter-bomber pilot thought he could complete the mission, he would, assuming that all of the ground forces had cleared the area in accordance with the plan. He'd never really see the small band of Inuits and SEALs trapped on the cliffs in the whiteout.

All the more reason to get to it, and get to it quickly. He turned and motioned Senior Chief Huerta up to the front of the line.

"Here," he said, pointing at a deep rift in the jagged ice. "A fracture line."

The SEAL studied the narrow chasm thoughtfully. "Might could do it with explosives," he suggested.

The Inuit shook his head. "We'd get a surface shear. Sure, a lot of debris would rain down, but that's not nearly what we're aiming for. Is it?" It was his turn to study the other man carefully.

The two of them were about the same age, which should have given them a good deal in common. And it did, the Alaskan native decided, although he didn't know if the other man would understand that. Family, phases of life, the way they coped with their harsh environment— while the SEAL may have seen more of the world than the island-bound native, the harsh realities of the sea and ice were the same for both. No amount of training, experience, or philosophy could change that.

"No, we need more force," he continued. He pointed down at the slope in front of him. "See that? I want the forward thirty feet of this cliff to shear off."

"Okay. You're the expert around here." Huerta trudged back to his knapsack, motioning his men around him. Together, they carefully unpacked the array of sophisticated targeting laser devices they were carrying.

They fanned out around the area, each one carrying one of the precious target designators. Ten minutes later, all four devices were pointed in different locations, each one throwing a ruby-red spot on the edge of the rift.

The SEALs rejoined the natives, and both took a moment to proudly survey their handiwork. "They'll be dropping dumb bombs, but these laser pointers will give them a damned clear landmark." He gestured at the spires and jagged outcroppings of rock around them. "Without this, all this terrain looks too much alike. Hell, the target point isn't even visible until you break out over that last ridge."

Finally, Morning Eagle glanced up at the sky again. "We leave now," he said forcefully. "We have maybe thirty minutes."

"I expect you're right. And I don't wanna take the chance that you aren't."

Morning Eagle took point, and carefully began retracing his path to the east, over the harshest surfaces of the icy environment.

Even for the Inuits, accustomed to this terrain, it was tough going. Twenty minutes later, all the men were soaked with sweat inside their protective gear. To stop now would be suicide. Only their body heat kept the sweat from freezing into an icy, killing sheen of ice. They trudged on, their breathing becoming more labored, heavy droplets of moisture fogging the air as they panted.

Finally, they reached the edge of the ice floe and started their way downward. Ten minutes later, they were gathered around the small boats the Inuits had provided.

The SEAL senior chief glanced up at the sky again. "Do we start back to your island now?"

Morning Eagle shook his head. "Too late." He pointed at one massive billow now ten degrees off their vertical. "Whiteout before we're halfway there. We might make do with the compass, but I wouldn't want to take the chance. Not unless we really have to."

"Well, as long as our playmates don't know we're here, we won't have to take that chance. I haven't seen them make a patrol on this side of the island once."

"Then we settle in to wait. An hour, maybe two, when the weather breaks—" He let the sentence trail off. Whiteouts had been known to last for days, holding every man, woman, and child trapped inside the camp. While some of the tribe possessed an uncanny sense of direction, and could find their way back to camp no matter what the weather conditions, Morning Eagle was not one of those. He respected the power of the weather, and chose to live with it rather than against it.

"We wait," Huerta echoed. The two teams of men, so alike and so different, quickly combined their gear and began building a small camp that would keep them alive.

Until the weather clears, Morning Eagle thought.

"How certain are you that they'll come to investigate the cliff, anyway?" he asked the SEAL.

The chief shrugged, then grinned. "Not certain. But it's what I'd do."

"Why?"

"While the fellows were busy setting up the designators, I took a little stroll over to the edge of the cliff. If you'd been watching, you would have seen me leave a little present there for our friends."

"A present?" Morning Eagle was momentarily confused. "What kind of present?"

"Nothing complicated. Just an all-frequency static transmitter. Remote controlled, it is." He fished into his parka jacket and pulled out a small set of controls. "All I have to do is toggle this switch, and that little bitch starts sending a jamming signal on every frequency these guys are likely to be using. The first thing they'll notice it on is their handheld radios. And if I were maintaining a garrison here, I'd damned sure want to find out what was jamming my communications. Especially since it was supposed to be an uninhabited island."

Morning Eagle regarded him appraisingly. "Nice trick."

"We get some nice toys now and then. This is an old standby, but it still works just fine."

0950 Local
Tomcat 201

"I don't like this one damned bit," Bird Dog grumbled. He cast an anxious glance back at the wings, trying to see if there was any ice forming. A visual inspection was not necessary—his instruments would have told him immediately if there was a problem, but there was nothing more reassuring than getting a visual on a clean, ice-free wing. "The meteorology boys really screwed this one up."

"Not that we had a lot of choice about it," Gator said. "You think we have problems, how do you think those helo pilots feel?"

Bird Dog repressed a shudder. "Not good. I wouldn't trade places with them for anything. You got solid contact on Batman?"

"Yep. Five-hundred-feet separation, just like we briefed. You're in solid. Okay, starting the approach," Gator said briskly. "The sooner we get this done, the sooner we're out of here. Just follow Batman on in."

"You got any indication of target designation?" Bird Dog asked.

"No, not yet. Still too far away. And look at the time—Batman's running a few minutes early."

"Well, we could grab some altitude and orbit for a while," Bird Dog said, "but I don't fancy charging through those clouds any more than I have to. And neither does he."

Both men knew that the moisture-laden clouds seriously increased the danger of icing on the wings. While the deicing gear on the Tomcat was fairly decent, it had never been designed to cope with frigid temperatures like these, or with multiple passes through arctic clouds. As far as they were concerned, it was just another chance for things to go wrong.

"Best not," Gator said finally. "Let's settle in a pattern out here, far enough to be out of visual range. That'll have to do for now. Besides, we haven't detected any radar sweeps coming off the island. I'm willing to bet as long as we're out of visual range, we're safe."

"You got it, partner," Bird Dog responded. He ascended to fifteen thousand feet and began a right-hand orbit, carefully keeping an eye on the approaching clouds. "They get much closer, and we'll have problems," he remarked.

Gator grunted. "We should be inbound by then."

They left unspoken the possibility of having to abort the mission. True, the admiral had made it plain that it was Batman's call. Neither crew was to pointlessly risk the safety of the multimillion-dollar aircraft and its highly trained crew of two if there were no chance of accomplishing their objective. However, it would be a cold day in hell—Bird Dog smiled grimly at the appropriate metaphor—before either of the two would willingly break off.

"How's she flying?" Gator said, more to break the silence than out of any real curiosity.

"Heavy as a pig," Bird Dog answered. "I hate playing bomb cat."

The versatile F-14 Tomcat had been designed as both a fighter and bomber aircraft. During the days when the A-6 and A-7 aircraft were in use in the fleet, practicing the arcane skills of bombing had been largely a matter of form. However, as the older attack aircraft were phased out, and the newer FA-18 Hornet entered the fleet, the Tomcat community found itself under serious attack. After ironing out some minor avionics glitches, Tomcat squadrons aggressively attacked the problem of becoming as proficient in ground-to-air attacks as they were in aerial combat. Within a couple of years, they were matching every test of accuracy and reliability neck for neck with the Hornet. Indeed, carrier battle group commanders preferred Tomcats over the Hornet, since the latter aircraft's payload and endurance was seriously limited. The Tomcat, while a much larger spotting problem on the deck, generally proved itself more than worth the extra space, based on its capacity for ordnance.

Of course, Bird Dog reflected, it was tough to tangle with a Hornet. The smaller aircraft had a maneuverability and weight-to-power factor that made it a tough target for any Tomcat. Still, they managed to hold their own as well there. If you could outlast a Hornet, sooner or later he'd have to leave to go gas up.

And when you've got an opponent like a MiG, with their higher fuel endurance, the Tomcat was the only choice. Like it had been in the Spratlys. While the Hornets had covered their asses from time to time there, in the end the Tomcat had proven victor of the skies.

"Okay, time," Gator announced. "Batman's starting his run in. He says it looks like it's clearing up around the island. You vector on down and get on his ass just like we briefed, Bird Dog."

"Hell, he's the bird dog on this mission," the pilot grumbled. "I'm just batting cleanup."

"You mix any metaphors you want as long as you get me back to the boat," his RIO answered.

1000 Local
West End, Attu

"Commander, I think you'd better come here," the senior Spetsnaz commander said.

"Problem?" Rogov paused from inventorying the stores, and walked over to the small group of worried commandos. "What?"

"Listen." The commando thrust his handheld radio toward Rogov. "Started five minutes ago." He turned up the volume on the radio.

Rogov shook his head. "I don't hear anything except static."

"That is the problem, exactly. Someone is trying to jam our communications."

"Jamming? But how—" Rogov whirled around and glared at the SEAL still held captive at the end of the cavern. "I see," he said, his voice more calm.

"It appears to be a static source. It hasn't changed in intensity, and it's still strongest from a single direction."

"So what can you do about it?"

The commando shrugged. "There are no choices. There are intruders on the island, and we've lost communications. My standing orders are for my patrols to take cover in the event that something such as this should happen. I suspect they even now have our entrance under surveillance, and are prepared to kill anyone that approaches that door."

"You find this transponder," Rogov said harshly. So close, so close to success, and now this. Unreasoning rage boiled in his stomach, making its way slowly to his head. "Find the men who brought this and kill them. Do you understand?"

The same unnerving smile Rogov had seen on the submarine returned. "It's what we do best, Colonel," he said, looking eager.

1015 Local

Huerta looked up at the sky. "An hour, you think?" As much as he'd like to believe that, it didn't seem possible. Gusting williwaw winds were already pounding the thin shelters, screaming through every tiny crack between the two sections mated to form a fragile barrier against the environment. He'd risked one peek outside, for what it was worth. Now more than the horizon had disappeared—all he could see was blinding snow and ice pelting him in the face, banging against the two flaps tied together to form the door to the shelter. The other clamshell shelter, only four feet away, was invisible. There was no chance that they were moving anytime soon.

"Maybe not soon," Morning Eagle said, unconsciously echoing the SEAL's thoughts. "Sometimes these blow over quickly."

"And other times?" the SEAL demanded.

Morning Eagle shrugged. The SEAL felt rising frustration, which he stifled.

Truly, there was no help for it. The storm would end when it ended—not a moment sooner. Giving the young Inuit an ass-chewing for underestimating its duration would do no good. After all, they would have gone ahead with the mission anyway, even if they'd had an accurate weather forecast. No way they were leaving the boss behind—no way.

The SEAL rummaged in one pocket of his parka, finally found what he was looking for. He extracted two high-calorie protein bars, and offered one to the Inuit. The other waxed covering was dull army green, and the bar itself tasted like it would match the protective wrapper. "Beats whale blubber," the SEAL offered.

The Inuit unwrapped his bar, studied it, sniffed it, and then took a small, tentative bite. He chewed for a moment thoughtfully, and an odd expression, half apology, half disgust, rose in his eyes. "Not by much," he said, then swallowed hard.

1020 Local
Tomcat 201

"The weather's not holding," Bird Dog said, in a singsong tone of voice. "Although why I expected anything different, I'll never know. How much time do we have left?"

"Three minutes," Gator answered. "That is, if you think we can make it."

"Oh, we'll make it in all right," Bird Dog said grimly. He pulled the Tomcat out of its orbit and pointed its nose toward the island. The eastern half of the small outcropping was already obscured by the storm. The clouds had advanced at least halfway across the rocky cliffs that were their destination. "Let me know the moment you have a lock on the lasers."

"Right."

As they approached the island, winds buffeted Tomcat,

tossing the ungainly, heavily laden jet in the skies in a seemingly random pattern. Bird Dog swore softly, and focused his concentration on his controls. He tried to feel the jet, to anticipate her movements, and to correct for the sudden and sickening drops in altitude. This close in, it wouldn't do. At the altitude at which they were going to have to be, a sudden downdraft could be deadly.

"Two minutes, thirty seconds," Gator said calmly, his voice a reassuring presence in the decreasing visibility and increasingly violent movement of the cockpit. Bird Dog didn't answer, instead concentrating on the wildly roller-coastering motion of the aircraft.

One hundred feet above the churning ocean, Bird Dog watched the island rush toward him with terrifying swiftness. His hair-trigger reflexes shouted warnings, screaming at him to pull up, pull up. He waited, knowing in just a few seconds he would, pulling the Tomcat into its parabolic maneuver that would toss the weapons precisely toward the laser-designated point. Ahead of him, he saw the ass end of the JAST bird.

"Two more miles." He tensed, readying himself for the final maneuver.

Suddenly, his targeting gear screamed warnings. The churning clouds to the north had finally made a quick dash over the island, completely obscuring the small red points of light aimed on the rift.

"Shit! We're icing," he heard Batman snarl over tactical. "That damned deicing kit—it was giving us some problems on the deck, but I thought they'd gotten it corrected. Bird Dog, it gets any worse and we'll have to abort. I can't take this bird in like this."

Bird Dog swore violently and made a lightning-fast decision.

Too much was riding on this mission. The safety of the team on the ground, the fate of the captured men, and indeed, America's first response to an incursion on her territory. He stared ahead at the point where the target had been before it was obscured by blowing clouds of ice and fog, memorizing its location, praying that the hours of training over Chocolate Mountain would pay off. He screened out the loud protests and questions from Gator, knowing that in a few seconds the RIO would look up and see his dilemma. It wasn't impossible to get the bombs on target without the laser designator. Just very, very difficult, as decades of strike warfare in earlier wars had proved. It took good reflexes, a superb sense of direction, and an instinctive ability to calculate the myriad factors that went into a launch. Airspeed, altitude, effect of gravity on the missiles, and the safest direction to exit the target area. He felt his gut churn. That was the critical part, at least for the two aviators in Tomcat 201. Getting clear of the spewing debris, rock, and ice before it could FOD one of the turbofan engines was critical.

Forty-five seconds remaining. He squinted, ignoring the sweat breaking out on his forehead, rolling down into his eyes and stinging. In front of him, the JAST aircraft broke off its attack run and turned back toward the carrier.

1021 Local
Attu

"There he is!" Morning Eagle pointed at the sky. The Tomcat was a tiny black dot, skimming over the ocean, blending in with the dark, blue-black, whitecapped waves.

"Too low," Huerta said. He shook his head. "He'll have to abort—there's no way he can do it."

Morning Eagle stared at the aircraft, which was now large enough that he could make out its features. The sleek, backswept wings, the double bubble of the canopy perched almost too far up on the aircraft, its sleek, aerodynamically sound nose. And the weapons, the most important part of the aircraft for his purposes today. He stared at the undercarriage, which looked bulky and ungainly. The two huge bombs, flanked by the smaller air-to-air missiles, hung down below it like some phallic symbol.

"Look out!" Huerta shouted. He took two steps forward, grabbed Morning Eagle, and pulled him back away from the rift. "We've got to get the hell out of here."

Morning Eagle blinked, startled out of his fascinated reverie of the deadly aircraft. He whirled, following Huerta, and took five steps forward before the world disappeared in a blinding whirl of white.

1022 Local
Tomcat 201

"Bird Dog! You get the hell out of there!" he heard Batman snap. "You don't have a solid fix on the target. You miss, and you hit friendly forces. Break off; we'll try again when the weather clears."

"Can't," Bird Dog said tersely. "I've got a solid lock on this—I can feel it." He tried desperately to regain his fix on the target, momentarily distracted by the sight of white-clad figures scurrying away from his impact point— the IP.

Damn it all, what the hell did they think they were doing? he thought angrily. Couldn't someone have briefed them? The SEAL should know better at least than to stand that close to an IP. Even with advanced avionics and pinpoint targeting, there was still an error of five to ten feet built into launch calculations. Even under the best circumstances—and these were hardly those—there was a good chance he'd miss the exact spot at the rift. He shook his head angrily.

There was no help for it now—he was too heavy and too low to recover. In order to gain altitude quickly and clear the worst of the peaks, he had to get rid of the bombs. And it made no sense to jettison them harmlessly, not this close to the IP. He concentrated, bearing down on the target.

1023 Local
Attu

"Whiteout," Morning Eagle screamed. He swung his arms wildly, felt them hit something, and pulled it toward him. Huerta grasped at him like a drowning man. With a firm grip on each other, they dropped to the ground, lessening their wind profile.

Huerta heard Morning Eagle shout something, the words unintelligible, swept away by the gale-force winds. He shook his head, then realized Morning Eagle couldn't see the gesture. He reached for the other man's hand and held it up, pointing it in the direction of the aircraft.

And the rest of their team—they'd been well back from the rift, he remembered, reviewing the last scene he'd been able to see clearly in his mind. With a little bit of luck, and some decent piloting, they'd be safe as well.

The laser designators. For a moment, he felt a flash of real fear, remembering how close the Tomcat had been when he'd last seen it. He turned his head, looking in the direction of the rift. There was nothing there except a solid white wall of flying ice crystals in the snow. Frustration replaced fear, as he realized the laser targeting information would no longer be visible to the pilot.

Absent skill, there was always luck. The chief SEAL started to pray.

Tomcat 201

"You're never gonna make it, Bird Dog," Gator said, his voice insistent. "Dump 'em."

Bird Dog shook his head, not bothering to answer. Concentrating on the spot where he'd last seen the targeting data took every ounce of concentration he had. He flipped the ICS switch off, locking out Gator's voice completely. They'd either make it or they wouldn't, and there was nothing Gator could tell him in the interim to change the odds either way.

Five . . . four . . . three . . . two . . . NOW. Bird Dog toggled the weapons release switch and felt the hard thump of ordnance leaving the undercarriage as the bombs dropped free. He wrenched the Tomcat up into a sharp climb, already feeling the difference that the loss in weight made, climbing for altitude as hard as he dared push the Tomcat. The sleek jet shook as it approached the stall envelope. Bird Dog dropped the nose slightly, hoping it was enough. He spared one glance at the altimeter—three thousand feet—and then cut the Tomcat hard to the right, praying he cleared the tallest spires.

Attu

The hard thunder of military engines at full afterburner cut through the high-pitched scream of the wind. It was a sound at least as much felt as heard, a deep, bone-jarring growl and rumble that cut through viscera and skin alike, settling into the bones with a comforting aftertaste.

He made it, the Chief SEAL thought, marveling. How many pilots could have pulled that off? For a moment, a deep surge of pride replaced the fear and anxiety he'd felt watching the aircraft approach. Damn, some days it was good to be an American. If he ever got out of this, he was going to do his damnedest to make sure that pilot got a commendation.

Suddenly, the ground underneath him exploded, shaking and rolling like the worst earthquake he'd ever experienced in California. He gasped and threw himself flat on the ground, no longer caring whether he lost contact with Morning Eagle's hand. The hard ice surface rose up underneath him, smashing him in the face, and he felt the delicate bones in the bridge of his nose splinter. A falling rock bashed him in the leg, settling over his lower right shin and ankle. The SEAL screamed, feeling the wind whip away the sound as soon as it left his mouth. He clamped his mouth shut as icy air surged into his mouth, straight down his air passageway, and chilled his lungs. Stupid to survive the actual strike and then be killed by ice crystals forming in his lungs, he thought grimly, falling back on years of training and experience to override survival instincts. He clung to the ground for dear life and waited.

Bird Dog leveled off at eleven thousand feet, and suddenly started shaking. He was safe; he was safe. Until that moment, he hadn't realized how doubtful he'd been that they'd make it.

Below them, the whiteout whipped violently, obscuring sea and island alike. The noise, however, had faded as the aircraft had climbed. Finally, he noticed an odd noise in the cockpit. It took him a moment to puzzle it out. Then an involuntary grin cracked his face. He reached over and flipped on the ICS switch.

"—and if you ever pull this bullshit again, I'm not going to wait for a court-martial, I'm going to personally—" Gator's voice was saying.

Bird Dog cut him off. "Cool your jets, Gator, we made it." He moved the yoke back and forth experimentally, testing his control over the Tomcat to reassure himself. "See?"

Gator's voice broke off. "And just what the hell did you think you were doing, making a blind approach in the middle of a storm cell?" the RIO demanded. "You should have broken off like Batman said."

"Not a chance. Those men were depending on us."

He heard Gator sigh. "Well, I guess they were at that," the RIO said finally. "How close do you think you got?" he continued, his professionalism overriding what must have been a terrifying ride for the backseater.

"Pretty damned close, I think," Bird Dog said. He felt a sudden surge of joy. "Damned close. In fact, it felt like it went spot-on."

"It's not like we can fly over and do a BDA—a bomb damage assessment," the RIO said. "But from what I could see from back here, it looked good to me, too. Let's get back to the boat and wait for the weather to chill out."

"Bad choice of words," Bird Dog responded. He put the Tomcat in a gentle curve, the motion seeming unusually cautious after the wild maneuver he'd just pulled off.

"You icing?" Gator said anxiously.

Bird Dog glanced at his instruments, then out the window at the wing. "Looks like a little—but not enough to hurt us, now that we're out of the storm. The deicers will take care of it."

"You're damned lucky you've got me back here, you know that?" Gator said.

"Oh, really? Why is that?" Bird Dog answered, as he laid in a level course for the carrier.

"Because any other backseater in his right mind would've filled his shorts about two minutes ago," Gator said, amusement in his voice. "It'd serve you right, flying in a stinking cockpit for a couple of months. They never can get the smell out."

"I guess there's always something to be grateful for," Bird Dog answered. "Now, let's just hope we did the job on the ground," he continued, his voice suddenly sober.

Attu

The Cossack commando barely had time to glance up as the Tomcat screamed in over the barren landscape, only fifty feet above him. He swore reflexively, and dived for the ground. The low, ominous rumble of the engines reverberated through his body. He buried his hands under his arms and waited.

The initial blast tossed him two feet off the icy surface of the island; gravity slammed him back down hard enough to knock the wind out of him. He gasped, trying to breathe, and finally drew a deep, shuddering lungful of air.

The noise hit him again first. He wondered for a moment whether the Tomcat had come around to make a second run on the cliffs. He looked up, trying to focus on the landscape in front of him.

To his horrified eyes, it looked like a wave. Something he'd see in the warmer coast waters of the Black Sea, a phenomenon that belonged somewhere other than this desolate, forsaken island. The land curled slightly at the top, leaning over the rest of the cliff, increasing its similarity to an ocean breaker.

The commando shouted, his words already lost in the massive cacophony of forty thousand tons of avalanche. Two seconds later, the massive wall of ice and snow cut off his words. Forever.

The ground played trampoline for almost three minutes before the violent motion subsided into a series of sharp jolts. At the same time, the wind dropped perceptibly, though the searing blindness of the whiteout remained. Huerta kept his eyes firmly shut, guarding delicate tissues with one hand over his face. The other flailed about him, searching for Morning Eagle.

Finally, after a series of gentle rumbles no more than 4.0 on the Richter scale, Huerta took a chance and stood up. His feet swayed under him slightly, and he had to bend forward to keep his balance in the gusting winds. Still, at least he could move. He opened one eye cautiously. The whiteout was receding, and he could now see almost five feet in front of him.

He scanned the landscape quickly. Crumpled against a rock, curled into a small ball, was Morning Eagle. The Chief SEAL walked over, dropped to his knees, and felt for a pulse. It pounded hard and strong under his fingers, and he breathed a sigh of relief. He checked the man for injuries quickly, a difficult process in the heavy winter parkas. Finally, satisfied that there was no life-threatening damage, the SEAL stood. He touched his pocket, felt the reassuring bulk of the handheld radio. He held it out, toggled it on, and started walking over toward the rift that had been their aim point.

He took two steps, and then stopped short and gasped. Despite his long experience with naval ordnance, the damage was astounding.

The first forty feet of the cliff had sheared off, cascading down the side of the hill. They'd barely been far enough away to avoid being caught up in it. He glanced back at Morning Eagle, wondering if the man would ever realize how lucky they'd been. That was one damned fine pilot.

He lifted the radio to his mouth. "*Jefferson*, SEAL Team One," he said in the clear, hardly caring whether or not anyone else could hear them. "Request medical evacuation. Assessment of bomb damage follows—on target, on time. Out."

With that done, he crossed back to Morning Eagle and sat down beside him. Pulling his pistol out of his other pocket, he sat down to wait.

1035 Local
USS *Jefferson*

The Combat Direction Center exploded in wild cheers and victory cries. The TAO stood up, glanced sternly around the spacious compartment, and tried to frown disapprovingly. However, he couldn't repress the mad exultation coursing through his own body, and settled for a cursory wave of his hand.

The chief sitting next to him took it in, his own rebel victory cry just dying on his lips. "Let's let them celebrate now, sir," the chief said. "You take your victories where you can get 'em."

The TAO nodded and stared back at the large blue screen dominating the forward half of the room. The small symbol for friendly aircraft separated itself from the mass of land, and was tracking slowly back toward the aircraft carrier. "You take your victories where you can get 'em," he echoed softly, and picked up the mike. There was one aircrew that was going to be doing just that in a matter of seconds.

1050 Local
Attu

"Hang in there, buddy," Huerta said softly. He patted Morning Eagle on the arm gently. In the last few minutes, the man's breathing had gotten deeper and more stentorian. Although his pulse was still strong, Huerta was gravely worried about the condition of the young native. "They'll be comin' for us soon—you wait. We don't ever leave our friends behind. Not ever."

Huerta stared at the horizon, now growing dark as the sun crept down below it, hoping that the SAR aircraft would make it out in time.

CHAPTER 13
Friday, 30 December

Rogov crept through the massive jumble of ice blocks, barely daring to breathe. The explosion had shaken him, much more than he anticipated. While it had seemed reasonable that the Americans might attempt something like this, the sheer magnitude of the avalanche and the deafening noise had shaken him.

He heard voices, maybe thirty yards off. He ran his hands over himself one more time, checking to see that he was intact and that his identification had been removed. He took a deep breath, then another. While the loss of the twenty-eight Spetsnaz commandos clustered at the base of the cliff meant nothing to him personally, it presented some tactical problems. He'd counted on being able to pass more of them off as injured Inuits, at least enough to simultaneously take the bridge and Combat and the admiral's quarters. He shook his head. The only predictable thing about unconventional warfare was that it was unpredictable. On a mission such as this, it was expected that he would adapt, overcome, and adjust to any changes in circumstances.

He looked behind him, counting heads. Eight Spetsnaz were up and moving, a few of them shaking off minor injuries. He checked their faces, noting the look of cold resolve in each man's eyes. He nodded. Commanding men such as these, he could do nothing less than his best.

He gave the signal, and the Spetsnaz commandos dispersed, creeping ever closer to the small, abandoned group. When they were ten feet away, more or less, they arranged themselves on the ground. Rogov heard low moans start to issue, more inviting evidence of injured allies for the Americans. He rearranged his face in an expression of pain, found a convenient ice spire to drape himself over, and moaned. In truth, there was not much pain he had to simulate, since the aerial bombardment had shaken him up badly, giving him a few additional bruises. He grimaced. All the better for realism. Injuries, but nothing so serious as to slow them down.

He looked down at the old Inuit lying at his feet. Better to let him live for now, use him to support the deception. If he could keep the helo's crew focused on the injured old man and his obviously Inuit features, they might miss any clues to the real identity of the rest of the supposed natives.

But the SEAL? Where was he? Rogov scanned the landscape around him quickly, looking for his other prisoner, then made a rapid time-distance calculation. There wasn't time to look for him, not and make the airlift quickly. Furthermore, the American SEAL would surely have given them away at the very first opportunity. A loose end, and one that he would have eliminated quickly if the man had been in sight.

No time. Rogov shrugged. The hostile land would kill

the man as quickly as a bullet, although he would have preferred the reassurance of the latter to the former.

If they had the chance, the Americans would kill him for this, he knew. There would be no trial, no investigation, no complicated legal maneuverings. A quick death sentence, one that the SEAL's teammates would impose the moment they knew what had happened.

But then again, they wouldn't be given that opportunity. Rogov had other plans immediately following his arrival on board USS *Jefferson*.

1102 Local
Tomcat 201

"Tomcat Two-oh-one, say state," the operations specialist on board *Jefferson* inquired anxiously.

Bird Dog glanced down at the fuel indicator and swore quietly. Between the exhilaration of the attack and checking for icing on the wings, he'd forgotten the most basic safety in flight protocols. His fuel was now creeping dangerously low, his reserves sapped by the extended time at afterburners necessary to escape the target site.

"Three point two," he answered calmly. "Might be nice to get a drink before we try to get back on board."

"Roger," the OS said, and gave the vector to the KA-6 tanker.

"Got plenty of gas for one pass," Gator said. "But I agree—no point in taking any chances."

Bird Dog laughed. "That's not what you said five minutes ago," he said, an injured tone in his voice.

"Intercept with the tanker in two mikes," the TAO reported to TFCC. "And the SAR helicopter is airborne now, en route to the island. Medical is standing by."

Tombstone settled into the elevated brown leatherette chair in TFCC and studied the screen carefully. Injuries—it was to be expected. But according to the SEAL team reports, there were enough uninjured men to attempt penetration of the intruder fortress. The avalanche had decimated the forces sufficiently to allow them to proceed, and they were on track to evacuate the wounded immediately, absolutely imperative in this climate. He shook his head, wondering why he had an uneasy feeling in the pit of his stomach. Aside from the daredevil maneuvers of the young Tomcat pilot—he almost smiled, remembering the stunts Bird Dog had pulled on their last cruise when Tombstone had been in command of the carrier group—things had gone pretty much as planned. Why, then, couldn't he relax?

"Too long out of the saddle," he said out loud, to no one in particular.

"Sir?" the TFCC TAO said, turning to look back at him.

Tombstone flushed. "Nothing," he muttered, swearing silently. What the hell was this, voicing the random concerns and thoughts that flitted through every commander's mind? Had he been away from real operations for too long?

"How long until the SAR helicopter arrives?" He asked to cover his embarrassment.

"One minute, Admiral," the TAO said crisply. "They should be back on board in five minutes." The TAO glanced back at him curiously.

"Very well." Tombstone willed himself to sit still and concentrate on the screen. Whatever niggling concerns were in the back of his mind, no one else seemed to share them.

1112 Local
Tomcat 201

"Got a visual," Bird Dog said. He pulled back on the throttle, slowing the Tomcat to rendezvous speed. "A quick plug, a fast drink, and we're out of here," he said over tactical.

"Gee, Bird Dog, you're a cheap date," the female copilot of the tanker quipped. "Might want to do something about that. I hear they've got all sorts of solutions for that sort of male problem these days."

Gator laughed, while Bird Dog fumbled for a smart-ass reply.

1131 Local
Attu

The helicopter hovered overhead, kicking up snow and ice in the downdraft of its powerful rotors. Huerta swore and motioned it up. The pilot complied, and the draft, only slightly less gusting than the whiteout storm, abated slightly. "You guys who called for a ride home?" his radio crackled. "Where do you want the pickup, here or down on level ground?"

Heurta glanced up at the helicopter, thinking it through. Of the ten men around him, all but Morning Eagle were moving around well enough to get down the slope, even with the clutter of debris that now covered it.

"On the flat," he decided. He motioned to the men and trotted over. "Let's get him down there," he said, pointing to Morning Eagle. The two men grunted something unintelligible and started fashioning a rough structure out of tent fragments and ski poles.

Huerta spared a few moments to appraise their gear. Good solid stuff, he thought, one part of his mind coldly evaluating its tactical usefulness. Moments later, Morning Eagle was slung over the stretcher, strapped down by more torn fragments of tent. "Let's go," he ordered. He took point, leading the small band through a relatively flat part of the debris.

Had he not been so shaken by the avalanche, focused on the mission ahead, and still suffering a few minor scrapes and bruises by the bombardment himself, Huerta might have stopped to wonder about the equipment he'd just seen. And if he had, he might have remembered that the Inuits who had made the journey over the seas with him had been carrying outdated Navy equipment, not modern combat gear. And that would have struck him as strange.

1135 Local
Tomcat 201

"Easy, easy," Gator cautioned.

"I'm okay," Bird Dog snapped. And he would be, in just a few minutes, if he could get his goddamned hands to quit shaking, his gut to stop twisting into a knot.

Intellectually, he knew it was just the aftereffects of the adrenaline bleeding out of his system, but the feeling frightened him nonetheless. And made him angry—how he'd managed to navigate the aircraft through the near-impossible bombardment mission, only to fall apart during level flight.

Not that tanking was that easy a task. Aside from a night landing on a carrier, it was one of the most dangerous and difficult evolutions a carrier pilot underwent. Approaching another aircraft from behind, slowly adjusting the airspeed until the two were perfectly matched, and then plugging the refueling probe of a Tomcat into the small, three-foot basket trailing out the end of a KA-6 tanker called for steady hands and a cool head. He couldn't afford to be distracted, not now, not this close to another aircraft. Too many collisions took place just at this point.

"Hold it!" Gator said sharply. "Bird Dog, back off and take a look again. You're all over the sky, man."

Bird Dog swore softly. "I'm okay, I'm okay," he insisted.

"You're not." Gator's voice was firm. "Just ease off—let's try this again." Gator's calm, professional tones couldn't mask the real note of concern in his voice. "You're a little heavy—all that ice hasn't melted yet, and it's affecting your flight characteristics, but it's real doable—just take it slow, let me kick the heaters up another notch."

Bird Dog concentrated on the dancing basket in front of him. It was, he realized, not the basket that was moving but his dancing Tomcat. He tried to quiet the tremor in his hands, the jerk in his right foot.

"Think of something calm," Gator's voice soothed.

"Man, you just blew the hell out of a lot of bad guys back there. Think about that."

Bird Dog concentrated, focusing on the moments immediately after he'd dropped the weapons. It had been a clear, cool feeling, one buoyed up with exhilaration and joy far beyond anything he'd experienced in the air before. Even shooting down his first MiG hadn't come close to knowing he'd just done a hell of a job under impossible circumstances. He focused, letting the feeling come back, letting the raw sensation of power replace the tentativeness in his hands and legs.

After a few moments, he took a deep breath. "Okay," he said, his voice now calm and strong. "I've got it."

After what he'd been through, plugging this little basket would be a piece of cake. He grinned, relishing the challenge, and slid the Tomcat smoothly forward. The refueling probe rammed home, jarring the aircraft slightly.

"Good job," Gator said softly. Not for the first time, he marveled at his pilot's ability to focus, to compartmen-talize and stay right in the moment. Whether Bird Dog knew it or not, Gator decided, he was one hell of a pilot.

Not that Gator was going to tell him that. The RIO glanced down at his gauges and saw a solid lock and fuel flowing into the aircraft. "How much you going to take on?" he asked Bird Dog.

"Six thousand pounds," the pilot said, his hands and feet moving quickly to make the minor adjustments in airspeed and altitude to keep the aircraft firmly mated. "That gives us enough fuel for a couple of passes. If we need them."

And they would not, Gator decided, relaxing. The

mood that Bird Dog was in, he might not even need the arresting wire to get on board.

1136 Local
Attu

"How about a lift?" the helicopter pilot shouted over the noise. Rogov smiled, held out his hand, and tried to look as friendly and undangerous as he could.

"Thank you," he said, hoping the slight accent in his voice would be interpreted as native islander. Evidently it was, since the pilot returned his smile and gestured to one of the canvas-strapped seats lining the interior of the helicopter. "We've got a corpsman and doctor on board," the pilot added.

"One is badly hurt," Huerta said, pointing at Morning Eagle, pale and motionless on the stretcher. "The rest are just banged up and bruised."

"Eskimos, huh?" The pilot studied his new passengers, then shrugged and turned back to the controls. "We'll be there in five mikes."

Huerta sat poised in the hatch to the aircraft, watching the others file aboard. Oddly enough, Morning Eagle was among the last in line, still carried by the same two Inuit. He saw Morning Eagle start to move, then one of the stretcher-bearers shifted, blocking his line of sight. When he next got a good look at him, Morning Eagle was no longer moving.

"Come on, come on," Huerta shouted, gesturing at the men. "We've got most of them, but who knows how many else there are?"

The men started to move more rapidly and quickly

took seats along the sides. Moving fast, Huerta noted, for men that had looked so stunned half an hour earlier. He shrugged. The human body was more resilient than anyone gave it credit for, particularly when the mind knew what the body didn't. He'd seen the men drive themselves long past the point of exhaustion, held upright and moving only by the sheer force of will. Any man could do it—SEAL training taught them how.

"That's the last of them," Huerta shouted to the pilot. He moved toward the last seat in the aircraft. As he was midway down the fuselage, the waiting men suddenly moved. Three men stood up, grabbed him, and threw him to the deck, pinning him down. He started to struggle, then something hard hit him on the right side of his head. He lay motionless, unconscious, on the deck.

Two more of the supposed native forces moved forward, gently easing their pistols up against the necks of the pilot and copilot. Rogov approached them and stood midway between the two seats. "Now, the carrier," he ordered, in a voice that left no doubt as to what the consequence of disobedience would be. "Do not touch that," he said sharply as the copilot's hand reached out for the IFF transponder. "I know you have special codes that will tell the ship that you are under force. Do not attempt to use them. If necessary, my men can fly this craft themselves."

The pilot and copilot exchanged an angry, helpless look, then the pilot nodded. "Do what the man says, Brian," he said levelly. The copilot nodded and returned to reading the preflight checklist in a slightly shaky voice.

Too bad there's no checklist for hijacking, the pilot thought grimly, as he made the routine responses to the checklist items. And there was no way to let *Jefferson* know what was happening, not without risking the lives of the remaining friendlies on board. If there *were* any others, he added to himself, wondering if he and the copilot were the only Americans still left on board the helicopter.

1140 Local
USS *Jefferson*

"Helo inbound," the TFCC TAO reported.

Tombstone acknowledged the report with a curt nod. He studied the friendly aircraft symbol that had just popped up on the display. "Ask them how many souls on board," he said. "And ask CDC if they're going to get that Tomcat on board before the helo makes its approach. I don't want a cluster fuck over this, people."

"Tomcat Two-oh-one on final now," the TAO responded instantly. "The tanker is going to wait until after the helo is on board, then we'll clear the decks for her. I think there're some casualties on the helo, so we'll want to get them in as soon as we can, but there's a good window of time for Bird Dog to take one pass."

"That's all it usually takes him," Tombstone said.

"Tomcat Two-oh-one."

"Roger, ball, Tomcat Two-oh-one, five point four, two souls." Bird Dog radioed to the landing signals officer, or LSO. Tomcat 201 was one mile behind the carrier, coming up fast on the broad, blunt stern. His call indicated he'd seen the meatball, the giant Fresnel lens mounted on the port side. The intricate combination of lens and lights gave the pilot a quick visual reference as

to whether or not he was on glide path. When he was
making a proper approach, at a safe altitude, the light
would glow green. Too high or too low, and the pilot
could see only the red lights. With the LSO having the
final word, and acting as a final safety check and flight
coach, all under the watchful eyes of the air boss, final
approach on a carrier was one the most carefully monitored flight patterns in the world.

Not that accidents didn't happen, Bird Dog thought
grimly. Calm down now, boy, don't get too excited. Just
hit the three-wire, nice and sweet, like you've done a
hundred times before.

Of course, experience was no guarantee that nothing
would go wrong. Just two weeks ago, an FA-18 Hornet
pilot hadn't been paying close enough attention to the air
mass that always churned and bubbled in the wake of the
aircraft carrier. He'd lost concentration, and a sudden
downdraft had caught him unprepared. Still at 140 knots
airspeed, he'd smacked his Hornet straight into the stern
of the carrier, crumpling airframe and man into a twisted
mass now resting somewhere on the ocean floor.

Bird Dog shuddered, forcing the picture out of his
mind. It happened to other people, not to him. He felt his
concentration quiver, then steady and become absolute.
His world narrowed down to the Fresnel lens, the aft end
of the carrier, and the quiet, soothing voice of the LSO in
his ear.

"A little more altitude, altitude, coming on in, you've
got it," the LSO said, chanting his familiar refrain of
orders and encouragement.

Even without the LSO's comments, Bird Dog knew he
had it nailed. He felt the Tomcat grab for the deck, heard
the squeal of rubber meeting nonskid, and had just a

moment to wonder at how gentle first contact had been when the tailhook caught the arresting wire.

"Three-wire," Gator crowed from the backseat. "Knew you could do it!"

Bird Dog slammed the throttle forward to full military power, a normal precaution against the tailhook bouncing free from the wire. Only after the arresting wire had brought him to full stop, and he received a signal from the plane captain, did he throttle back, carefully backing out of the arresting wire, raising his tailhook, and taxiing forward. He followed the directions of the Yellow Shirt and brought the jet to a stop near the waist catapult.

"Stay in your aircraft, Two-oh-one," he heard the air boss order.

He swiveled around to look back at Gator. "What the hell?"

"We're bringing in a helo, casualties on board," the air boss continued, ignoring the comment Bird Dog had inadvertently transmitted over the flight deck circuit. "You did a good job up there—sit tight for a few minutes and let us get the injured out of the way, then you can exit the aircraft."

Bird Dog twisted further away and saw a helicopter on final approach to the carrier. It was heading for spot three, midway down the long deck in the spot closest to the island. He sighed, turned back to face forward, and slumped in his seat. The events of the last several hours were finally catching up with him. He shut his eyes and relived it for a moment, seeing again the landscape disappearing in a white, furious cloud, feeling again the uncanny sense of certainty and direction he'd gotten just off of the IP. It was magic when it all worked out, no doubt about it, though how he'd ever pulled it off, he'd never know.

"Bird Dog, I—" Gator cleared his throat. "What I said earlier, about trading you in for another pilot. I didn't mean it, you know."

Bird Dog hid his grin. Let Gator be the one twisting on the spit for once. No point in making it easy for him. "I don't know, Gator," he said doubtfully. "It sounded to me like you meant it. Maybe I ought to think about finding a new RIO, one who's got some confidence in my airmanship."

"Anybody who can make the attack you made today— well, I'll fly with you anytime, Bird Dog. I mean it."

Bird Dog turned around in his seat again and eyed his RIO straight on. Gator had already unsnapped his mask and shoved his helmet back on his head. A few curls of dark brown hair escaped from the front of it. His face was shiny with sweat and probably felt as grimy as Bird Dog's did.

Bird Dog performed a contortion, managing to reach a hand into the backseat. "We're a team, Gator. And you ever try to bail on me again, I'm going to punch you out by yourself over hostile territory."

1155 Local
Seahawk 601

"I won't do it." The pilot stared straight ahead, hands and feet moving reflexively to keep the helicopter in level flight. "I'm not gonna be the first pilot in naval aviation history to land terrorists on board a carrier."

Rogov took his own weapon and placed the muzzle

against the pilot's temple. "Are you that eager to die?" he demanded.

The pilot was pale and sweating, and the helicopter started to bob erratically.

"Easy, Jim," the copilot said, putting his hands and feet on the controls and taking over. "Just do what the man says."

The pilot shook his head. "No," he said, his voice gaining strength. "I won't. And you shouldn't, either." The muzzle at the right side of his head prevented him from looking at the copilot.

Crack! The single shot from the 9mm was clearly audible over the interior noise of the helicopter. The pilot slumped forward, then sideways, banging against the controls. The man standing behind him reached over, unfastened the harness, and yanked the body out. Blood streamed from the head wound, splashing on the commandos as they dragged him away from the controls.

Rogov turned to the copilot. No words were necessary.

The copilot fought for control of the helicopter, trying to correct, then overcorrecting, the motion induced by the pilot's last clutch at the instruments. Twenty seconds later, with the helicopter once again in level flight, he'd arrived at his decision. "Okay," he said quietly, his words inaudible but his meaning somehow reaching Rogov. "I'll take you in."

The helicopter heeled around and headed for the carrier. The radio squawked as the operations specialist anxiously queried the helo. The air boss had noted its erratic motion in the skies and demanded an explanation.

"Tell them it's nothing; the pilot had a moment of vertigo," Rogov suggested. He made it an order by motioning with the pistol. The copilot complied, trying to compensate for the PIO—pilot-induced oscillation—resulting from his trembling hands. He felt sweat bead up on his forehead, then trickle down his face.

Two minutes later, the helo hovered neatly over spot three. At the signal from the LSO, it settled gently to the deck.

The moment it touched down, Spetsnaz poured out of the open hatchway, catching the flight deck crew and medical team by surprise. They brushed past their rescuers, heading for the nearest hatch into the island. By the time the air boss could scream an angry question, and the flight deck crew could react, the first commando had already descended two ladders. The others were fast on his heels.

The terrorists descended two ladders and took a sharp right, a left, and another right. The lead commando paused, getting his bearings. Yes, this was the Flag Passageway, the dark blue tile gleaming as he remembered it from his tours. "That way," he snapped in his native tongue, pointing to the right. Twenty paces down the corridor was the door to the Flag Mess, which opened into a rabbit warren of compartments including the admiral's cabin, the admiral's conference room, and the TFCC beyond. If this ship was anything like the ones he'd visited before, none of the connecting doors would be locked.

The commandos pounded down the corridor, cut through the Wardroom, startling two lieutenant commanders who'd stopped in for a cup of coffee. A replay of a Padres baseball game was playing on the VCR, and one officer dozed quietly in a corner.

After a quick look at their collars, the commando determined that none of them was the quarry he sought.

He burst into the admiral's cabin, checked the private bedroom, then immediately headed for TFCC. By this time, alarms were beginning to sound, putting the ship on general quarters. *Intruder alert, intruder alert,* the 1MC blared.

The first alarm caught Tombstone by surprise. His head snapped up, and he whirled toward the entrance of TFCC. Two operations specialists were already moving toward it, one recently abandoning his post at the JOTS terminal to secure the area.

They were fast, but not fast enough. Just as they were shoving the heavy, five-inch-thick steel door shut, the first commando hit it hard with his shoulder. Simultaneously, he wedged his gun into the space between the door and the doorjamb, preventing it from closing. The two enlisted men, unprepared for the full weight of four highly trained terrorists against the door, fell back. Rogov, followed by six commandos, burst into TFCC.

"Excellent," he said, staring at Tombstone. "You have just made my job much easier, Admiral, by being where you are supposed to be."

Tombstone stood slowly, imposing iron will over his face. "Who are you, and what are you doing on my ship?" he demanded.

The Spetsnaz commando took a deep breath, as though regrouping. "Who we are is not important, Admiral. What is important is that we have you—and your watch-standers." He motioned at the aide people scattered around the room. While he was talking, six other commandos streamed into the base. "The emergency exit—back behind the screen," the commando said, pointing toward the rear of the room. The second team leader nodded and took his men over to it. The dogging mechanism on the door moved easily, and seconds later they were walking into the carrier CDC. From what he could hear, the Spetnaz surmised that they experienced as little physical resistance to the invasion as the flag spaces had.

"They'll kill you for this," Tombstone said levelly. His eyes searched the commando's face, looking for any break in the passivity he saw there. "What's more, there's nothing you can do with this ship. I will give no orders on your behalf, and none of my staff members will obey you. What will you accomplish by this?"

Rogov stepped into the compartment from behind the commandos, and Tombstone immediately recognized that he was the man in command. The Cossack stared at Tombstone for a moment, as though assessing him. Finally, he spoke.

"For your purposes, Admiral, what we want is not nearly as important as what we have. That is to say," he said, making a gesture that included the entire room, "your people and your ship."

1158 Local
Tomcat 201

"What the hell's taking them so long to clear us?" Bird Dog grumbled. All he wanted now was about six hours' uninterrupted rack time, followed by a couple of sliders, the carrier version of a hamburger. And some autodog, he decided. Yes, that sounded good—a whole ice cream cone full of the soft brown ice cream that had earned the disgusting slang name. He sighed, settling in to do what all Navy officers learned to do early in their career—hurry up and wait.

"Wonder what the hell's going on back there?" Gator said curiously. Bird Dog glanced in the mirror and saw his RIO had turned around in his seat and was staring at the helicopter landing spot. "Awful lot of people around there. Hell, we're at General Quarters."

He turned around and settled back in his seat. "You hearing anything?" he asked, putting his own helmet with its speakers back on.

"Oh, shit," Bird Dog said softly. "Gator, they're gonna launch us again."

"Launch us? But we just got here. What the hell—" Gator fell silent as he listened to the instructions coming over his own headset. "Armed terrorists on the ship?" Gator said disbelievingly. "I don't believe—Bird Dog, at least get them to put some weapons on the rack before we launch again," he finished, resigning himself to the inevitable. "Although what good it's gonna do with terrorists in the ship, I'll be damned if I know."

"Start the checklist," Bird Dog ordered, all traces of his earlier fatigue now vanishing in a fresh wave of adrenaline. "I don't know either, but if the air boss wants it, we're out of here."

Gator complied, and began reading the prelaunch checklist from his kneeboard. Before he was finished, Bird Dog started taxiing for the catapult. Ordnance technicians scurried about the aircraft, short-cutting most of their standard safety precautions to slap Sidewinders and Sparrows onto the wings.

"No Phoenix?" Gator asked.

"No. And just as well, if you ask me." Shooting the long-range Phoenix missile was okay for making long-range aircraft go on the defensive, but for what he had in mind he preferred a knife-fighting close-in load out.

"That tanker's still in the air, at least." He glanced down at the gauge. "We've got enough for a launch, with some time overhead, but I'm going to want to be going back for a fill-up real fast."

"Air boss says they're in TFCC and CDC," Gator reported. "We'll have to get the air boss to coordinate it."

"He mentioned that earlier—said the tanker's in the starboard marshall pattern already, waiting for us. They're gonna shoot us off, and then get as many of the ready aircraft launched as they can. Although where we're supposed to go if they don't get our airport sanitized, I'll be damned if I know."

Four minutes later, only partially through the checklist, Tomcat 201 hurled down the flight deck on the waist catapult and shot into the air.

"Where to now?" Gator said.

Bird Dog shrugged. "First we go get a drink, amigo," he said. "Then we see if *Jefferson* is getting her shit together, then we worry about where we go. A CAP station, maybe, in case there's adversary air inbound."

"It's a plan. Not sure I can come up with anything better at this point," Gator agreed. "I'll help you spot in on the tanker."

1200 Local
TFCC USS *Jefferson*

Rogov leveled his weapon at Tombstone. He took a deep breath, and when he started speaking, his voice was firm and forceful. "You will turn this aircraft carrier toward the west," he ordered. "Due west. Heading for Petropavlovsk."

"Petro?" Tombstone said, stunned. "Surely you don't think you can force us to attack Petro."

"It's been in your war plans for twenty years, now, hasn't it?" Rogov countered. "That was one premise of the entire Cold War scenario—that the Pacific Fleet would attack and capture the Soviet Union's easternmost stronghold, containing the submarines there and destroying the amphibious forces and airpower. After so many years, I would hope you knew how to do that." He stopped and considered Tombstone's shocked look. "I will know how, at least. And with an operational American carrier under their control, no Cossack will ever have to curry favor with a foul Russian bastard."

"You'd turn the *Jefferson* into a Cossack carrier?" Tombstone asked, dumbfounded at the idea.

"And why not? A cohort of Roman soldiers, a platoon of mounted Cossack—men of war have always had their methods of taking the war to their opponents. Today, the modern equivalent is the aircraft carrier. Who better to understand how to use this vessel? We're not putting your own war plans to a real test. Instead, you will approach to thirty miles off the coast of Petro, and wait for further instructions." He fixed Tombstone with a steely glare. "Do not test me on this, Admiral. If necessary, I can have two hundred more Spetsnaz on board within eight hours, more than enough to assist me in controlling your crew. Additionally, if you force me to such measures, we will begin executing one of your crew every five minutes until you agree to comply. We will begin with the women," he ended, gesturing toward a woman dressed in a flight suit standing in the corner of TFCC. "With her, I think."

Tombstone felt the blood drain from his face. He resisted the impulse to turn and look at that bright red hair on the diminutive form one last time. Tomboy had stopped by TFCC to follow Bird Dog's return to the ship.

"I see I have your attention," Rogov observed. He glanced from Tombstone to Tomboy, and then back at Tombstone. A careful, considering look crossed the Cossack's face. "So it is like that, is it?" he murmured. "Guard him." He pointed at two Spetsnaz.

The designated men swiveled around and trained their weapons on Tombstone. Rogov crossed the room quickly, grabbed Tomboy by her hair, and yanked her head back. He pulled her to a standing position and twisted his hands to turn her to face him. "So this is an American pilot," he noted, touching the gold wings over her left breast.

"I'm not a pilot," she said sharply. "I'm a naval flight officer—a radar intercept operator, if you must know."

Rogov's hand flashed out, and he smacked her across the face. "Then you have learned some bad habits, riding always in the backseat. While I am here, you will speak when spoken to, and at no other time. Is that clear?"

Tomboy stood mute, her face pale except for the red mark on her face where Rogov's hand had landed. He jerked her up sharply by the hair, causing her to wince.

"Is that clear?" he repeated slowly.

"Yes," Tomboy spat.

"Good." Rogov shoved her back in her chair. "In my tribe, a woman is not permitted to wed until she has killed. A pity you have no such customs here." He turned back to Tombstone. "And that you have so little control over your face and emotions, Admiral," the Cossack sneered. "It is always dangerous to expose one's weaknesses to an enemy, is it not?" Rogov turned back to his squad. "If the admiral does not order the ship to turn west in the next thirty seconds, you are to shoot her. Take her into the conference room, since I do not want a ricochet to damage the equipment."

He turned back to Tombstone. "And I will ensure that you accompany them. I would not want you to miss the lesson especially arranged for you."

Tombstone prayed that the fear and anger pounding through his body weren't showing on his face. In his most impassive voice, he said, "She's a naval officer, nothing more. You can't force me to do anything by harming her."

He felt Rogov's gaze prying at the facade he carefully held in place. "Perhaps so," the Cossack said finally. "Perhaps. Let me increase the stakes. Tell me, Admiral, have you been notified of a missing civilian vessel in the area? A large fishing vessel?"

Cold coursed through his body. "No, I haven't," he lied.

"I think you have. That fishing vessel was merely a demonstration of what one submarine can do to a ship. I believe you call the boat an Oscar."

"I fail to see what that has to do with me," Tombstone answered.

"That same submarine is now fifty miles astern of you. If you fail to comply with my orders, I will send every man and woman on your ship to the bottom of the ocean."

CHAPTER 14
Friday, 30 December

"Get us back in the fight," Bird Dog snapped. Every second of the last five minutes of tanking, he'd felt increasingly impatient. Somewhere not so far away, the Bear-J orbited menacingly, datalinking down to the submarine aft of the carrier. Eliminate the targeting information, and the submarine was less of a threat.

"Bear's on three-one-zero true, range ninety-two miles," Gator announced. "No LINK data from *Jefferson*, but I'm holding him bigger than shit."

"He's alone?"

"Looks to be. Shouldn't be much of a knife fight."

"He carries some self-defense missiles, but I can shoot from outside his engagement envelope," Bird Dog answered. "Right?"

"I think so. Probably."

"What kind of answer is that?"

"The best one I can give you," Gator said, exasperated. "Look, I can read the latest Intel reports as well as the next guy, but are you willing to bet your ass—not to mention mine—on what they say? They've missed this

277

whole skirmish developing, but you want me to tell you their offensive weapons data is the gospel? Sorry, Bird Dog. There're not enough detections on Bear-J's for me to be real happy about this."

"They might have long-range air-to-air missiles? Hell." Bird Dog slammed the Tomcat into a steep climb. "Nice of you to finally mention it. I think I'll just grab a little airspace while I can. And I thought this was going to be like shooting fish in a barrel."

"It probably *will* be," Gator shot back. "I just don't want you getting too complacent up there. Chances are that you can stand off at maximum range and blow his ass out of the air."

"I'll try the Sparrow first. Just inside thirty miles—no, let's go on into twenty. That'll give us a margin of safety." The semiactive radar-homing AIM-7 missile used continuous wave or pulse-doppler radar for target illumination. It was more effective in a nonmaneuvering intercept than in a dogfight, as the Navy's experience in Libya and Iran had proven. Later engagements during Desert Storm showed improved performance from the new solid-state electronics and better pilot training, but most pilots were still reluctant to count on it close in.

"Might as well," Gator agreed. "If nothing else, you'll dump some weight off the wings and improve our fuel figures. Be more maneuverable, too, since you'll dump five hundred ten pounds per missile."

"Like I need maneuverable against a Bear."

"And like I said, there's a chance he can fight back. You got missiles inbound, maneuverable's a real good thing to be."

"If he's carrying long-range air-to-air missiles, that might explain why he's out here without fighter protection," Bird Dog said suddenly. "That's been bothering me, trying to figure out why he'd be out here all alone."

"It might at that," Gator said, ending the sentence with a harsh grunt as the G-forces tugged at his guts. "That never did make much sense. The Russians aren't ones for subtle, probing feints. They'd rather slam you with three waves of Backfires and MiGs."

"Okay, let's assume he's got something new on his wings. I think we have to, seeing as how we're the only CAP out here. Is he going to let me get inside Sidewinder range?"

"Ten miles? Maybe. But remember, his exhaust isn't going to be screaming out at the infrared homer like a jet on afterburner. You might want to get in closer. Besides, one hundred eighty-six pounds of Sidewinder's not going to slow you down like a Sparrow still on the wings."

"This is crazy," Bird Dog said suddenly. "We're talking about ACM with a *Bear*. Let's get real."

"Like you said, we're the only friendlies out here. If that means we got to be a little more cautious than usual, then we live with it."

"How far now?"

"He's at forty miles," Gator replied. "Still in a starboard turn—no, wait. He's shedding some altitude. Now at fifteen thousand feet."

"Okay with me. I'm going to get a broadside shot at him."

"I don't like it. What's he doing at fifteen thousand? And still descending."

"Where's the sub?" Bird Dog asked.

"Twenty miles to the north. The Bear's pattern's been taking him almost directly overhead."

"And that Oscar might have surface-to-air missiles on her, too. Just dandy."

"Something to watch out for," Gator agreed. "Range now thirty miles."

"I'm ready. We'll go in to twenty."

The seconds clicked by too slowly. Bird Dog bit his lower lip, tried to will time to move faster. The selector switch was already toggled to the Sparrow, and his finger was poised to twitch. That's all it would take—an almost infinitesimal movement of his finger, he'd take the easy shot at the Bear, and then they could—could what? With the carrier under the terrorists' control, there was no assurance that they'd have anywhere to land. Adak was too far, and ditching in the hostile sea below was unthinkable.

"*Now*," Gator snapped.

His finger moved of its own accord, toggling the weapon off the wing. The Tomcat jolted abruptly to the left as its center of gravity shifted.

"He's still heading for the deck, increasing his rate of descent," Gator reported. "Now passing through five thousand feet."

"Sparrow'll catch him," Bird Dog said grimly. "Mach 4 ain't peanuts."

"Shit, he's got almost zero speed over ground," Gator muttered. "He must be damned near vertical."

"Wouldn't you be? His only chances are getting lost in sea clutter or having the Sparrow go tits up. I've still got a lock—let's put the other one on his tail."

"Now."

"Fox Two." The Tomcat rolled to the right as the other Sparrow leaped off the wing. "Now give me a vector up his ass. Next shot's a Sidewinder right up his exhaust pipe."

"Intercept two miles behind—come right to zero-two-zero. Three minutes."

Bird Dog twisted the Tomcat around in the air and put the aircraft into a steep rate of descent. "Got a visual," he reported, staring at the tiny black spot against the sea. "On the missiles, too."

"Tracking, tracking—aw, shit! Fucking sea clutter, shipmate. Lost lock on both missiles. You're going to have to get him with the Sidewinder."

"Sidewinder, my ass," Bird Dog muttered. "I'll ram this little bastard if I have to. No damned turboprop's wiggling away from me. How the hell would I ever live it down in the Ready Room?"

"Altitude," Gator warned. "Fly the aircraft first, shoot weapons second."

Bird Dog eased the Tomcat out of the steep dive, letting his airspeed bleed off.

And still the Bear descended, finally arresting its dive just fifty feet above the water. He heard Gator mutter, "Jesus, even Bird Dog's not that crazy."

The massive command-and-control aircraft seemed to skim just above the tops of the waves, looking more like a hovercraft than an airplane. Bird Dog approached from the rear, still descending, hunting for the perfect altitude to allow the Sidewinder to lock onto the Bear's exhaust. Finally, he heard the distinctive warble from the weapon, telling him it had acquired a targeting heat source.

"Got lock," he announced, then thumbed the weapon off of the rail. The missile, carrying an annular blast warhead with perforated metal rods in it, barely twitched the Tomcat as it ignited.

Bird Dog watched the missile's tail flare, quickly kicking the Sidewinder up to its Mach 2 terminal velocity. It warbled once, then headed straight for the Bear's exhaust.

Then the unthinkable happened. The Bear, clearly aware that it was being targeted with a heat-seeking missile, dipped even lower toward the water. Bird Dog saw the pilot jerk the nose hard up, risking a stall but counting on ground effect to substitute for lift. As the nose came up, the rest of the aircraft teetered back down. The port engine and wing smashed through a wave, spewing black smoke instead of hot exhaust as it emerged.

The Sidewinder wobbled again, evidently confused by the loss of the infrared source it'd been homing on. The perturbation increased, and the flight path of the stark white missile wandered around the dark ocean below.

"The other engine, the *other* engine," Bird Dog screamed. He started swearing.

"Come on, come on, baby," he heard Gator crooning.

Neither threats nor encouragement worked. The starboard engine, still burning hot and bright, was hidden from the missile by the Bear's wavering attitude. The Sidewinder fizzled, then wandered off toward the horizon, intrigued by the one decent heat source it could sense—the sun.

"You've got one left," Gator said.

"Bastard's too low," Bird Dog said. "God, who would have thought? I've heard of a COD smashing through waves after a cat shot, but never anything as big as that Bear."

"Take the shot," Gator urged. "He can't pull that stunt again—both port engines are out. He'll never make it back to wherever he came from if he loses another one."

"And we won't make it if we run into something else up here," Bird Dog pointed out. "He's low and slow, Gator. I'm going to take him with guns."

"And you're not going to need those? Same principle applies."

"Less likely to need them than that Sidewinder. Besides, he's an easy target on two engines. His airspeed has already fallen off to three hundred knots."

"Okay, okay," Gator said. "I'm getting more and more nervous about being out here. Just get that bastard before his submarine buddy decides to have a go at the carrier."

"Lining it up now." Bird Dog brought the Tomcat around in a hard port turn, cutting away from and then back toward the Bear for a beam shot. The 675-round M61A1 20mm Vulcan multibarrel cannon—hell, it might not be as flashy as a Sidewinder, but one or two rounds into a critical hydraulics line or a fuel tank would work just as well.

Tomcat 201 bore down on the stricken Bear, and Bird Dog carefully lined up his shot, leading the Bear by a few hundred feet. Let the aircraft fly through the pattern, make him part of the firing solution. Slow and easy, slow and—

"Break right, break right," Gator howled over ICS. "Now!"

Bird Dog acted immediately, snapping the Tomcat into a hard roll away from the target before he'd even gotten off one short burst. "What, *what*?" he screamed.

"Submarine's surfacing. Look over to your left. You recognize that cute little bit of gear on its sail?"

"Like I've got eyes on the tailpipes? Listen, I was a little busy up here—"

"And that's why I was watching elsewhere. Since you can't see it now, let me describe it for you. A small radar unfolding from the sail, a black box just aft of it—sound familiar?"

Bird Dog felt cold. On his last cruise, he and Gator had almost been shot down by one of the first deployed antiwar systems on a submarine. "And that Bear was leading us right into his kill zone, just like we were saying."

"The only thing good in the whole equation is that the Bear is too low to be holding radar contact on *Jefferson*. He can talk to that sewer pipe below him, but all he's got is old info."

"But that might be enough—hold on, I'm going back around for that Sidewinder shot. We don't have a choice on this now, not a smart one."

"Get low," Gator suggested. "He's not going to pull that jet-ski impersonation on you again."

"Concur." Bird Dog descended back down to five hundred feet, carefully staying three miles away from the submarine. "He's going to have to overfly, then come right or left to turn and come back over him." Bird Dog kicked into afterburner range, felt the Tomcat leap forward and shove him back in the seat. "Suppose we just meet him down at the end of his racetrack?"

The Tomcat overshot his prey, then pulled up into a tight starboard orbit three miles in front of the Bear. Two minutes later, as the Bear started its turn back toward its guardian submarine, Bird Dog toggled the last Sidewinder off of the wing from an altitude of two hundred feet.

The missile had less than one mile to go to reach its target. Even if the Bear had had some other tactic in mind, there was no time. Bird Dog saw the Bear frantically ejecting flares and chaff, hoping to decoy the Sidewinder, but the missile flew a perfect profile straight into the engines beckoning so loudly in the infrared spectrum. Bird Dog yanked the Tomcat up just as the Bear disintegrated into a flaming mass of metal and machinery.

"Scratch one Bear," Gator said. "Good shot."

"Do me a favor, Gator. Just one—I'll never ask anything of you again."

"What?"

"Let's just tell the boat that the missiles fell off the damned wings or something. I'm never going to live it down if the skipper finds out I shot a full load at that damned Bear."

"Let's go find us some gas. I'll think about it."

Bird Dog groaned.

1230 Local
Tomcat 201

Bird Dog plugged and sucked on the tanker uneventfully. The sight of fuel gauges indicating a full load gave him a definite sense of comfort. At loitering speed, that bought them at least four hours in which to decide what to do. By that time, hopefully the carrier would have gotten the terrorist situation under control. Absent any other good plan, Bird Dog headed for the starboard marshall stack, entering it at the standard altitude and commencing to orbit.

"That submarine would explain a good deal about the carrier's cooperation with those terrorists," Gator said. "Having a cruise missile sitting on your ass is no joke."

"We were loaded up for antiair," Bird Dog swore. "A couple of Rockeyes on the wings would have been a hell of a lot more help a little while ago."

"Well, why don't we go back and get some?" Gator asked. "After all, we don't seem to have any weapons at all right now."

"Trap on the carrier?"

"You have somewhere else in mind? There aren't a

287

whole hell of a lot of choices out here, Bird Dog," Gator said sarcastically. "Besides, you have any better ideas?"

Bird Dog shook his head. He might not have a good idea, but he could see a hell of a lot that could go wrong with this one. Who knew how much control the carrier had over its own flight operations, with the terrorists on board? Additionally, what were the odds that they could land, get rearmed, and launch again without someone objecting?

"I guess it's worth asking about," he said finally. "Who do we have comms with?"

"Just the air boss. From what he says, he hasn't heard from the bridge, Combat, or TFCC in twenty minutes. I think that's probably a good indicator of their tactical status."

"If they don't have control of the bridge, how are they gonna get us the right winds to land?"

"What, a little wind bothering you now? We can land in just about anything except a tailwind, you know. Still—well, let's give them a call and see what they think of the idea. We'll worry about the details later."

Bird Dog picked up the radio to contact the air boss. As crazy as it sounded, if the Tomcat could do something about the submarine on the carrier's tail, it might improve the situation.

1231 Local
USS *Jefferson*

The air boss shifted uneasily in his seat and glared down at the deck. With the carrier heading west, the anemometer indicated a tailwind of thirty knots across the deck.

Even if he had an aircraft ready to launch, there was no way they were getting off the deck. Not with that wind.

And where would they go, anyway? The nearest air base was well out of tactical range, unless the carrier launched tankers to support a divert. No, he decided, better keep the aircraft on deck.

"Sir. A strange request from Tomcat Two-oh-one," the operations specialist said. He pointed toward the air boss's communication panel. "Button three, boss."

The air boss picked up the receiver, acknowledged the call-up, and listened quietly for a few moments. A slow smile spread across his face. After a few short comments, he hung up the receiver and turned to his tower crew. He surveyed them quickly, finally fixing his eyes on Petty Officer First Class Berkshire. The operations specialist sported an Enlisted Surface Warfare insignia on his neatly pressed dungaree shirt.

"Berkshire! Get over here," the air boss said. "Time for you to lay some of that black shoe magic on me. Here's what I want to do. . . ."

Thirty minutes later, the enlisted men and women had rigged up a sound-powered phone circuit between the tower and after-steering, the auxiliary compartment in the aft end of the ship that housed the rudder mechanism and alternative steering capabilities.

"With the bridge and Combat out of control, I reckon that makes me about the senior officer around," the air boss said. He straightened and took a deep breath. "But this is a hell of a lot different from flying an F-14. People, you got any good ideas, I wanna hear them immediately. Don't make me look stupid on this."

Berkshire, now seated in the miniboss's chair, swallowed nervously. "Boss, I had to stand some conning officer watches to get my pin, but that's been a couple of years."

The air boss turned and glared at him. "Are you saying you don't remember?"

"No, it's just that . . . I . . ." The technician's voice trailed off.

Berkshire started to wilt under the air boss's glare. His hand reached up involuntarily and touched the ESWS insignia ironed on his shirt. It did mean something, didn't it? His mind flashed back to the endless hours of study, the grueling written exam, and the six-hour oral examination he had to pass to win his water wings.

Yes, it did, he decided, feeling his confidence return. He'd survived hours of questioning by the captain, the executive officer, and the senior enlisted men aboard. They wouldn't have qualified him if they didn't believe in him, didn't trust him to know his stuff. And now was the time to prove it.

"Yes, boss, I know what to do," he said confidently. "The first thing you want to do is shift the steering to after-steering. We've already done that. Now you'll want to test your rudder. I'll relay your orders for you to after-steering—put 'em in the right language, and make sure we're not doing anything, uh—uh—"

"Stupid?" the air boss queried. He nodded sharply. "That's exactly what you're supposed to do, Berkshire. Keep me from doing anything stupid. And don't you forget it."

"Right, then. The first thing you'll want to do, boss, is order five degrees right rudder. I'll pass that on to them, and you watch the repeater to make sure we change course. Then, we'll go back the other way. That way, we know we can maneuver. Make sure the linkages are all set correctly."

"Make it so," the air boss answered, turning to his right so that he watched the forward part of the ship.

"There's only one thing that worries me a little, boss," Berkshire continued. "Usually, you want to do a visual check on both sides of the ship to make sure there's no traffic around you before you turn. We don't have a clear look at the right side of the ship, so we're going to be working on faith. Not a bad bet in this neck of the ocean, since there's not likely to be any traffic around, but it's something to be aware of."

"Turn this puppy right five degrees," the air boss responded. "I'll take full responsibility for any mishaps."

Berkshire nodded. "Right five degrees rudder," he translated for the after-steering crew.

Both men watched the repeater twitch, then move slowly to the right, indicating the ship was responding to rudder control from after-steering. They repeated the maneuver, using increasing degrees of left and right rudder, until finally Berkshire was satisfied that they had control of the ship.

"Now find me some wind," the air boss ordered. "You know what we need."

"The easiest way to do that is to just start a turn and watch the relative wind indicator until you get what you want," Berkshire responded. "I can do the calculations manually, but—"

"Do it the fastest way," the air boss answered. He glanced up at the sky, as though looking for Tomcat 201. "Let's get those boys down on deck, rearmed, and back in the air."

1310 Local
Tomcat 201

"Will you look at that?" Gator said.

Bird Dog nodded and adjusted his own flight pattern to compensate for the carrier's movement. "Trying to get her nose into the wind, is she?"

"Looks like it to me. Bird Dog, since we're the only damned aircraft in this pattern, how about we settle in two miles astern? Save us some time when we want to start making our approach."

"Good idea." Bird Dog relayed their plan to the air boss, then moved the Tomcat back aft of the carrier. With no other aircraft in the pattern, he started executing a lazy figure eight instead of the standard oval orbit track.

The call came ten minutes later. "Tomcat Two-oh-one, you're cleared for final," Bird Dog heard the air boss say.

"Ready, partner?" he asked Gator.

"As ready as we'll ever be. Remember, we're going to be getting on board without an LSO. You keep a close watch on that meatball."

"And you speak up if you see anything going wrong," Bird Dog responded. "Unless there's anything else, let's get it done. We've got ordies with armament waiting for us on the deck."

Bird Dog headed the Tomcat away from the carrier, taking it out to the five-mile point. He slowly decreased his altitude, finally settling in right on glide path two miles behind the ship. He headed for the boat, keeping a careful eye on the stern, making minute course and altitude corrections that his gut told him were right.

Finally, at the half-mile point, he got a clear visual on the meatball.

"Oh, shit," he swore. "Gator, the meatball is down."

"What? You mean—"

"The last idiot out of the LSO platform turned it off. I'm not getting any indications at all."

Gator was silent for a moment. "How do you feel about making an IFR approach?" he asked finally.

"I don't see that I've got much option, do I? At least I got some practice recently, over that damned island. Hell, landing on the carrier, at least I can see it."

"Okay, let's go for it. They got power on the arresting cables?"

"Yes, the air boss said they were already set for us. I gave him my final weight just a second ago."

"Let's do it."

1311 Local
TFCC, USS *Jefferson*

Tombstone observed the large blue tactical screen in the front of TFCC cut of the corner of his eye. He tried to avoid giving Rogov any indication that he was watching closely the events transpiring there. He wished he knew what the hell was going on. He'd seen from the course repeaters that the carrier had changed course, and that the wind over the deck was now acceptable for most landings and takeoffs. Recalling the lessons he'd learned while in the pipeline for commander of the carrier group, he decided that the bridge—or whoever was in control of the ship—must have shifted steering back to after-steering. The bridge itself was clearly under the terror-

ists' control, which he knew not only from what he'd
overhead over the radio, but by the rule-of-thumb approach he saw the carrier taking toward good wind.

The symbols on the screen were virtually motionless,
the carrier moving so slowly that her track was barely
perceptible. Only one other symbol moved—that of a
friendly aircraft. He watched it break out of the marshall
pattern and head for a holding pattern aft of the ship.
His eyes widened as he caught a glimpse of its next
movement—it turned south, slowly approaching the carrier. Surely they couldn't be—how could they—no, it had
to be. Whatever was going on on the rest of the ship, it was
clear that somebody had decided to continue flight operations even under the hostage situation.

Tombstone felt a moment of grim pride. It was one of
the strengths of naval leadership, the ability to take
charge of any disastrous scenario and try to wring
tactical advantage from it. He wondered who had the
balls to make this call, and resolved that, no matter how
it turned out, that man—or woman—was getting a
commendation.

Some tiny movement of Tombstone's eyes must have
betrayed him. Rogov turned and stared at the tactical
screen. "What is this?" he snapped, finally noticing the
small symbol moving toward the aft end of the carrier.

He turned back to Tombstone, enraged. "How did
you—"

"I didn't do anything," Tombstone responded coldly.
"Regardless of how your organization works, my men
are trained to take charge. That's what's wrong with your
whole scenario, Comrade," he said, giving the last word
a heavy inflection. "You may kill me, you may kill
everyone in TFCC, but the remaining men and officers

will take charge and carry out the mission of this ship."

Rogov whirled to the three remaining Spetsnaz. "Get up on the deck," he ordered, pointing at the door. "As soon as that aircraft's on deck, kill the flight crew and disable the aircraft. Go on, you heard me."

"But, Colonel—" one of the commandos started to say.

Rogov cut him off. "I will maintain control here." He raised his weapon, displaying it for the other three. "Regardless of the admiral's brave words, his crew here will not attempt anything foolish with their admiral's life at stake. Now go."

The three commandos left the small compartment at a run, quickly heading for the flight deck.

They burst out onto the tarmac, orienting themselves toward the rear of the carrier. Tomcat 201 was a small speck, quickly growing larger.

"Who the hell is fouling the flight deck?" the air boss shouted. Berkshire peered over the edge of the tower and examined the figures below.

"I don't know, boss, but I don't think they're ours. Our plane captains normally don't carry machine guns on the flight deck."

"That bird's only one mile out. If those fellows start shooting—" He left the sentence unfinished.

Suddenly, an idea occurred to Berkshire. "Boss . . ." he started hesitantly, then raised his voice. "This is out of my area, but doesn't the Tomcat have a gun on the front, sort of like a cannon?"

"Yes, it does. But what—ah." The air boss picked up the microphone to the flight deck circuit. "All hands clear the deck. That's an order. Now!" He turned to Berkshire. "With any luck, they won't understand English, or they won't think it applies to them. Either way, we'll give that Tomcat a clear field of fire. Now, let me see if I can explain this to the pilot without having him think I've gone insane."

1315 Local
Tomcat 201

"He wants us to do what?" Gator asked. "A strafing run?"

"That's what the man said," Bird Dog responded. "Look, I can see them now. Right next to the island."

"Bird Dog, you hit one full fuel tank and we're talking a major conflagration on the flight deck. Then where do we land? Have you thought of that?"

"Then I'll just have to be sure not to miss," Bird Dog replied with a good deal more confidence than he actually felt. "I remind you, Gator, you're talking to the man who can pitch a thousand-pound bomb in an ice storm without a visual. Now just let me show you what I can do with a cannon."

1320 Local
Flight Deck, USS *Jefferson*

The commandos crossed over the yellow lines that marked the border of the operating area of the flight deck. They darted aft, staying on the starboard side of the ship, just to the right of the landing aircraft's projected flight. With less than a minute remaining until the aircraft crossed in front of them, they reached the number three arresting wire, raised their Kalishnikovs, and pegged the Tomcat in their sights.

"The cockpit and the fuel tanks," the commando ordered. "If the pilot survives, we will teach him a lesson later. For now, we must ensure that the aircraft is completely disabled. Disobedience deserves a harsh lesson."

On either side of him, his companions nodded. With a target this big, there wasn't much chance they would miss.

"A few more seconds," the commando shouted. Thirty knots of wind across the bow blurred his words. "If we can hit him before he's on deck, we'll prevent any serious damage to the carrier. But wait until he's in range."

1326 Local
Tomcat 201

"Those little bastards," Bird Dog muttered. "Gator, something just occurred to me—if I fire at them head-on, I'm risking nailing another bird with a ricochet or a bullet."

"Well, there just might be a way to avoid that."

"How?"

"Bird Dog, what are you going to—" The rest of the RIO's comments were cut off by a sudden hard turn. The G-forces slammed him into the side of his seat, and his vision grayed. He grunted, trying to force the blood back up to his brain and prevent a gray-out.

Bird Dog kicked in the afterburners, pulling the slow-moving Tomcat into a sharp left-hand turn. He dropped the nose slightly, a dangerous maneuver at that low an altitude, but critical to avoiding stall speed. As soon as he felt the Tomcat pick up airspeed, he returned to level flight.

Seconds after that maneuver, he pulled the Tomcat's nose up sharply, praying that their airspeed was sufficient to sustain flight. Over, over, climbing into a steep Immelmann, Bird Dog drove the F-14 into the air. Finally, as the aircraft reached the apex of its turn, it was almost out of airspeed. It hung motionless for a second at three thousand feet, then nosed over, inverted, back down toward the water. Bird Dog brought every sense to bear on the shuddering aircraft, carefully gauging the exact moment at which he could start pulling out of the steep dive. He didn't have enough airspeed yet to remain airborne in level flight, but pulling up too soon would just induce a deadly stall. Finally, at the last possible moment, he pulled the aircraft up, barely avoiding the icy sea below.

Fifteen hundred feet away from the carrier, the aircraft decided to remain airborne. The afterburners quickly picked the speed up to well over 160 knots, increasing it steadily as the plane approached the aircraft carrier.

Three hundred feet away from the flight deck, Bird Dog toggled the weapon switch to guns. He waited one more second, then depressed the fire switch, applying small amounts of rudder to sweep the pattern of gunfire back and forth across the aft end of the flight deck.

Bright sparks of light flashed against the black tarmac, evidence of both ricochets and the tracer rounds embedded in every fifth round. He quickly got his range, bracketing the Spetsnaz, then, in one final sweep, nailing them dead-on. The three figures crumpled slowly as he screamed across the flight deck.

1327 Local
Flight Deck, USS _Jefferson_

How could it be? the commando thought, consciousness fading fast as the blood drained out of his body and onto the icy tarmac. He moved his head slightly, and could see one pool already congealing into thin crimson ice. The aircraft had fired on its own flight deck—it wasn't possible, it wasn't—he closed his eyes as a fresh wave of pain moved through him. It quickly increased in tempo until his world was no more than a red haze gnawing away at every nerve ending in his body. He tried to scream, found his vocal chords wouldn't respond, then tried to move a hand up to his face. Nothing seemed to work, not even his fingers. The most he could do was open his eyes and stare in the direction that he was facing. The pain grew to incredible proportions, even worse because of his inability to give voice to it. When he saw the black shape moving along the horizon, he could have cried with relief. Soon the pain would end.

The Tomcat was coming back for another strafing run.

1328 Local
Tomcat 201

"That finishes that." Bird Dog tried to feel the same sense of victory he'd felt on the bombing run over the island, but it was slow in coming. It was one thing, he thought, to scream in above the landscape and drop ordnance on anonymous opponents on the deck. You didn't look at them, didn't see their faces turn pale and eyes grow wide as you approached. It was—sanitary, somehow.

But this had been different. Even at 250 knots, he'd had a few seconds to look at the faces of his opponents. No matter that their Kalishnikovs were turning to bracket him, and that if they'd had their way he'd have been a small greasy spot on the surface of the ocean. No, it was still different, he decided. Watching their faces, seeing them crumple in response to his gunfire, and coming back over for a second pass on the motionless figures made it personal.

"The submarine?" Gator prompted.

Bird Dog cast an uneasy look in the rearview mirror. "Yeah, yeah, the submarine." He banked the Tomcat to the right, coming back around toward the stern of the boat. From fifteen thousand feet of altitude, the Oscar was still visible, her conning tower just breaking the surface of the ocean. The 540 foot-long submarine looked small next to the carrier, but Bird Dog knew that it was among the largest submarines in the world. Certainly the largest, most potent antiship boat. Looking at her now, even from five hundred feet up, he could well believe that one torpedo from her tubes could crack the keel of the carrier, rendering his airport permanently inoperative. "Let's go get those Rockeyes."

Forty-five minutes later, rearmed with Rockeyes, Tomcat 201 was airborne again. Bird Dog pulled out from the cat shot and arrowed straight out toward the submarine.

"You're too close," Gator warned. "Move out to at least a mile and a half."

"I'm going, I'm going. I just wanted to get a look at her first. Those guys on the deck back there . . ." He let his voice trail off.

"Ugly, wasn't it? Just as nasty as what we'd look like right now if they'd had their way about it. Same thing with the submarine."

"I know. But that's one good thing about flying backseat, Gator—the only thing. You don't have as good a view of it."

"Save the soul-searching for later, buster," the RIO snapped. "We've got our range now, now, now. Get that bastard off the wing."

Bird Dog toggled the weapons selector switch to select the Rockeye stations. Waiting until his targeting gear beeped a solid, reassuring tone at him, he fired. The Tomcat lurched as the heavy missile streaked off the wings. Bird Dog waited two seconds, targeted the second missile, then fired again.

"Jesus, look at those bastards," he breathed. Although he'd fired several practice Rockeyes before, they hadn't been the true heavyweights of an actual missile.

The bright burn from their rockets seared his eyes, and he looked away for a moment. When he glanced back, the missiles were still in sight, something that wouldn't have happened if they'd been antiair missiles. The huge anti-ship and -submarine Rockeyes moved much more slowly through the air. Almost too slow, it seemed, to stay airborne. Compared to the quick flash of a Sparrow or Sidewinder, they looked like dirigibles.

Ten seconds later, the first missile struck. It impacted

the water just forward of the submarine, just missing its intended target.

The explosive force of the warhead lofted the bow of the submarine up, and the forward part of the hull broke the surface of the water. The second missile arced down, spilling bomblets in is wake. Two seconds later, it hit the exposed hull of the submarine dead-on.

Water geysered up and out, reaching a height of almost seventy-five feet and spewing water droplets over a two-hundred-yard radius. A buffet of displaced air caught the Tomcat, rocking her gently, and Bird Dog banked hard to the right to avoid the airborne blast of seawater.

"Time for some BDA," Gator suggested.

Bird Dog nodded, somehow relieved that this kill was not as up close and personal as the last. He put the Tomcat into a gentle orbit a thousand feet above the surface of the ocean, and waited.

The forward portion of the hull was completely gone. The aft part stayed afloat for a few minutes, even bobbing up to the surface for a moment as the men inside it evidently blew all their air tanks. A hatch on the back popped open, and three figures struggled out, turning to haul a large package out with them. A life raft, Bird Dog surmised, although whether or not they would have time to open it and still survive the air temperature clad only in their thin submariner overalls was open for debate.

Evidently the impact from the Rockeye had cracked the hull in too many critical spots. Bird Dog saw huge gouts of air bubbles stream out of the hull, and the stern half sank appreciably in the water. Thirty seconds later, it was completely awash. The three men who'd exited the submarine still struggled with the life boat package, their movements now noticeably slower and lethargic.

The poor bastards, he thought, still trying to stay focused on what the Oscar had intended to do to *Jefferson*. At least they'll go fast—and they're not trapped inside the hull, waiting for the water to leak into their compartment. I'd rather freeze than drown any day, he concluded.

Four minutes after the first Rockeye had hit near the submarine, it was all over. The men were floating on the surface of the water, their abandoned life raft, only partially inflated, bobbing gently among them. The remaining portions of the submarine's hull slipped quietly beneath the sea, although air bubbles and occasional gouts of water still rippled up.

The two aviators, as though by silent agreement, watched the submarine die before turning to consider their own situation. Finally, when there had been no air bubbles for several minutes, Bird Dog said, "Let's call Mother and let her know."

"Okay. I'll do the honors."

Bird Dog heard Gator's voice going out over Tactical, advising the air boss—temporary commander of the carrier battle group—of what had occurred. He listened to the brief conversation, patiently orbiting in a standard marshall pattern, albeit at a lower altitude than he normally would have done had there been other aircraft in the pattern. Finally, he heard the air boss say, "Bring her on home, gentlemen. We've still got a few problems, but I think we'd best get you on deck."

"Sounds good to me," Bird Dog said wearily. "And this time, boss, we're getting out of the cockpit right away."

1410 Local
TFCC, USS *Jefferson*

"We've lost communications with our submarine," Rogov said heavily. He glared at Tombstone Magruder. "I warned you what the consequences would be if you interfered." He raised his 9mm slowly, and held it against the side of Tombstone's neck.

"No!" Tomboy shouted. She started to stand up.

Rogov turned to face her, training the weapon on her. "Even better. You first."

A movement in the corner of the room caught Tombstone's eye, momentarily distracting him from the life-and-death scenario being played out in front of him. He glanced up, saw a black form move through an escape shuttle located behind the JOTS terminal, and a hand with a dully gleaming black shape pointed at Rogov. There was a short, quiet bark, too soft to seem like gunfire.

The bullet caught Rogov in the throat, slamming him across the small compartment and into the far bulkhead. Before he fell, his head rolled back, ending up resting along his spine, held to his body by only a few thin strips of skin and sinew. From chest to chin, his throat was almost completely gone.

The gruesome, decapitated corpse slid slowly down the wall, catching for a moment on a yellow emergency lighting battle lantern before hitting the deck. Blood poured out of the shattered neck at a tremendous rate, stopping only when his heart gave up the struggle to keep it circulating through the body.

The black-clad figure climbed the rest of the way through the escape hatch, and then stood and stretched. "I couldn't wait any longer," Sikes said simply, looking back and forth between the two. "It was a chance, with him so close to you, but I couldn't wait. You know that."

Tombstone nodded. "Another few seconds and it would've been one of us. You did all right, Sikes."

The SEAL nodded at Tomboy. "Good thing you spoke up. It distracted him just long enough for me to get a shot off. If you hadn't—well, better lucky than good."

Tombstone turned to Tomboy. "TAO—get someone in here to clean up this mess," he said, surprised at how steady and calm his voice sounded even to himself.

Tomboy nodded. "Aye, aye, Admiral," she said. "But there's something else I need to do first." She crossed three steps over to Tombstone, carefully stepping over the mutilated body on the floor, and let her arms snake around him. Tombstone resisted for just a second, then pulled her toward him as though he'd never let her go.

CHAPTER 16
Friday, 30 December

"You got them all?" Tombstone said into the handheld radio.

"Yes, sir. Nasty bit of work. You've got two injured up here, one pretty seriously. The corpsmen are already here—first impression is that they'll make it," Sikes replied. "You've got the bridge of your ship back, Admiral. And four nasty characters in custody."

"Good work. And just for the record, it's not my ship for much longer. About ten seconds, I'd say." Tombstone glanced across the room at Batman, who was pacing back and forth in the admiral's cabin. His *own* cabin, Tombstone reminded himself, not mine. Not anymore— and never again. This one last brief command of the carrier group had been a fluke.

"You ready to relieve me?" Tombstone asked Batman. "If you're going to wear out that strip of carpet, you might as well be the one who has to explain it to the shipyard."

"You bet! For a moment there, I was afraid you wouldn't give her back."

"The thought crossed my mind. But I've had my tour—*Jefferson* is all yours." Tombstone paused as a thought suddenly occurred to him. A cold, distant shadow flitted across his face. "Almost. There's one last thing I have to take care of."

"What? You're not pissed about the JAST bird going sneakers up, are you?" Seeing the look on Tombstone's face, Batman added hastily, "Not that I really care. Being project manager for JAST was last tour, not now."

"No, nothing to do with your baby at all. It's just I've cleaned up the mess I left in your cabin—I ought to finish the job." Tombstone reached for the telephone, then paused. "Can you wait another five minutes? No longer—and you'll be glad you did."

"Wha—?"

Tombstone cut him off. "I just remembered another little mess I left on your ship. And I'm going to need the lawyers to straighten it out."

"You're sure?" The JAG officer looked doubtful, then shook his head. "Washington's going to scream bloody murder over this one."

"Let them scream," Tombstone answered coldly. "Those people endangered the safe operation of this ship with their stupid stunt. I want criminal charges brought against all of them—and I want my name on the charge sheet. How long will it take you to get moving on it?" He glanced over at Batman. "My relief's chomping at the bit."

The JAG held out the manila envelope he'd been carrying in his left hand. "Admiral, after our last conversation—well, I took the liberty of—I thought you might be asking for this as some point. I think you'll find everything in order."

Something softened slightly in Tombstone's eyes. "Why, Captain. By any chance have you anticipated my desires in this matter?"

The lawyer nodded. "I like to be prepared for anything, Admiral."

"And what, may I ask, is in the other folder?" Batman broke in. "Commendations for all of them?"

The lawyer looked faintly alarmed. "If I'd thought of it, there would be. No, the only other option I've prepared is an airlift request—with and without armed guards."

Tombstone nodded. "You get those armed guards ready to go. I think I'm going to need them."

Fifteen minutes later, Tombstone watched from Vulture's Row as four civilians wearing flight deck cranials paraded across the flight deck toward the waiting COD. Two master-at-arms carrying sidearms flanked them. Each of the civilians had his or her hands clasped behind the back in a peculiarly uniform-looking arrangement. From the 0-10 level, the handcuffs were invisible.

"Pamela's going to be damned pissed at you for a long, long time, Stoney," Batman remarked. "Though I do admit the handcuffs were a nice touch. Something in your personal life you want to share with your old wingman?"

Tombstone shot him a wry look. "You got it all backward. If you think Pamela's going to stay mad at me, then you know nothing about the media and reporters. Hell, I've just put her on the top of every news show in the world. Can't you see the headlines—Journalist Imprisoned on U.S. ship? And ACN is going to have an exclusive."

Batman looked doubtful. "I don't know about that. She

looked pretty damned mad when you had that petty officer search her."

"It wasn't even a strip search—though now that you mention it . . ." Tombstone looked thoughtful.

"I don't think you ought to press your luck on this one," Batman said hastily. "Besides, it's my ship now."

Tombstone slapped him on the back. "Damned sure is. Now you see why I made you wait that extra five minutes?"

"I do—and thank you. I wouldn't have had the nerve—and I wouldn't have missed the expression on her face for anything."

The two men fell silent, too tired to try to talk over the noise of the COD taking the cat shot. Finally, as the rugged little C-2 started to gain altitude and veer away from the boat, Batman asked, "So what about the rest of this mess? The Cossacks, I mean."

Tombstone shrugged. "Above my paygrade. I imagine the State Department's going to want a whack at them, along with every intelligence organization in the country. They're not going anywhere, not after sinking that Greenpeace boat. The rest of the business will be written off to a misunderstanding, to engineering casualties and such. Nobody's going to want to give up the peace dividend over the Aleutian Islands."

Batman gazed off at the horizon. "The Cossacks— who would have thought a splinter group like that would almost start another Russian-U.S. conflict? Just a tiny group of extremists, when you think about it. Good thing we don't have that kind of ethnic conflict in the States."

Tombstone looked sober. "I wouldn't be so sure of that. Think of the damage some of these white suprema- cist groups could do to our national interests. They've already managed to commit one atrocity, the Oklahoma City bombing. They're there, and they're dangerous."

"Too bad the military can't do anything about domestic terrorism," Batman said thoughtfully.

Tombstone snorted. "I think we've got enough to do already, don't you?"

Here's a special excerpt from
A FLASH OF RED
by Clay Harvey

**"One of the best thriller debuts in
years."**—Jack Higgins

**"Taut, knowing, and headlong.
Welcome aboard!"**—Robert B. Parker

**"From the quick-clutch first sentence,
Harvey establishes himself as a writer possessed
of cool control . . . The muscular story line zips
along in pared-down prose."**—*Publishers Weekly*

**"Fast-moving . . . An excellent
thriller."**—*The Denver Post*

**"Will keep you flipping pages furiously
into the night."**—*Rapport*

Available August 1997 in bookstores everywhere
from Berkley Books

I didn't want to shoot him, I really didn't. He gave me no choice, poking the barrel of his revolver straight at me and yelling, "Get out of the truck!"

God knows I've killed enough men. They often come to me in the night, disembodied. But not faceless. Never faceless.

At home there was a four-year-old who called me Daddy.

Six months ago a drunk driver took his mom.

Crossed the median, *Wham*, just like that.

For three days he didn't speak. When he did he just asked, "Why?"

It nearly killed me.

Now here was a guy who might take his daddy. *Bam*, just like that.

No. . . .

When I pulled into the bank's parking lot en route to the drive-in window, I found myself behind a bronze Olds four-door of late vintage which sat, engine idling, a few yards this side of the window, blocking both "open" lanes. Odd. Maybe the driver was making out a deposit slip and had failed to notice that the car in front of him had finished conducting its banking business. Assuming of course that there had been a car in front of him.

I reached over and punched off the radio with my thumb, stilling the silken cello of Yo-Yo Ma. A thin veil of exhaust fumes rose from the Olds's tailpipe, muting the dying rays of the sun. I waited a few seconds, almost honked my horn, noticed that the driver was not looking down but was rubbernecking like a first-time bather at a nude beach, his head never still. Very, very nervous.

A marked police car sped by the bank, blue lights ablaze but bereft of siren accompaniment. On the way to an accident? The strain of its presence was too much for the driver of the Oldsmobile. He stood on the gas, his car fishtailing and fighting for traction as its tires painted twin black marks on the asphalt. Five seconds, tops, and he was squirting out of the parking lot, barely avoiding a rusted Nissan whose occupants saluted him in concert, poking their middle fingers skyward. Undaunted by their derision, he roared off westward, the compass heading opposite that of the departed police car.

Strange, these goings-on.

Having a keen sense of self-preservation augmented years ago by Uncle Sam under conditions that were less than serene, I stayed right where I was. Did *not* pull up to the drive-in teller's window to make a withdrawal, withdrawing instead from my glove compartment a Colt .45 automatic. I racked its slide to chamber a round, then rested the gun—still in hand—on my right leg. And awaited developments.

Which were not long in coming. Out the side door of

the bank, perhaps thirty feet from my truck, popped a medium-sized man sporting lavender sweatpants, an olive turtleneck sweater, an orange ski mask, and a stainless-steel Smith & Wesson .357 Magnum. I transferred the .45 to my left hand, holding the gun against the door panel out of sight. With my right hand, I shifted into reverse. For many reasons, I wanted no part of a robbery in progress. My best way out would be to make a run for it, with backward being the safest route.

Lavender Pants stared in the direction of the now out-of-sight Oldsmobile, stomped his foot, and mouthed the common street euphemism for excrement. Clearly upset, this colorfully clad miscreant.

He reached up, grasped the ski mask at his crown, jerked it off angrily, exposing a coarse black beard mottled with gray. His right ear boasted four jeweled adornments that were completely ineffectual at belying his obvious aggressiveness.

Trying my best to blend with the scenery, I assessed the probability of ducking low in the seat, punching the throttle, and driving my way out of this situation without acquiring painful perforations to my anatomy. I judged my chances to be slim.

What if I backed up, swung around, put some sheet metal, sponge rubber, and upholstery between his gun and my skin? *Might work,* I thought, just as he yelled. "Get out of the truck!"

Ah, well.

I now had two viable options, in my view. One, I could drop the .45 onto the floorboard and relinquish my truck, hoping he wouldn't shoot me, pistol-whip me, or secure me as a hostage. Such an alternative went against my gut feeling, my knowledge of human nature, my philosophy of social decorum, and my extensive—albeit long-past—training in handling violent confrontations.

I went with option two.

I shot him in the beard.

The impact of the heavy hollow-point bullet snapped his head back. He gave a spasmodic kick with his right foot, then fell over backward, his revolver clattering on the concrete. I didn't see him hit the sidewalk, being too busy getting the hell out of my truck.

The side door of the bank had slammed open just as old Lavender Pants and I were getting acquainted. Not figuring the tall, ski-masked individual standing in the doorway to be the governor with my lottery check, I just fired the one shot and exited stage right, through the passenger door. Real fast.

It couldn't have taken me more than three seconds to clear the truck, but by the time my shoes hit the tarmac I had two pounds of shattered glass in my hair. My ancient Toyota pickup was being demolished by a hail of jacketed 9mm bullets as I crouched beside its protective right front wheel. *Sounds like an UZI,* I thought, as I knelt there trying to make myself tiny. The barrage ended as abruptly as it had begun, the sudden silence punctuated by the clack of changing magazines. I duckwalked to the front bumper. The report of a single shot rang out; the nasty little bullet whacked into the offside of my truck, stopping the motor forthwith. *Probably hit the fuel tank pump. Better it than me.*

Why just one shot? Gun jammed? Did he have a handgun as well as the UZI? A partner? I risked a peek around the front of the truck, poking my head out and tucking it back in like a rattlesnake on speed.

I saw just the lanky guy, snapping back the bolt on his

automatic weapon. As I took a longer second look, he pulled the trigger, receiving for his effort a heavy *click* as the firing pin snapped forward on an empty chamber.

No jam, I reflected. *He didn't shove the magazine home.*

Steadying my left elbow into a headlight recess, I silhouetted the black sights of my pistol against the milky white of his jacket while his attention was directed at his recalcitrant firearm, and yelled, "Drop it!"

Hard to intimidate a man with an UZI. He lifted his head, looked me fixedly in the eye, smacked the magazine's floor plate with the heel of his left hand. The magazine snapped into place.

As he reached upward to retract the bolt, I shot him where his heart should've been. He grabbed his chest with his left hand, staggered, nearly dropping the gun, then sagged to both knees, his right hand closed tightly on the trigger, spraying 9mm slugs into the cement walkway, wickedly whining ricochets merging with staccato muzzle blasts as the gun purged itself. I shot him again, hoping to stanch the burst, my second bullet producing no visible effect. The shooting did not stop until he fell forward onto his face and lay still.

I watched him over my gun's sights for what seemed like several minutes. No one moved within my range of vision. Especially me.

The squeal of tires brought my head around as a shiny red Volvo wagon spun out of the parking lot on the other side of the bank, then disappeared from view. It was hard to tell from where I crouched, but there appeared to be three people in the car, including the ski-masked driver.

I stood up, keeping a wary eye on my downed assailants. A marked police car bounced over the grassy verge separating the bank parking lot from the street, blue lights flashing. They'd likely been called to quell a robbery. Had they been informed it had escalated into a shoot-out? I laid my gun carefully atop the hood of my defunct Toyota and stepped out of reach, so as not to make anyone more nervous than they already were. There I waited with my hands well out from my body, palms forward, for the long-familiar but nearly forgotten adrenaline surge to abate.

"You're a what?"

"A writer."

"What kind of writer?"

"Books, magazine articles, monographs . . ."

"The hell's a monograph?"

"Short treatise on a specific, limited subject. Like fly-fishing."

"You write about fishing?"

"No."

"Then why'd you bring it up?"

"Never mind."

No mental giant, Detective Carl McDuffy. He leaned against the only table in the room—a metal industrial-strength job bolted to the tile floor—arms folded across his flat chest. Longish red hair spilled down his brow into his eyes. He brushed it away with an index finger. Whatever happened to department regulations? Good grooming? Unobstructed vision?

I had been escorted to this room, deep within its confines of the Greensboro police annex, by a uniformed patrolman who had subsequently turned me over to the scarlet-plumed McDuffy. Immediately following the shoot-out at the bank, approximately four million police officers had arrived amid much screeching of tires, flashing of lights, and drawing of guns. I had stood politely—and safely—beside the remains of my faithful Toyota while steely-eyed guys and gals in blue surrounded, searched, identified, and grilled me, making me feel as popular as a Twinkie salesman at a Weight Watchers convention.

After determining that I had been duly disarmed, subjugated, and scrutinized, the bulk of the policefolk turned their attention to more important matters. What little information I could catch, as I waited there under guard, indicated that a multitude of witnesses had related to the gendarmerie the following: Four men had staged a holdup at the bank; two of them had attempted an exit through the west entrance of the bank building, encountering a good deal of difficulty; I was personally and solely responsible for said difficulty and either "incredibly brave" or "a fucking idiot," depending upon whose opinion you subscribed to; the remaining pair of robbers had grabbed an unfortunate teller and her car keys, and escaped through the east-side entrance.

A final, almost tearful comment was proffered by the branch manager, a professorial, tuberous stub of a man dressed in a pale green suit of neither plant nor animal origin. The gist was that despite the best efforts of the "gentleman in the diminutive truck" (me) to "thwart" the robbery, two "dregs of society" had, alas, "absconded" with funds the "precise aggregate of which has yet to be determined."

Pedants, everywhere you look.

Shortly following the manager's somber fiscal revelation, I was whisked off to the station house and ensconced in the lackluster interrogation room in which I

now sat. It was large enough, barely, to contain the metal
table, three chairs with yellow plastic seats shaped like
ice cream scoops, and maybe four or five adult-sized
humans if they all used Dial. White walls and ceiling,
maroon-tiled floor, no windows, one door. On the long
institutional table were two small aluminum ashtrays, a
pack of Juicy Fruit, and McDuffy's rear end.

Would they offer me gum? Probably no.

Through the one door strode a big man wearing a
medium gray suit of fashionable cut, a pink shirt, and a
tie featuring many colorful geometric shapes. His angu-
lar face had been recently shaved, his hair newly shorn to
the length of a drill sergeant's. Prominent ears, blue eyes,
blunt fingers, and, I would soon learn, an equally blunt
manner. He was maybe a half-foot taller than I—making
him six two—and carried at least 235 pounds lightly on
big feet, like a puma. Much gold jewelry in evidence,
none of it in his earlobes. Or nose. He padded across the
room, rounded the table, sat.

The big man said, in a guttural rasp that could have
come from a jaguar if jaguars could talk, "Carl, get off
the table."

Instant compliance. McDuffy shifted his carcass upright and milled around like a shy, pimply teenager at the
senior prom. Obvious who was in charge here.

Again the throaty voice: "I am Lieutenant John T.
Fanner, Homicide. Your name, I have been told, is Tyler
Vance. Is that correct?"

Tough. No-nonsense. Intent on setting the pace. We'd
see about that.

I said, "Pass the gum?"

"I beg your pardon?"

"Gum. There's some on the table. Hand it over. My throat's dry."

They glared at me, flint-eyed.

"The two of you keep looking mean at me, I might faint from terror, fall over, maybe sustain a bump on my noggin, be compelled to sue." I planned to win them over with my keen wit.

"Here, smartass," McDuffy said, tossing me the pack of Juicy Fruit. Had I won him over? No matter; I had the gum. Popped a piece into my mouth and chewed contentedly.

"Are you comfortable? Is your throat relieved?" asked Lieutenant John T. Fanner.

I smiled pleasantly.

"I assume that we may now continue. I would like to talk with you about your shooting two citizens."

I snorted. "Those *citizens*"—I stressed the word theatrically—"tried their damnedest to shoot *me*. At least, one of them did. The other might have been satisfied with taking my truck."

"The were less than completely successful, since you are here and they are not." He talked like Mattie Ross in *True Grit*, using no contractions.

"Well, my truck is certainly the worse for wear," I countered.

"Just how did you determine that the intentions of the first man you shot were not only unlawful but threatening?"

"The guy came out of the bank wearing a ski mask, brandishing a magnum six-gun, obviously looking for a getaway car which had just got away, peeling rubber all over the parking lot in its haste. That seemed a little suspicious to me, how about you?"

"How did you know that the vehicle was in fact a . . . as you put it, getaway car?"

"I'd been watching the driver since I pulled up behind him. He was sitting well back from the drive-in window, motor running, looking this way and that. Nervous as a rabbit up a flagpole. When a cop car whizzed by on Cornwallis, he took off in a big hurry.

"The bearded guy showing up, face covered and waving his .357 around and all, confirmed my suspicions. When he told me to get out of my truck, I demurred."

"You certainly did," said Fanner.

McDuffy waded in. "If he was wearing a mask, tough guy, why didn't it have a hole in it where you shot him?"

"Because he jerked it off in disgust when he saw the Oldsmobile was gone," I answered. "By the way, it was a late model, maybe two, three years old, copper or bronze in color. Didn't catch the plate."

"You sure it was an Olds, not a Chevy?" McDuffy pressed.

"Well, I can't be certain," I said, "but it had 'O-L-D-S-M-O-B-I-L-E' on the back in great big letters. Maybe it was a Studebaker."

"Why would he go to such trouble to conceal his identity just to expose himself at the first sign of trouble?" Fanner asked.

"I didn't say he was smart, just mad. Maybe his mask itched. How the hell do I know? You think I shot the guy for nothing?"

"No, I do not think that," said Fanner. "I simply wanted to hear your side of it. Several witnesses corroborate your story."

"Then why am I still here?" I said, and stood up.

McDuffy stepped in front of me. Close. Too close. A

conditioned response, long dormant, welled up in me, tightening my chest. For an instant I surveyed his anatomy, mental faculties on auto scan, seeking the proper spot for instant incapacitation without an attendant risk of death.

Well, only a slight risk.

"What I want to know," he said, poised like a bantam rooster protecting the henhouse, "is why you shot the dude in the face instead of his shoulder or something. Seems like you wanted to kill him, not just stop him."

"Ever drawn your gun other than to clean it, McDuffy?" I looked him over ruefully, then shook my head. "My guess is no."

His face was suddenly inches from mine, ruddy, irate, quivering with anger. "What's it to you?"

"McDuffy!" Fanner snapped.

But McDuffy didn't budge. I put my hands in my back pockets, slowly, afraid to have them out in the open. He had no idea how vulnerable he was, the rube. He thought he was a tough nut to crack.

Fanner's chair squeaked on the tile floor as he shoved it backward. McDuffy swiveled his head in the direction of the sound, then back to me, torn between anger and subordination. And saving face. For a moment, I thought he was going to take a swing. The moment passed. He turned on his heel and went to a corner of the little room, breathing deeply, only partially subdued.

Probably liked to think of himself as explosive, what with the red hair and all. And he was, but only in the way a Fourth of July firecracker is explosive. If his temper went off, I doubted much carnage would ensue.

Fanner was quite another matter. He'd be capable of

more mayhem in his sleep than McDuffy could manage
in the throes of uncontrollable fury.

"I am curious. Would you answer Sergeant McDuffy's
question, please?"

"You mean why I didn't try to cowboy my way out,
shoot the gun out of his hand, wing him in the uvula?"

He almost smiled, but caught himself. "More or less,
yes."

"The quickest way I know of to lose a gunfight—aside
from throwing up your hands, wetting your pants, and
yelling 'HELP!'—is to try to shoot your opponent
around the edges, hoping not to kill the poor soul, who is
after all, only trying to shoot you. The man was virtually
at arm's length, Fanner, revolver in hand, and he had all
the room in the world to maneuver. My own gun was
below the windowsill, in my weak hand, and me with no
room to move and no effective cover. The only thing I
could do to survive was put him out of commission
really, really fast. So I did."

"I'll say"—from McDuffy's corner.

"You worked all of that out while you were sitting
there under his gun?" asked Fanner.

"Yes."

He pondered that, studying me closely. Then he said,
"I would like to hear about the gun. How did you happen
to have it so close at hand?"

"I was planning to cash a royalty check I'd just
received in the mail. Since it was for nearly forty-five
hundred bucks, I carried my own, shall we say, insurance, right there on the seat beside me." Well, not exactly
on the seat, but carrying one in an unlocked glove
compartment is illegal in my state. A small fib, but who
was to know?

"What did you want with forty-five hundred dollars in cash?" McDuffy asked.

"I was thinking about buying a Studebaker," I answered.

He gave me a withering look. I tried not to wither, at least not right there in front of him.

From Fanner: "Are you perchance a Vietnam veteran? You are too old for Desert Storm, unless perhaps you serve in the guard or reserves."

I didn't like this shift of direction, but I concealed my discomfiture artfully, resorting to acerbic levity. "Thanks. Pardon me while I take a sip of Geritol. I went regular Army right out of high school, stationed in Korea for eighteen months—'73, '74."

His blue eyes probed.

"Korea, in the 1970s. There was not much action then. At least not publicized. Were you infantry?"

I nodded uneasily.

"Stationed at any time north of the Imjin River? Did you ever patrol the demilitarized zone?"

Fanner was no dummy. Nor was he uninformed.

"No," I lied.

"Never in a firefight?"

"No." Another lie. Seemed to be becoming a habit.

"Hmm," he responded thoughtfully, tugging at his ear. I didn't think he'd bought it, not all of it. He suspected I was holding back. He was right. I had no choice; information about my Korea escapades was classified. Highly classified. Divulging information—however tenuous in specifics—to a civilian could land me in Leavenworth or some other federal funhouse. No thanks.

Besides, after thirteen months of cleaning house for Uncle Sam, I'd developed a deep-rooted aversion to talking about it, even during my final military debriefing. Not only that, I'd refused to continue covert ops in the Korea DMZ, even under the threat of court-martial and serious jail time, not because of a failure of nerve but an extreme repugnance toward my duties as military-trained attack dog. The gory details of my tenure as a solitary operative in the "Z" still haunted me. They always would.

Fanner said, "I suppose that is all. This appears to be a case of self-defense, justifiable homicide witnessed by a number of solid citizens. Physical evidence supports that premise. There will likely be a grand jury hearing, going through the motions. Such an event will work in your favor should a family member sue you for wrongful death."

"Now there's a happy thought," I said.

"Unfortunately, things like that happen all the time." He held out a pawlike hand. I shook it. His grip was akin to getting your hand wedged in a car door, but he didn't abuse it. I was glad. Might want to use that hand later.

He turned to McDuffy. "Arrange a ride for Mr. Vance—his vehicle seems to be in disrepair. And keep your temper on a leash." With that, he turned and left the room.

McDuffy turned up the wick on his Clint Eastwood stare. It wasn't difficult to keep my knees from buckling, though it was tough sledding indeed not to laugh out loud.

"Where to, bucko?" said McDuffy.

"My address is in your report. When do I get my gun back?"

"Never, I got anything to do with it. Evidence disappears all the time, security not being all that tight around here."

He stepped closer. "I don't give a muskrat turd what Fanner says, you're a cocky bastard that needs deflating. Whack two guys, then walk. Shit. That's not your job. It's mine.

"Go out to the front desk and wait. I'll find someone to take you home, some rookie doesn't care who he rides with."

He put his face close to mine and added, "But I'm betting I'll be seeing you here again, soon."

"Then I hope you'll brush your teeth," I said, and walked out.

#1 NEW YORK TIMES BESTSELLER

SENTINEL

ONE NATION

BEN CARSON, MD, raised by a poor single mother in Detroit, recently retired as the director of pediatric neurosurgery at Johns Hopkins Hospital after a groundbreaking medical career of more than thirty-five years. Now a *Washington Times* columnist, he is the author of five previous books, including the *New York Times* bestsellers *Gifted Hands*, *America the Beautiful*, and most recently, *One Nation*, coauthored with his wife, CANDY CARSON. A former member of the President's Council on Bioethics, he is the recipient of the Presidential Medal of Freedom, the highest civilian honor in the country. Dr. and Mrs. Carson together founded the Carson Scholars Fund, dedicated to recognizing the academic achievements of deserving young people. They have three grown children and two grandchildren and now live in West Palm Beach, Florida.

ONE NATION

—

WHAT WE CAN ALL DO TO

SAVE AMERICA'S FUTURE

BEN CARSON, MD,

WITH CANDY CARSON

SENTINEL

SENTINEL
An imprint of Penguin Random House LLC
375 Hudson Street
New York, New York 10014
penguin.com

First published in the United States of America by Sentinel 2014
This paperback edition with a new preface published 2015

ISBN 978-1-59523-112-3 (hc.)
ISBN 978-1-59523-122-2 (pbk.)

Printed in the United States of America
1   3   5   7   9   10   8   6   4   2

Set in Garamond MT Std
Designed by Alissa Rose Theodor

Dedicated to the millions of Americans who fought, sacrificed, and died to provide freedom and prosperity for us and our progeny.

CONTENTS

■

CONTENTS

PREFACE TO THE
PAPERBACK EDITION

I wrote *One Nation* to address what each citizen of our great country can do to save America's future. In early 2015, I delivered an address expanding on the themes of my book and touching on issues of national security that I had not included in it. I hope that the following words, taken from that important speech, awaken you to the dire state of our nation and encourage you to read on.

—Ben Carson, May 2015

It seems like every year we're getting closer and closer to some very critical moments for our country. It also seems that we're moving closer to a real crisis in our national leadership, and just thinking about the failures of the Obama administration is depressing. I think that's why liberals are ready for Hillary, and I think that's why the Left loves to re-label and rename things

these days. For instance, if you're pro-life, then you're anti-woman. If you're pro–traditional family, then you're a homophobe. If you're white and you oppose a progressive black person, you're a racist. If you're black and you oppose a progressive agenda, you're crazy. And if you're black and you oppose a progressive agenda and are pro-life and pro-family, they don't even know what to call you. I mean, you end up on some watchlist for extremists.

The real extremists are not sensible citizens looking out for their country. The real extremists are literally looking to destroy our country, and our current leadership is ignoring the threat. Our commander in chief and his staff must recognize the threat of militant Islamic terrorism. And let's not get distracted by assuming that the threat is just from ISIS or other organizations that are not connected with any state governments, such as Al Qaeda and Boko Haram. We need to recognize that the Shia leadership of Iran is every bit as dangerous—and perhaps more dangerous—to the world as ISIS, Al Qaeda, or Boko Haram. We cannot take our eye off the ball as Iran continues to develop nuclear weapons. I'm not ready for us to ignore Benjamin Netanyahu while Iran works to develop the Bomb.

What am I ready for? I'm not ready for Hillary, but I am ready for a country that puts our Constitution first—every part of it. And for those who have any doubts, that includes the Second Amendment. I'm ready for a country where we pay our way as we go, and we stop creating huge amounts of debt for future generations to have to pay off. I'm ready for a country where we take the restraints off the most dynamic economy the world has ever known and allow that economic engine to actually work for us. I'm ready for a country where we develop our natural

energy resources. We have been blessed with them; let's not make that a curse. It doesn't mean we can't look for alternatives and take care of the environment. Some people think it's one or the other, but it's not. That's why God gave us our amazing brains—so we can do more than one thing at one time.

I'm ready to see leadership on the world stage, not just politicians sitting around and waiting to see what other people do and then reacting to it. I'm ready for leadership in our nation that acts and doesn't only react. I'm ready for school choice. We need to recognize that education is the great liberator in our country—no one needs to be a victim. I'm ready for putting healthcare in our hands and not in the hands of some bureaucrat. I'm ready for a balanced budget and for a fair taxation system that allows us to get rid of the IRS. I'm ready for a strong military and for taking care of our veterans the way they should be cared for. I'm ready for honesty and integrity and common sense and courage, because courage is what we really need. Freedom is not free—we must fight for it. We live in the land of the free and the home of the brave, but we cannot be free if we're not brave. And being brave is something we ALL can do to help save America's future!

INTRODUCTION

——

THE 2013 NATIONAL PRAYER BREAKFAST

I was totally shocked when in the fall of 2012 my office received a call inquiring whether I would be willing to give the keynote address for the 2013 National Prayer Breakfast. I had already had the pleasure and honor of being the keynote speaker for the 1997 National Prayer Breakfast when President Clinton was in office. That speech was well received, even by President Clinton, despite my pointed comments about integrity in public office. "I just want to know who is responsible for putting this guy on before me," he quipped when he came to the podium after my talk. The audience roared with laughter and he went on to give his usual very good speech. The event had gone as well as it could have, but I didn't give a second thought as to whether I'd be asked again.

Stunned by the request, I asked if anyone had ever done it twice and I was informed that only one person fit into that category and that was Billy Graham. I prayed about it and felt that there was a reason why I was being asked for a repeat performance. I talked by telephone and in person with members of the National Prayer Breakfast staff and they informed me that many senators thought that I was the right person not only to

encourage people but also to help bring a sense of unity back to our nation's capital. I was honored to accept the challenge and immediately begin praying for the necessary wisdom and words to gently address the spiritual, financial, and moral decline of America, a difficult task in the highly partisan atmosphere that exists in Washington, DC, today.

The event organizers were obviously familiar with many of my public speeches in which I had taken no prisoners. I call it as I see it without dancing around a topic in order to spare everyone's feelings. They were therefore somewhat concerned that I might say something that would offend the president. I indicated that I had no intention of offending anyone, the president included. Nevertheless, the organizers were still quite interested in receiving a copy of my transcript just to be on the safe side. I informed them that the 1997 National Prayer Breakfast committee had also wanted a copy of my notes but because I don't speak from a transcript, I wasn't able to provide them with a copy at that time either.

The breakfast was held at the Washington Hilton in the District of Columbia. The predictable protocols were shared by security and the Secret Service the evening before the event. And in the morning, I had the opportunity to chat with other participants in the Green Room over breakfast appetizers. I recalled that the menu in 1997 was considerably more varied and robust, and thinking that the fact that the selections were meager was a good thing since the federal budget is under a lot of pressure. I also remember the affability of the president and first lady in the 1997 receiving line. They were both very gracious and easy to talk to. This year, President and Mrs. Obama were not present in the Green Room, so there really was no opportunity to meet them or chat beforehand. However, there

were many well-known dignitaries in the platform party there. Once we were on stage, I was seated on one side of the podium between Vice President Biden and Senator Schumer of New York, while the president was seated on the other side of the lectern between his wife and Senator Sessions of Alabama.

Before my speech, Bible readings and inspirational comments were made by a variety of people. I was introduced, followed by very generous applause, and began my speech by reading several Bible verses that seemed particularly applicable to the leadership in Washington, DC, today. The text of the speech follows:

Thank you so much. Mr. President, Mr. Vice President, Mrs. Obama, and distinguished guests ... which includes everybody. Thank you so much for this wonderful honor to be at this stage again. I was here 16 years ago, and the fact that they invited me back means that I didn't offend too many people, so that was great.

I want to start by reading four texts which will put into context what I'm going to say.

Proverbs 11:9: Evil words destroy one's friends; wise discernment rescues the godly.

Proverbs 11:12: It is foolish to belittle a neighbor; a person with good sense remains silent.

Proverbs 11:25: The generous prosper and are satisfied; those who refresh others will themselves be refreshed.

2 Chronicles 7:14: Then if my people who are called by my name will humble themselves and pray and seek my face and turn from their wicked ways, I will hear from heaven and will forgive their sins and heal their land.

You know, I have an opportunity to speak in a lot of venues. This is my fourth speech this week. And I have an opportunity to talk to a lot of people. And I've been asking people what concerns you? What are you most concerned about in terms of the spirituality and the direction of our nation and our world? I've talked to very prominent Democrats ... very prominent Republicans. And I was surprised by the uniformity of their answers. And those (answers) have informed my comments this morning.

Now, it's not my intention to offend anyone. I have discovered, however, in recent years that it's very difficult to speak to a large group of people these days and not offend someone. People walk around with their feelings on their shoulders waiting for you to say something. "Ah, did you hear that?" and they can't hear anything else you say. The PC police are out in force at all times. I remember once I was talking to a group about the difference between a human brain and a dog's brain, and a man got offended. He said, "You can't talk about dogs like that!" People just focus in on that ... completely miss the point of what you're saying. And we've reached the point where people are afraid to actually talk about what they want to say because somebody might be offended. People are afraid to say "Merry Christmas" at Christmastime. Doesn't matter whether the person you're talking to is Jewish or, you know, whether they're any religion. That's a salutation, a greeting of goodwill. We've got to get over this sensitivity. You know it keeps people from saying what they really believe.

You know, I'm reminded of a very successful young businessman. And he loved to buy his mother these exotic gifts

for Mother's Day. [One year] he ran out of ideas, and then he ran across these birds. These birds were cool, you know? They cost $5,000 apiece. They could dance, they could sing, they could talk! He was so excited, he bought two of them. Sent them to his mother, couldn't wait to call her up on Mother's Day, "Mother, Mother, what'd you think of those birds?" And she said, "They was good." [laughter] He said, "No, no, no! Mother, you didn't eat those birds? Those birds cost $5,000 apiece! They could dance, they could sing, they could talk!" And she said, "Well, they should have said something." [laughter] And, you know, that's where we'll end up, too, if we don't speak up for what we believe. [laughter] And, you know, what we need to do—[applause]what we need to do in this PC world is forget about unanimity of speech and unanimity of thought, and we need to concentrate on being respectful to those people with whom we disagree.

And that's when I think we begin to make real progress. And one last thing about political correctness, which I think is a horrible thing, by the way. I'm very, very compassionate, and I'm not ever out to offend anyone. But PC is dangerous. Because you see, in this country, one of the founding principles was freedom of thought and freedom of expression. And it muffles people. It puts a muzzle on them. And at the same time, keeps people from discussing important issues while the fabric of this society is being changed. And we cannot fall for that trick. And what we need to do is start talking about things ... talking about things that are important. Things that were important in the development of our nation.

One of those things was education. I'm very passionate

about education because it made such a big difference in my life. But here we are at a time in the world—the information age, the age of technology—and yet 30% of people who enter high school in this country do not graduate. 44% of people who start a four-year college program do not finish it in four years. What is that about? Think back to a darker time in our history. Two hundred years ago when slavery was going on it was illegal to educate a slave, particularly to teach them to read. Why do you think that was? Because when you educate a man, you liberate a man. And there I was as a youngster placing myself in the same situation that a horrible institution did because I wasn't taking advantage of the education. I was a horrible student. Most of my classmates thought I was the stupidest person in the world. They called me "Dummy." I was the butt of all the jokes.

Now, admittedly, it was a bad environment. Single-parent home . . . you know my mother and father had gotten divorced early on. My mother got married when she was 13. She was one of 24 children. Had a horrible life. Discovered that her husband was a bigamist, had another family. And she only had a third-grade education. She had to take care of us. Dire poverty. I had a horrible temper and poor self-esteem. All the things that you think would preclude success. But I had something very important. I had a mother who believed in me. And I had a mother who would never allow herself to be a victim no matter what happened . . . never made excuses, and she never accepted an excuse from us. And if we ever came up with an excuse, she always said, "Do you have a brain?" And if the answer was yes, then she said, "Then you could have thought your way out of it." It

doesn't matter what John or Susan or Mary or anybody else did or said. And it was the most important thing she did for my brother and myself. Because if you don't accept excuses, pretty soon people stop giving them, and they start looking for solutions. And that is a critical issue when it comes to success.

Well, you know, we did live in dire poverty. And one of the things that I hated was poverty. You know, some people hate spiders, some people hate snakes . . . I hated poverty. I couldn't stand it. [laughter] But, you know, my mother couldn't stand the fact that we were doing poorly in school. And she prayed and she asked God to give her wisdom . . . what could she do to get her young sons to understand the importance of developing their minds, so that they could control their own lives? And you know what, God gave her the wisdom . . . at least in her opinion. My brother and I didn't think it was that wise. Because it was to turn off the TV, let us watch only two or three TV programs during the week, and with all that spare time read two books apiece from the Detroit Public Libraries and submit to her written book reports which she couldn't read, but we didn't know that. She'd put check marks and highlights and stuff—but, you know I just hated this. And my friends were out having a good time. Her friends would criticize her. They would say, "You can't make boys stay in the house reading books, they'll grow up and they'll hate you." And I would overhear them and say, "Mother, you know they're right." But she didn't care, you know.

But, after a while, I actually began to enjoy reading those books, because we were very poor. But between the covers

of those books I could go anywhere, I could be anybody, I could do anything. I began to read about people of great accomplishment. And as I read those stories, I began to see a connecting thread. I began to see that the person who has the most to do with you and what happens to you in life, is you. You make decisions. You decide how much energy you want to put behind that decision. And I came to understand that I had control of my own destiny. And at that point I didn't hate poverty anymore, because I knew it was only temporary. I knew I could change that. It was incredibly liberating for me, made all the difference.

To continue on that theme of education, in 1831 Alexis de Tocqueville came to America to study this country. The Europeans were fascinated. How could a fledgling nation, barely 50 years old already be competing with them on virtually every level? This was impossible. De Tocqueville was going to sort it out. He looked at our government and he was duly impressed by the three branches of government—four now because now we have special interest groups, but it was only three back in those days. He said, "WOW, this is really something," and then he said, "but let me look at their educational system," and he was blown away. You see, anybody who had finished the second grade was completely literate. He could find a mountain man on the outskirts of society who could read the newspaper and could have a political discussion . . . could tell him how the government worked.

If you really want to be impressed, take a look at the chapter on education in my latest book, *America the Beautiful*, which I wrote with my wife—it came out last year, and in that education chapter you will see questions extracted from

a sixth-grade exit exam from the 1800s—a test you had to pass to get your sixth-grade certificate. I doubt most college graduates today could pass that test. We have dumbed things down to that level. And the reason that is so dangerous is because the people who founded this nation said that our system of government was designed for a well-informed and educated populace. And when they become less informed, they become vulnerable. Think about that . . . our system of government. That is why education is so vitally important.

Now some people say, "Ahhh, you're overblowing it, things aren't that bad, and you're a doctor, a neurosurgeon. Why are you concerned about these things?" Got news for you. FIVE doctors signed the Declaration of Independence. Doctors were involved in the framing of the Constitution, the Bill of Rights . . . a whole bunch of things. It's only been in recent decades that we've extracted ourselves, which I think is a big mistake.

We need doctors, we need scientists, engineers. We need all those people involved in government, not just lawyers. I don't have anything against lawyers, but you know, here's the thing about lawyers . . . I'm sorry, but I got to be truthful . . . got to be truthful—what do lawyers learn in law school? To win . . . by hook or by crook . . . you've got to win. So you got all these Democrat lawyers, and you got all these Republican lawyers and their sides want to win. We need to get rid of that. What we need to start thinking about is, how do we solve problems?

Now, before I get shot, let me finish. I don't like to bring up problems without coming up with solutions. My wife and I started the Carson Scholars Fund 16 years ago after we

heard about an international survey looking at the ability of eighth graders in 22 countries to solve math and science problems, and we came out number 21 out of 22. We only barely beat out number 22 . . . very concerning.

We'd go to these schools and we'd see all these trophies: All-State Basketball, All-State Wrestling, All-State this, that, and the other. The quarterback was the big man on campus. What about the intellectual superstar? What did they get? A National Honor Society pin? A pat on the head, "There, there little nerd?" Nobody cared about them. And is it any wonder that sometimes the smart kids try to hide? They don't want anybody to know that they are smart? This is not helping us as a nation. So we started giving out scholarships from all backgrounds for superior academic performance and demonstration of humanitarian qualities. Unless you cared about other people, it didn't matter how smart you were. We've got plenty of people like that. We don't need those. We need smart people who care about other people.

We would give them money. The money would go into a trust. They would get interest on it. When they would go to college they would get the money. But also the school gets a trophy, every bit as impressive as any sports trophy—and it goes right out there with the others. They get a medal. They get to go to a banquet. We try to put them on the same kind of pedestal as we do the all-state athletes. Now I have nothing against athletics or entertainment, please believe me. I'm from Baltimore. The Ravens won. This is great—okay. But—but what will maintain our position in the world? The ability to shoot a 25-foot jump shot or the ability to solve a quadratic equation? We need to put the things into proper perspective.

Many teachers have told us that when we put a Carson Scholar in their classroom, the GPA of the whole class goes up over the next year. It's been very gratifying. We started 16 years ago with 25 scholarships in Maryland, now we've given out more than 5,000 and we are in all 50 states. But we've also put in reading rooms. These are fascinating places that no little kid could possibly pass up. And uh, they get points for the amount of time they spend in there reading, and the number of books they read. They can trade the points for prizes. In the beginning they do it for the prizes, but it doesn't take long before their academic performance begins to improve.

And we particularly target Title I schools where the kids come from homes with no books and they go to schools with no libraries. Those are the ones who drop out. We need to truncate that process early on because we can't afford to waste any of those young people. You know, for every one of those people that we keep from going down that path, that path of self-destruction and mediocrity, that's one less person you have to protect yourself and your family from. One less person you have to pay for in the penal or the welfare system. One more taxpaying productive member of society who may invent a new energy source or come up with a cure for cancer. They are all important to us and we need every single one of them. It makes a difference. And when you go home tonight, read about it, Carson Scholars Fund, carson scholars.org.

But why is it so important that we educate our people? Because we don't want to go down the same pathway as many other pinnacle nations that have preceded us. I think

particularly about ancient Rome. Very powerful. Nobody could even challenge them militarily. But what happened to them? They destroyed themselves from within . . . moral decay, fiscal irresponsibility . . . they destroyed themselves. If you don't think that can happen to America, you get out your books and you start reading.

But you know, we can fix it. Why can we fix it? Because we're smart. We have some of the most intellectually gifted people leading our nation. All we need to do is remember what our real responsibilities are so that we can solve the problems.

I think about these problems all the time. And you know, my role model was Jesus. And He used parables to help people understand things. And one of our big problems right now (and like I said, I'm not politically correct, so I'm sorry), but you know—our deficit is a big problem. Think about it. And our national debt—$16 and 1/2 trillion dollars—you think that's not a lot of money? I'll tell you what! Count one number per second, which you can't even do because once you get to a thousand it will take you longer than a second, but . . . one number per second. You know how long it would take you to count to 16 trillion? 507,000 years—more than a half a million years to get there. We have to deal with this.

Here's the parable: A family falls on hard times. Dad loses his job or is demoted . . . gets part-time work. He has 5 children. He comes to the 5 children, he says, "We're going to have to reduce your allowance." Well, they're not happy about it but . . . he says, ". . . except for John and Susan. They're . . . they're special. They get to keep their allowance.

In fact, we'll give them more." How do you think that's going to go down? Not too well. Same thing happens. Enough said.

What about our taxation system? So complex there is no one who can possibly comply with every jot and tittle of our tax system. If I wanted to get you, I could get you on a tax issue. That doesn't make any sense. What we need to do is come up with something that is simple.

And when I pick up my Bible, you know what I see? I see the fairest individual in the Universe: God. And He's given us a system. It's called tithe. Now we don't necessarily have to pay 10% but it's the principle. He didn't say, "If your crops fail, don't give me any tithes." He didn't say, "If you have a bumper crop, give me triple tithes." So there must be something inherently fair about proportionality. You make $10 billion dollars you put in a billion. You make $10 you put in $1. Of course, you've got to get rid of the loopholes. But now some people say, "Well that's not fair because it doesn't hurt the guy who made $10 billion dollars as much as the guy who made $10." Where does it say you have to hurt the guy? He's just put a billion dollars in the pot. We don't need to hurt him.

It's that kind of thinking . . . it's that kind of thinking that has resulted in 602 banks in the Cayman Islands. That money needs to be back here, building our infrastructure and creating jobs. And we're smart enough . . . we're smart enough to figure out how to do that.

We've already started down the path to solving one of the other big problems: health care. We need to have good health care for everybody. It's the most important thing that a person can have. Money means nothing, titles mean nothing

when you don't have your health. But we've got to figure out efficient ways to do it. We spend a lot of money on health care, twice as much per capita as anybody else in the world, and yet not very efficient. What can we do?

Here's my solution. When a person is born, give him a birth certificate, an electronic medical record, and a health savings account [HSA], to which money can be contributed, pretax from the time you are born, to the time you die. When you die, you can pass it on to your family members so that when you're 85 years old and you've got 6 diseases, you're not trying to spend up everything. You're happy to pass it on and there's nobody talking about death panels. That's number one.

Also, for the people who are indigent, who don't have any money, we can make contributions to their HSA each month because we already have this huge pot of money. Instead of sending it to some bureaucracy, let's put it into HSAs. Now they have some control over their own health care and what do you think they're going to do? They're going to learn very quickly how to be responsible. When Mr. Jones gets that diabetic foot ulcer, he's not going to the emergency room and blowing a big chunk of it. He's going to go to the clinic. He learns that very quickly . . . gets the same treatment. In the emergency room they send him out. In the clinic they say, now let's get your diabetes under control so that you're not back here in three weeks with another problem. That's how we begin to solve these kinds of problems. It's much more complex than that, and I don't have time to go into it all, but we CAN do all of these things because we are smart people.

And let me begin to close here by another parable: Sea

Captain. And he's out on the sea near the area where the *Titanic* went down. And they look ahead and there's a bright light right there . . . another ship, he figures. He tells his signaler, "Signal that ship: Deviate 10 degrees to the south." Back comes the message, "No, you deviate 10 degrees to the north." Well, he's a little bit incensed, you know. He says, "Send a message, 'This is CAPTAIN Johnson. Deviate 10 degrees to the south.'" Back comes the message, "This is Ensign 4th Class Reilly. Deviate 10 degrees to the north." Now Captain Johnson is really upset. He says, "Send him a message, 'This is a naval destroyer.'" Back comes the message, "This is a lighthouse." Enough said.

Now, what about the symbol of our nation? The eagle. The bald eagle. It's an interesting story how we chose that, but a lot of people think we call it the bald eagle because it looks like it has a bald head. That's not the reason. It comes from the Old English word *piebald*, which means crowned with white. And we just shortened it to *bald*. Now, use that the next time you see somebody who thinks they know everything. You'll get 'em on that one.

But, why is that eagle able to fly . . . high . . . forward? Because it has two wings: a left wing and a right wing. Enough said.

And I want to close with this story: Two hundred years ago this nation was involved in a war, the War of 1812. The British, who are now our good friends, thought that we were young whippersnappers. It was time for us to become a colony again. They were winning that war . . . marching up the eastern seaboard, destroying city after city. Destroyed Washington, DC, burned down the White House. Next stop . . .

Baltimore. As they came into the Chesapeake Bay, that armada of ships . . . war ships as far as the eye could see. It was looking grim. Fort McHenry standing right there. General Armistead, who was in charge of Fort McHenry, had a large American flag commissioned to fly in front of the fort. The admiral in charge of the British fleet was offended, and said "Take that flag down. You have until dusk to take that flag down. If you don't take it down, we will reduce you to ashes."

There was a young amateur poet on board by the name of Francis Scott Key, sent by President Madison to try to obtain the release of an American physician who was being held captive. He overheard the British plans. They were not going to let him off the ship. He mourned. As dusk approached he mourned for his fledgling young nation, and as the sun fell, the bombardment started. Bombs bursting in air . . . missiles . . . so much debris. He strained, trying to see, was the flag still there? Couldn't see a thing. All night long it continued. At the crack of dawn he ran out to the banister. He looked, straining his eyes, but all he could see was dust and debris.

And then there was a clearing and he beheld the most beautiful sight he had ever seen . . . the torn and tattered Stars and Stripes still waving. And many historians say that was the turning point in the War of 1812. We went on to win that war and to retain our freedom. And if you had gone onto the grounds of Fort McHenry that day, you would have seen at the base of that flag, the bodies . . . of soldiers who took turns propping up that flag! They would not let that flag go down because they believed in what that flag symbolized. And what did it symbolize? One nation, under God, [ap-

plause] indivisible, with liberty and justice for all. Thank you. God Bless.

Many have commented that the president appeared to be uncomfortable during my speech, but I was not paying particular attention to him or his reactions, as my comments were really directed more at the American people than the people on the dais. At the conclusion of the program, the president approached me to shake my hand and thank me for my participation. He did not appear to be hostile or angry, but within a matter of minutes after the conclusion of the program, I received a call from some of the prayer breakfast organizers saying that the White House was upset and requesting that I call the president and apologize for offending him. I said that I did not think that he was offended and that I didn't think that such a call was warranted.

Although I thought the speech was good—the audience response was overwhelming, I had no idea that it would go viral and that literally millions of people would be talking about it over the next few days. This reaction was a reflection of the fact that the American people are excited to know that they are not the only ones who value common sense. People are also excited when they see one of their fellow citizens unintimidated by political correctness and unafraid to express his opinions.

The conservative news outlets were very excited about the talk and in fact the *Wall Street Journal* penned an article entitled, "Ben Carson for President." Requests for my appearance on television and radio exploded and there was and continues to be much speculation about my political future. Over the years, there have been many attempts to get me to throw my hat into

the political arena. I have been offered support from around the country and tremendous financial resources if I decide to run for national office. But I have not felt called to run. I suspect that there are many others who think logically and are interested in a political future who might be better candidates than myself. Nevertheless, if I felt called by God to officially enter the world of politics, I certainly would not hesitate to do so.

However, at the moment, I believe the more important thing that can be done with the platform I have been given is to try to convince the American populace that we are not one another's enemies even if a (D) is by some of our names and an (R) by the names of others. Knowing that the future of my grandchildren and everyone else's is put in jeopardy by a continuation of reckless spending, godless government, and mean-spirited attempts to silence critics leaves me with little choice but to continue to expound on the principles outlined in my prayer breakfast speech and to fight for a bright future for America.

SAVING OUR FUTURE

Godliness exalts a nation, but sin is a disgrace to any people.

PROVERBS 14:34

Several years ago I took a trip to Alaska, and my hosts offered to send me on an excursion in their private plane to see the glaciers in the area. I was extremely excited and eagerly accepted the offer. I was less excited when I saw the single-engine prop plane that would be used by the pilot. He assured me that he had flown this mission many times and that the plane was very safe, so we headed out.

As the plane took off, I marveled at the beautiful scenery. As we flew over the mountaintop and dropped into the valley, it almost seemed as if we were on another planet. The glaciers were awe inspiring and I quietly thanked God for the opportunity to view these natural wonders.

As I was enjoying the sights, heavy cloud cover descended on the valley severely obscuring our view. The small plane was not equipped for instrument-only flight, so the pilot announced that we were going to climb through the clouds as rapidly as we

could without going into a stall, and that we should clear the mountaintops that surrounded us. He spoke calmly, but I could detect the uncertainty in his voice. Deeply concerned, I entered into prayer and reminded myself that God is in charge even when we are in grave danger.

After several intense minutes of upward flight, there was a break in the clouds and we cleared the mountain peaks by just a few feet. Relieved, I thanked the pilot for his quick and decisive action that saved our lives. I was never so happy to be on the ground as when we landed at the small airstrip.

Our nation is in trouble today, and our only chance is to take quick and decisive action the way the pilot did in Alaska. Shrugging and hoping that something good would happen was not a viable choice for us as our plane hurtled toward the mountain, and it is not a wise choice for us today. Doing everything we could while beseeching the mercies of God paid big dividends in the Alaskan sky, and prayerful action could make all the difference in the problems America faces now.

Many Americans argue that our nation's future does not need to be saved and that we are in very good shape. They think that only partisans are skeptical about our future and that people say negative things in order to make the current administration look bad. They see the beautiful view that is America, but they don't have the common sense and wisdom to look for the lowering clouds that obscure the mountains.

It is true that we are enjoying the benefits of the system set up by our founders, and we are relatively quite comfortable because previous generations have made good choices. Nevertheless, the fog has been gathering for years, and we must act

quickly and decisively to deal with substantial issues if we don't want to destroy our children's future.

A quick glance at a newspaper should be enough to perceive the warning signs. As far as education is concerned, we have made a lot of progress in being politically correct, but very little progress in basic education, particularly in areas like math and science. The secular progressive movement completely denies any moral backsliding and feels that we have made substantial progress as a nation with respect to great moral issues like abortion, gay marriage, and helping the poor, but in reality we are losing our moral compass and are caught up in elitism and bigotry. On top of that, our national debt and the passage of Obamacare are threatening the financial future of our nation. Worst of all, we seem to have lost our ability to discuss important issues respectfully and courteously and cannot come together enough to begin to solve our problems.

We each need to take an active role in changing the course of our nation if we are to live up to the motto "one nation under God, indivisible, with liberty and justice for all." We are the pinnacle nation in the world right now, but if the examples of Egypt, Greece, Rome, and Great Britain teach us anything, it is that pinnacle nations are not guaranteed their place forever. If we fail to rediscover the basic principles of common sense, manners, and morality, we will go the same way they did. Fortunately, our downward pathway is not an inexorable one. It is not too late to learn from the mistakes of those who preceded us and take the kinds of corrective action that will ensure a promising future for those who come after us.

Communities, political parties, business organizations, the

news media, educational institutions, and the government can all work to turn our nation around, but the most important changes will be made by you and me, the American individuals. Each of us can control only our own behavior, but if we all take action individually, our actions will collectively have a significant impact on the direction of our nation. As individuals, we can educate ourselves and our children, cultivate the art of compromise, pray for wisdom, and hold our representatives accountable. Each of us can positively affect our nation just by making ourselves (and those in our spheres of influence) aware of the fact that we are being used as pawns by those who try to tell us what we should think as opposed to using our own common sense.

As an example of cloudy thinking that threatens common sense, consider the recent furor over voter ID cards. I travel to many nations of the world, and recently I've taken it upon myself to ask citizens of those other countries how they prevent voter fraud. I have yet to find a nation that does not require some type of official voter identification card or mechanism to ensure that the voter is who they say they are. This is basic common sense, yet some members of our society who have co-opted the media have convinced ordinary Americans that there is some type of discrimination going on when we require the same thing of those voting in our country. This would not even be an issue if political groups weren't trying to curry favor with certain groups of voters. Instead of being whipped into a frenzy over a nonissue, it is my hope and prayer that individual Americans will educate themselves on this issue, seek to understand one another's values, allow common sense to prevail, and reject those who try to politicize almost everything to their own advantage.

When I was a child, there was a common saying: "Sticks and stones may break my bones but names will never hurt me." I'm not sure that children today have ever heard that expression and certainly the adults don't seem to know it any longer. Special interest groups tell our country's citizens that they should be easily offended by simple words or suggestions. By taking umbrage so readily, people shift the discussion from the subject matter to the person making the comment, which is a desirable thing to do only if you don't have a good argument. This is also a good way to keep people at one another's throats constantly so they can't form a united front and deal logically with the many real issues facing the nation. Individually, Americans need to choose to be the bigger person, overlook offense, and be willing to have candid discussions about volatile issues.

There have been many stories recently about the bullying epidemic that seems to be occurring in our public school system. We should not be terribly surprised by this because children emulate what they see adults doing. One does not have to look at television for very long or listen to the radio for an extended period before one sees supposedly rational and mature adults vehemently attacking one another, calling each other names and acting like third graders. I have grown used to dealing with people who resort to name-calling at the drop of a hat by saying, "Now that you have had an opportunity to engage in a gratuitous attack, is it possible for us to return to the subject matter at hand?" I refuse to engage in the grade-schoolyard tactics of name-calling and mean-spirited comments when we have so many important issues to solve. We can help our nation quite a bit if we refrain from getting into our respective corners and throwing hand grenades at each other, and instead try to

understand the other's viewpoint, reject the stifling of political correctness, and engage in intelligent civil discussion.

A suitably thick skin, common sense, and manners are of limited use without education. I'm always fascinated by some of the "man on the street" episodes on *The Tonight Show with Jay Leno* or *Watters' World* on Fox, where Jay or Jesse asks people for very basic information regarding the significance of a particular day or some historical event and many of them have no clue about the right answer. Our nation's founders felt very strongly that our system of government could only survive with a well-informed and educated populace. They understood that if the populace reached the point of not being able to critically analyze information, it would easily fall prey to slick politicians and unethical news media. All citizens need to arm themselves with a basic knowledge of American history and stay abreast of current events, analyzing them with respect to history. Knowledge is power and at a time when the people are becoming increasingly impotent while the government grows larger and more powerful, it is vital that we arm ourselves with knowledge.

Finally, each of us must have courage. I have encountered countless thousands of Americans, as I've traveled around the country recently giving speeches, who resonate very strongly with the concepts that I'm putting forward but who have been beaten down. They have mistaken the false unity of political correctness and submission for the true unity that comes with liberty, justice, and responsibility. This unity doesn't succeed without some conflict, but it is far healthier than silence and is worth the fight. I've been spreading the word that we must have enough backbone to stand up to the secular progressives who insist on fundamentally changing America into something that

we would not recognize as our hard-won government of, by, and for the people. Because there are consequences for standing up for your beliefs in the current distorted version of America, one has to be very courageous when standing up to malicious influences or even while engaging in healthy dialogue with our neighbors about important issues.

The bottom line is that our country is in the process of undergoing fundamental radical changes while rapidly moving away from the "can-do" attitude that made us the most prosperous and beneficent superpower the world has ever known. If each of us sits back and expects someone to take action, it will soon be too late. But as of today, it is still not too late to join the battle to save our nation and pass on to our children and grandchildren something we can all be proud of.

PART ONE

—

CAUSES OF DISUNITY
AND DECLINE

POLITICAL CORRECTNESS

Those who love to talk will experience the consequences, for the tongue can kill or nourish life.

PROVERBS 18:21

When I was a teenager, my neighbor had a dog that appeared to be quite vicious. If anyone walked near that home, the dog would come running toward the fence, barking and snarling, sending the passerby rapidly along his way. His ferociousness actually changed the behavior of people in the neighborhood, who began to avoid walking down the alley when the dog was outside.

Feeling that the dog should not be ruining the neighborhood, I began reading books about dogs and their behavior to see what I could do. I discovered that dogs tend to react to the reaction of the human or other animal it is trying to frighten— if the person they bark at shows fear, the dog decides its antics are effective. If the person shows no fear, the dog will give up.

It took a lot of courage, but I decided to repeatedly walk by the fence and completely ignore the dog. It took about a month before the dog realized that I would not react, but eventually he

stopped trying to frighten me and would simply lie down quietly as I walked by.

Today's political correctness operates in the same way as that dog. Self-appointed political correctness police (PCP) have set up speech guidelines that go far beyond the requirements of kindness, good manners, education, and tact. They forbid the use of the word *slavery* by conservatives, the mention of Nazism by conservatives, or the mention of homosexuality in anything other than a positive context, to name a few of their rules. Going even further, they continually grow their list of terms they believe are offensive, tripping up innocent people with their increasingly strict speech code. By bludgeoning people who violate these rules, the PCP establish a chilling control over the speech of a nation that was founded on the principles of freedom of speech. Intent on managing the national conversation, they mock and belittle anyone who violates their tenets of speech or behavior with such ferocity that few people will dare trespass their boundaries. For example, a few years ago, Lawrence Summers, then president of Harvard, mentioned that men and women might be wired differently. His comments drew a fierce attack from the PCP that may well have influenced his decision to resign his position.

I had my own run-in with the PCP when I said that I thought Obamacare was the worst thing in our country since slavery. My point was that we the American people were turning over to the government control of our most precious resource—our health. The implications of such a shift of power (where we have no choice but to purchase the only prescribed product—Obamacare), are profound in a society that is supposed to be free and centered around freedom of choice. Once we give the

government this kind of power, it is naïve to believe that it will stop here in its quest for total control of our lives. The PCP wanted to immediately divert the argument away from this fundamental truth, so they said I thought Obamacare was an evil equal to slavery, when I was merely pointing out that this particular attempt at health care reform takes us the first step away from liberty.

Many well-meaning Americans have bought into the PC speech code, thinking that by being extra careful not to offend anyone we will achieve unity. What they fail to realize is that this is a false unity that prevents us from talking about important issues and is a Far Left strategy to paralyze us while they change our nation. People have been led to become so sensitive that fault can be found in almost anything anyone says because somewhere, somehow, someone will be offended by it.

To stop this, Americans need to recognize what is happening, speak up courageously, avoid fearful or angry responses, and ignore the barking and snarling as we put political correctness to bed forever. This is the reason why I choose to continue speaking out despite the many efforts of the secular progressives to discredit and silence me. It is also the reason why I continue to encourage Americans to stand up for the freedoms that were hard-won and must be preserved if we are to remain a free society.

Political Correctness Stifles Dialogue

Open discussions of political and social issues are key to healthy unity. Society works very much like a marriage in the sense that open communication facilitates harmony. In almost all marriages that end in divorce, there is a serious breakdown in com-

munication, followed by false assumptions and outright warfare. One of the first things a marriage counselor does is get the warring parties to sit down and open up to each other. Two people may perceive the same event very differently, and gaining an understanding of the other person's perspective can be the first step to healing a broken marriage. If fear or anger prevents either person from expressing his or her perspective, there is no hope for the relationship.

In our country today, we act much like those warring spouses who want nothing more than to get rid of each other. Political correctness has thrown a veil of silence over our important discussions. Rather than asking those with whom we disagree to clearly state their case, we set up rules of political correctness that mandate that their perspective must be the same as ours. We then demonize those with whom we disagree and as a result fail to reach any consensus that might solve our problems.

The only people who can resolve this problem are "we the people." We do not have to yield to pop culture, Hollywood, politicians, and the media who are the primary enforcers of political correctness. We need to simply ignore the "barking" and act like mature adults who can tolerate hearing something about which we disagree and still remain civil and open-minded.

Who Benefits from Hypersensitivity?

While most people buying into the PC code are well meaning and just want to get along with everyone, the ones who bark and snarl the most are those on the Far Left who cultivate political correctness in order to forward their own agendas. In his famous book, *Rules for Radicals*, Saul Alinsky, an activist and orga-

nizer of the Far Left, makes it clear that leftists trying to effect change are to have no conversations with their opponents, because open discussion could lend credence to their opponents' arguments and humanize them in the sight of the public. He argued that activists must demonize their opponents and get the larger society to recognize the activists as the ones who will deliver society from the demons. As Alinsky suggests, cultivating hypersensitivity to perceived slights by conservatives is a convenient way to halt important conversations and to demonize opponents.

Unfortunately, hypersensitivity is not limited to those on the Left. Conservative politicians have also adopted the strategy of feigned offense. The Right tends to be hypersensitive about blaming Bush for economic problems and the double standard of the media. Even though these problems are real, hypersensitive conservatives sometimes see bias where it doesn't exist, defend Bush when they don't need to, or even shut down a discussion because of a perceived slight.

While we all have a tendency to say "See, they did it too!" in order to justify wrongdoing, we must start focusing on what is right or wrong and not on what someone else did. It is imperative that each of us, whatever side we are on, begins to act like adults who can find real solutions instead of pointing the finger at others or running away crying because someone disagreed with us.

It's Not All About You

When talking about hypersensitivity in our society, it is important to distinguish between those who are truly sensitive to com-

ments and those instigators and manipulators with feigned sensitivity and outrage. To the first group I would say it's time to grow up and start thinking about what you can do to contribute to society's well-being instead of choosing to be a victim of speech that is sometimes intentionally cruel and at other times completely innocent. The best way not to be easily injured by others' speech is to step out of the center of the circle so everything is not about you. By thinking about others and looking at things from other people's perspectives, there is much less time to feel that someone is picking on you or your interests.

In a previous book, I mentioned that when I was an intern at Johns Hopkins back in 1977, the sight of a black physician was decidedly rare. Often when I would go onto a hospital ward while wearing my surgical scrubs, a nurse would say, "I'm sorry, but Mr. Patient is not quite ready to be taken to the operating room yet," assuming that I was an orderly. After many years of hard work to achieve the title of doctor, many might say that I would have been justified in reacting angrily to the suggestion that I was an orderly, especially given the racial overtones of the misunderstanding. However, I tried to look at things from the nurse's perspective. The only black males she had seen come onto that ward wearing surgical scrubs were orderlies who were coming to pick up or deliver a patient. Why would she think differently in my case? A highly sensitive individual would have created a scene and everyone would have felt uncomfortable. I would simply say in those situations, "I'm sorry that Mr. Patient isn't ready yet, but I'm Dr. Carson and I'm here for another reason."

The offending nurse would often be so embarrassed that I actually felt sorry for her or him and would say, "It's quite all right and you don't need to feel bad." I would be very nice to

that person, and I would have another friend for life. That was a whole lot better than having someone who would always feel ashamed, embarrassed, or hostile when they saw me.

Some might say that by allowing ignorant slights or insults to go, I capitulated to the racism of the day, but that's not the case. Instead, by realizing that the nurse's statement really wasn't a reflection of careful judgment about me, I was able to remain calm and gently correct the offender. I guarantee you that both the nurse's mistake and my response reduced the lingering effects of racism in her mind just as well, if not better, than an angry outburst on my part would have.

Political correctness aside, people do say ignorant, insensitive, and even malicious things. However, most of our public fights over racism, sexism, and every other "ism" could be easily resolved if the injured party expected the best of the offender and corrected the offensive statement in a kind and rational manner. We all have choices in the way we react to the words we hear. Our lives and the lives of all those around us will be significantly improved if we choose to react positively rather than negatively.

Faux Hypersensitivity

To the second group of hypersensitives, those who are feigning hurt to make a point, I would say you need to decide where your priorities are. Are you interested in the unity and our nation's well-being or is it more important for you to further a political agenda that is not consistent with the founding principles of unity in this country? Political correctness and hypersensitivity block discussion of important social issues while

they are being changed—exactly the time when it is most important to discuss them.

An excellent example of how these people work occurred about a month after the National Prayer Breakfast when on national television I was asked about my opinion regarding gay marriage. I immediately stated that I believe marriage is between a man and a woman and that no group has the right to change the definition of marriage to suit their needs. By way of example of groups that engaged in nontraditional sexual relationships, I mentioned NAMBLA (North American Man/Boy Love Association) and people who engage in bestiality. My point was to emphasize that marriage is a long-standing tradition and there is no necessity to change the definition now, regardless of which group wants to change it.

The secular progressives seized upon the opportunity to distort the meaning of what I said and deviate the conversation away from the definition of marriage by instead focusing on me and trying to paint me as a homophobe who thinks that gay marriage is equivalent to bestiality. Nothing could be further from the truth. I appeared both on CNN and MSNBC to explain that I didn't think that there was equivalency between the groups mentioned in my answer and to state unequivocally that I had no intention of offending anyone, but I still believe in traditional marriage. The objective media found that explanation satisfactory, but the secular progressive media continued to state that I think that gay marriage and bestiality are the same. This is a very instructive example of how they distort words and meanings, and then cling to the created lies in an attempt to destroy enemies.

Around the same time, a group of gay activists at the Johns

Hopkins School of Medicine began their mission as instigators, accusing me of being a homophobe. I was scheduled to be the commencement speaker at the Johns Hopkins School of Medicine as well as at the Johns Hopkins School of Education, but decided to withdraw because of the controversy the instigators had successfully created. After years of hard work by the students, I did not want their graduation ceremony to be about me rather than about them and their achievements.

I received several messages from students who were very disappointed that I would not be speaking at their commencement. Some even threatened to protest if I did not speak. The thing that saddened me most was the fact that many of them indicated that they were afraid to speak out because of potential repercussions from the administration. I certainly like to think that these fears were unfounded, but the fact that they exist at all is troubling. Like so many thousands of Americans I have encountered across the nation, these students had been beaten into submission by secular progressives who have no regard for such fundamental American principles as freedom of speech when that speech is not in agreement with their philosophies. Political correctness has effectively removed their point of view, as well as their rights, from the debate.

Prior to my decision to withdraw as commencement speaker, I spoke to some prominent members of the gay community at Johns Hopkins. In doing so I found out two important things: First, bestiality is particularly abhorrent in the gay community and the mention of it evokes a very emotional response. Had I known that, I would have avoided the topic, since the last thing I wanted to do was to cause unnecessary offense and distract from the matters at hand.

Second, I asked if there was any position a person could take that did not include approval of gay marriage that would be acceptable to the gay community. After some consideration, I was told that there really was no other acceptable position. This explains why there was such a ferocious attack on my comments—there really was no argument that could have been made that would not have drawn an emotional response instead of a rational argument.

Responding to the PC Police

Not only is it important for Americans to communicate about difficult issues, but the method and tone of communication are also very important. Abrasive and reactionary speech can be at least as bad as silence, feeding right into the hands of the PCP. Saul Alinsky advised his followers to level sharp attacks against their opponents with the goal of goading them into rash counterattacks that would then discredit them. To avoid falling into this trap, those of us who are interested in civil discussion should prepare ourselves to refrain from reacting in fear or anger to those who disagree with us or even attack us.

I frequently remind my attackers that our greater purpose is to engage in intelligent conversation and solve problems. Most who disagree with me are good, intelligent people who also want to solve problems in a reasonable manner. As for those who are not so well intentioned, it is very difficult for them to continue attacking someone who is calm and reasonable. They usually realize fairly quickly that they are the ones who look like fools if they refuse to engage in problem solving.

It is particularly important when dealing with adversaries to

know what points you want to make while remaining focused. This makes constant interruptions, attacks, and attempts to change the subject more difficult. If you are an effective representative of American values, the secular progressives will make every attempt to destroy your character by exposing any mistakes, misstatements, or misdeeds from your past. Naturally, there are no perfect people, present company included, which makes the threats of exposure extremely potent. If a misdeed from your past is exploited, it is best to admit to it, condemn it, and ask, "What more do you want?"

Sometimes I am asked, "How do you maintain your cool when faced with ridiculous claims and statements by your opponents?" There was a time when I was a hothead, and my temper wreaked havoc in my life until I learned to take myself out of the center of the circle. The real key to staying cool and calm is to relinquish selfishness and always consider the feelings of others. When someone is being particularly mean and nasty, I simply think to myself, *He or she used to be a cute little baby, I wonder what happened?* Thinking about that question will soften your attitude and lessen the likelihood of an inflammatory confrontation.

As we discussed earlier in this book, offense and sensitivity are frequently feigned for the purpose of garnering sympathy and further reinforcing the validity of political correctness. However, two can play that game. When the offended party proclaims the injury you have wrought upon them with your words, say something to the effect of: "I can see that you were deeply hurt by my choice of words. It was not my intention to hurt you and for that I am sorry. Now I would like for you to know what I intended to communicate to you and I will use

different words that will hopefully convey the spirit of my thoughts and allow our discussion to continue." If the offended party was truly offended, that will be a sufficient statement, but if they were only pretending to be offended, they will continue to harp on their perceived mistreatment. This exercise is useful because it helps you learn what you are dealing with. If it is just a misunderstanding, frequently the conflict can be alleviated by this kind of open communication.

True Wounds

Sometimes a true wound can be so deep that it clouds the thoughts of the injured party to the point that they can no longer be objective. In such cases, continued explanations tend to result in diminishing returns or even exacerbations of the misunderstanding. I vividly remember the case of a disabled woman whom I greatly admire because she adopted many children with disabilities that were even greater than hers. Many of her children had complex neurosurgical problems that engaged my skills for many hours at a time. After caring for her many children over the years, one of them experienced a shunt malfunction that caused rapid accumulation of pressure in the head due to the spinal fluid's inability to escape. I rushed into the hospital in the middle of the night, even being stopped by the police for speeding. We operated on the child and repaired the shunt, but unfortunately the child suffered some brain damage and was never quite the same again. Despite explanations and a long-term relationship, I never saw that mother or any of her children again. I believe the emotional trauma was understandably more than

she could handle. Sometimes you just have to realize that you cannot heal all wounds no matter how hard you try.

In today's political scene, some people are so traumatized by perceived past injustices that they cannot conceive of any good thing that a group member who they believe has been unfair to them can do. They tend to demonize these individuals for past wrongs perpetrated by others and there is no changing their minds. It is important for the demonized group to understand this mentality and patiently attempt to undo the damage that has resulted in such attitudes. Both Republicans and Democrats can benefit from this advice.

Our Heritage of Free Speech

Whether by creating hypersensitivity or drawing angry reactions, Alinsky's organizers' goal is to make the societal majority feel that their opinion is the minority opinion and that the organizers' opinion is the majority opinion. The ability to co-opt the mainstream media in this endeavor is a gigantic coup. If the majority of people who are rational, reasonable, and full of common sense feel that their opinions are out of sync with everyone else, it is easy to shut them up and beat them into submission. This is what has occurred in America today. Hopefully by bringing this to light, more people will see the necessity of seizing the banner of bravery just like Nathan Hale, Patrick Henry, and many others in the past who stood up to tyranny.

Why was freedom of speech so important to our nation's founders? Many had come from countries like England where verbally opposing the king frequently resulted in a jail sentence or even death. The founders also felt that the free exchange of

ideas would result in better government and would prevent government from becoming too big and self-important. These are the very reasons we must once again insist on freedom of speech and expression, and we should be repulsed by the very idea of political correctness that muzzles the populace. Our government does not directly jail dissenters, but it can do so indirectly by expecting the IRS to harass those who oppose its policies. This should be something that completely outrages every American who understands the hard-fought freedoms of our nation, but many have been lulled to sleep by the gradual increase of political correctness and have yet to notice that our fundamental freedoms are in jeopardy.

It is tempting to simply acknowledge the corrosive effects of political correctness on freedom of speech and say that we will deal with this at some point in the future. The problem with that line of thinking is that the future may not arrive before catastrophic events intervene.

If we are to survive as a united nation, we must learn how to engage in civil discussion of our differences without becoming bitter enemies. We cannot fall for the Saul Alinsky trick of not having a conversation while trying to demonize each other. Let's talk about the tough issues without scrutinizing every word and castigating anyone who dares to violate the PC rules. There is nothing wrong with disagreement—in fact, if two people agree about everything, one of them isn't necessary. I believe we are all necessary so let's toss out the hypersensitivity and roll up our sleeves and start working together to solve our problems. If each of us is willing to extend the benefit of the doubt or overlook verbal missteps, political correctness will become impotent.

Action Steps

1. Try to identify one instance of artificial outrage. Explain to one other person why this is a contrived issue and outline the way it agitates people and cultivates political support for the agitators.
2. Readily apologize to a person who is offended by something you said. Explain what you had hoped to convey.
3. Attempt to politely disagree with someone who makes a political statement with which you disagree. (Be sure that you choose an appropriate setting.) Engage in a civil discussion of the matter.
4. Read Saul Alinsky's *Rules for Radicals* to get an idea of how the political correctness police work.

ELITISM

Pride goes before destruction, and haughtiness before a fall.

PROVERBS 16:18

Coming from inner-city Detroit and going to Yale University represented an astronomical change in my surroundings and life. One of my freshman roommates had a twin brother matriculating at Princeton and a father who was a prominent physician. The other roommate was from a business family. They all seemed very rich to me, being the son of a divorced mother with less education than the maids who cleaned their houses. But my roommates' wealth and status was minor compared with some of the really rich kids on campus. Many were from very well-known families and traveled around with an entourage of sycophants and admirers. It was not unusual to see parents visiting campus in Rolls-Royces and limousines when I was a freshman and a sophomore. I was surrounded by elites.

But the way the elites presented themselves was changing. By the end of my sophomore year, the campus was already

starting to become radicalized. The Black Panthers were idolized, and the most admired people on campus dressed like hippies and flower children. Marijuana and acid rock had become fashionable, and outward shows of affluence were frowned upon. Elitism on campus, which had previously been defined by wealth, was now defined by identification with the downtrodden people in society and a determination to use one's superior education and compassion to help them. As this generation of elites grew up, they began to occupy positions of importance in society, becoming college professors and administrators, national television producers, business managers, and politicians. Even though many still enjoyed the fruits of economic prosperity, they continued to identify with those people they considered to be oppressed by the system.

The makeup of today's elite class is psychologically and sociologically more complex than what I have just presented, but its development in the Ivy Leagues of the 1960s can explain the dichotomy between what the wealthy members of this class say and what they do. For the most part, they are incapable of seeing any hypocrisy in their own lives while examining with a microscope every facet of their perceived opponents' lives. They are very happy to give away other people's money, but guard their own purse strings possessively. The sad thing is that they have become so wise in their own eyes that they have lost objectivity, thus frequently rendering themselves quite useless when it comes to truly improving the lot of the downtrodden in our society.

Do the Elite Really Know Better Than the Rest of Us?

This arrogance is the chief characteristic of the elites I am concerned about. Wealth, education, and influence are all well and good, but when they lull those who hold them into a state of self-satisfaction where they are convinced of their own perfect wisdom and virtue and shield them from life's realities, we have a problem. Today's elites constantly talk about hubris in their opponents but seem unaware of their own lack of humility. They are thoroughly convinced that they are intellectually superior to those people who believe in God, creation, and the Bible, and many use positions of authority at colleges and universities to strictly enforce "open-mindedness" by pillorying any student or colleague who dares question their ideological rantings. The elite class also exists in the mainstream media where elite journalists try to be objective but simply cannot escape the influence of so many years of social propaganda. I believe that in their heart of hearts elites see themselves as society's savior, but they are blinded by pride to the results of their actions.

Not all elites are blinded by what they are doing. Very recently I was speaking to a major producer of a major left-wing television network who admitted that the electronic media today is a major propaganda tool used to manipulate society. We have never had this kind of access to the minds of the people and no one really knows the extent to which public opinion can be controlled. Most frightening, these secular progressive elites, as well as some right-leaning elites in the media, are willing to push the limits in order to see just how effective they can be with the imposition of their will upon the people.

Not all media personalities fit this characterization. Perhaps the greatest television journalist of all time, Walter Cronkite, was decidedly left wing in his political outlook, but was so professional in his reporting that most people were unaware of this. Unless the other elites can ever see the possibility of a flaw in their belief systems or are willing to be objective in their reporting, they are largely unreachable and have little intersection with common sense.

Politically, elitism knows no single party. Establishing policies that create dependency, like easy food stamps and subsidized health care for families making in excess of $80,000 per year, seems to stroke the egos of both Republican and Democrat elites who believe they are God's gift to mankind. However, if they examine the long-term consequences of what they are doing, some may begin to understand that true compassion warrants the investment of intellectual capital into finding ways that people can be elevated and imbued with the can-do attitude.

The Elite Oppression of Minority Communities

In order for elitism to flourish, there has to be another class of people who are willing to acknowledge the superiority of the chosen ones. Elites cultivate this obeisance by providing goodies to the less fortunate ones. In our society today, those goodies consist of multiple kinds of entitlement programs. As the dependency on these programs grows, the position of the elite class is solidified because they will always be seen as the providers who need to be protected from any threats of power redistribution. The elitists constantly find ways to proclaim their goodness and

their necessity for the well-being of the "oppressed," while at the same time declaring how evil their opponents are, and how those evil people would utterly destroy any hope of a reasonable life for the oppressed if they were to gain power.

The truth is, the liberal policies of the elite class have done little to improve the lot of those who depend so much on them. In America's black communities, where the goodies have been flowing for decades, rather than seeing improvements in terms of upward mobility, we are seeing deteriorating family structure, increases in violent crimes, growing poverty, and growing dependence. Even with such a blatant record of failure, there is slavish devotion to the elite class who continue to promise more goodies in exchange for votes.

Black leaders like Booker T. Washington, George Washington Carver, and Dr. Martin Luther King, Jr., among others, were great proponents of self-reliance and self-help. I believe they would have been horrified to see the condition of the black community in America today despite their efforts to bring true economic liberation to this important group of Americans. Many of the elites from both parties embrace these men as heroes but propose social policies that do not encourage self-reliance; policies these men would never have approved. Based on their policies, I believe that they subconsciously think that some people are not capable of helping themselves.

Most of the elite are not humble enough to accept these kinds of criticisms and make changes. I guess that is why they are considered elite. Since we can't expect them to change, it's up to the rest of us to do all that we can to help those dependent on the elites to get on their feet. The elite class can't last long without the votes of these communities.

Escaping Subservience

One of the most important ways the African American community in particular can end its dependence on the elites is to lower the number of out-of wedlock births. As a result of the number of black babies born out of wedlock in recent years, there is a gigantic economic hole from which many in the community will have to. climb out of to achieve the American Dream. That ascension needs to start immediately by teaching young women the importance of self-respect and the consequences of single motherhood—usually the end of the mother's educational endeavors, limiting her economic success and often condemning her child to poverty. (A 2013 article in *US News and World Report* by Steven Nelson titled "Census Bureau Links Poverty with Out-of-Wedlock Births" examines this phenomenon, which has been corroborated by many other journalistic sources.) At the same time, we need to provide affordable child care to enable single mothers to further their schooling and prepare for an increasingly technologically sophisticated world. We also have to demonstrate to these mothers that men are not going to disappear or be afraid of them after they obtain advanced education. This is a total myth and if anything, advanced education increases the opportunity to meet someone with similar accomplishments and goals. We must do everything we can to convince these young ladies that they are priceless and can make great contributions to all of mankind. When these valuable citizens gain appropriate self-esteem, they will avoid many careless mistakes and think more independently, weakening the hold the elites have on them.

Young black women aren't the only people needing to be

freed from the elites. A quarter of the young men in the black community are involved with the criminal justice system, which in many cases compromises their job prospects for the future. Worse than that is the fact that many end up being violently killed or taken off the streets by incarceration for long periods of time. In either case, tremendous intellectual talent is being wasted by a society that can ill afford such losses. Rather than imitating the elite and trying to make these young men feel like victims of discrimination or racism, we must look for ways to empower and help them realize their tremendous value to society.

Both the men and women in these communities need to be educated about basic economics and wealth creation. One of the reasons the Jewish, Korean, Vietnamese, and other communities have been able to thrive in the United States is that they have learned how to turn over the dollar in their own communities two or three times before sending it out into the larger community. By patronizing the constituents of their own neighborhoods, they allow local merchants and businesspeople to thrive, which not only provides jobs for others in the community but also gives them an opportunity to invest and grow their businesses. The more they grow, the more opportunities they are able to provide to those around them. I have a friend who started his own business as a young black man and has subsequently retired as a multimillionaire, and at least two other African American–owned businesses were started by others who got their initial breaks from him. Economic prosperity for one can mushroom into opportunities for many when greed and vice are not involved. Furthermore, this kind of thinking provides economic independence, and economic independence promotes ideological freedom, rather than creating voting blocs

that can be taken for granted. If politicians have to compete for support, they will have to show results, which will be a big win for the black community.

Although understanding economic principles of wealth development is very important to oppressed communities and will go a long way toward liberating them from the influence of the elite class, even more important is education. When Frederick Douglass was a slave, the master's wife began teaching him to read after recognizing his exceptional intellectual gifts. When the master found out about this he was angry and instructed his wife to desist immediately, because he felt that education would light the fires of desire for freedom. He was absolutely right in this assessment, so Frederick Douglass went on to find other ways of educating himself. As a consequence, he was not only able to obtain his own freedom but played a vital role in the abolition of slavery as well as in the women's suffrage movement in the United States. He also lived in Europe and wielded significant influence there; many feel that his involvement and notoriety profoundly affected the decision of the British not to support the Confederacy during the Civil War.

During the fifties and sixties many people of all nationalities sacrificed life, limb, and physical freedom to win basic rights for blacks in America. Those rights included educational pursuits. During slavery, reconstruction, Jim Crow, and beyond, many blacks would have sacrificed almost anything for an opportunity to be educated. Sometimes, particularly when traveling north with their masters, slaves were able to witness how articulate and sometimes prosperous free, educated blacks were. They began to equate education with freedom. Even as a child growing up in Detroit and Boston, almost all of the adults in

our neighborhood emphasized the importance of education and how it would allow me to go far beyond anything they had achieved. Today, even though those educational doors are no longer blocked, many of the people who sacrificed to open those doors would be disappointed to see the indifference with which many of the younger generation treat education.

It is time in America to empower the people through education, sound economic policies, and the return of honest and responsible media reporting. This will be no small undertaking, because the intellectually elite class will not relinquish their stranglehold without a fight. We must be encouraged by the fact that this is the United States of America: a place for, of, and by the people . . . and there is no place for elitism in our country.

Action Steps

1. Identify a member of an elite class and ask the person how he or she would recommend that you assist those stuck in poverty.
2. If you are a member of the elite class, ask yourself honestly what you have personally done in the last year to help lift someone from poverty.
3. Read and think about 2 Chronicles 7:14.
4. If you are offended by the previous suggestion, ask yourself why.

4

IGNORANCE AND FORGETFULNESS

Throw out the mocker, and fighting, quarrels, and insults
will disappear. Anyone who loves a pure heart and gracious
speech is the king's friend. The Lord preserves knowledge,
but he ruins the plans of the deceitful.

PROVERBS 22:10-12

When I was a student at Southwestern High School in inner-
city Detroit in the mid-to-late sixties, I was far from popular. By
that time my lackluster academic performance during the early
years had completely reversed and I was a quintessential nerd. I
even carried a slide rule in a holster on my belt and belonged to
the Chess Club. I grew quite accustomed to being ridiculed for
not being "cool," but I was generally left alone because of my
accomplishments in ROTC and because I was friends with
some of the really tough guys, since I helped them with their
school assignments.

When my wife and I attended my twenty-fifth Southwestern
High School class reunion in 1994, I was astonished to see that

so many of the really cool guys were now deceased, but I was even more amazed at the number of my former classmates who came up to me and said, "We are so proud of you and we tell our children and grandchildren about you all the time, and don't you remember how we used to encourage you when you were a student at Southwestern?" Of course I was polite, but I certainly didn't remember many encouraging words and in fact I vividly remember just the opposite.

It is natural to want to identify with success and distance oneself from failure and embarrassment and to avoid difficulty. This is why people undergo memory alterations as time passes and why we selectively forget painful knowledge. In medicine it is particularly important not to do this because people's lives could needlessly be put at risk by failure to accurately remember lessons of the past. I explicitly remember the case of an achondroplastic child (dwarfism) who I determined was in need of a highly specialized type of surgery to alleviate pressure on the brain stem. I wrote a letter and spoke to the gatekeeper at the insurance company to no avail. Because they wanted to save money, the insurance company determined that their in-network pediatric neurosurgeon could do the job. They were wrong and ended up paying twice, because I had to do corrective surgery. If they had heeded the medical knowledge that had summarized past lessons about this condition and its treatment, including the need for significant experience and a team approach, needless trauma and expense could have been avoided. Instead, they ignored key facts, willfully ignoring information that would have benefited a child's health and their bottom line.

Ignorance, whether it takes the form of revisionism or laziness, can hurt our nation too. If we don't know our true national history, we won't be able to recognize the way in which America is drifting. If we don't have enough basic information to manage our lives, we will give up our freedoms to those who promise to take care of us. It is time for us to stand up and educate ourselves and our children before we allow misinformation and ignorance to destroy our democratic republic.

Historical Revisionism

People frequently rewrite history to increase self-esteem and to clear their consciences of guilt for historical misdeeds. Historical revision can also go the other way, as historians attempt to discredit figures from the past. Early American history has been rewritten many times in both ways, to suit the beliefs of historians with different educational and philosophical agendas. For this reason, I rarely accept a single account of any historical event. Fortunately one can quickly get a sense of the truth by examining accounts from several different trusted sources.

There seems to be general consensus around the fact that the founders of this nation were men of great vision and intellect. They thoroughly studied the many civilizations that preceded us to try to determine the common pitfalls inherent in establishing a new government. With hard work, a lot of arguing, and finally an ecumenical prayer to God, they were able to put together a sixteen-and-one-third-page document known as the Constitution of the United States of America,

one of the most admired governmental documents in history. This document encapsulated their vision of a nation where the freedom of the people to pursue their dreams was of paramount importance. It created a government that existed for the purpose of protecting the people from foreign invaders, protecting their assets and property, and facilitating their pursuit of happiness. The Constitution mandated minimal government interference in the everyday lives of the average citizen and arranged for the federal government to remain small, allowing state governments to be responsible for most of the legislation.

Our founders were deathly afraid that our government would do the same thing that virtually all other governments had done previously: expand continually, developing a voracious appetite for the resources of the people. They also feared that as the government expanded it would encroach upon the rights of the citizens. Finally, they were petrified that people would be complacent as the government expanded and would gradually relinquish their rights for a false sense of security. These great men wrote the Constitution the way they did to prevent the worst of their fears from coming true, creating a great and noble framework for virtuous government.

Some historical revisionists have denigrated the efforts of these great men and emphasized the fact that many of them were slaveholders or had some other flaw commonly seen in the culture at that time. The same historians also highlight our cruelty to the Japanese during World War II where we used hideous internment camps and detonated the only nuclear weapon against fellow human beings in history. They shine a bright

light on the history of racism that was rampant throughout America, especially before the crusades of Dr. Martin Luther King Jr., and they repeatedly remind us of the atrocities witnessed during the Vietnam War, which we lost. By emphasizing these things and other wrongdoings, revisionists attempt to paint the United States as an opportunistic, uncaring, and savage nation in dire need of change.

There is no question that the United States, like every other nation, has made mistakes. However, what should be emphasized is that we are the first pinnacle nation of the world to wield such enormous power without brutally dominating other nations. We have helped rebuild nations ravaged by wars in which we took part and we have refused to confiscate oil, minerals, and other treasures found in nations we have helped or defeated. I believe it is fair to say that we are the most benign superpower the world has ever known. Furthermore, it is important that we maintain our pinnacle status, because if we lose it, we will be replaced by another world power that is unlikely to be nearly as benign.

In America, we have a proud history of accomplishment and of helping to save the world from tyranny. Our military is second to none and our technological achievements have transformed the world. We have moved from a nearly apartheid state to a multicultural society with enormous potential and strength that can be significantly enhanced by the kind of leadership that emphasizes a vision that unites everyone as opposed to exploiting differences to advance political causes.

If most of the people in the country believe that America is generally fair and decent, it becomes more difficult for Saul Alinsky types to recruit change agents and for those on the

Far Left to undermine our Constitution. Hence the constant bad-mouthing of our nation to impressionable young people, preparing them to be ripe for manipulation at the appropriate time. In the recent past, the Occupy Wall Street movement, which was replicated in many parts of the country, shows how easily physically destructive actions that compromise the rights and property of others can be incited in those who have been educated this way and also have an entitlement mentality.

Forgetting Our Christian Heritage

Some historical revisionists have also attempted to diminish the role of God and religion in our nation's past. A careful examination of the records, however, makes it quite clear that religion was a very important factor in the development of our nation. In 1831 when Alexis de Tocqueville came to America to try to unravel the secrets to the success of a fledgling nation that was already competing with the powers of Europe on virtually every level, he discovered that we had a fantastic public educational system that rendered anyone who had finished the second grade completely literate. He was more astonished to discover that the Bible was an important tool used to teach moral principles in our public schools. No particular religious denomination was revered, but rather commonly accepted biblical truths became the backbone of our social structure. Our founders did not believe that our society could thrive without this kind of moral social structure. In fact, it was our second president, John Adams, who said of our thoroughly researched and developed governing document, "Our Constitution was made only for a

moral and religious people. It is wholly inadequate to the government of any other."

Adams's quote makes it clear that the founders did not want to extract God from our lives, but rather intended for his principles to be a central feature of our society. What they wanted to avoid was a theocracy-like state where the church dominated public policy or where the government dictated religious practice. That was the whole point of the separation clause of the First Amendment. The secular progressives have zoomed past the intent of the law and tried to replace it with their anti-God propaganda reinforced by bullying tactics. If Americans fail to educate themselves in American history, the revisionists will win this fight.

And right now it looks like they are winning. The secular progressive movement in America has been successful in removing all vestiges of faith in God from the public square. The very fact that people hesitate to say "Merry Christmas" to strangers lets you know just how successful they have been. Why are they so determined to remove God from our lives? They recognize that if we have no higher authority to answer to than man, we become gods unto ourselves and get to determine our own behavior. In their world, "If it feels good, do it." They can justify anything based on their ideology because in their opinion, there is no higher authority other than themselves to overrule them. They have a visceral reaction to the mention of God's word, because it tears at the fabric of their justification system.

Forgetting Dr. Martin Luther King Jr.'s Advice

The left wing secular progressives love to invoke the name of Dr. Martin Luther King Jr., but only in their historical revision would his views be compatible with theirs. The last thing he would have wanted to see was the culture of dependency that has developed among the very people he fought so hard to free. A strong opponent of godless ideology, Dr. King also rejected the idea that human beings are not responsible for their actions, arguing, "One of the most common tendencies of human nature is that of placing responsibility on some external agency for sins we have committed or mistakes we have made."

Later in the same speech, Dr. King spoke of several Americans who rose from less than optimal circumstances of heredity and environment to become successful and greatly admired individuals. Helen Keller, who was blind and deaf from infancy, was able to overcome these hereditary traits to become one of the most admired people in the world! Franklin D. Roosevelt had infantile paralysis, but rose to become president of the United States. Marian Anderson was born in poverty in Philadelphia, but developed her voice to the point where she became one of the world's greatest contraltos. Italian composer Toscanini was said to have commented that a voice like hers comes only once in a century! King continued in the speech by citing Jesus Christ as the best example of one who overcame nonoptimal circumstances. His parents were not of high social standing or people of wealth . . . not aristocrats or belonging to any prestigious groups.

Dr. King concluded: "Not environment, not heredity, but personal response is the final determining factor in our lives. And herein lies our area of responsibility."

According to Dr. King, your life is what you make it. Education and career development is the responsibility of the individual, not their parents, teachers, or anyone else, though many would claim that heredity and environment can absolve people of responsibility. Although these two entities can affect one's life, the most important factor is our response to challenges that arise. If you prepare yourself academically and experientially through various work situations, you can become whatever you dream. That's the American Dream. I believe the current leadership in America's black community could learn a great deal about effective leadership by studying some of the writings and the real history of Dr. King.

Ignorance: The Reason History Repeats Itself

Historical revisionists don't need to put in any effort if no one cares about history in the first place. Many people find history boring and think that pop culture is much more relevant to citizens today. There certainly is nothing wrong with being up to date on the current social issues that affect our lives, but in order to have the proper perspective on current events, we need to know what happened in the past. For example, it is much easier to understand today's unrest in the Middle East when you know about the establishment of a sovereign Israeli territory in 1948 and the intense turmoil and controversy sur-

rounding the placement of that nation in an unwelcoming environment.

And it is much easier to understand why a 7 to 8 percent unemployment rate today is much worse than a rate like that many years ago, because economists were not nearly as facile as they are currently with manipulating numbers. A good student of history would understand that the labor force participation rate is a more accurate indicator of the level of employment nationwide. That number has been steadily declining since 2009. This indicates that many people are simply giving up on working and as a result are not being counted when calculating the unemployment rate that is widely reported. However, the labor force participation rate captures these individuals and is one of the most accurate reflections of the state of employment. These are just two of many examples of the kinds of things informed citizens should know in order to properly interpret what they read in newspapers or hear on the news networks. Many pundits are all too happy to take advantage of the lack of such knowledge in order to manipulate an unsuspecting populace.

Another excellent reason to be familiar with history is to avoid repeating the same mistakes. The stock market crash of 1929 exacted a severe toll on the people of our nation and our legislators realized, in hindsight, that some of our banking and investment policies had contributed to the crash. Several laws were crafted, including the Glass-Steagall Act, which separated commercial and investment banking activities. Sixty to seventy years later we forgot about many of the horrors of those difficult financial times as well as the reasons why we

imposed appropriate regulation on speculative financial activity involving private resources. It only took about twenty years before we faced another near crash. The new regulations that had been put in place were even harsher than the ones that followed the crash of 1929. Perhaps this was an overreaction, but none of it ever had to happen again if our leaders had been more diligent in their study and understanding of history as well as their understanding of human nature, which is characterized by such traits as greed and selfishness. I am not one of those persons who thinks that no regulations are necessary on behalf of the government, but I believe careful attention to history and regular meetings with experts of differing views can provide a great deal of safety and help us avoid unnecessary pain.

We cannot ignore the socially tragic events of our past, but they can be taught in the context of learning experiences that improved our unity and vision. For instance, we were dragged, kicking and screaming, into both world wars because of our isolationist policies. Many of our allies and some of our own citizens were not happy with our reluctance to enter the fray, but we naïvely thought that we could remain neutral and even benefit financially by selling supplies and arms to anyone with money. From these experiences, we learned the importance of putting the fire out before it gets too big. We also learned that isolationist policies are not a luxury to be afforded the pinnacle nation in the world. With power comes great responsibility and the need to lead rather than simply react to volatile international situations with the potential to affect our security. This does not require our involvement with all the international conflicts in the world, but

strategic overt or covert intervention can preclude future difficulties. Even as this book is being written, massive demonstrations and horrific fighting is taking place in Egypt where ultimate control remains uncertain. We clearly don't know which side to support in the conflict and it is therefore wise to adopt a wait-and-see attitude. This is a marked contrast to the situation that occurred in Iran four years ago when the populace was rising up against an unjust government and we stood by and did nothing as the people were slaughtered by the military. If we use these occurrences as learning experiences that enhance our future international relationships, it will be worthwhile.

We live in a sophisticated world with many moving parts and it is no longer acceptable or advisable for Americans to know more about the candidates on *Dancing with the Stars* than they do about current affairs and who their representatives are. More important, we can evaluate what we hear in the news and from political candidates only if we are able to put it in the context of historical knowledge. The more we know about the great things that our nation has accomplished, the more pride and patriotism we cultivate among the citizenry.

Action Steps

1. Read some of Dr. Martin Luther King Jr.'s speeches and see if you can determine why he could be considered a conserative.
2. Determine to stay abreast of current events by reading an objective newspaper or watching an objective news broadcast daily. Avoid news sources that leave out major stories because they don't fit a political agenda.

3. Consider whether you have ever suppressed knowledge or arguments that disprove a viewpoint that you hold.

4. If you identify an area where you have revised history or selectively ignored a fact, admit it. Challenge those with whom you disagree to do the same.

BIGOTRY

It is sin to despise one's neighbors; blessed are those who help the poor.

PROVERBS 14:21

When my mother, brother, and I returned to Detroit after living in Boston for a couple of years, we moved into a multifamily dwelling in a racially mixed neighborhood. It was the early sixties, I was ten years old, and the civil rights movement was still in its adolescent stages. We lived adjacent to the railroad tracks, which served as the line of demarcation between primarily black and primarily white communities. Since our home was on the white side of the tracks, my brother and I attended Higgins Elementary School, where there were only a handful of black students, most of whom were assigned to the special education section. I was very slight in build, so I was assigned to a regular classroom even though my academic performance was abominable, because the administrators recognized that there was a lot of violence in the special education classrooms and that my size might not be conducive to long-term survival.

Racial stereotyping was common and widely accepted among both adults and children and racially charged comments were often heard.

The black kids were greatly outnumbered in our neighborhood and tended to be rather docile and submissive in order to avoid trouble. On the other side of the tracks there were a number of black gangs that tended to be quite aggressive toward one another and toward whites. There was a community center nearby on the black side of the tracks that was well equipped and attracted youngsters from both communities with its after-school activities. On most days everyone got along at the center, but whenever there was an interracial fight the spectators promptly chose sides based on race. The adult supervisors would intervene quickly, but at times the feelings were so intense that fights between black and white gangs ensued, sometimes with significant injuries.

Although I never joined one of the gangs, I knew a lot of people who were in them and was privy to the conversations of both black and white gang members. Hate speech and animosity were rampant on both sides, with an abundance of derogatory and hateful names being casually tossed about. Because of my religious upbringing and the constant preaching of my mother about God's love and the need to treat everyone equally, I never bought into the race baiting and hatred that I saw all around me. Nevertheless, I became very aware of the negative opinions and inappropriate emotional attitudes in both the black and white communities. I saw black gangs plotting against white individuals in the same way that white groups plotted against black individuals. In other words, the prejudice, hatred, and racism were not exclusive to only one group.

I can vividly remember being the only black student in my eighth-grade math class at Wilson Junior High School in Detroit. We had a substitute math teacher from one of the Slavic countries who just could not comprehend how I was able to constantly achieve the highest math scores on all the tests. She was constantly sending notes home to my mother about the miraculous achievements in my academic endeavors. I seriously doubt that she was a bad person, but she had been fully indoctrinated into the belief that blacks were intellectually inferior, so my success was a miracle in her eyes.

I also remember seeing black kids throwing rocks at Hasidic Jews simply because they dressed differently and because no one was stopping them from engaging in such racist and mean-spirited acts. In retrospect, one of the cruelest things I've ever witnessed was the taunting, teasing, and harassment of elderly people who had difficulty getting around. These are only a few examples of the latent prejudice that exists in our society.

In my experience, bigotry tends to be a product of ignorance. The more sheltered one is, the more likely one is to have negative views about someone who belongs to an unfamiliar group. Areas where bigotry is damaging the unity of American society are race, religion, gender, age, and sexual orientation. Let's look at each of these individually.

Racism

Racial bigotry is certainly much less common in America today than it was when I was growing up. Because segregation was so prevalent, there were not a lot of opportunities for members of

different races to work together and socialize together. Since whites held the most powerful and lucrative positions in society, most of them were certainly in no hurry to share those positions with others. Blacks, on the other hand, were becoming progressively more educated and therefore impatient to share the fruits of their labors. This eagerness was frequently misinterpreted by whites who coined the term *uppity* to characterize those blacks who, in their opinion, didn't "know their place." Those blacks who were very docile and cooperative were frequently rewarded with better jobs and more money, while the less subservient blacks were humiliated and disrespected.

It was common for whites to believe that blacks were dirty, unintelligent, and sexually promiscuous. These beliefs informed hiring practices and property distribution. Many of the whites in those days found ways to rationalize their unjust treatment of fellow human beings, arguing that they were not racists but rather protectors of traditional values. It wasn't unusual for some whites to say that blacks should be grateful to have been brought out of the African jungles where they faced a very meager existence. (Talk about historical revisionism and elitism, especially since the lives of blacks in Africa were complete; they had knowledge of how to live off the land, something that American whites of that time would probably have had difficulty doing if they were placed there.)

Unfortunately, blacks also harbored some false assumptions about whites. As a youngster I frequently heard that white people carried lice and that you had to be very careful when you were around them or you would get them too. It was also frequently said that whites were greedy and cruel. Obviously, none

of the things that were said about either group were true, but these kinds of bigoted notions were passed down through the generations, thereby poisoning race relations.

Though the days of legalized segregation are over, racist bigotry and prejudice still exist today, both in overt and covert ways. I can remember times when I would be walking in a white neighborhood and in short order a police car would show up, undoubtedly summoned by a concerned onlooker. Unfortunately, this and worse still happens today, as evidenced by the Trayvon Martin case. A neighborhood watchman, George Zimmerman, suspicious of the young black man who was walking through the neighborhood late at night, shot and killed Martin after an altercation. The real tragedy is that a young life was lost and another life ruined because both individuals made assumptions about the other that were probably untrue. I hope this tragedy is not useless and we can learn something about how neighborhood watchpersons should be trained by police and what types of weapons, if any, they should use. I love the idea of tasers for neighborhood guardians, because they usually are not lethal.

More subtle than assuming someone to be a criminal because of his or her race, expecting someone to vote a certain way or follow a certain philosophical line of thinking simply due to skin color is every bit as outrageous and unfair as Jim Crow laws. To facilitate dependency by giving able-bodied people handouts rather than requiring they work for pay is every bit as cruel (even if unintentionally so) as the activities practiced by racists of the past. If the guilty parties could exercise enough humility to recognize that they might actually be doing harm to those they purport to help, I'm certain that things could be

done fairly quickly and in cooperation with others of goodwill to improve the plight of millions of Americans.

Religious Bigotry

Religious bigotry is also a problem today. While we might think we only see it in the streets of Iran or Egypt, and congratulate ourselves for being extremely tolerant when it comes to religious freedom, we still need to make progress in this area. A close look at our attitudes nationally reveals a drastic need for improvement in our understanding of religious tolerance as a fundamental pillar of the American Constitution.

It is widely believed that throughout history more people have been killed in the name of religious causes than any other cause. Often religious crusaders are so certain that only they can be right, that they will stop at nothing to either convert others or eliminate them. Certainly the Islamic extremists of today feel that way, just as the Christian crusaders felt years ago. This history of intolerance by some religious adherents has understandably caused many people to shun religion and to look unfavorably upon those seen as religious.

As a Christian, I can fully understand the aversion to religious extremism and hypocritical religious propaganda put in place to create wealth and maintain positions of a very few leaders. Jesus Christ would also have an aversion to this kind of false religion. He preached love, acceptance, and forgiveness. Even though he was all-powerful, he led a humble life directed toward improving the lot of others, but the Christian movement that he started has been so distorted by some that it is sometimes hard to recognize.

If one is able to cut through all the garbage and analyze the real principles set forth by Christ, they can be distilled into two major entities: love of God and love of your neighbor. That means respecting what God has told us and being caretakers of all He has created. And it also means being respectful of every man and being fair to all people regardless of how they may differ from you. It means leaving the judging to God and not trying to impose our ideological beliefs on others. This last point is one that is particularly important for those entering the political arena and who may at some point assume power.

Whether or not one likes Christianity or any other religion is not the point, however. Our Constitutional Bill of Rights states that "Congress can make no law respecting an establishment of religion, or prohibiting the free exercise thereof." In other words, our government should not support particular denominations or religious groups, but neither should it prevent anyone from expressing their religion.

Unfortunately, our nation seems to have forgotten the latter part of that statement. The media is peppered with stories about communities or organizations demanding the removal of patriotic symbols or crosses from private property simply because such symbols are offensive to some. Recently a community in the Northeast was forced to remove a memorial to fallen soldiers because the memorial was reminiscent of a Christmas tree. In this case the bias was so great against the concept of Christmas that it trumped respect and honor for our fallen military personnel.

In the rotunda of the original Johns Hopkins Hospital is a twelve-foot statue of Jesus beckoning those in need to come to him. When that statue was first placed, several physicians and

scientists vehemently protested its presence, stating that Hopkins was a scientific institution and there was no room for religious symbols. The controversy grew so ferocious that the decision was made to remove the statue. Ironically, the protest against the removal of the statue was even more vehement and the statue was brought back and has remained in that location to this day.

As upsetting as religious bigotry is in the private sphere, it is an even more serious concern in our government. There is nothing in our Constitution that supports the banning of manger scenes or other signs of Christmas in public places, yet some have called for their removal. For example, at Palisades Park in Santa Monica, California, manger scenes had been on display every Christmas for over fifty years, but they were banned in 2012. And this type of intolerance is proliferating throughout the country.

The fact that some people want to take the words *under God* out of the "Pledge of Allegiance" and others want to remove the words *In God we trust* from our money, demonstrates the depth of misunderstanding of the First Amendment's separation clause. The spirit of religious freedom supports various kinds of religious expression, and instead of trying to restrict one group or another from celebrating their religious beliefs through symbolism, we should be encouraging free expression on behalf of every group.

Totalitarianism always starts with restrictions on the rights of others. We must avoid this at all costs. George Washington even said, "If the freedom of speech is taken away, then dumb and silent we may be led, like sheep to the slaughter."

It is appalling how far our country has strayed from the

principles of the founding fathers. In Michigan, in 2013, a high school banned its football team from praying on the field. The practice of team members opting to pray together was started when one of the students had requested that the team pray for an ill family member after a game. The ten-year-old tradition was banned because of "concern" by the family of a current team member who brought the practice to the attention of the ACLU. And in Washington, the capital of our country, our congresspeople are not allowed to say "Merry Christmas" in their mail unless they pay for the postage out of their own pockets. The Congressional Franking Committee, which reviews all mail, will not "frank" (send free of charge) any congressperson's mail that has "Merry Christmas" or any other holiday greeting in it.

These are examples of the kind of bias that ignores the rights and freedom of those who disagree with the purveyors of prejudice. The bias exists on both sides of the political spectrum as demonstrated by the horrible things the Christian Right said about Bill Clinton because of his affair with a White House intern, when in fact several Republican leaders were also engaged in extramarital adventurism. It would probably be a good thing for both sides to stay out of private issues that don't affect one's duties. Many on the Right exhibit bigotry by assuming that those who believe in the sacredness of big government programs have socialistic tendencies. This is of course not true and many people who have grown up with significant government assistance simply don't know any other way of life and are patriotic American citizens. We all need to take a deep breath and concentrate on educating the populace about true liberty and justice while respecting one another's religious—or nonreligious—beliefs. No

one's religious beliefs should have to be hidden in a truly free and open society, but if we the people do not stand up against the religious bigotry that exists right now, we may end up without any religious freedom at all.

Sexism

Sexist bigotry is another problem, despite the tremendous strides we have made toward achieving equality of the sexes in America. I can easily remember when people were shocked to see a female commercial airline pilot or executive in a large organization. Female surgeons were almost unheard of when I was a child. Today more than half of the medical students in America are female and the chiefs of surgery at many large institutions, including Johns Hopkins, are women. As was the case with blacks, once people had an opportunity to work closely with members of the opposite sex, it became readily apparent that they were just as competent as anyone else.

Nevertheless, there remain in our society people who doubt the ability of women to be good police officers, firefighters, or military combatants. They claim that women are too weak for such jobs. Anyone who is truly objective would have to admit that there are many men who are too weak for such jobs and there would be no rationale for putting such men in those positions just as there is no rationale for putting such women in those positions. On the other hand, there are many women who are stronger than most men and can easily handle these roles. We need to start evaluating people based on their abilities and not on their sex or other congenital characteristics.

Keep in mind that not all the sexist bias is directed toward one gender. In recent years, sitcoms and commercials have portrayed men, particularly fathers, as buffoons. People seem to derive great pleasure from mocking men's foolishness while extolling women's wisdom and cleverness. While they may feel that this type of sexism is fine because there was discrimination against women for so many years, this is a childish mentality. Both men and women should be treated with dignity and respect. When men and women are able to work together as equals by bringing their specific skills and talents to the table, a type of synergy develops that can be beneficial to everyone.

Ageism

Ageism is another form of bigotry today. In the early 1900s, the average age of death in America was less than fifty years. Now that mark is approaching eighty years of age. As a result, we are seeing larger numbers of elderly individuals in our society. I sometimes observe younger people acting quite impatient when they are behind an elderly individual who is moving slowly up a ramp or flight of stairs. Instead of showing disrespect, these young people need to think about the fact that they, too, one day will be relegated to the slow lane and will be appreciative of patience by others.

Younger people need to realize that the opportunities they have today exist largely because of the hard work and sacrifices of those who preceded them. Certainly we would not enjoy the kind of freedom we have today if our ancestors had not valiantly fought and defeated the axis powers of World War II. Not

only should we be thankful to the brave men who fought and died for our sakes but we should remember the millions of women who occupied the vacancies in the factories created by the military draft. From their strength and determination were created more airplanes, tanks, and mortars than anyone could have imagined, thus supplying the fuel for military victory. As a mark of respect, we should be more than happy to care for these elders who have done so much for us.

On the flip side, many older people have negative impressions of younger people and their work ethic, or their use of drugs, and their musical selections. If they stimulate their memory banks they will discover that when they were young, older people said some similar things about them. Of course we all have biases based on where we are in the stages of life. Wisdom gives the kind of perspective that allows one to appreciate others wherever they are along life's journey.

It is also important for the generation in power currently to realize that it has an obligation to the next generations, which if unfulfilled will likely create a level of animosity toward them that is unprecedented. Thomas Jefferson said it was immoral to leave debt to the next generation. He would be speechless if he were resurrected today and saw that we are leaving the next generation a $17 trillion national debt. If the next generations were paying closer attention, it is likely that they would be protesting the unbridled borrowing against their future. The stark reality is that if we don't immediately assume fiscal responsibility and adopt policies that are conducive to economic growth, an economic disaster will ensue that will affect all generations. This is another area where a little common sense will go a long way.

Homophobia

Finally, there's the issue of bigotry regarding sexual orientation. As I stated earlier, people who have differing opinions about gay marriage are likely to always exist. There has been a long and shameful history of gay bashing in America that thankfully is waning. However, this bigotry can still be seen in the assumption by many on the Right that gays should not have access to children because they are more likely to commit rape or engage in aberrant sexual indoctrination. If this is true, it should be relatively easy to prove statistically, but such proof has yet to be provided.

Unfortunately, the mantle of hatred has been taken up by the other side, which feels that hateful speech and actions toward anyone who doesn't embrace the gay agenda is justified. Obviously hatred on either side of the opinion ledger is unacceptable and should be shunned by all.

Defeating Bigotry

Unless we are able to apply both condemnation and praise equally and objectively, we will do nothing except exacerbate the social relationships that are vital to a healthy society. The problems facing America are so overwhelming that we can ill afford to expend energy on issues stimulated by bigotry of any type. Unless we are able to focus on the big-picture items, like many societies before us, we will be agents of our own destruction. I strongly believe that if we adhere to the creed "one nation, under God, indivisible with liberty and justice for all," that we can avoid the pitfalls that have so effectively disabled the pinnacle

nations that preceded us. Let us live the words, rather than just allow them to roll off our tongues without thinking.

Action Steps

1. When ready to call someone a nasty name, stop and evaluate the situation from that person's point of view.
2. Stand up for the rights of someone with whom you disagree.
3. Identify an area where you have participated in bigotry and plan two concrete actions you can take this week to remedy the situation.
4. Be aware of bigotry shown toward you and plan two concrete ways to civilly confront the bigots.

NO WINNERS IN POLITICAL FIGHTING

A troublemaker plants seeds of strife; gossip separates the best of friends.

PROVERBS 16:28

I worked as a supervisor of highway cleanup crews around the Detroit area during the summers of 1970 and 1971. Mostly from inner-city Detroit, the young men in these crews were not overly ambitious and enjoyed having a good time. At first they were always interested in knowing the minimum amount of work required of them in order to be paid. They were quite clever in devising schemes that would meet that minimum requirement without exerting excessive effort.

Since they were particularly averse to working long hours in the hot sun, I proposed a framework that would allow them to do the bulk of their work early in the morning before rising temperatures made work unpleasant. Instead of paying them by the hour, I would pay them for a full day's work when they had collected a certain amount of trash. Prior to such an offer, they

each worked independently while surreptitiously keeping an eye on how much work was being done by the others. Now they became more insistent on efficiency and the best way to quickly complete the work. They devised methods of working together, which greatly enhanced not only their efficiency but their satisfaction. Working faster and more effectively than any other crews became a badge of pride for them and they actually looked forward to their work, while at the same time establishing very cordial working relationships with one another. There were occasional days when dissension arose in the ranks and on those days there was a noticeable decline in the crew's effectiveness. If an outside force wanted to lessen the effectiveness of a crew, they would sow seeds of discord, and simply watch them grow.

The work crew mirrors the political landscape in our country. When working toward the common goal of American people's welfare, Republicans and Democrats get along relatively well. Even though they have philosophical differences they are able to work together to pass legislation that is beneficial for everyone. When special interest groups influence one side or the other, creating dissension, Congress doesn't work well at all. Unfortunately, polarizing influences—such as unions that want what they want, gay rights groups, isolationists, and others who cannot or will not consider the opinions of others—have become stronger in recent years, robbing from the pool of moderate legislators and increasing the numbers of extreme legislators. Their efforts explain why it is so difficult to come to consensus on almost anything.

"My Way or the Highway"

Washington, DC, is dysfunctional today because the primary two political parties have become opponents instead of teammates with different approaches to the same goal. In a speech not long ago, President Obama referred to the Republicans as enemies. While it was wrong of him to refer to them as such, many of the party probably see themselves as his enemies, largely because of the Affordable Care Act, the biggest governmental program in the history of the United States, which was passed without a single Republican vote in the House or the Senate. Never before has any major society-changing piece of legislation been passed in this country without bipartisan effort. During the bill's passage, I had an opportunity to speak with one of the president's senior staffers and said that this unilateral act would create an unprecedented level of dissension and rancor that could preclude cordial working relationships for an extended period of time. The response I got was "So what? That's nothing new."

This "my way or the highway" approach has resulted in disaster. Influenced by special interest groups, like some of the insurance companies that stood to benefit from the exchanges if they worked well, the Trial Lawyers Association, which supports anything that doesn't include tort reform, and many liberal universities, which blindly support anything disguised in the mantle of liberalism, Democrats tried to create a bandwagon effect to alleviate any anxiety felt by the public. But by rushing to pass the bill while they still controlled the House and Senate, the Democrats passed a program so massive that many components of it have not even been tested. As Nancy Pelosi once famously said, "We have to pass it, so we can see what's in it."

As we are finding out what's in it, more groups, including labor unions that originally supported it, are withdrawing their support. A program that was supposed to reduce costs and allow people to keep their insurance if they wanted to, is raising costs and making it impractical for people to keep their previous insurance. It is also rapidly expanding the number of part-time workers in our country because the law does not require employers to provide health care insurance for part-time workers. The result will funnel almost everybody into government health care.

Although some of the Democrats may have felt temporary joy when they passed the bill, in the long run, they destroyed harmony. The Democrats now have an albatross around their necks with Obamacare and will forever be blamed for destroying a reasonable health care system that needed improvement, but was working for 85 percent of the populace. The Republicans were shut out of the process and have been largely marginalized, and they continue to weaken themselves with internal squabbling. Everyone loses when our politicians and our people engage in this kind of political infighting.

I can remember a time when senators and congresspeople from different political parties were friends and happily worked together to help our nation prosper. In recent years politicians have capitulated to divisive forces that drive wedges into every crack and then hype the differences of opinion to force each side deep into their ideological corners, making it difficult to compromise without appearing to surrender. A prime example is the federal budget battles we seem to face annually. They have become games of brinksmanship where both parties participate in a game of chicken. The goal is not

to solve problems but rather to pin on opponents the blame for lack of progress or for a government shutdown. Those representatives who play this game rather than represent the will of their constituencies should be voted out of office regardless of their party affiliation, and should be replaced by people who understand the dangers of fiscal irresponsibility and moral decay.

Many of our politicians seem to relish their role as dividers today. It is essential to the viability of a united nation that we learn to recognize their tactics and resist. If we are fragmented, we cannot provide a united response to tyranny, and we certainly cannot get things done effectively.

Division Tactics

A favorite tactic of dividers is the demonization of their opponents. It is rare for them to engage in a rational conversation but they are eager, particularly when surrounded by people of like mind, to viciously castigate those with opposing views. Usually the questionable motive they ascribe to their victim is the very same thing they are guilty of themselves. It is sometimes tempting to get into the mud pit with them and hurl insults, but this serves to lower one to their level and accomplishes nothing. For instance, recently a prominent congresswoman stated that it was not possible to cut one penny from the federal budget, and implied that those advocating this were heartless. The sad thing is that anyone who thinks at all knows that this is not true, but they are more loyal to their party than to truth or the well-being of future generations.

Another tactic of the dividers is to hold up one of their own

as an example of someone who has been treated unjustly in some fashion, and say that this is what their opponents want to do to everyone. Last year, Democrats claimed that a Georgetown law student was poorly treated by those who did not wish to make free birth control pills available to her. Not only did they say that Republicans discriminated against her by refusing to pay for her birth control but they suggested that this refusal meant the Republicans were engaged in a "war on women." The argument had very little substance or truth but was nearly wholly focused on victimization and blame.

Demagoguery is another tool of dividers. Dividers on both sides of the aisle make sweeping and often obviously false statements about their opponents, recognizing that most people understand that this is foolishness, but a growing number don't think for themselves and blindly trust their political leaders, believing everything they say. These gullible voters believe emotionally manipulative arguments presented by strong leaders, especially when the arguments are repeated frequently and are not called into question by most of the media.

Yet another device used by the dividers is quoting their opponents out of context. The extreme media uses this technique frequently and when they are caught, they simply say "My bad" and quickly move on. All of these techniques are designed to call into question their opponent's character and set them up as enemies of the people who should be resisted on every level. It is my fervent hope and prayer that "the people" will soon awaken and recognize that they are being manipulated by real enemies—those who are constantly trying to divide us and make us believe that we are one another's enemies.

"We the People" or "They the Government"?

Over the course of time many Americans have forgotten that "we the people" are actually at the top of the food chain as far as authority is concerned in this nation. The Republicans don't run our nation. The Democrats don't run our nation. We do. However, by dividing and engaging in political squabbles, we have allowed the government to grow so large and powerful that it has now become the boss, progressively taking charge of all of our lives. It has reached the size where it is incredibly dangerous for one half of the dividers to take control, since they can then wreak havoc on the lives of those who oppose them.

For example, the IRS targeted Tea Party organizations for intense scrutiny and unfair treatment. To add insult to injury, the head of the IRS pleaded the Fifth Amendment rather than answer questions about her involvement in the scandal. Other government officials have said they had adequately investigated the problem and were sure no one in the government's executive branch knew anything about the decision to persecute American citizens. However, congressional testimony has subsequently revealed that the offending agents did receive instructions from higher-ups in Washington.

What can we do about this type of situation? In times like this, the people must understand their power and their responsibility. This means getting together in groups like early citizens of this country did, discussing the problems and working together to put pressure on their elected representatives to use all available legal avenues to flush out the truth and punish the culprits. If illegal actions by dividers are just allowed to fade away with little or no consequences, we can be guaranteed to

have repeat performances and significant exacerbations of this kind of abuse.

In the 2012 presidential election, tens of millions of Americans did not vote even though they were eligible to do so. I have had an opportunity to talk to thousands of such people who have become so discouraged and disillusioned by the bickering of their representatives that they have simply given up on our nation and its promise to be centered on the people. I encourage those people to fight rather than give up, but this should be a fight for unity, not for a party. If Americans simply choose to vote for the person who has a *D* or an *R* by their name, we will get what we deserve, which is what we have now.

I would love it if party labels were not allowed on ballots and people were forced to actually know who they were voting for. Blind loyalty to a party platform is tantamount to relinquishing the important duties of intelligent voting. Leaders of both parties want to have voters who will blindly follow them and not even consider what's being said by their opponents. This was not the intention of the multiparty system. Rather it was to make sure that different sides of the issues were carefully examined, allowing the average citizen to then make an intelligent choice. I believe that it would be beneficial to the future of our nation to find ways to increase the likelihood that voters would actually know about the person for whom they are voting, rather than their party affiliation.

Strength in Unity

In 1968 I was a diehard Detroit Tigers baseball fan. I listened to almost every game and could tell you quite a bit about each of

the players. That year the Tigers won the American League pennant for the first time in thirty-seven years, which resulted in great unity across racial and socioeconomic barriers throughout the city. Even more remarkable was the team spirit that created almost miraculous comebacks in what appeared to be impossible situations. Every night there was a different hero and the esprit de corps was magical. The World Series was played against the St. Louis Cardinals, who amassed a three-games-to-one lead. Although things looked grim for the Tigers, no one in Detroit was willing to give up on them, because of the incredible comebacks they had witnessed all season long. Because of that unity and belief in one another, and the backing of the fans, the team won the last three games, taking the World Series crown in seven games. Anyone who does not believe in the power of unity certainly did not experience the 1968 Detroit Tigers.

That same kind of unity is possible among the people of our nation with the right kind of leadership. But we the people must for ourselves determine that we will be indivisible regardless of the leadership, and we must exercise our ability to identify the divisive forces and vote them out of office.

If we are to put an end to division, people from all political persuasions will have to stop fighting one another and seek true unity, not just a consensus that benefits one party. Right now, some of the Democrats say, "We all want to help people," but their next sentence is about how Republicans want people to die. One Democratic representative famously said, "The Republican health plan is for people to die quickly." Republicans, on the other hand, often talk about how Democrats want to change America into a socialist country. They may not intend

to sow seeds of discord but the constant spewing of hatred is having a deleterious effect on the unity of the nation. The America haters and extremists may not be that concerned about the well-being of the country, but reasonable people from both political parties must be able to see the big picture and not fall into the traps set by those who wish to divide and conquer. We must be able to sit down and engage in civil discussion without casting aspersions on others.

Action Steps

1. Pretend that you are in a different political party from yours and that you must give a rational defense of something you currently strongly disagree with that the other party embraces.
2. Ask the people who spend the most time around you to let you know if and when you are being intolerant.
3. Determine to study at least two alternatives to the Affordable Care Act.
4. Invite friends and neighbors over for a civil political discussion.

7

ENSLAVING OUR CHILDREN— DON'T SELL THE FUTURE

Good people leave an inheritance to their grandchildren, but the sinner's wealth passes to the godly.

PROVERBS 13:22

I have a lot of very wealthy friends and have watched with interest over the years how they raised their children. One family I knew always provided their several children with the best of everything including limousine drivers and top-of-the-line clothing. There was always an abundance of maids, gardeners, and other people to care for personal needs. Unforeseen circumstances abruptly ended their life of luxury and no significant inheritance was left for the children. If they had lived a slightly less extravagant lifestyle and put away a small fraction of their enormous income each month, the tragic event would not have had such a profound effect on their lives. Living large and disregarding the future was a major mistake for this family, and it continues to be a predominant issue for today's families from all socioeconomic groups.

Unfortunately today in America, many parents appear to be more concerned about their own lifestyles than the financial landscape they are leaving behind for those who will follow us. Our national debt, which is the accumulation of annual federal budget deficits, is now approaching $17 trillion with a trajectory that could take us well beyond $20 trillion within the next few years. These astronomical numbers represent new financial landmines unlike anything we have encountered previously. We do not know what the result of this kind of debt will be, but it can't possibly be good!

Debt Leads to Disaster

There are recent examples of what happens to nations that continue to accumulate debt without regard to its consequences. Like ancient Rome, modern Greece continued to expand the dole for all citizens while increasing taxes on businesses and doing nothing to foster the economy's growth. As it became clear to lending nations that this pattern was continuing with no imposition of fiscal responsibility, they became less willing to make additional loans to the Greek government, precipitating a crisis. As the Greek government worked to cut down on spending, Greek citizens rioted in the streets to protest austerity measures that decreased the monies they felt they were entitled to receive from the government.

It is hard to believe that our leaders in both political parties do not understand that they are jeopardizing the financial future of the next generations by allowing continued debt accumulation, even if they are slowing the rise of that debt. The government recently announced it will pay down our debt by

$35 billion in the next quarter. This sounds good, but that equals about 0.02 percent of the total amount owed. They will probably pat themselves on the back and proclaim what a great job they are doing while at the same time borrowing even more during the next quarter rather than continuing the downward trend in borrowing.

Our Ballooning Debt

Here are some interesting facts of the last few years, demonstrating how exponentially the problem is increasing: In 2007 the United States federal debt was 64 percent of the gross domestic product (GDP). By 2012, the federal debt had risen to 103 percent of GDP. It is still growing, although admittedly at a slower pace. The implementation of Obamacare and the progressive aging of the populace at large will do nothing to help these numbers.

And as of March 19, 2012, the national debt had increased more during the three years and two months of the current administration than during the eight years of the previous administration. Anyone with a modicum of common sense can see that this is a huge problem and that whoever downplays it or uses rosy language to assuage the anxiety of the populace is disingenuous at best.

Many, particularly in the Democratic Party, seem to feel that this level of debt is not a serious problem because the U.S. government has the ability to print money. Unfortunately, this solution cannot be sustained indefinitely because the more money we print, the more we devalue the dollar, thereby gradually

weakening our financial foundation. Since Franklin D. Roosevelt decoupled the U.S. dollar from gold, our currency has been backed only by our good name. Not only has this resulted in fiscal policy problems, but it has also steadily increased the gap between the wealth of the rich and poor in this country and provided the opportunity to do a lot of fancy currency manipulation. Nothing good will happen if we continue along this reckless course of fiscal irresponsibility.

Economic Growth as a Solution

I believe there is some relatively painless budget cutting that can be done, because there is a fat layer in virtually every governmental budget, but the real emphasis should be on growing the economy, which has been extremely sluggish for the last several years. I have great respect for economists and their complex theories, but I don't believe sophisticated theories are necessary to spur economic growth in our country. We have the highest corporate tax rates in the world, which obviously encourage many U.S. companies to conduct business outside of America. We also have high individual taxation rates and high rates for small businesses. None of this is conducive to economic growth, particularly during times that resemble a recession.

· Couple this with excessive governmental interference in business and the imposition of a national health care program that adds substantially to the cost of each employee and you have a formula for persistent anemic growth. If the rest of the world, and especially China, loses confidence in America's abil-

ity to handle its fiscal responsibilities and calls for repayment of the money we owe them, an unimaginable economic crisis would likely ensue.

Ignore the "Spiders"

When I was nine or ten years old, some friends and I were climbing a rock mountain located in Franklin Park in the Roxbury section of Boston. We felt we were invincible and paid little attention to the signs forbidding such activities. I had climbed those rocks on many occasions and really didn't even consider the possible consequences of falling—death or great bodily harm. This particular day, I was very high on the rock face when the ledge I was standing on broke, leaving me dangling with my hands tightly gripping the protruding rocks. At that point I realized that my life was in danger and it was my own fault. I earnestly prayed to God asking Him to save me and promising that I would never engage in such stupid activities again. Suddenly off to my right, I saw a cubbyhole large enough to admit my hand, providing me a better position from which I could place my feet and continue my climb. I have never been a fan of big, hairy wolf spiders and the cubbyhole featured a nest of them, but considering the alternatives, they looked like beautiful, welcoming creatures and I happily placed my hand in their domain. Gaining that leverage, I was able to complete my ascension to the top of the mountain for the very last time. I was never even tempted to climb it again.

Our government reminds me of myself in this story as it pushes its debts higher and higher, ignoring the warning signs posted by history. Feeling invincible, it brushes off concerns

about the fragility of financial markets easily panicked by rumors as a result of the vulnerability created by debt. It ignores the U.S. Constitution, our chief warning sign, which describes the responsibilities of the government toward the people, attempting to preclude a massive and intrusive governing structure that would require so much spending.

If we fail to heed these warnings, unexpected disaster will leave us desperately grasping for solutions. Eventually, something is going to slip. Just as entering the domain of the spiders was not a pleasant option for me as a child, adopting a policy of fiscal responsibility is an unpleasant option for our government, which seems to have difficulty distinguishing needs from wants, but there will be no other option.

The difference between my story and the government's situation today is that I learned my lesson after I was miraculously spared, while our government seems incapable of understanding the danger ahead. The debt burden it is creating will have to be paid by someone at some point in time. When we look at history, we see that the ancient Greeks had a complex and large governmental structure that necessitated an ever-growing tax burden on the populace, eventually reducing many of them to serfdom. Although the serf-like population was provided with certain handouts by the state, it was essentially rendered into slaves to the government. Are we in the process of doing the very same thing even though we have examples from the past of the consequences of such a direction?

I do not doubt the sincerity of individuals in both political parties who want to use government to enhance the lives of the citizenry, but I seriously doubt their understanding of our nation's founding principles. We the people need the application of

smelling salts to awaken us from a slumber that imperils the financial freedom of the next generations. Only through careful analysis of what is going on today and comparison of today's events with the things that have gone on in societies that preceded us, will we be able to recognize and correct our course. We are engaged in nothing less than a war of philosophies, one of which will lead to prosperity and continued freedom, and the other, which will lead to fundamental changes in who we are and our role in the world. We get to decide which of these futures we want to leave to our children, but we only have a short time to make that decision.

A Balanced Budget

Balancing the budget is not a goal out of reach. The last time the United States experienced an annual budgetary surplus instead of a deficit was during the Clinton administration, when the House of Representatives was controlled by budgetary hawks and the White House was controlled by a president who was pragmatic and not an ideologue. Even though Democrats and Republicans had different ideas regarding fiscal policy, they were not so entrenched in their positions that they couldn't understand the other side and compromise. If that spirit of cooperation had continued with multiple years of budgetary surpluses, by now we would have had a much smaller national debt or perhaps as in 1835, no national debt at all, as occurred under the watch of President Andrew Jackson.

Although our financial problems may seem large and complex, there is nothing about them that is not subject to commonsense solutions. The question is are we willing to abandon

ideological gridlock and learn to compromise for the sake of those who follow us in this nation? Also, do we know the meaning of the word *sacrifice* anymore, and if not, are we willing to learn what that word means and to enact policies that are truly compassionate toward our progeny? We have time to do it if we are willing to act now before the crisis occurs.

If we spend our money wisely, we can still be quite comfortable without stressing about budgetary shortfalls. We don't even have to be heartless when it comes to reducing the size of government, even though those who promoted such massive growth were not particularly caring regarding our long-term financial well-being. If we simply do not replace those workers who retire, natural attrition will quickly work in our favor. It might be necessary to retrain and shift some younger workers into areas that need them, but the result will be the same: a slow shrinking of government bloat. These kinds of simple and compassionate solutions cannot only make a big difference in the budget but will improve the esprit de corps.

During the recent sequester and government shutdown, the executive branch of government, which has the power to decide where to focus the budgetary cuts, made little or no attempt to target the cuts in such a way that they would have a minimal effect on the population at large. Whatever the reasons for this lack of compassionate effort, maturation on both sides of the political aisle should lead politicians to more intelligent budgetary solutions. Everyone knows there is waste and duplication in virtually every federal program. To deny this is a complete divorce from reality. Nevertheless, there are those who insist on continually raising the federal debt ceiling and consequently the federal debt. The directors of every federal program know

where the excesses are and if directed to cut a certain small percentage of their budget, could do so without wreaking havoc on the program and its beneficiaries. In order to be fair, the argument should not be about which programs to cut, but rather about what percentage gets trimmed from every federal program with no sacred cows. Such cuts should be made every year until we eliminate the federal budget deficit.

The people who should be the most concerned about our growing national debt and our future obligations are the young people in our society who will be saddled with massive taxes if we don't alter our course. When I was in college, students were much more involved in what was going on in the country and there were frequent marches and protests. Other than the misguided Occupy Wall Street movement, there has been very little heard from the next generation about current fiscal issues. It is essential for the next generation of young people to start paying closer attention to what is going on in our country and in the world because it will profoundly affect their future. They need to make their voices heard in order to create some guilt among the members of my generation who are greedily spending their future resources.

Action Steps

1. Try to live for one week without accumulating any additional debt.
2. Calculate how long it would take to pay off a national debt of $17 trillion if we pay $1 billion per day with no further deficit spending. This does not begin to address the over $90 trillion in unfunded liabilities associated

with entitlements. Determine which candidates in the next election would take quickest action to reduce the debt.

3. Discuss fiscal responsibility with a young person in your sphere of influence this month.

4. When you engage in your next financial endeavor, ask yourself, "How will this affect the next generation?"

PART TWO

—

SOLUTIONS

PUSHING BACK

If you fail under pressure your strength is not very great.
Rescue those who are unjustly sentenced to death; don't
stand back and let them die. Don't try to avoid responsibility
by saying you didn't know about it. For God knows all
hearts, and He sees you. He keeps watch over your soul, and
He knows you knew! And He will judge all people according
to what they have done.

PROVERBS 24:10-12

When I was in middle school in Detroit, school life was reasonably peaceful except for the existence of bullies. There was one
particular young man whom I will call Jonathan, who took
great delight in beating me and pushing me around as well as
heaping verbal abuse on me and others. It reached a point where
I would alter my pathways in order to avoid him. I tried to stay
out of his sight as much as possible and generally kept very quiet
when he was around. One day on the way home from school,
he began picking on me for no reason and I simply decided that
I had had enough and I challenged him to a fight. He did not

wish to fight and decided to leave me alone, not only on that day, but every day after. The situation could have ended up quite differently with my taking a severe beating, but even if that had been the case, I had decided that I would withstand as many beatings as necessary to make it clear that I would no longer be his punching bag.

Even after Jonathan stopped bothering me, there were others to take his place, but that all ended soon after I joined the ROTC in the latter part of the tenth grade and rapidly rose through the ranks. My uniform was covered with ribbons, medals, and ropes that were quite impressive and the bullies had so much respect for that uniform that they showed me great deference.

Today, we Americans may feel bullied by the PC police, elites, historical revisionists, bigots, dividers, and spenders mentioned in the previous sections. We may be discouraged or afraid, but we must take action. As I learned from my experience with Jonathan, there are two ways of dealing with bullies: standing up to them and gaining their respect. Being quiet or trying to ignore them usually doesn't work and frequently emboldens them to keep trying to get a reaction from the victim. Taking calm, mature, rational action is the only way to stop them.

Media Bullies

One of the biggest bullies is the media, which has a tremendous advantage because of the regular platform from which it launches attacks against victims who don't have a national broadcast stage to disseminate their defense. Like Jonathan, the

media will continue its relentless attacks on those it does not approve of until they submit or mount a credible counterattack. It is rare that its victims have an equally loud microphone to refute the accusations leveled by their attackers. This means the victims must take maximum advantage of every weapon they do have.

Social media provides one very effective way to gain allies against the media bullies. These allies can help one another collectively recall blatantly untrue positions that have been advocated by the bullies in the past. They can also help organize boycotts of the offending media outlets once a critical mass of individuals has been convinced of the problem. Members of the media are very sensitive to ratings and their behavior can be changed by a strong group of individuals with a large following who threaten to boycott them. If social media is used to persuade large numbers of people to stop watching an offending program, the program's ratings, which determine whether the program will continue, will fall. In the end, most members of the media are more concerned about survival than ideology and will listen when the boycotts are successful, even though they will not admit that the ratings resulted in the changes they subsequently made.

Political Bullies

Politicians are even more sensitive than the media to organized resistance. They count on the fact that most people are not paying close attention to their votes and their actions and frequently are clueless regarding whether their representatives actually reflect their values. They know that many people go

into the voting booth looking for a name that looks familiar or one that is affiliated with their political party and simply vote on that basis with no further critical analysis. When well-organized groups within their constituency begin to point out to others their critical shortfallings, they start to panic and will frequently put out television or radio ads trying to reassure voters that they are on their side.

It is hoped and anticipated by the current administration, as well as previous administrations, that the majority of American citizens will be much more interested in what their professional sports teams are doing than they will be in holding leaders accountable. The current crop of politicians and many of those who preceded them are not necessarily bad people, but they believe that they know what is best for people and act on their beliefs rather than fulfilling their role of service to them. By stonewalling and depending on the short memory and attention span of the average citizen, it is quite possible for them to skate by with no consequences for their transgressions.

The way to push back against such officials is to track their votes and demonstrate a consistent voting pattern that is not in the interest of their constituencies. Exposing the negative pattern to the public using social media, radio and television ads, and newspaper articles can wake up apathetic voters and inspire them to take action. The side using this strategy most effectively is likely to be victorious, which means the majority can actually lose if they just sit by and assume that voters will check the records themselves.

As the opposition, we have to be just as persistent as the supporters of the representatives who truly do not represent their constituents. By that I am referring to the people who say

one thing to get elected, but then follow the dictates of party leaders rather than the people's will. As I said earlier, I would love to one day see elections in America where we do not indicate party affiliations on the ballot. This would force people to actually research the candidates and make intelligent choices. Until then, we must push back hard to inform our fellow citizens of problems with our leaders.

Citizens also have to be organized enough to keep records of their representatives' responsiveness so they can vote them out of office if necessary. It would be amazing how responsive representatives would become if this were done on a regular basis. What I am talking about is not complex, but does require real energy and willingness to fight for a truly free society. It has been done before: American farmworkers and environmentalists were able to get the toxic pesticide azinphos-methyl (AZM), a chemical warfare agent, removed from the agricultural market through persistent lobbying that led to legal action. Today we need to follow the example of those Americans and heed the words of cultural anthropologist Margaret Mead, who said, "Never doubt that a small group of thoughtful, committed citizens can change the world; indeed, it's the only thing that ever has."

Academic Bullies

Another area where a great deal of bullying takes place is on university campuses. Several recent surveys have shown that the vast majority of college professors are liberals. Being a liberal is not a problem unless you only teach from a liberal perspective and penalize students with different views. Unfortunately, university professors generally are not held to high standards of fair-

ness by their administrations because the university officers are also liberal.

Case in point: A conservative student at Florida Atlantic University was suspended from school because he refused to participate in a class "exercise." His professor asked the class to write "Jesus" on a piece of paper, place this on the ground, and stomp on it. The student respectfully introduced himself as a devout Mormon, and requested to be excused from the exercise. After the professor insisted, the student went to the professor's superior only to be suspended from school.

What can students and citizens do to fight back against political bias on campus? Fortunately the board of trustees at most institutions of higher learning have a significant number of moderates and conservatives as members. These are frequently people who have had great financial success and have experience in the evenhanded application of rules. Grievances concerning political bias should be brought to these individuals in a formal way and they should not be filtered through a university official. Electronic, print, and social media should also be used to publicize the state of affairs if efficient action is not taken by the board of trustees. Most universities are terrified of substantiated negative information about their practices and will act if grievances are brought in a responsible way to their attention. Inaction by the grieved parties will only guarantee continuance of the grievance.

Bullies in Business

Business entities such as stores and organizations that sell products are especially vulnerable to publicized accusations of bul-

lying and unfairness. Their public persona is their most valuable asset and they can ill afford boycotts or public demonstrations against them. For example, a few years ago a large big-box store chain banned its employees from saying "Merry Christmas." The negative press associated with this was so significant that they relented the following Christmas season, an excellent lesson for other retailers.

One of the best examples in American history of collective community action to change grossly unfair practices was the Montgomery bus boycott in the 1950s. The most powerless members of the community, namely the blacks, were able to bring the racist business community to its knees by effectively withholding financial resources, which are the lifeblood of any business. If it is difficult to rally support against what you feel is an unjust practice, it might be wise to reexamine the situation and get other opinions to determine whether you are justified in your opinion.

Unintentional Bullying

Sometimes bullying is not blatant or even intentional. In 2004 my colleagues and I took on the case of the Block conjoined twins from Germany. They were type 1 vertical craniopagus, which means they were joined at the top of the head facing in the same direction. By this time I had learned a great deal about conjoined twins and decided on a new approach. Since the neurosurgical department at Johns Hopkins is rated number one in the country and because I had so many incredibly talented colleagues, I felt it would be wise to involve as many of them as possible in the attempted separation. Some people were re-

nowned vascular neurosurgeons, while others specialized in tumors and tissue separation and others were very skilled with osseous endeavors. By slotting each team into the operation when we reached the part where their expertise would be most valuable, we were able to proceed rapidly with the separation and in fact were ten hours ahead of schedule when the heart of one of the twins (who had had multiple cardiac problems during anesthetic procedures prior to the operation) stopped.

Fortunately CPR was successful, but I knew we had to do more to take care of the problem. I was quite concerned about the heart problems of the one twin and suggested that we consider placing a temporary pacemaker before continuing the operation in a couple of days. One of the anesthesiologists involved was quite adamant that we did not need a pacemaker and that that was his area of expertise. The pediatric cardiologists had mixed views about what should be done. Eventually we proceeded with the rest of the separation without a pacemaker. Unfortunately, at the conclusion of the operation the twin with a weak heart once again suffered a cardiac arrest but this time could not be revived. Fortunately the other twin did well, but we were all quite devastated by the loss of our patient.

In this case I felt quite strongly that a pacemaker should have been placed and that it would have given us a better chance of avoiding tragedy. Afterward I realized that I had too easily yielded to someone who claimed to be a greater authority on the issue. I clearly should have pushed harder for my point of view since the benefit-to-risk ratio would have been favorable for pacemaker versus no pacemaker. By the same token, in situations outside the operating room it is valuable to look at the benefit-to-risk ratio to determine how hard to fight. Of course

one needs to be well informed on the issues before making such an analysis, but the rewards can be substantial.

People are unintentionally bullied all the time by political correctness, which keeps them from saying what they really want to say, because they feel that they will be ostracized and disliked. Everyone likes to feel as though they are a part of the community and appreciated, and that makes them relatively easy to bully into compliance and/or silence. Instead of succumbing to bullies, Americans need to grow backbones, examine their understanding of an issue, and push back if they are sure they are right. Being temporarily unpopular for your political view is a small price to pay for moving our nation back from the brink of disaster.

Our Heritage of Courage

The American colonialists were quite content with British oversight until that oversight became burdensome with ever-increasing taxes and abuse of power. If the British government's thirst for the resources of the colonialists had not grown so large, Americans might never have sought independence, but it is the natural tendency of all governments to grow, and they require revenue to do so. Fortunately for America, the rebellion against the English crown was successful and a new era of freedom sprang up on this continent.

The same thing is happening in America today that happened to the colonialists of old. As our government grows larger and more complex, it will require increasingly larger proportions of the people's earnings. Also, as the rights of the government increase, the rights of the people decrease. The question is will the American people of today be as courageous

and tough as the colonialists were and are they ready for the ultimate push back? Are they ready to stand boldly for those things they believe in without fear of consequences and are they willing to fight with all tools available to them against those who wish to change the nature of the country from people-centric to government-centric?

Dire Consequences of Giving In

Throughout history many societies have failed to push back and have allowed an overly aggressive government to expand and dominate their lives. Nazi Germany is a perfect example of such a society. One can only wonder what would've happened if people had not tolerated the foolishness of Adolf Hitler's appeal to the baser instincts of greed and envy and his institution of an official weapons confiscation program. He made one group of Germans feel that the success of another group was impeding their own financial progress. He trumped up reasons to confiscate the populace's weapons to quell any subsequent ideas about resistance. His regime may have started out innocently enough, but because the people did not oppose a progressively overreaching government, the entire world suffered a great Holocaust. Some may say that I'm being overly dramatic in comparing U.S. circumstances with Germany's state of affairs before pure evil gained the upper hand there, but few people have recognized the precursors of national societal tragedies and even fewer have done anything about them. Bullies do whatever they can get away with and keep pushing the boundaries until they meet resistance. It is the people's job to stop them before they become uncontrollable.

Push Back Peacefully and Consistently

Lest anyone get the wrong impression, I am not advocating armed insurrection, but rather just making ourselves aware of what is going on vis-à-vis our freedom. It is ineffective to sit around and complain while the encroachment continues. Instead, concerned citizens should be educating their neighbors, circulating petitions, having community discussions that involve their elected representatives, and using social media to get others involved in the struggle to return power to the people and reduce government's size and influence. Every activist has a sphere of influence and at the very least can inform friends about voting issues.

Fighting back against bullies does not always result in immediate victory and, in some cases, you will be soundly defeated. However, bullies like soft targets and if you continue to fight every time they infringe on your rights, you will eventually wear them down and they will look for easier targets. Bullies are cowards, and they will not pick on those who fight back for long.

Win Through Respect

Standing up to bullies doesn't always mean fighting them directly. As I mentioned at the beginning of the chapter, there is another option: gaining their respect. One of the best examples of this kind of pushing back is about a young female substitute teacher at my high school in Detroit. Substitute teachers were often treated quite roughly, but this teacher, who was very short in stature, commanded classrooms where you could hear a pin drop because even the biggest and toughest guys were afraid of

her. She was not a mean person, but she consistently refused to tolerate disrespect and insubordination. She was very warm toward students who behaved themselves. One might say she became the bully, but in fact, she was just taking a strong, principled stand that demanded respect, while at the same time being respectful of others.

In fighting back against the secular progressives who wish to control our lives with big government, it is important not to emulate their behavior with respect to denigrating their enemies with name-calling and lies. Instead, be calm and courteous and even nice, because as the Bible says in Proverbs 25:21-22, "If your enemies are hungry, give them food to eat. If they are thirsty, give them water to drink. You will heap burning coals on their heads, and the Lord will reward you." In other words, your enemy will feel much worse if you treat him nicely than if you retaliate. This does not mean that you shouldn't expose what your enemies are doing and that you shouldn't have a plan of counterattack that is wise and well thought out.

Know Your Enemy

A final word on bullies: It is very important to know who your "enemies" are. They are not your average fellow Americans. Don't mistake neighbors who simply disagree with you for bullies—they are your teammates who happen to have different points of view. Disagree with them, try to educate them, learn from them yourself, but don't fight them. Instead, push back against the real bullies—those people and influences that wish to fundamentally change America to another type of society. They can belong to any political party and frequently they dis-

guise themselves as great humanitarians. Unless you understand the philosophy of freedom that created our nation and carefully compare new ideas and actions against that philosophy, it becomes very difficult to determine who and what forces are trying to change the nature of our country. Keen observation of current events and diligent study of history and current events is the best way to determine who the enemies of the American Dream are. Once you identify these bullies, you can stand up to them with courage, and they will back down.

Action Steps

1. Devise a rational plan to confront a bully in your life.
2. Discuss responses to bullying with young people in your sphere of influence.
3. Examine your own behavior for bullying. If any behavior could come even close to being considered bullying, determine to stop the behavior for a month and see whether your life improves.
4. Based on this chapter, try to identify some media and/ or political bullies and discuss your findings with others.

9

RESPECTFUL DISAGREEMENT

> So discuss the matter with them [your neighbors] privately.
> Don't tell anyone else, or others may accuse you of gossip.
> Then you will never regain your good reputation.

PROVERBS 25:9-10

Recently I had an opportunity to seek funding for the Carson Scholars Fund from a very large and well-funded foundation. I explained that the purpose of the fund is to honor students from all backgrounds who achieve at the highest academic levels and also care about others, placing them on the same kind of pedestal upon which we place athletic superstars. By receiving recognition, money, a medal, the trophy, and an opportunity to attend an awards ceremony, the students frequently rise from nerd to symbol of excellence in the eyes of their peers, and they inspire other students to work toward academic and humanitarian excellence. The other part of the program concentrates on placing reading rooms all over the country to encourage the love of reading. Special emphasis is placed on Title I schools, where many students come from homes with no

books and attend schools with no libraries and are unlikely to otherwise establish a love of reading. The extremely elevated high school dropout rate of these schools hurts not only the students but the well-being of the entire country, and we want to help.

I told the foundation staff that their support would allow us to dramatically increase the scope of the program, which is currently active in all fifty states. In response, the staff members were very complimentary about the program and the progress that had been made in a relatively short period of time, but they indicated that their priorities were more global and immediate in nature and would not be able to offer any financial assistance to Carson Scholars.

I feel that the most urgent need in our society is to develop the right kind of leaders for tomorrow, since they will have a tremendous impact not only on the United States but also the world. The foundation staff felt that there were too many problems needing immediate attention and that they could not focus on programs whose effect would be felt in the future. We parted ways cordially and with no hard feelings even though I was disappointed. We both had good intentions but different ideas about priorities. I believe this foundation is composed of good people who expend enormous energy and resources for the good of others and I will continue to have great respect for them regardless of their philosophical priorities.

Though today's politicians would have you think otherwise, it is eminently possible to have substantial disagreements with others and remain friendly and cooperative. This is a lesson that must be quickly relearned by American society if we are to be successful going forward. People will always have different

ideas about what is important, but those differences should not trump a cordial working relationship.

Pro-Life versus Pro-Choice

One of the biggest issues dividing Americans today is abortion. Pro-life groups feel that life begins at conception and is very precious and should be protected. They believe that a fetus is a living human being with certain natural rights including life and protection from cruelty. Recent scientific observations have led observers to conclude that a fetus can experience pain as early as ten weeks of gestation. This means that most abortion procedures produce extreme discomfort for the fetus before it dies, making abortion even more abhorrent to pro-life groups. Because of these convictions, some members of pro-life groups oppose abortion under all circumstances, while others believe abortion is wrong but are willing to tolerate abortion in the case of rape, incest, and/ or risk to the mother's life. It is important for the pro-choice groups to understand that the pro-life group is not being mean and obstinate, but truly believes that babies are being slaughtered by people who primarily care about their own convenience.

On the other hand, the pro-life group needs to understand that the pro-choice group does not really believe that the fetus is a real human being entitled to natural human rights. They are not necessarily being mean or selfish, but rather just have a different understanding of when life begins.

This is a difficult issue on which to reach compromise, but that should not mean the members of opposing sides demonize each other. I suspect that over the course of time, the age line for abortions will continue to shift depending on political

winds and further scientific information regarding fetal existence. The important thing is for both sides to understand the
reasoning that forms the foundation for the beliefs of the other
side. It is only through attempted empathy that the two sides
can work cordially together.

Welfare

Another contentious issue is whether welfare should be extended to able-bodied adults. In recent years the welfare rolls
have rapidly expanded, dramatically adding to the national debt.
Those who are in favor of welfare reform tend to claim that
people on welfare are lazy and that those who want to continue
supporting them are wasteful spendthrifts. Those on the other
side tend to call their opponents hard-hearted skinflints who do
not care about the poor. The reality is that none of this name-
calling is necessary.

If those on each side of the issue would try to place themselves in the shoes of those with whom they disagree, much of
the rancor would dissolve. If you suddenly fell on hard times, it
is very likely that you would welcome public assistance, even for
an extended period. If, as is true in many cases, you could live
better on the welfare system than you could working a low-
wage job, what would you do? Certainly if one has small children to care for, elderly parents, or a sick family member, it
would make a lot more sense to stay home and accept the public
assistance than to try to work. I certainly would not criticize
someone who has made such a decision under these circumstances, and it is important for those who are not on public assistance to understand this kind of reasoning.

On the other hand, if you had been on public assistance for a while and suddenly got off it because you got a low-paying job (or more than one to make ends meet), you probably wouldn't be overly excited about being forced to support those who are less fortunate. If you are making a good salary, you may be happy to share with the less fortunate, or you might feel taken advantage of by a system that requires more of your resources to support ever-expanding government entitlements. Those on welfare should make an attempt to understand how these people feel as well.

Doctors Versus Patients

Another example of an issue on which we can respectfully disagree and still work together is tort reform. One of the real drivers of medical costs is the practice of defensive medicine. Many lawyers are happy to bring a lawsuit against a doctor or his practice knowing that they will receive 30 to 40 percent of the award. Eighty to 90 percent of neurosurgical malpractice cases are without merit but that matters little to these lawyers because the majority of cases are settled, since the doctor, the hospital, and the insurance company are not interested in being tied up in a court case for several months. Once the monetary demand drops to an acceptable level, they would rather pay the settlement and move on.

In order to protect themselves from lawsuits, many doctors order a lot of unnecessary tests and screenings so they can't be accused of negligence, driving health care costs up. Doctors also purchase extremely expensive insurance to guard themselves against lawsuits, which further inflates what they charge

patients. Worst of all, some of the best doctors have quit practicing after enduring unjustified lawsuits, further impoverishing our already broken health care system.

Those against tort reform argue that we need the lawsuits in order to police the medical industry. They feel that unscrupulous medical professionals would treat patients poorly without the threat of a lawsuit over their heads. Those on the other side of the argument would say that in countries where there is no medical malpractice crisis, the doctors have not abandoned common decency and caring about their patients. Both are reasonable positions, and if the opposing sides would disagree respectfully, they might be able to pass reform similar to that passed in California, which halted a substantial exodus of physicians from the state. Instead, every time tort reform has been introduced to Congress, certain senators have filibustered the issue to death instead of discussing the issue reasonably.

The Rich Versus the Poor

One of the biggest bones of contention in our nation revolves around the definition of fair taxation. According to some, fair taxation means taking progressively more from the rich and redistributing it to others after the government takes its "fair share." Others argue that we should reward the wealthy with tax breaks, trusting that the wealth will "trickle down." I believe there is a third way that becomes evident once you consider the viewpoints of both the rich and the poor.

I think if a poor person puts herself into the shoes of a rich person, she would feel largely responsible for the well-being of society because her profitable lifestyle has resulted in signifi-

cant income to sustain the rest of society. If a rich person were put into the shoes of a poor person, he would likely already have a significantly developed work ethic and rather than complaining about having to contribute anything from his meager salary toward societal maintenance, he would be thinking about how to enhance his income and his life. Both would realize that the rich and the poor all have rights and responsibilities in society.

Considering the views of both the rich and the poor, I would argue that fair taxation means that everyone contributes according to their ability, or in other words, proportionately. I like the idea of proportionality because that was put forth in the Bible in the concept of tithing. All taxpayers were required to give 10 percent of their increase. If they had no increase they had to give nothing, and if they had an extralarge increase, they still only had to provide 10 percent of their increase. This system recognized that the wealthy were not above the law—no tax breaks and no political clout for having given a larger amount. It also recognized that the poor were not "below" the law—as dignified human beings, they had responsibilities to give, even if just a little.

If our society used this system, a Wall Street mogul who made $10 billion would be required to give $1 billion and a Harlem schoolteacher who made $50,000 would be required to give $5,000. Even though one would give hundreds of times more than the other, they would both have one vote and the same rights and responsibilities before our government. This fits with the American idea that everybody contributes to the overall good of society with the talents he or she brings to the table, no matter how much money each has. Schoolteachers

offer much in terms of training the next generation, whereas billionaires offer much in terms of providing resources to maintain infrastructure and so on that benefit everyone.

Not everyone agrees with this plan. Some feel that it is fair for those with incomes under a certain dollar amount not to pay any federal tax. They say that these people are too poor and it would be a great burden to require them to contribute to the common pot. While I appreciate their compassion, serious problems arise when a person who pays nothing has the right to vote and determine what other people are paying. It does not make sense for me to vote on how much you should give if I don't have to give anything. In fact, in such a situation it is likely that I would be more than willing to vote to raise your taxes while I simply reap the benefits.

Unfortunately, redistributionism is a very good strategy for cultivating the favor of large blocks of voters. Under this system, voters will always be loyal to that politician who promises to keep taxes low or nonexistent while taking from the "evil rich" to support the government. Voters with lower incomes will always have the incentive to vote for higher taxes on the wealthy, and that system would result in a smaller and smaller tax base supporting an increasingly large financial burden.

As soon as you introduce a graduated income tax as opposed to a proportional income tax, you also introduce your own biases. Although it sounds magnanimous to say the rich should bear virtually all of the tax burden and the poor should not have their lives complicated by paying any taxes, this is actually quite demeaning to the poor and is basically saying to them, "You poor little thing, don't you worry because I will take care of you since you can't take care of yourself." Robbing people of dignity

by making them feel like freeloaders is not compassionate, but it can be quite effective in assuaging the guilt of some of the economically well-off individuals in our society.

Not only is this kind of taxation both divisive and unsustainable, it is especially offensive to individuals like me who have worked extremely hard throughout life to achieve success and who give away enormous amounts of money to benefit others. This system unfairly assumes that people like me are only greedy and uncaring. Wealthy people in the United States have created more charitable organizations and been more philanthropic than any other group in the world. We should celebrate their achievements rather than envy them.

Sure, some wealthy people are selfish because they are human beings subject to the same imperfections as everyone else. Fortunately, even these people have to give back to society; they need house cleaners, pilots, gardeners, chauffeurs, cooks, and a host of other people to maintain their lifestyle. Even if they don't have a charitable bone in their body, they still provide employment for others. We are more likely to get such individuals to begin thinking of others if we treat them fairly rather than if we demonize them, just as the poor are more likely to want compromise if we don't assume they are all lazy and undeserving of help.

The Importance of Humility and a Listening Ear

There are many more contentious issues that divide the American people, but all of them should be subjected to open civil discussions in which each side tries to look at the issue from the perspective of the other. This can only be done if each party is

willing to exhibit some humility. That means being willing to let someone else be right sometimes and being willing to listen.

I was recently on a national talk show in which I represented one side of a particular argument and a congresswoman represented the other side. She was so intent on demonstrating the superiority of her position that she repeatedly rudely interrupted while I was speaking without even realizing that we were largely in agreement. I can certainly identify with this attitude, because I held an extreme version of it as an adolescent in Detroit. I arrogantly thought that I knew more than others and I frequently would not even entertain their views. I often found myself in trouble, because I would become angry and react in a violent or other aggressive manner, in one case almost killing a classmate with a knife.

I had been minding my own business when a classmate came along and began to ridicule me. I had a large camping knife in my hand and without thinking, I lunged at him, plunging the knife into his abdomen. He backed off, certain that he had been mortally wounded before discovering that the knife blade had struck a large metal belt buckle under his clothing and broken. He fled in terror but I was even more terrified when realizing that I had almost killed someone. That incident led me to prayerfully consider my plight and to ask for God's guidance and help. I came to understand that very day that I was always angry because I was selfish. I felt that someone was always infringing on my rights, getting in my space, messing with my things, disregarding my positions, and so on, which offended me, leading to inappropriate behavior. Through wisdom provided by God it dawned on me that I should step outside of the center of the circle so that everything wasn't always about me. I

learned to consider the viewpoint of others and it dramatically altered my behavior. Most people who know me today cannot believe that I was ever plagued by a violent temper. Proverbs 16:32 says, "It is better to be patient than powerful; it is better to have self-control than to conquer a city." Anyone can act irrationally, but it takes a wise and truly strong individual to remain controlled, logical, and willing to truly hear what the other person is saying.

Strategies for Cordial Disagreement

Compromise is most likely when both parties respect each other no matter how much they disagree. In stressful situations where you need a consensus, respect sometimes means saying nothing and refraining from name-calling even when irritated. By doing so, you not only manifest respect for others but for yourself as well. The best way to respond to distracting personal attacks is to practice bringing the conversation back to the issue at hand. Never fall into the trap of engaging in personal attacks while letting the topic of conversation slip into the background. Doing so allows your opponent to escape the need to explain her position. If she has a good argument, she would be eager to pursue it rather than trying to change the subject to you and your character.

When seeking respectful dialogue, another good tactic is to focus on the big picture and de-emphasize small details. I liken the silly arguments that some people engage in to a passenger ship that is about to go over Niagara Falls while the passengers and crew are arguing about the barnacles on the side of the ship. They continue a discourse that could have some value

down the road, but they fail to adjust the course of the ship and everyone perishes, rendering the barnacle issue completely irrelevant. Don't lose sight of the issue at hand.

I have found that the best way to proceed with civil discussions about issues on which people disagree is to first concur on what is important to both parties. Next determine who is harmed by each position and agree not to intentionally harm others. Last, exhibit tolerance without discarding core values.

The Second Amendment debate is a good illustration of this process. Some people feel that there should be no restrictions on the rights of citizens to have any kind of weapon they choose. They firmly believe that the Second Amendment was established to allow citizens to protect themselves from foreign or domestic threats including an out-of-control central government. They do not believe it reasonable for such a government to hold all of the powerful weapons, while they are left with only hunting rifles.

The other side dismisses such arguments as paranoia and believes in stringent gun control and restrictions on the types of weapons and amount of ammunition individuals can possess. They believe that we could quell the epidemic of mass murders by keeping dangerous weapons out of the hands of unstable individuals.

Both sides can agree that we do not want dangerous weapons in the hands of unstable individuals and this should be the starting point of any conversation. The first group would probably agree that freedom is the most important thing, while the second group might feel that safety is the most important thing. Their discussion should center around how to preserve Second Amendment freedom while ensuring safety for the largest num-

ber of citizens. During those discussions both should agree to hold personal freedom and societal safety as their targets. Nothing should be done to intentionally affect those two things in a negative way. This is a civilized way to have a productive discussion and is the first step toward finding compromise.

Recall that I love to say, "If two people agree about everything, one of them isn't necessary." Disagreement is part of being a person who has choices. One of those choices is to respect others and engage in intelligent conversation about differences of opinion without becoming enemies, eventually allowing us to move forward to compromise. "A house divided against itself cannot stand," and a nation that tears itself apart will not survive.

Action Steps

1. Take the first step and offer to put your differences aside with someone you frequently argue with. Refuse to argue with them for at least one month.
2. If engaged in a pointless argument, change the subject to something about which there is agreement.
3. Try to conceive of a plan that might work for both sides when you see the next political argument on television.
4. Try listening twice as much as talking since you have two ears and only one mouth.

THE ART OF COMPROMISE

Without wise leadership, a nation falls; with many counselors, there is safety.

PROVERBS 11:14

Although we had very little money, my mother would save every penny over several years in order to be able to purchase a new car when the old one she was driving was on its last leg. She did not believe in buying used cars, because she felt that the previous owner probably would not have gotten rid of it if it was functioning optimally.

Once when I was a teenager I went with her to look at a car. It was a beautiful vehicle, yellow with black interior and a black vinyl top. I was quite excited, because I had recently acquired my driver's license and was already starting to imagine myself cruising down the streets of Detroit in a brand-new automobile. The problem was that the car was several hundred dollars more expensive than the cash she had on hand.

My mother could bargain with the best of people, and after a couple of hours had worn the salesman down to the point

that he was ready to make a deal after she showed him the cash. I was absolutely jubilant until I heard several days later that the salesman had lost his job for giving my mother too sweet a deal. I'm certain that if my mother had had more money, she would have been willing to compromise, but she believed in only paying cash for cars and would not qualify for a loan anyway. As a matter of principle, she did not believe in borrowing money to pay for anything other than a house, because she had seen too many people ruin their lives with financial overreach.

Many people feel that driving a hard bargain is a sign of strength and perseverance, and in many cases they are correct. However, my mother and I learned the hard way that it is not always the kindest thing to do. My mother certainly did not intend to get the man fired and offered to give the car back, but for some reason, since the deal had already been consummated, that was not possible. While my mother was pleased she had been able to buy the car, she wished she had not pressed so hard. Sometimes compromise is the best way to go, even when you think you could get your own way without it.

Many people have recently commented on how difficult it is to get anything accomplished in Washington anymore. The art of compromise appears to be vanishing with both political parties adopting a "my way or the highway" attitude. In much of the legislation that has been passed in the last few years, one side is pleased and the other side is disgruntled. This is an acceptable outcome, as long as each side is civil and works honestly with the other. Unfortunately today, both parties seem to be content with gridlock if they can't get what they want and have stopped giving ground in order to be a part of an impor-

tant solution. Rather than sulking, they should be seeking compromise in every possible way. For that to happen, both sides must have some incentive to move through respectful disagreement to produce an actual agreement.

Timing Is Everything

I remember as a child in Boston going to Haymarket Square on Saturday evenings with my mother and my aunt and uncle, as well as my brother. This was the weekly trip to buy produce and I always found it exciting, especially during the closing hour when the farmers were ready to go home and wanted desperately to avoid carrying unsold produce back home. The same sellers who a couple of hours earlier were disinclined to sell five tomatoes for a dollar were now willing to give away a dozen tomatoes for the same price. You might say they were highly incentivized to make a deal.

In the same way, situations change for legislators and it is good to revisit issues periodically where no compromise was possible earlier. A good example of this is the fierce opposition to Medicare when it was first introduced. While some lawmakers refused it initially, it soon became apparent that there were no other good alternatives being offered, and the need for the program grew as our population began showing significant signs of aging. Over time, the incentive for compromising grew, the opposition waned, and the program was accepted by both legislative bodies.

Starting Small

When I was a freshman in high school, my Latin class had to break up into teams and complete a complex project depicting some important facet of the Roman Empire. I was paired with a couple of people who had always been my academic competitors and with whom I did not get along particularly well. Despite our dislike for one another, we got to work and decided to create a replica of the Roman Colosseum. We experimented with all types of ingredients and finally decided to construct walls with dough, clay, and sand. We used wire and popsicle sticks for scaffolding, and really tested our artistic talents in the creation of people and ferocious animals to populate a structure that was rather magnificent, if I do say so myself. In the process of doing the research and figuring out how to make our project structurally sound and aesthetically pleasing, we began to realize that we liked one another and started to associate as friends as much as project mates.

I believe the same thing could happen in Washington with our legislators if they put aside their differences and worked together in a systematic fashion to solve a problem. Perhaps they could start with a small issue and work their way up gradually to large and very meaningful problems. I believe they would discover in working together that they are not nearly as different from one another as they had previously thought.

Recent Examples of Compromise

Interestingly enough, there already have been a number of such projects, and the records are available for our study. We have the

opportunity to see what kind of people have been representing us, and whether they are interested in serving the needs of the populace or whether they are more closely tied to the special interest groups that continue to fund their reelection. We have all the ammunition we need to make important decisions about our nation's direction.

In our recent history, there have been some notable events that brought both parties together with an amazing show of unity and success. The Iraqi invasion of Kuwait led to a bipartisan determination to expel Saddam Hussein and his army from the land of the peace-loving people of Kuwait. Even more unity was demonstrated after our nation was attacked by radical Islamic elements on September 11, 2001. People were able to look at the big picture in these situations and quickly establish common goals that were reached through cooperative efforts. In the latter case a second war ensued that probably was not necessary, but there was bipartisan agreement on its initiation, although bitter partisan battles over the war effort later broke out.

During the Clinton administration there was significant rancor between the two parties over efforts to reform social welfare programs. Both sides made significant concessions and successfully improved the program while decreasing the welfare rolls. At the beginning of the welfare fight, both sides were entrenched and it appeared that no progress would be made, but President Clinton exercised real leadership by sitting down with Speaker Gingrich and discussing how to make changes that would make the program affordable while still helping those individuals who were truly in need. These kinds of cooperative efforts actually led to a budgetary surplus for the first time in many years. There is absolutely no reason why the same

type of success cannot be achieved today if the two sides were willing to look at the big picture and put aside pride in order to solve problems, with no one achieving total victory and no one suffering total defeat.

Gay Marriage

One large issue that is ripe for compromise is the issue of gay marriage. I liken the gay marriage argument to a new group of mathematicians who claim that $2 + 2 = 5$. The traditional mathematicians say that $2 + 2 = 4$ and always has been, and always will be 4. The new mathematicians continue to insist on their version of mathematics so the traditional mathematicians eventually relent and say, "For you guys, $2 + 2 = 5$, but for us it will continue to be 4." The new mathematicians are not satisfied with that compromise and say that $2 + 2$ must also be 5 for you and everyone else and if you won't accept that then you are a "mathist" (as opposed to a racist, sexist, or some other kind of "ist") or mathophobe. The two sides will most likely never reach an agreement as to the actual equation. If, however, they discuss the matter rationally without demanding that political correctness silence the other's opinions, they may move through respectful disagreement to practical compromises that are acceptable to both sides.

I firmly believe that marriage is between a man and a woman. However, I see no reason why any two consenting adults, regardless of their sexual orientation, cannot be joined together in a legally binding civil relationship that provides hospital visitation rights, property rights, and so on without tampering with the definition of marriage. This would give the gay

population what they want, while leaving the traditional definition of marriage intact. This is what compromise is about. The "my way or the highway" mentality on either side of the argument only leads to gridlock and animosity. This is a practical way to apply common sense to a complex social issue.

National Debt

Another issue where compromise is badly needed is rapidly accumulating debt. The Democrats, led by the president, appear to be relatively unconcerned about the debt and are happy to continue spending, borrowing, and expanding entitlements. The Republicans, on the other hand, are extremely concerned that we will eventually have to pay the piper if we continue to expand our national debt, and that we will burden future generations with financial obligations that will extinguish the American Dream. One side is concerned about preserving entitlements and the other is concerned about preserving our nation's future.

A little wisdom and some review of the actual facts would be useful in the pursuit of joint solutions. We have a $17 trillion national debt that continues to grow. We have ever-expanding entitlement programs that are extremely expensive. Small businesses are frightened of government and its plans to implement a health care system that will be expensive and intrusive. This also includes its many enforcement provisions that will be overseen by the discredited IRS, which at the time of this writing is under investigation for illegal activity. Big businesses have trillions of dollars sitting on the sidelines waiting for a friendlier business environment before investing. None of us, regardless

of our political philosophy, can possibly be content with such a situation. The injection of a little common sense into the discussions would prove beneficial.

As far as the growing debt is concerned, it should be treated the same way that personal debt is treated by thinking and pragmatic families. First they assess their income and output. If the output is greater than the income, they either decrease the output, find a way to increase the income, or both. If after several months their deficit spending continues, they realize that their plan is not working and honestly reappraise and adjust it accordingly. The last thing they do is double down on an ineffective plan while sticking their head in the sand. An unwise family in this situation, however, would continue on, while stating emphatically that they were not spending as much as they had been and that eventually the budget would come under control. They would claim that it would be too painful to significantly cut down on the spending and that anyone requesting such action is obviously heartless. They would also talk about growing their income, but would not change what they were doing to make that a reality. When they saw that things were not working out according to their predictions, they would never consider that they were following an inappropriate course of action, but instead would blame others for impeding them.

There's no question that our government needs to cut wasteful spending. Obviously the cutting should occur in areas of duplication of services, extravagant entertainment for government officials, fraud, unnecessary programs, and so on. In the recent sequestration efforts, the current administration intentionally targeted cuts that would be felt acutely by the public who would then agree that making any cuts was too painful.

Included in these cuts was elimination of White House tours for ordinary citizens. This is something that many school groups plan for years and it is not too expensive. Additionally, in light of this particular cut, many individuals and groups volunteered to provide the funds necessary to keep the White House tours open, but such offers were refused. Another cut was in TSA (Transportation Security Administration) personnel to make the experience at the airport even more painful for travelers. I personally find these tactics extraordinarily insulting to the populace's intelligence, most of whom can easily see through this gamesmanship. The sad thing is that there are large numbers of people in American society today who are fooled by these infantile tactics and don't question anything, as long as they get their government support.

Much more important, however, than cutting money from the budget, is expanding the economy with resultant significant income to the government. We do not have to reinvent the wheel to accomplish this. We simply need to create a friendly environment for business and entrepreneurship and stop trying to regulate the lives of responsible American citizens. These were principles that were followed (early in American history) during the rapid expansion of business and industry throughout our nation, which rapidly propelled us to the pinnacle of the world economically.

First of all, we need to recognize that the United States has the highest corporate tax rates in the world. Our rates even exceed those of openly socialist countries. A few years ago Canada and several other countries significantly slashed their corporate rates, which had the desired effect of attracting American business. Our American leadership has talked about cutting

corporate tax rates, but nothing has been done. We are capable of moving very quickly in a crisis, such as 9/11, but extreme lethargy characterizes our usual pace of governmental progress. This is an issue that should not be controversial for those who are socialists in our Congress.

More controversial, however, is the issue of cutting tax rates for individuals and small businesses. The Democrats feel that those with very high incomes should pay most of the taxes since they can afford to do so. The Republicans feel that enabling people to keep the vast majority of what they earn is more conducive to growth and encourages people to work hard. Again, a little common sense goes a long way. Taxation needs to be fair for everyone and not just for a favored group. This is the reason I like the tithing model set forth in the Bible, as I mentioned earlier. As soon as you depart from a proportional taxation system, you introduce ideological bias, making arguments endless. Also, everyone must have skin in the game when it comes to taxation. People with a lot of money have a large amount of skin in the game and people with very little money only have a small amount, but everybody is taxed proportionately, which makes it fair.

Unfairness is introduced when the tax code is riddled with loopholes that are accessible to some but irrelevant for others. Those with good tax lawyers and accountants can substantially reduce the taxes they pay, which is grossly unfair to those unable to take advantage of such things. Lowering tax rates and eliminating loopholes at the same time is a no-brainer that has been advocated by both Republicans and Democrats, but once again nothing is done. Even with the loopholes, the top 10 percent of the populace in terms of income pay 70 percent of

the income taxes while earning 46 percent of the taxable income, which means they are indeed paying more than their fair share.

The Simpson-Bowles commission, which was a bipartisan congressional group, laid out the rationale for cutting taxes and eliminating loopholes quite cogently and in a way that provided a victory for both sides, but the recommendations were rejected by the executive branch of government and by members of Congress from both sides. This is a good example of the "my way or the highway" philosophy that runs rampant in Washington today. Ideology generally does not yield to logic and common sense. Because the Simpson-Bowles plan and other plans like it significantly reduced government spending and thus government growth, those politicians who feel that government is the solution to every problem and want to massively expand the government's reach into every aspect of our lives could not possibly agree with a reasoned approach to getting our deficit under control and growing the economy. At the same time, those who want to rapidly reduce the federal debt and shrink government might be noble in their goals, but must be patient and gradually accomplish their objectives, because a rapid reduction in the size of government could create significant unemployment and other logistical problems that could be avoided with some compromise.

The Problem of Pride

In the Bible, in the Book of Proverbs we are told that God hates pride and arrogance. These are the very characteristics that surround the ideologues on both sides who feel that their way is

the only right way. How many wonderful relationships never developed because each of the two parties was too proud to make the first move? How many wonderful marriages were ruined because pride erased the words "I'm sorry" from a couple's vocabularies? I vividly remember a case where a couple lost their home to foreclosure because they refused to accept a bid from a buyer that was lower than their asking price. Pride is the quickest compromise killer.

When this kind of silliness is not only present but abounds in our congressional and executive halls, how can we ever expect to make progress? The answer to this problem is simple. It is found in the Bible, again in the Book of Proverbs where chapter 22, verse 4 says, "True humility and fear of the Lord lead to riches, honor, and long life." Humility doesn't mean that you can't have an opinion or advocate a position, but it does mean you are willing to consider the opinions and positions of others in a serious way and then move forward to a meaningful compromise. If the politicians can just drop some of the hubris and once again serve humbly for the good of the people, solutions will rapidly follow. We the people must make ourselves aware of whom the politicians are who totally disregard our welfare and cast their votes in their own interests. Those people need to be thrown out of office on a wholesale basis regardless of their party affiliation.

Action Steps

1. Try to identify some national politicians who are humble.
2. Identify your principles that can't be compromised. Then

consider what ideas used to implement those principles could be compromised.

3. Make the first step toward compromise of an idea that has put you at odds with someone you know.

4. Examine your own attitude for arrogance. When you identify an area of pride, practice gratitude for what you have been given. Recognize your own fallibility.

BECOMING INFORMED

Only simpletons believe everything they are told! The prudent carefully consider their steps.

When I was young, I thought classical music was only the background noise for cartoons, so when my brother Curtis returned from one of his stints in the navy with an album titled *The Unfinished Symphony of Franz Schubert*, I was quite astonished. This was a strange choice for someone who had grown up in Detroit, also known as Motown. In Detroit "classical" music was produced by the likes of Stevie Wonder, the Supremes, the Temptations, the Four Tops, Gladys Knight, Martha and the Vandellas, and the Jackson Five.

Nevertheless, I listened to the Unfinished Symphony, and it appealed to me. I was interested in learning more about classical music because they frequently asked questions on my favorite television program, *GE College Bowl,* about different classical composers and their creations. Inspired by Curtis, I purchased a record album of Rossini overtures that included the theme

from the *Lone Ranger*. I played that record every day until I could name each overture and became immensely fond of this music, which led me to begin listening to classical music stations and making classical music a big part of my life. I'm glad I cultivated the interest, since classical music affected my life in many ways and, most important, created some wonderful friendships, including a lasting relationship with a young Yale student by the name of Candy Rustin, a classical violinist who is now my wife of thirty-eight years.

Many people criticized me and thought that I was weird because of my love of classical music, but if I had listened to them and remained in the ideological box they created for themselves, I would not have expanded my horizons in a way that turned out to be positive for me. Today I frequently find myself reminding young people to expand their horizons of knowledge and not listen to those who tell them to limit their interests to things that are "culturally relevant." I tell them that if you want to be relevant only in your household, then you only need to know the things that are important in your house, and if you want to be relevant in your neighborhood, you need to know what's important in your neighborhood. The same thing applies to your city, state, and country. And if you want to be relevant to the entire world, program that computer known as your brain with all kinds of information from everywhere in order to prepare yourself.

Someone might say, "Don't learn all that stuff because you will overload your brain." As a neuroscientist I can tell you unequivocally that it is impossible to overload the human brain with information. If you learn one new fact every second, which is virtually impossible, it will take you approximately three mil-

lion years to approach brain overload. The human brain has billions of neurons and hundreds of billions of interconnections. It can process more than two million bits of information per second and can remember everything you have ever seen or heard.

All of this information is retained indefinitely. I could take an eighty-five-year-old man and place depth electrodes into a certain part of his brain followed by appropriate electrical stimulation and he would be able to recite back verbatim a book he had read sixty years ago. Most of us can't retrieve the information our brain stores that easily, but surely we can improve.

Many people comment on what percentage of the brain we actually use, but no one knows the actual number. We do, however, know of many accounts of individuals who have done unbelievable things when it was a matter of survival. That alone tells us that we generally operate significantly below capacity and that we can always learn more.

Education as the Foundation of Our Government

The founders of our nation understood that such a society could not long exist without a well-informed and well-educated populace who used the amazing brains God gave them. Even people with only a grade school education in America in the 1800s were extremely well educated. That education in turn allowed them to make informed decisions in the voting booth, protecting them against tyranny.

There are many sinister forces that are vying for power in

our American society. Most of these are associated with politically ambitious individuals who are far more concerned about power and prestige than they are about the people's welfare. Uninformed citizens tend to be trusting of some of these forces without doing due diligence in terms of studying their previous performance or their associations with dubious characters. An uninformed voter, for instance, might ignore the fact that their favorite candidate had a long history of associating with radical elements, because the candidate proclaims his good intentions and promises them justice. A well-informed voter who favored the same candidate might engage in further investigation on his own, discover that the candidate represented an organization found to be engaged in illegal practices, and change his vote as a result of the discovery.

Congress today has less than a 10 percent approval rating, yet its members are reelected 90 percent of the time across the nation. This means they have been successful in fooling the voters, but it does not mean that this should or will continue. Until the laws of this country are changed, we the people still have the ability to select our representatives. This is not only a right, but a responsibility, and we can only exercise that right responsibly when we are well informed.

Know the Record, Not Just the Party

To be informed voters, Americans need to learn to look beyond party affiliation. A significant number of voters enter the voting booth looking for a name they recognize or a party affiliation and they cast their vote based on these superficial factors. Hon-

est politicians should be uncomfortable cultivating these types of voters. Dishonest politicians actively try to encourage such voters to support them by offering promises of jobs, free or low-cost health care, easy access to citizenship for aliens, free equipment such as telephones, and government aid to purchase food and other necessities. These bribes are extraordinarily appealing to people who feel disempowered, yet entitled. The politicians know that all of these promises will not be fulfilled or will only be fulfilled temporarily before money runs out, but they don't really care as long as they are voted into power. The poor voters in many cases are too stressed to even notice the poor performance of their representatives and eagerly listen while those same representatives shower them with even more empty promises.

Unfortunately, many Americans don't even know who their representatives are, nor are they aware of their voting record or general philosophy about life in our nation. Because the world is so interconnected, a well-informed individual cannot be an isolationist. They clearly must be aware of what is happening in the rest of the world and should be able to articulate opinions on major subjects of interest at any time. This way, they will be able to tell whether their opinions are in sync with those of their state and congressional representatives.

All of this is to say that we as Americans should vigorously pursue knowledge of history, current events, science and technology, finance, geography, philosophy, and religion—actually, anything and everything. Cultivating wide-ranging curiosity and careful study will provide the background we need to correctly analyze the words uttered by politicians and people in the media.

Don't Replace Your Brain with a Computer

I've heard it argued that a broad base of knowledge is not nearly as important as it used to be, because most people have smartphones and can instantly access the Internet. While it may be a waste of time to memorize certain types of information since we all have virtual encyclopedias in our pockets, there is no substitute for an ingrained broad base of knowledge. That built-in knowledge allows a person to immediately assess the veracity of something they are hearing for the first time rather than just swallowing it hook, line, and sinker. While we may be able to look up answers to many questions, the study of psychology has demonstrated that what we already know influences the way we process new information. For instance, if we know there is a rabid dog loose in our neighborhood, we will regard any stray dog with a great deal of caution and suspicion, whereas if we are notified that a valuable prize-winning dog is lost in our neighborhood with a big reward out for its return, we are likely to regard that stray dog differently. Having a good knowledge base rather than relying on the ability to look everything up on Google definitely affects our instant analysis of new information on an everyday basis.

Dangers of Ignorance

Unfortunately, uninformed citizens frequently are the most vociferous in voicing their opinions. They cannot back up those opinions with facts but often are not interested in listening to common sense that opposes their beliefs. I remember a young man, very popular during late middle school and early

high school years, who provides a vivid example of this behavior and its consequences. He had a following and clearly was the leader of the pack. He also was quick to voice his opinions about almost everything and was overly impressed with his own physical abilities. One unfortunate summer day, he was bragging about his swimming abilities and when challenged, was determined to demonstrate that his detractors were wrong. On a dare, he attempted to swim to one of the pillars holding up a large bridge and then swim back to shore. Unfortunately, he was caught in the undertow of the river and drowned. His tragic death illustrates what can happen when one pursues goals without appropriate information. One may think that a river looks like a gigantic swimming pool, but a little investigation should lead one to the understanding that there are many forces in a river that are not found in a swimming pool.

While a lack of education can lead to hasty action, it can also lead to lethal inaction. During the last presidential election in America, tens of millions of eligible voters simply did not vote. Many have become frustrated with the whole political scene and do not want to participate, while many others feel that the elections are fixed and/or their vote would not count anyway for a variety of reasons. I cannot emphasize strongly enough to such individuals that your failure to become informed and vote accordingly only exacerbates the situation. If only those completely swayed by the promises of demagogues vote, we will soon be in trouble far deeper than what we have already experienced.

What an Educated Citizen Knows

Becoming an informed citizen not only makes you a wiser voter but can enhance all of life's experiences, from planning a career to raising a family. Time and space won't allow me to provide an exhaustive outline of the things informed citizens should know, but here are a few of the basics:

- Basic world and American history
- Basic world and American geography
- Basic household economics (key principles like balancing a checkbook and knowing that you do not buy a house that costs more than two and a half times your annual income could have spared many Americans a lot of trouble before the housing crisis)
- Basic understanding of how credit works and how debt accumulates
- Names of state and national representatives
- Basic nutrition and disease management
- Traffic rules for pedestrians and vehicle operators
- Basic math including the calculation of percentages
- The ability to read at an eighth-grade level

You may be surprised at the elementary nature of some items on this list, but a surprising number of adult Americans are lacking in these areas despite being well versed in the minor characters of popular sitcoms. Obviously there are a host of other things that would be useful to know, but I've deliberately chosen this list, since anyone who is honest and informed at the basic levels described above will be a formidable individual who

is difficult to manipulate and would be a prized supporter for any honest political candidate.

Education Is the Door to Prosperity

It is especially imperative that we emphasize to members of oppressed communities that education affects your entire life. There are many studies available to show vast lifetime economic differences between those with a high school diploma versus a college degree versus a professional degree. (Education in highly skilled trades also pays off very well economically.) The first twenty to twenty-five years are spent either preparing yourself educationally or not preparing yourself. If you prepare well, you will have sixty years to reap the benefits. If you prepare poorly, you will have sixty years to suffer the consequences. When you look at it that way, a little investment in hard work for a relatively short period of time pays huge dividends, while failure to prepare is equivalent to choosing to be a victim of society. We must get our young people to understand that they are the ones who get to make the choice about the lifestyle they will lead. As long as they remain free of legal entanglements, no one can stop them from pursuing their dreams. My life is a testament to this.

Education also opens many doors of personal fulfillment and joy that have nothing to do with economics. I believe it would be highly instructive and beneficial to many of the young people in our nation to live abroad in a third world nation for several months and then return to the United States. Like many immigrants who come here, I believe they would immediately

realize how many opportunities they have and how many choices are theirs for the taking.

It's Never Too Late to Learn

The basic elements necessary to become an informed citizen are readily available in the public school systems, but unfortunately some people do not pay attention in school, and 30 percent of those who enter U.S. high schools do not graduate. Fortunately, all hope is not lost for such individuals, because there are many ways that one can acquire the basic knowledge listed in the bullet points above. Information on those topics can be found for free online, though it's important to choose reputable sources. Many things posted on the Internet are simply opinions presented as facts and it is important to cross-reference information several times before accepting them.

Television and radio programs can provide much information on current events, but since there is so much bias in the media, it is important to listen to several sources representing both sides of an issue in order to be informed. Listening only to one cable news outlet is probably not wise if you want to learn about all sides of an issue. The same is true of printed media. I recently had dinner with two senior editors of a major national newspaper and I asked them if they were unbiased. They both proclaimed that they were objective and saw no bias in their reporting, despite clearly partisan leanings in their paper. To avoid absorbing a biased point of view, make sure you vary your media sources.

Perhaps the best source of information are books from rep-

utable publishers. As a boy I made extensive use of the public library, where I could access thousands of books for free. Even such books can give a slanted view, making it wise for the reader to read many books. One way to find out what books are fair and accurate is to ask librarians. In most cases they don't mind being references even if you are not checking out a book from their library. It is also a good idea, when trying to decide how reputable a particular publisher is, to determine the number of books they have in the section of the library that you are interested in. There are numerous small, upstart publishing houses that make claims that cannot be substantiated about the quality of their publications, but if you see their name on numerous titles, it is likely that they are quite reputable and that they engage in due diligence before publishing any work.

Don't Be Fooled

People who try to manipulate public opinion are much more effective when they appear to present new information to people who should have already known the subject matter. They also like to make accusations against their enemies, repeating them loudly and often with the hope that people will begin to believe them. They know that even though they frequently need to retract these accusations, they can print retractions weeks later on the bottom of page 23 of the newspaper where it is unlikely to be noticed.

In addition, the manipulators in the media intentionally ignore or downplay transgressions and prevarications on behalf of the people they agree with while making an enormous fanfare about any imperfections found in their perceived enemies.

The media hated George W. Bush and made a big deal about the victory pose he assumed during the Iraqi war on the deck of a battleship with a sign behind him declaring, "Mission Accomplished." Of course that war went on for several more years with many casualties and enormous expenditures of taxpayer dollars. The same media has largely ignored the fact that Barack Obama stated that with the death of Osama bin Laden and the drone strikes of several other Al Qaeda leaders that we were winning the war and our enemies were on the run. If anything, Al Qaeda is becoming stronger with many people vying for the leadership role. Also, the same media that portrayed Watergate as the scandal of the century sat quietly by as the current administration proclaimed the IRS harassment of the administration's enemies "a phony scandal." By not focusing on the "fast and furious" scandal, the Benghazi debacle, the IRS scandal, the government surveillance revelations, and so on, the hope is that the public will simply forget about these horrendous shortcomings and move on. This will work only if American voters remain uneducated.

What Does a Good Education Look Like?

I recently visited the College of the Ozarks in Branson, Missouri. Like Berea College in Kentucky, they require all students to work at least fifteen hours per week. Their nickname, Hard Work University, is well earned. They are a Christian college that is both true to its convictions and selective—they only accept one out of ten applicants. They are definitely not politically correct and place strong emphasis on the founding principles of our nation and on Christian doctrine. The students, faculty, and

administrators are the most courteous and friendly people you could ever hope to meet. One might say these students are being indoctrinated the right way. They are taught fiscal responsibility and all graduate with no debt.

If we don't start following the College of the Ozarks' example of teaching our young people about the values and principles that made our nation great, those values and principles will be replaced by something else that is unlikely to be inspiring and elevating. We have to be just as proactive as the secular progressives who have put us in the position we are in now and have been over the last few decades. We must not be ashamed of who we are or what we believe, in fact we should be extremely proud of our historical accomplishments. There is no room for gloating, but we must remember that if we don't put appropriate facts and people before our young people, someone else will substitute their version of *Utopia*.

To be successful we must take politics out of education and concentrate on empowering the entire American populace. This is the only way that the people's will can be ensured so that we can have the kind of nation that was envisioned by our founders. We must take advantage of all the educational tools available to return us to a place where our public education system is the envy of the world. The rapid development of virtual classrooms and smart computers that are able tutors can be a godsend that will be well worth the cost, enabling us to be serious about our obligation to educate people. Part of that education includes preparing people for jobs of the future, which will decrease unemployment and increase fulfillment while brightening future generations' prospects. Last, we should shine the bright light of truth on the forces of manipulation that run

rampant throughout our society today. Improvements in education, combined with wisdom and knowledge, would then turn our country around.

Action Steps

1. Challenge yourself to learn a new fact about American history each day for one month.
2. Resolve to replace television and Internet surfing with reading for a month.
3. Learn the names of your state and federal government representatives and research their voting records.
4. Cross-reference each use of statistics in a news report to determine whether the reporter is spinning the facts.

WISDOM AND KNOWLEDGE

How much better to get wisdom than gold, and understanding than silver!

PROVERBS 16:16

When I was in medical school, a prized possession was a copy of the last year's examination in the various courses. Many students would memorize the questions and answers from previous years and feel that they had a significant advantage at exam time only to discover that they answered incorrectly on numerous occasions. They were culling the old exams for knowledge, but not using wisdom in the process.

Wise persons would understand that the professors knew that students would acquire old exams and try to remember the correct answers. They would also realize that professors tend to be smart people and would likely slip in something that would change the question ever so slightly, requiring a different answer. The wise students really didn't care very much about the previous year's answer, but spent a lot of time analyzing the question to determine what body of knowledge they would

need to correctly answer such a question. They would then make sure that they had a thorough understanding of that body of information, recognizing that it is important and would be tested for again. Needless to say, those students tended to do very well. Without a doubt, students who did poorly were very knowledgeable and generally had been high achievers throughout their lives, but they were looking for a quick solution without fully understanding and dissecting the questions.

Not Just the Facts

Many people use the terms *wisdom* and *knowledge* interchangeably. They are, however, quite different, and having one in no way confers the other. Knowledge is familiarity with facts. The more knowledge one has, the more things one is capable of doing, but only with wisdom is one able to discern which of the many things they are capable of doing should be pursued and in what order.

Wisdom is essentially the same thing as common sense, the slight difference is that common sense provides the ability to react appropriately, while wisdom is frequently more proactive and additionally encourages the shaping of the environment. As such, wisdom is the most important commodity for anyone who is planning to be successful in any endeavor.

Solomon, the son of King David in the Bible, is considered by many to be the wisest man who ever lived. His wisdom led to great wealth and renown. Many will remember that his first challenge as king of Israel was to determine what to do in the case of two women who came before him, both claiming to be the mother of the same baby. Had he based his decision on

knowledge alone, King Solomon would have focused on the women's testimony by interrogating them. Instead, after hearing all the arguments, King Solomon declared that a swordsman should split the baby and give half to each woman. One of the women thought that was a fair solution and the other was horrified and immediately relinquished her claim on the baby. In his wisdom, he used his knowledge that the real mother would truly love the baby and prefer to give it to the other woman rather than killing it.

You've probably noticed that I frequently quote Solomon, the writer of the Book of Proverbs in the Bible. Since the day that I tried to stab another teenager, I have started and ended each day reading from the Book of Proverbs, which was instrumental on that particular day in helping me realize how foolishly I had been acting. I also believe that God has a sense of humor, because he inspired my parents to give me the middle name of Solomon knowing that I would have this great affinity for the Book of Proverbs, one of the greatest repositories of wisdom. Like Solomon, I, too, gained great notoriety as a surgeon who divided babies, who in this case were conjoined at the head.

Even though my mother had very little formal education and thus little knowledge, she was extremely observant and very wise. Since she worked as a domestic in the homes of very successful people, she decided to observe how they managed their lives to achieve success. She compared their actions with those of the many unsuccessful people who populated our surroundings, and after careful analysis concluded that the big difference was reading and studying. Hence her insistence that my brother and I read two books per week. Although this move was quite

unpopular, it yielded tremendous results for both my brother, Curtis, and me. My mother's wisdom prompted her to use the little knowledge she had to greatly benefit her sons.

While wisdom dictates the need for education, education does not necessarily make one wise. I remember a man when I was growing up who was extremely well educated and had two master's degrees. He could wax eloquently on many subjects but had a very difficult time sustaining himself economically. In fact, he would frequently mooch off of anyone who would take pity on him. On the other hand, many of the greatest achievers in our society never finished college. That includes Bill Gates Jr., Steve Jobs, and Dan Snyder, who is the owner of the Washington Redskins. This does not mean that higher education isn't highly desirable and beneficial, but it does indicate that the wise use of knowledge is more important than knowledge itself.

As my wife and I traveled around the country over the last few months, we encountered large and enthusiastic crowds, many of whom feel that I should run for public office. I believe what they are really clamoring for is not me per se, but for the return of common sense and intelligible speech to solve our ever-increasing problems.

Many Experts Lack Wisdom

It is always interesting to watch the "experts" expound on various topics from the economy to national defense to social issues, and so on, sometimes presenting a host of statistics and little-known studies as proof of their expertise. They claim that their knowledge and all those letters behind their name give them unquestionable authority to declare truth. Some of these

experts continue to claim that our economy remains sluggish because we are not borrowing and spending at a greater rate. They want another stimulus package and if that doesn't work, I can guarantee you they will want yet another. I will admit that these people are very knowledgeable, but I severely doubt that they possess wisdom. I believe my mother with her third-grade education could come up with a better plan than theirs. When someone does challenge them, they love to say, "That person is not an expert and can't possibly know what she's talking about."

I have to chuckle when some of them say that "Ben Carson is a neurosurgeon and can't possibly know anything about economics." Many of these same people were involved in crafting the Affordable Care Act even though their training is not in health care. They say that economic principles have broad application and therefore their recommendations are legitimate. I say that common sense has broad application and can be used in all areas. In fact, I would choose common sense over knowledge in almost every circumstance. I also like to point out that five physicians signed the Declaration of Independence, our founding document, and they certainly were not shy about expressing their views regarding the principles that should govern our nation.

A Vision for a Wiser Health Care System

As a doctor, I believe I have acquired some wisdom that can be applied to our need for a well-functioning health care system for the nation. The agenda needs to be the health of the people as opposed to a political feather in a cap, and being a

doctor, I would make that a priority more naturally than would a politician. Unfortunately, the Affordable Care Act was more of a victory for the Obama administration than for the American people.

In order to have good health care, you need a patient and a health care provider. Originally, the middleman facilitated the relationship between a person and their doctor, but now the middleman is the primary entity, with the health care provider and the patient at his beck and call. The middleman gains financially by denying health care to clients, even when they are supposed to be facilitating the health care process. The whole system is upside down and it is no wonder that it is dysfunctional.

If we are to reform the system, we must know what the overriding goals of reform are. First, not only do we need to stop the rapid rise of health care costs, we need to decrease these costs. Second, we need to make sure that everyone has access to basic health care. Third, we need to restore the doctor-patient relationship and put patients back in charge of their own health. (These are not given in order of importance.)

As I said at the National Prayer Breakfast, I believe everyone should have a health savings account (HSA) and an electronic medical record (EMR) at the time of birth as a first step toward reform. The EMR should only be in the patient's possession in the form of an electronic chip embedded into a card or device that can be shared with a health care provider at the patient's discretion. It would not be available to the IRS or any other governmental agency, and the database would of course need to be as secure as possible to protect personal information from hackers. The HSA could be populated with funds supplied by

an employer, the owner, relatives, friends, and governmental sources.

Since we already spend twice as much per capita on health care in America as does any other country in the world, even if we put substantial monies in everyone's HSA, there's a strong possibility that our shared national health care cost would still decrease. Because there are many responsible individuals and employers who would be willing to contribute to the HSA's, it would only be necessary for the government to make contributions in the cases of individuals incapable of making a living. In Singapore, the government deducts regular contributions to the medical savings accounts from each worker's paycheck. Singapore is capable of providing excellent medical care for all citizens for less than a quarter of what we pay.

With each person owning his own HSA in the United States, most people would become interested in saving by shopping for the most cost-effective high-quality health care plans available. This would bring the entire health care industry into the free-market economic model resulting in price transparency and creating a system where services and pricing are more closely related to value. In our current third-party insurance-based health-care payment system, it would not be unusual to find a hospital in one part of town that charges $66,000 for an appendectomy while in the same city another hospital charges only $14,000 for the same operation. Since a third party is responsible for the payments, the patient doesn't really care which of the two hospitals is used, and spends an unnecessarily large amount of money.

Approximately 80 percent of all encounters between the health care provider and the patient in a system where HSAs are

widely used would be covered by the private account with no need to involve a third party. Since most of the relationships would be doctor-patient relationships, the doctors certainly would not order things without regard to price, and patients would not permit excessive depletion of their HSA's by careless expenditure. With everybody becoming cost conscious, price transparency would be of paramount importance and fair competition would cause prices to be consistent and reasonable.

It is natural to ask what happens if a man needs an operation and does not have enough money in his HSA to cover the cost? The system would be designed in such a way that allows members of his immediate family to shift money from their HSA accounts to his without any penalties. In essence, this would make each family unit its own private health insurance company with no unnecessary middleman increasing costs. I would also make it possible for people to pass the money in their HSAs to family members at the time of their death. This would largely eliminate incentive to spend the money in the account in order not to lose it.

A portion of the money in the account could be used to purchase bridge or catastrophic insurance, which would be relatively inexpensive since it would only be used for those 20 percent of cases too expensive to be covered by the typical HSA account. This would work in a manner similar to homeowners insurance that has a high deductible. If that homeowners insurance was used for every type of repair needed on the home with little or no deduction, the cost would be astronomical. Since it is used only for major and expensive home repairs and because routine repairs are taken care of primarily by the homeowner, the cost is reasonable.

sense would dictate a piecemeal implementation of such a massive program since it profoundly affects virtually every American family. As the program is being rolled out, even its most fanatical supporters are starting to see major flaws and losing their enthusiasm for what is destined to be a disaster.

Many promises were made about the program including the famous presidential promise that "If you like your current insurance, you can keep it." On an almost weekly basis we hear about organizations that are dropping or altering the insurance they offer and about health care providers who are retiring or changing the way they practice. This means that millions of Americans who were satisfied with their health care plans now have to make costly and worrisome changes. Many who previously had health care insurance have been demoted to part-time status, so not only do they lose their insurance, but they lose substantial income. The very fact that everyone is looking for exclusions so they don't have to participate right away should be a red flag to any objective observer.

Learn from Mistakes

One of the prime indicators of wisdom is the ability to see a mistake and back away while learning from it. As Proverbs says, "As a dog returns to its vomit, so a fool repeats his foolishness." Ideology frequently renders one incapable of learning and instead makes its ideologues expert excuse makers. They always have someone or something to blame for the failure of their ideas, which in their opinion can't possibly be flawed in any way. You will hardly ever hear the words "I'm sorry," or "I was wrong" coming from their lips. When you see people who fit

this description, common sense should tell you they are not to be trusted. Sometimes they are gifted with flowery speech and a pleasant persona, which makes them even more dangerous and misleading, particularly for the trusting souls who want so much to believe in them. There is nothing wrong with wanting desperately to believe in someone or some idea, but the application of common sense should tell anyone with a modicum of objectivity that if that person or those ideas consistently yield bad results, their allegiance should be reconsidered.

Set Priorities Wisely

Another key characteristic of wisdom is the ability to prioritize. One must have perspective in order to know which things are most important. Several administrations have talked about the importance of energy independence, yet we remain as dependent on foreign oil as we were years ago. This is because of a problem with priorities. The Environmental Protection Agency feels it has a duty to protect every aspect of the environment under all circumstances, and that priority has been placed above energy independence.

It is estimated that the amount of oil in the Dakotas and Montana is eight times greater than the amount of oil in Saudi Arabia. Yet the EPA has made it difficult for us to take advantage of the enormous amounts of shale oil available in that area of our nation because of pollution problems, and our government has not done much to find a new solution.

With the knowledge of the shale oil and the problems, a wise overseer would be encouraging the development of safe and clean ways to take advantage of this energy bounty rather than

trying to shut down proponents of its use. If you were a seller of jewels and decided to extract them from a cave by using dynamite, but then discovered that the jewels would be ruined by the dynamite blast, you could just give up and say these dynamite blasts destroy air quality and don't yield quality jewels. Or if you were wise, you could say let's look for better and safer ways to extract a valuable commodity.

I thoroughly believe that we have a duty to protect our environment not only for ourselves but for the next generations. However, we also have a duty to develop our economic potential and free ourselves of unnecessary stress and dependency on volatile foreign sources of energy. As a bonus, energy independence for us means decreased revenues for radical terrorist elements who aim to destroy our way of life. Wisdom would lead us to find solutions reflecting those priorities.

Humility Comes Before Wisdom

How does one acquire wisdom? First and foremost, one must be humble enough to recognize that one doesn't know everything. "The more you know, the less you know." This saying means that a wise person understands that on any given issue, there is still much knowledge to be acquired, while the foolish glory in their limited knowledge. It is essential for the prosperity of our nation that our leaders be endowed with knowledge and wisdom.

The acquisition of knowledge is relatively straightforward, but wisdom has to be sought prayerfully from many sources. First, anyone who is trying to live her life wisely should imitate my mother and observe carefully what is going on around her.

If you can learn from the triumphs and mistakes of others, you can move further and faster along the path of success. Second, you can also learn a great deal from your own failures if you are willing to admit failure. Finally and most important, consult God, the source of all wisdom. I ask God for wisdom and guidance on a daily basis, and His answers were instrumental during my surgical career, especially when dealing with situations that were unique and extraordinarily complex. His wisdom is at least equally important in my retirement. Pray for wisdom and believe that you will receive a positive answer to that request as the Bible commands in James 1:5. He always provides what is necessary and will guide us in the best way to serve Him and love our neighbors.

Action Steps

1. Ask an older and wiser person for his or her perspective on a controversial issue.
2. Read the first four chapters of the Book of Proverbs in the Bible this week. Glean the wisdom that is there for the taking.
3. Think of a recent mistake you made and determine to learn from it.
4. Consider your priorities—should you be spending your time differently?

MY BROTHER'S KEEPER

Those who oppress the poor insult their Maker, but those who help the poor honor Him.

PROVERBS 14:31

In the mid-1960s my aunt Jean and uncle William were finally able to escape the inner city of Boston and move to a rural home in the town of Holly, Michigan. They had lived in Michigan before moving to Boston a decade earlier and had always dreamed about returning home. Uncle William still had a lot of friends in Michigan and under his supervision, and with a lot of backbreaking effort, they were able to build a reasonable home.

Uncle William had a brother by the name of Albert who was developmentally disabled, or retarded, as they used to say. There was no possibility of Albert's ever being able to care for himself and my uncle felt it was his responsibility to make sure that all of Albert's basic needs were met. He and my aunt constructed a small home on the property for Albert, and he was pretty reclusive. Even though Albert could not read, write, or even com-

municate in a way that most people understood, he was capable of hard work, including transporting heavy objects, loading and unloading trucks, and other activities where brawn was more important than brains. Albert was always proud when he put in a good day of labor and he enjoyed a good meal. He trusted Uncle William and was very obedient.

The children, including yours truly, were frightened of Albert at first, but as time went on we got to know that he was actually quite benign and very shy. By the time I went off to college at Yale, I had grown quite fond of Albert and my girlfriend Candy, who later became my wife, liked him also.

Albert had never worked outside of the home nor had served in the military, so there was no source of public assistance to help with his care. My relatives never complained about the care they provided for Albert and in fact they felt it was their duty.

My aunt and uncle are examples of a mind-set that seems to be dying out in recent years. Until recently, it was expected in America that families would take care of their own disabled or poor, regardless of whether the government provided any assistance. There was a strong sense of responsibility for family and neighbors in need, a sense that unfortunately is much rarer today. Instead of caring for the disabled and elderly, many Americans expect the government to care for them, resulting in a lowered standard of care and a ballooning national debt. Compounding the problem, many others have embraced models of government assistance that actually push the poor into deeper cycles of poverty. Until these patterns are broken, our nation will continue to decline.

Socialism: A Deterrent to Charity

In many socialist societies the basic needs of the elderly and poor are provided by the state. This is expensive, a problem that is partially resolved by denying certain medical treatments to the elderly. Socialism demands that every member of society have their basic needs provided for by the government, but it is nearly impossible to stay ahead of the expanding costs in this type of governing structure so the citizens become enslaved by governmental debt.

Does capitalism offer a better solution? The answer is a resounding yes, as long as personal responsibility and compassion are included. Capitalism practiced without such elements has given the entire idea of a free market a bad rap, when in reality, every economic system is insufficient and undesirable when it is devoid of virtue. Capitalism certainly should not mean "every man for himself" but should instead allow every man to freely earn and freely share with his neighbor.

Respectful Care for the Elderly

Caring for one's family is a basic responsibility that is becoming increasingly crucial in today's economy. Rapidly shifting population demographics indicate a need to reconsider how we care for the elderly in our nation. Less than half of the population can now look forward to a comfortable retirement at age sixty-five because retirement plans have been derailed by a stagnant economy with no signs of a lasting and meaningful recovery. Many older couples can certainly pay their mortgage, car notes, utility bills, and supply food and some level of entertainment

without much difficulty as long as they continue to work. With the job market undergoing many changes, it will be hard for many elderly individuals who do not have appropriate skills to keep up and they may be forced into retirement.

Unfortunately, the proliferation of nursing homes and elder care facilities in our society indicates that many families are reluctant to exercise enough compassion to care for their own parents and relatives. In some cases people must work outside the home to earn a living and have relatives who cannot be left alone, and these cases are understandable, but those who expect others to care for their parents and don't even visit them should remember that these people took care of them when they could not care for themselves.

In cases where the problem is due more to circumstances rather than lack of character, we need to work together to find solutions. The task of providing full-time care for the elderly or disabled has become progressively more difficult in families where everyone is working outside the home and no one can be a full-time guardian for the person(s) in need. Fortunately, there is an old saying that "necessity is the mother of invention." The importance of caring for one's own remains unchanged, and our society needs to create new ways of doing this.

In some ways, this is already happening. A whole new industry known as adult day care arose because of this necessity. It has created many jobs and provided a stimulating and safe environment for millions of elderly and incapacitated individuals. Many of these adult day care centers are independently owned and operated with little or no assistance from the government. Community living with the ability to pool and share resources can provide a healthy social environment while reducing finan-

cial obligations. A variety of such communities can be built around the nation quite economically, allowing freedom and peace of mind to those who deserve a period of relaxation in their lives. These are the kinds of organizations that should be encouraged as time goes on, particularly in light of the growing number of elderly individuals in our society. If we just depend on government programs as the number of elders increases faster than our young population, it will accelerate our rate of debt accumulation, which will negatively affect us all.

We also need to encourage everyone to feel a responsibility toward taking care of their elderly parents and disabled relatives. It should be anticipated that the day will come when it will be necessary to do this, as it probably will be for each of us to be taken care of by sons and daughters, nieces and nephews, in-laws, or other relatives in the future. This care can be expensive, but it is not nearly as costly as nursing homes and other full-time care facilities. If these expenses are anticipated and resources are set aside accordingly, undue hardship and guilt can frequently be avoided.

I know there will be some people saying, "I can barely care for my own needs, how can anyone expect me to provide for someone else, even if they are my parents?" During the time in America when these kinds of questions were not asked, people didn't necessarily have to have multiple vehicles, flat screen televisions, multiple cell phones, iPads, and a host of other "necessities." This begs the question: Is it more important to take care of your extended family or have the creature comforts pop culture demands?

Compassion for the Poor

Anyone familiar with the Bible knows that our responsibilities to care for others don't end with our families. There are numerous Biblical references to our obligations to care for the poor and to love our neighbors as ourselves. And even if you don't believe in God and/or the Bible, there are commonsense reasons to exercise compassion toward the poor. Most of us have an innate sense that it is right to care for those less fortunate than ourselves, and even those with the hardest hearts should understand that elevating the social status of the poor is better for the economy as a whole.

Compassion, however, should mean providing a mechanism to escape poverty rather than simply maintaining people in an impoverished state by supplying handouts. By doing this we give them an opportunity to elevate their personal situations, which eventually decreases our need to take care of them and empowers them to be able to exercise compassion toward others.

The Problem of Government Dependency

Having established that we should care about our neighbors, the next question is who is my neighbor and where does my responsibility end, leaving the government in charge? My answer will come as a great surprise to many, but I do not believe the government has any obligation to take care of able-bodied citizens who are capable of providing for themselves. Private citizens, on the other hand, should be encouraged but not coerced to provide as much aid and opportunities to their neigh-

bors as they are capable of. Indiscriminately providing for the needs of people who can provide for themselves is not only unwise, it is cruel because it tends in many cases to create dependency and robs people of their God-given dignity.

The only reason I can imagine that it would be a good idea for government to foster dependency in large groups of citizens is to cultivate a dependable voting bloc that will guarantee continued power as long as the entitlements are provided. The problem of course is that such a government will eventually "run out of other people's money," as Margaret Thatcher once famously said.

The Value of the Minimum-Wage Job

As I mentioned earlier, it is quite possible to obtain more money from the welfare system than one would get from a minimum-wage job. It is hard to criticize someone who takes advantage of such a situation. The problem with this line of thinking is that it relegates the value of job experience to a lowly position on the totem pole.

I have had many jobs on the way to becoming a physician, all of which provided some knowledge and skill sets that were useful, no matter how low-skilled and low-paid they were. My first jobs were as a lab assistant both in high school and at Wayne State University in Detroit, where I learned concepts such as sterility and how to set up laboratory experiments. During the summer between high school and college, I obtained a job as a payroll office clerk at the Ford Motors world headquarters, where I learned about many office machines and how to operate them. Next I had a job as a bank teller, where I

learned accuracy and efficiency as well some things about dealing with bank robbers. A job as a mailroom clerk taught me various ways of efficient filing and delivery, and a job as an encyclopedia salesman taught me much about presentation. One of my best experiences was as a supervisor for highway cleanup crews. I learned how to motivate individuals who were not interested in working and I learned the importance of teamwork in the generation of an efficient workforce.

My experience as an assembly line worker in an automobile factory taught me the importance of concentration, and my job as a student aid to the Yale University campus police gave me an opportunity to learn a great deal about security for a large organization. With that job there were also a lot of perks, like being able to get into concerts free of charge. And I derived great benefit from my job as an X-ray technician between my first and second years in medical school. Learning how to operate that equipment led to a subsequent new technique for visualizing a difficult part of the skull that facilitated a complex neurosurgical procedure. Later in life as an attending neurosurgeon, occasions would arise when X-rays had to be taken in the operating room and all the X-ray technicians were tied up elsewhere. I was able to save a great deal of time by being able to operate the equipment myself, which typically amazed the operating room staff.

I also had a job as a crane operator in a steel factory that helped me realize that I was gifted with great eye-hand coordination, a fact that later affected my career choice. Finally, a job as a school bus driver taught me to be extremely cautious around small schoolchildren.

On the surface it might appear that many of these jobs had

nothing to do with a successful career as a neurosurgeon, but closer analysis should lead one to the understanding that no knowledge is wasted knowledge. It can be used in virtually any career, and opens many doors of opportunity.

I don't wish to sound cold, but sitting around collecting welfare checks is unlikely to bolster one's résumé and expose one to job opportunities. When you make yourself valuable by acquiring knowledge and many skills, you make yourself more employable. Even if no one wants to hire you, you can create your own job. Being able to cut a lawn, weed a lawn, or garden, cook, clean, paint, wash cars, pick fruits and vegetables, and so on may not make you a millionaire, but certainly can pay the bills and put food on the table if you are not extravagant.

Sometimes one has to be humble enough to start at the bottom with a minimum-wage job even if you have a college degree. Once you get your foot in the door, you can prove your worth and rapidly move up the ladder. If you never get in the door, it is unlikely that you will rise to the top.

I have no doubt that there are millions of extremely talented and intelligent people who have dropped out of the labor force and are living on the dole. They are not counted as unemployed, which makes the government happy, because it can claim that the jobless numbers are improving. These people are doing no one, including themselves, a favor by depriving the labor force of their potential contributions. If you know such individuals, please share this chapter with them and encourage them to go out and make the American dream come true in their lives— that is one way of being your brother's keeper.

Rolling Back Welfare

One logical and compassionate solution to the problem of growing welfare rolls is to set a date several years away for the elimination of welfare payments for able-bodied individuals who could work and support themselves. This would give them time to prepare for the job market and it would also make people much more careful in their family planning. Some liberals would say that is mean and heartless, but some conservatives would say that continuing to sustain people in a dependent position with meager welfare payments is what is really cruel, because it frequently removes the incentive to engage in self-improvement activities.

People (Not Government) Helping People

When it comes to empowering those who have been rendered complacent by an overly generous system that cultivates their votes rather than their talents, churches and other charitable organizations can play an important role. Loving and caring relationships with those in need of jobs and self-esteem can bring hope and encouragement to the downtrodden, especially when combined with examples of success, the provision of opportunities, and training to achieve that success. It's all about people helping people, which is why such organizations exist in the first place and why they have tax-exempt status.

The Reformed Church of Bronxville, New York, has a mentorship program called "Coming Home," which aids formerly incarcerated individuals in their adjustment and acclimation

into society. Dawn Ravella, the director of mission and out-reach at the church said,

> The idea is to absorb them into a supportive community to help with the re-entry process, deal with the trauma and to help them get back on their feet.... It's so powerful what's happening here. We at the church thought we were starting this to help other people, and it's been transformational for us.
>
> This program has been duplicated in at least eight other churches in New York City.

And as far as helping the downtrodden, since 2005, 600,000 volunteers have worked 1.4 million man-hours under the auspices of Samaritan's Purse led by Franklin Graham, helping 24,000 families in 140 disasters across the nation. Also, their "Operation Heal Our Patriots" program liberates double-amputee veterans, enabling them to live more normal lives.

Some people are not religious and do not believe that religion is helpful, but hopefully such people are desirous of helping their fellow citizens achieve success in their lives. There is absolutely no reason why they cannot cooperate with churches and community organizations in a synergistic fashion to once again achieve a growing and vital economy that offers people a hand up rather than a handout.

I am particularly fond of churches because they are supposed to show kindness toward others, and if they do not, they can be embarrassed when that is pointed out to them, resulting in renewed efforts to help others. Other types of organizations, especially government agencies, are frequently staffed by people who only see it as a job, know they have job security, and there-

fore treat people without respect or compassion. If I had the authority to do so, I would plant random observers around governmental employees who could record their pattern of behavior and dismiss without recourse those people who manifested consistently unacceptable behavior. I believe that would quickly alter the nonchalant attitudes of government employees. I also believe that these employees would feel better about their jobs and themselves with the application of kindness and compassion to their daily chores.

What About Those Who Won't Take Responsibility?

I can't leave this topic without talking about those individuals in our society who are completely and utterly irresponsible. Who is responsible for taking care of those who have no intention of taking care of themselves? If they are not devoid of mental faculties, it is safe to assume that their behavior pattern is learned and that it can be unlearned by allowing them to experience the consequences of their choices. This is one of the ways that children are taught to be responsible and I believe it is a technique that will also work for adults who act like children.

Those who are horrified at such a suggestion should feel perfectly free to take these individuals under their wings and care for their needs. I believe in grace and am grateful for the undeserved mercy that I have received, especially mercy that forced me to better myself. However, to thrust this responsibility of caring for them on everyone else is unfair and encourages others to adopt similar irresponsible lifestyles.

We should be dedicated to providing for all of our citizens

life, liberty, and the pursuit of happiness. That means giving them the opportunity to pursue any course of action they choose for the purpose of bringing fulfillment to their lives, assuming it is legal. In no reasonable way can our responsibility as a society be interpreted as providing for the needs of all citizens, especially if they are ones who by choice make no attempt to provide for themselves. Again, this applies only to individuals who are fully capable of taking care of themselves.

True Compassion—A Rare Thing

Unfortunately, both Republican and Democratic politicians will have objections to the proposals I have made. I have heard some conservatives say all of us should have enough sense to adequately prepare for our retirement and if we fail to do so, we should have to suffer the consequences. Although there may be some merit to this sentiment, it does not show compassion. We are all human beings with shortcomings, therefore whenever we are capable of helping someone in need, we should do so even if his own mistakes produced the need, because this is what we would want them to do if the situation were reversed. I have heard some liberals say we have an obligation to fully take care of everyone regardless of lifestyle and poor choices. This lack of tough love encourages more irresponsible behavior and a progressively larger number of people to care for until all resources are exhausted. This seems compassionate, but instead is cruel like anything else that fosters dependency.

In short, yes, we are our brothers' keepers, but we have to be smart in the way that we keep them, and the compassion we

show must be in consideration of the long term, with a defined purpose of providing life, liberty, and the pursuit of happiness.

Action Steps

1. Check on an elderly relative or friend this week.
2. Go out of your way to help a stranger this week.
3. Commit a percentage of your time for volunteer work at a local charity this month.
4. Find out what your church or religious organization is doing for your community.

PART THREE

—

WHO WE ARE

WITHOUT A VISION

When people do not accept divine guidance, they run wild.
But whoever obeys the law is happy.

PROVERBS 29:18

When I was in middle school I was friends with a nice young
man named Charlie, who served as a punching bag for many of
the other students, including the class bully, Randy. One day
when the teacher was not in the room, Randy beat Charlie and
began strangling him. Many of the other students gasped in
horror and thought that they were going to witness a murder.
Fortunately, Randy came to his senses and desisted from his
attack. Charlie was visibly shaken but continued with his non-
confrontational demeanor until one day one of the smaller boys
attacked him and he decided to fight back. Not only did he win
the fight but he completely dominated the contest, leaving the
other boy in a state of total humiliation that was well deserved.
That day marked a turning point in Charlie's life and he became
a completely different person. His confidence grew and people

stopped picking on him. He also became a much better student and went on to become very successful in high school.

Charlie's metamorphosis occurred when he faced significant trials in his life head-on. His ordeal strengthened him, and his victory gave him a different vision for his life. He did not necessarily become a combatant, but he gained enough self-confidence to be able to live his life without fear. Once he had a glimpse of how good life could be out from under a bully's thumb, he began to take himself seriously. What happened with Charlie undoubtedly gave me the courage to resist a bully later in my life. Without his example, I might not have known it would be possible to stand up for myself, to envision a life free of being bullied.

Bullying by the British was a major impetus for the resistance movement that resulted in our ultimate independence and the establishment of our Constitution. An even bigger role was played in the establishment of a national vision by the desire for freedom. Our founders saw themselves as free people who could pursue whatever dreams inspired them. However, success is never achieved by people who only dream and do not act. My wife and I have some close friends who are examples of this truth. The husband was an attorney and the wife was an elementary school teacher. She was constantly talking about her dream of becoming a lawyer but she never really pursued that dream. I remember saying to her one day, "Just do it and stop dreaming." I reminded her that it only takes three years to complete law school and that three years goes by quite rapidly. She has been a successful attorney for many years and has established quite a reputation. Our founders were able to conquer their fears and act on their dreams on the way to establishing a

spectacular vision for America. They embedded that vision in the Constitution of the United States of America and intended for that document to be revered and held up as a guidepost for a truly free society.

Proverbs 29:18 (NKJV) says, "Without a vision the people perish." If a society doesn't have a shared understanding of its goals, it cannot move forward. To aimlessly drift along while reacting to events is a recipe for disaster. As Americans, we have the vision of our founders, codified in the Constitution and lived out by citizens who worked together, as a heritage. Unless we recover our lost vision, communicate it simply to the next generation, and seek out visionary leaders, our country will remain in serious trouble.

The Constitution as Vision

During the American Revolution, the colonies differed from one another in many ways but had a shared vision of liberation from a dominating British monarch. Each of the states had different mechanisms for achieving economic success and they had different feelings about the institution of slavery, but their overwhelming desire was to be able to pursue their dreams without outside interference. They were wise enough to recognize that their chances of success would be greatly enhanced if they worked together.

In 1787, the union almost split apart due to what were thought to be irreconcilable differences. It took the wise words of the senior statesman, Benjamin Franklin, to reinstate unity with his recommendation of prayer. He and other leaders were subsequently able to help frame one of the most concise and

inspirational national visions ever crafted, namely, the U.S. Constitution.

The Constitution was written primarily to protect the rights of the people and not the rights of the government to rule the people. It restrains the natural tendencies of government to expand while disregarding the rights of its constituents. Our freedoms are safe as long as we abide by its principles.

Drifting Away

Unfortunately, the executive, judicial, and legislative branches of government have become increasingly concerned with their image and their political parties, have drifted away from strict interpretations of the Constitution, and have substituted their own ideologies for the original vision. As a result, our government produces massively complicated taxation schemes, impossibly intricate and uninterpretable health care laws, and other intrusive measures instead of being a watchful guardian of our rights. Instead of providing an environment that allows diligent people to thrive on the basis of their own hard work and entrepreneurship, our government has taken on the role of trying to care for everyone's needs and redistributing the fruits of everyone's labors in a way consistent with its own ideology.

A New Utopian Vision?

Under this new vision for America, lawmakers are not particularly concerned with the people's will, since they firmly believe that they know better than the people. Confident in the superiority of their ideas, they cram measures like the Affordable Care

Act down the throats of protesting citizens and then have the nerve to tell the people that they'll like it once they understand it. This kind of paternal attitude is changing us from a representative type of governmental structure to a nanny state, where the government tells the constituency what's good for them and monitors and regulates every aspect of their lives.

The vision of this new form of government is a society where the basic needs of everyone are provided and no one needs to fret about anything, regardless of whether they choose to work hard and be productive or relax and enjoy life. This is a very attractive vision to those looking for a free ride. It certainly would not have been the kind of vision that hundreds of years ago would have caused many immigrants to cross treacherous seas and leave behind loved ones in order to try to provide a better future for their families.

The United States is not the first nation to alter its vision to include a more communal society, an alteration which on its surface seems like a noble goal. The problems with these utopian goals is that they never work in practice. For the government to be able to distribute goods to everyone, there must be significant production of goods and services. If producers know that the government is going to redistribute the wealth they accumulate, they have little incentive to increase production to meet the demand—they would be working more for the same amount of income. If the government decides to force the producer to manufacture more goods, a new problem arises: It is very difficult for a centralized government to know exactly how much to produce without the signals of a free market. Thus centralized economies usually end up with a mismatch between supply and demand.

Practical problems aside, there are moral problems with redistribution. Thomas Jefferson famously put it similarly when he said, "To take from one, because it is thought his own industry and that of his father's has acquired too much, in order to spare to others, who, or whose fathers, have not exercised equal industry and skill, is to violate arbitrarily the first principle of association, the guarantee to everyone the free exercise of his industry and the fruits acquired by it." The utopian vision of communal societies strongly disagrees with Jefferson's views and would advocate for equitable redistribution to prevent massive accumulation by any one group or poverty by another group. The communal philosophy does not recognize exceptional production by individuals or exceptional nonproduction.

When the vision of the U.S. government included guarding the rights of people but staying out of their way, America was an economic engine more powerful than anything the world had ever witnessed. That engine is still in place, and if the original vision can be restored, that engine could restart and quickly obliterate our national debt while helping our nation reclaim its rightful position of leadership and respect throughout the world. Our ability to care for the indigent would also be considerably enhanced and the number of indigent would be significantly decreased in a thriving job market.

Deep Division

Because of our neglect of the Constitution, it has been a while since the people of America could agree on a national vision. Perhaps the last time was toward the end of the Cold War when

our unity and strength radically changed the world's power structure for the better. There was a great deal of unity across party lines and the resultant national vision made us a formidable foe or a powerful ally. Today we are deeply divided along ideological lines, as discussed earlier in the book. As a result, our political climate changes dramatically every time power shifts from one party to another. Massive swings to the right are followed by massive swings to the left, destroying the unity that was our strength.

There are deep and sometimes hostile divisions between those who believe in God and those who are atheists. Even deeper divisions exist between those who believe in personal responsibility and those who believe that there is no problem with government dependency. Many believe that as the world's only superpower the United States should engage in strong international leadership, while others feel strongly that we should adopt a laissez-faire attitude. The right to bear arms versus the concern for public safety has produced a deep chasm as have attitudes about gay marriage, abortion, and other social issues. Every time the pendulum swings it leaves more deeply entrenched people at the extremities of the swing. This exacerbates tensions that used to be relatively minor differences.

Because we have strayed so far from the original intent of our nation's goals, and because philosophical differences are so deep and entrenched, the legitimate question is whether our disparities can be peacefully resolved, resulting in a long-term forward trajectory instead of massive pendulum swings. I believe it is possible for us to adopt a positive direction, but it will require exceptionally wise and courageous leadership.

A Constitutional Convention?

Recently, some radio commentators have suggested the need for another constitutional convention since the last one was more than two hundred years ago. While I would be delighted to see a new convention, I don't believe it is practical due to the size, complexity, dishonesty, and animosity that characterizes our political structure today. Fortunately, our founders were visionary and wise men who could foresee the turmoil we now face and anticipated almost everything that would be destructive to their vision except apathy on behalf of the populace in terms of protecting our freedom.

Revering the Constitution

I believe the only thing that will correct our downward trajectory is the rekindling of the enthusiasm for individual freedom and the reestablishment of the U.S. Constitution as the dominant document of governance. Unless the majority of Americans awaken from their complacency and recognize the threat to their fundamental individual liberties imposed by continued expansion of the federal government, nothing will save us from the fate of all pinnacle nations that have preceded us, those that tolerated political and moral corruption while ignoring fiscal irresponsibility.

We the people have lost the inspiration that produced the "can-do attitude" that was our foremost characteristic. We have capitulated to the forces of ever-expanding governmental control of our lives. But it is not too late for us to change. As a beginning, all American citizens must be familiar with our

Constitution, and they must be brave enough to stand up for its principles even if that makes them temporarily unpopular. They must be willing to share their knowledge with others and encourage frank discussions rather than "going along to get along."

Voting for the Constitution

The last point that I just mentioned is the safeguard that our founders built into our system of government to allow "we the people" to rectify an out-of-control governmental structure. As outraged citizens, we have the power to vote out of office any politician who refuses to uphold the Constitution.

One of the most important steps that must be taken if America is to remain free is stimulation of the large voter base that has basically tuned out of politics. One of the political parties or perhaps a new political party has to be dependable and courageously uphold the Constitution. The fact that the Republican Party in particular often seems to stand for principle, only to cave in to pressure at the last minute, has turned off a huge number of voters. A true reformation of the Republican Party would be a breath of fresh air for those voters. Those voters are also up for grabs for the Democrats if they decide suddenly that they want to be the party of the Constitution. In an ideal world, both parties would desire to uphold the Constitution, and their energies could be spent elsewhere, including solving our nation's problems instead of engaging in ideological squabbles.

Just prior to the start of the American Revolution, and throughout its duration, concerned citizens engaged in self-

education and education of others by convening community meetings, often in one another's homes, to discuss the desire for freedom and the threat posed by inaction. The same kinds of meetings were held throughout Europe during and after the Dark Ages in an attempt to keep Christianity alive. Both movements were successful because people became activists and used their collective skills, resources, and intellect to bring about the changes they desired. If Americans would meet together the same way and discuss which candidates would best honor the Constitutional vision, our future's security would be much improved.

In making decisions about who should be replaced, it is important for the people not to be deceived by those politicians who claim that the matters they are dealing with and voting on are too complex for the average citizen to understand. I believe our political role models should be people who understand and revere the U.S. Constitution and are willing to defend it from those who feel it is outdated. We need people who can articulate their beliefs in a way that is easily understandable, and people who are willing to point out who among their compatriots are deviating from the Constitution and why. People who are worried about reelection are terrible representatives, especially when they place reelection above principles. Until we the people learn to identify and support those political role models who truly represent our interests, we can expect continued deterioration of governmental trust and ongoing governmental expansion into every aspect of our lives.

In my opinion, if politicians are unable to explain a law or statute in a way that a seventh grader could understand it, then they don't understand it either and should be provided an op-

portunity to study after being voted out of office. Anyone who writes a law that cannot be easily understood by an average citizen is not worthy of leadership. The Constitution, which was written by extremely learned men, is quite easy to understand and should serve as a gold standard for the language and size of subsequent legislation that is introduced.

Visionary Leadership

Dynamic national leaders tend to be exceptionally good at painting a clear vision that inspires and motivates the populace. For the United States, George Washington was such a figure. He was extraordinarily brave and disciplined, and inspired confidence in his troops even though the odds of victory were often minuscule. He helped formulate the goals for our nation, which included a degree of personal freedom for all citizens, something rarely witnessed in the world previously. This understanding gave him the fortitude to resist the many calls for him to become a monarch.

The British adversaries of General Washington were used to beating their subjects into submission and treated the colonies like many of the other colonies around the world. But they had no overarching vision, putting them at a distinct disadvantage even though they were the most powerful fighting force in the world at that time, and their opponents were an ill-equipped, ragtag bunch of militiamen.

If today's Americans refuse to give up on the constitutional vision, explain that vision clearly, and elect leaders who will uphold it, we will likewise defeat the powers that would bring our country down.

Action Steps

1. Do you have a personal vision for the rest of your life? If not, stop and write out your lifetime, one-, five-, and ten-year goals.
2. Read the Declaration of Independence and the Constitution.
3. Examine candidates in the next election to see if any are potential visionary leaders.
4. Consider whether freedom or security is most important to you. Do you see the trade-offs between the two?

ROLE MODELS

Do not carouse with drunkards and gluttons, for they are on their way to poverty. Too much sleep clothes a person with rags. Listen to your father, who gave you life, and don't despise your mother's experience when she is old.

PROVERBS 23:20-22

As a child in Detroit and Boston, I had a rather limited worldview. The coolest people around were the drug dealers who drove big-finned fancy cars with huge white-walled tires, and always displayed the latest fashions, particularly in footwear and showy big straw hats. Also highly admired were the people who had risen to the rank of foreman in one of the many factories that fueled the burgeoning industrial-based economy. Most of the kids, including me, did not have a big vision of anything outside of our small world and being a dealer or foreman would have been great.

I was never heavily drawn toward drug selling or factory work, but instead I was fascinated whenever I heard stories about doctors, especially the ones I heard in church about mis-

sionary doctors who lived amazing adventures. My family certainly was not friendly with any doctors, but at the little community hospital in our neighborhood, one could occasionally see a well-dressed and polished physician driving off in a beautiful car. I was always eager to visit a doctor even if it meant getting a shot, and I was magnetically drawn to any doctor show on television, especially Dr. Kildare, who was a general practitioner, and Dr. Ben Casey, who was a neurosurgeon.

As mentioned earlier, in the fifth grade my academic performance was so poor that my mother (with her third-grade education) turned off the television and made us read books. I was rather disgruntled at first, but since I had no choice in the matter I began focusing on the reading so I could get my mother-required book reports done, even though she couldn't read them, which we didn't know. Within a matter of weeks, I began to actually know some of the answers to questions in various classes, which was shocking to the teachers and my classmates, and frankly to me as well.

I started out reading about animals because I love nature. I then moved on to plants and minerals before discovering what really affected me: stories about people. As I read about people of great accomplishment I began to understand that success is no accident that only happens to lucky people. Instead it became clear to me that the person who has the most to do with what happens to you in life is you!

Reading helped me realize that becoming a doctor was definitely within my grasp and that I could make this dream a reality if I was willing to invest the necessary time and effort. My vision was ever before me and buoyed me during times of discouragement. The environment can be a small factor but it

pales in comparison with the power of determination to achieve a dream.

I did not like poverty. In fact, I hated it until I began reading those books and realized that I had the power to control my own destiny and did not have to be a victim of circumstances. I know many successful people who grew up in poverty and also came to this realization sometime during their preadolescent years. What happened is that we developed a vision of what our lives could be and began to follow that vision, which required establishing plans and following them. When you have a vision, it is much easier to keep your target in sight and know when you are deviating from the plan.

Our Young People Need Vision

I've discussed how necessary a shared vision is to a country. It is equally important to make sure that the young individuals in the country are given role models, providing an inspiring vision of what their lives can be. As a teenager there was a period of time when I began to "hang out" with a gang after school and into the evening. The leader of the group was older than most of the kids at school because he had failed several grades. He was an extremely cool guy who not only had brass knuckles and a knife but he also possessed a shiny .22 caliber handgun. He demonstrated such extreme confidence that many of us followed him around like little ducklings. He either possessed or had access to cars and motorcycles and he always seemed to be flush with cash. For a kid surrounded by poverty and a sense of helplessness, being around a person like this was exciting and offered a false hope of quick financial security.

Fortunately, my fascination with his lifestyle was short-lived as I became captivated by the lives of great inventors, doctors, and explorers whom I was reading about in the library books. Once again my future was protected by academic pursuits, because that young man and many of his followers subsequently lost their lives to the violent subculture rampant in cities like Detroit.

It is common for young people to be deceived by glamour, power, or wealth when choosing their role models. I should quickly add that some adults are also easily fooled by such things. We have a duty as parents and guardians to strive to influence which people capture our children's imaginations. It means taking an active role in their lives and always being aware of who their friends are and what places they frequent. It also means trying to put them in the presence of people of great accomplishment whom we want them to emulate. These are things that used to be done quite routinely by caring guardians, but now many young people derive their identity from their peer group and their social network, which can be extensive.

Miley Cyrus Is Not a Role Model

If we don't help set role models for our children, the media will provide them—and they will not be the role models who will inspire our children to save America by living lives of wisdom, ambition, humility, and discipline.

Many sports stars are among our young people's heroes, but their character is often cause for concern. For example, before he died, I had an opportunity to have breakfast with Tom Landry, the famous former coach of the Dallas Cowboys. We

were talking about many of the spectacular players he had coached over the years, but I was unpleasantly surprised to hear that almost all those players had borrowed money from the coach or from others and were far from leading lives of comfort and productivity. I heard exactly the same story in talking to my friend Tony Dungy, who coached the Indianapolis Colts during their glory days. Many of these players are held up before our young people as great heroes because they can throw or catch a ball or perform some other athletic feat consistently and with great flair. Entertainers similarly are extolled as superior human specimens worthy of our praise, adoration, and attention.

Some of these people possess spectacular talent and I do not begrudge them the millions of dollars they receive for displaying those talents. I am, however, concerned about the godlike status bestowed on them when in most cases their intellectual contributions to the betterment of our society do not justify such deification. Like athletes, many entertainers are here today and gone tomorrow. It is a sad sight wandering through some of the Las Vegas casinos and seeing performers trying to get spectators to remember their glory days. I wish there were a television show that came on every day titled *Lifestyles of the Formerly Rich and Famous*. This would perhaps enable many of our young people to recognize the fleeting nature of some types of fame and begin to focus on developing their God-given intellectual talents so they can make a contribution to the betterment of society.

This is not to say that we don't need and value athletes and entertainers but we need to bring perspective to the table when talking about these kinds of careers. For example, only seven in one million will become starters in the NBA. Less than 1 per-

cent of student athletes attending college will have a career in professional sports due to the limited number of available slots. The average career span of a professional athlete is less than five years, and only one in ten thousand makes it in a lasting way in the entertainment field. Despite these discouraging odds, thousands of people dedicate themselves to being one of the few, while often neglecting preparation for the assumption of key productive roles in society.

More negative role models were identified in a parents' survey taken at the time of the penning of this book. Topping the list was former Disney star Miley Cyrus, who for years gave hope to parents as a wholesome character but changed into an R-rated performer without warning in August of 2013. And Chris Brown, the singer who assaulted Rihanna, had the distinct honor of being the top worst male role model.

Our government officials aren't much better. According to Emily Post, for proper etiquette our high-ranking government officials are to be addressed "The Honorable _____." However, with congressmen like Anthony Weiner with his sexting, former presidential candidate John Edwards's campaign finance fraud and infidelity, and Governor Mark Sanford skipping out of the country away from his family on Father's Day to be with a mistress, it is small wonder that our youth often have a difficult time finding their identities.

If sports stars and entertainers and even government officials are not the optimal role models, who should we be holding up as examples for society? A role model is someone whose life is worthy of emulation. Those would be individuals who not only are successful but who also contribute to the well-being of society at large. There is nothing that says these people need to

be famous and many of the best role models live right in our own houses.

My Mother: One of the Best Role Models I've Seen

My mother provided for my brother and me a wonderful example of how not to be a victim. Even though the odds sometimes seemed stacked against her, she would never give up. I remember when my brother started high school they placed him in the vocational track instead of the college prep track. My mother was more than a little upset and ruffled many feathers from the local school all the way to the Board of Education of Detroit to alter that situation. I remember another time when a hit-and-run driver hit her car and sped away. She backed up the car and chased him for thirty minutes through the streets of Southwest Detroit before he finally gave up. You certainly did not have to worry about whether she could defend herself physically if she caught him, even though she was only five foot three. The example of tenacity and courage that she presented certainly was not lost on me and is a large part of who I am today.

Teachers as Role Models

Even though my mother was a terrific role model, she did not have the wherewithal to be a good academic mentor. Fortunately, I had several teachers along the way who recognized some potential in a poor boy from the ghetto, and decided to invest much time and effort to make sure that I not only mastered my school work but also listened to quite a bit of advice they gave me about how to be successful in life. I was particu-

larly grateful for all the tips I received about college life and how to overcome the challenges it would present. Teachers frequently get a bad rap, but good ones can mean the difference between success and failure in many lives. When they are driven by their inherent goodness rather than some of the teacher unions, their potential for doing good is almost unlimited.

The Inventor as Role Model

When it comes to making contributions to society, inventors can serve as spectacular role models. People like Thomas Edison, Henry Ford, and Elijah McCoy, an inventor of locomotive lubrication systems, had profound effects on the way we all live. African American Garrett Morgan, widely known for his innovations with the traffic light, in 1916 demonstrated the effectiveness of his invention the "Morgan Safety Hood and Smoke Protector" (now known as the gas mask) by rescuing 32 men trapped 250 feet underground in a tunnel. Prior to that event, people had scoffed at his lifesaving innovation. This invention was then utilized by the U.S. Army, saving many lives during World War I, and is now commonly used all over the world by fire and police departments, as well as the military (http://inventors.about.com/od/mstartinventors/a/Garrett_Morgan.htm). Thomas Edison was a determined inventor who knew 999 ways a lightbulb did *not* work. His associate, Lewis Latimer, who came up with the filament that made the bulb last for more than a few days, happened to be born in Massachusetts of escaped slaves from Virginia. Although his parents had escaped six years before Lewis was born, he was still considered a slave and his freedom had to be defended by Frederick Douglass and William Lloyd Garrison in

Boston, actually purchasing his freedom himself, with the help of a local minister. After serving in the navy during the Civil War (he enlisted at age sixteen), he was honorably discharged.

Identifying Contemporary Role Models

All the people mentioned above embody the "can-do" attitude that helped America rapidly gain power and position in the world. Unfortunately, in the current atmosphere of division and demonization of political opponents and with the ever-present influence of political correctness, it is very difficult to identify generally admired people. But it is fair to say that most people admire courage and the willingness to sacrifice in order to achieve a goal. This is why people like Albert Einstein, Winston Churchill, Ronald Reagan, and John F. Kennedy are widely admired. They all had their flaws, as is the case with every one of us, but they all faced gigantic obstacles and were victorious. People like Helen Keller, Neil Armstrong, and many war heroes also demonstrated a level of courage that most of us can only dream about. Courage is admired so much because it is lacking in so many. People of courage tend to be much less concerned about their status with other people than they are with their ability to consistently uphold principles and values. Such people frequently are not appreciated during their lifetimes, but the pages of history are frequently kind to them. It takes some degree of wisdom to be able to identify the courageous role models living and working before our very eyes.

Action Steps

1. Discuss heroes and role models with the young people in your life. Ask who their role models are and recommend role models discussed in this chapter.
2. Discuss heroes and role models with the older people in your life and compare their answers with those of the young people. Are their role models similar or different?
3. Thank one of your role models for his or her example.
4. Examine your life. Could you be a role model for a younger person?

THE ORIGIN OF MORALITY

Those who follow the right path fear the Lord; those who
take the wrong path despise Him.

PROVERBS 14:2

When I was in my early teens, my brother and I acquired a BB
gun. We were excited and began shooting it behind the house,
using cans as targets. We were having so much fun that we
didn't think about where the errant BBs were going. The man
who lived across the alley came to our home holding a screen
with multiple holes in it. It looked amazingly like holes that
would be made by a BB gun. We didn't have money to replace
the screen, but agreed to do some chores for our neighbor.
Needless to say we stopped shooting the gun in the neighborhood.

However, our aunt Jean and uncle William lived out in the
country where there was plenty of space to shoot a BB gun and
we could hardly wait to get there. One Sunday morning while
we were spending the weekend with our relatives in the country, I spotted a red-winged blackbird that seemed to be an ex-

cellent target for an eagle-eyed BB gun marksman. I took careful aim at the beautiful creature sitting peacefully high above the fray in a tree. I really did not expect to hit the bird, but only seconds after I squeezed the trigger, the delicate form of the innocent creature fell lifelessly to the ground. I went over to the body and gazed at it with a combination of horror and pride. I was disgusted with myself for killing an innocent animal and I vowed never to shoot another bird and I never have.

Was I wrong to kill that bird and did it really even matter in the whole scheme of things? No one would really miss that bird except maybe the little chicks if this happened to be their mother out looking for food. Yet I couldn't find any way to assuage my guilt. The fact that I felt guilt obviously meant that I thought I had done something wrong—but how would I have known that? No one had ever explicitly told me not to shoot a bird, yet I had an innate sense that there was an absolute standard of morality that I had violated.

Who Says?

What is right? What is wrong? And who gets to determine the answers to these questions? For a nation to be truly united, most of its citizens must agree on the answers to these questions—or at least agree that there are answers to be found. For years, most Americans have turned to a belief in God and the Bible for answers. From the Creation story to the Ten Commandments to the Gospels to the Epistles, the Bible provided an explanation for the meaning of life and instructed us in moral principles. We held to a Judeo-Christian standard while respecting the beliefs of those who didn't share them, and that standard saved us from

confusion. Today, fewer people believe in the Bible, or even in absolute truth, and our rejection of an objective moral standard has thrown our society into disarray. If in fact we do really believe in God and His word, many of the moral "gray" issues of today become black and white.

Abortion

According to God's word, life begins at conception rather than at the time of delivery or at some arbitrary point during gestation. Psalm 139:13-16 indicates that God knew the writer of these verses while he was yet unformed. In Jeremiah 1:4-5, there is an indication that God knew Jeremiah before he was born and had a special purpose for his life. This is one of several biblical passages that indicate a continuum of life that starts before birth and continues after death. In the Book of Exodus, chapter 21, verses 22–24, it is made quite clear that God considers the life of the unborn to be just as valuable as the life of an adult. When you couple this belief with the commandment, "Thou shalt not kill" (Exodus 20:13), it is clear that abortion is rarely a moral option. Add the commandment to "Love your neighbor as yourself" (Matthew 22:39), and it becomes clear that we ought to help care for mothers put in a tough place by unwanted pregnancies.

Recently I visited a place called the Hope Center in Greenville, Tennessee, where young women with unplanned pregnancies are nurtured, mentored, and encouraged to give birth whether or not they plan to keep the baby. They make provisions for adoption if the young woman chooses not to keep the child and provide resources and support if she wants to

keep the baby. They also facilitate continued education and job training for these young mothers. The center is run by a Christian organization and they are doing exactly what they should be doing. We all need to be proactive in terms of providing solutions for those in our society who have made mistakes, rather than just criticizing them. This is what it means to be truly moral people.

Homosexuality

Another sticky moral issue is the topic of homosexuality. Many people do not understand why Christians object so strongly to gay marriage, but the answers are simply laid out in Scripture. First, several Bible verses reveal God's disapproval of homosexual behavior. For example, Leviticus 20:13 states, "If a man practices homosexuality, having sex with another man as with a woman, both men have committed a detestable act. They must both be put to death, for they are guilty of a capital offense." Jude 7, in the New Testament, says, "And don't forget the cities of Sodom and Gomorrah and their neighboring towns, which were filled with sexual immorality and every kind of sexual perversion. Those cities were destroyed by fire and are a warning of the eternal fire of God's judgment." Second, in Ephesians 5:31-32, Paul wrote, "As the Scriptures say, 'A man leaves his father and mother and is joined to his wife and the two are united into one.' This is a great mystery, but it is an illustration of the way Christ and the church are one." When you see that the Bible compares God's relationship with the church to the relationship between a man and a woman in covenant marriage, it is easy to see why those who believe that marriage

is an institution established by God might be less than enthusiastic about changing the definition of that institution. Some Christians may interpret the Scripture differently, but the text remains fairly clear: Condoning homosexual behavior goes directly against God's commands. Changing the definition of marriage distorts God's illustration of His relationship with us.

This is not to say that God does not love homosexuals, because He most certainly does, just as He loves everyone regardless of their behavior. And Jesus died to pay the price for the shortcomings of everyone. Since there are no perfect people, no one but God has the right to judge our lives outside of criminal activity. Only He knows the minute details of every life from conception to death and can judge matters of the heart.

However, this does not mean that we have to accept man-imposed changes to God's word. We all make choices in life. In this matter, one can choose God's word or the gay marriage agenda. Even though the two are not compatible, people on opposite sides of the issue do not need to be hateful toward the other side. It also should be made quite clear that upholding traditional marriage does not mean that one is a homophobe. It appears almost impossible for the gay community to understand this last point. Whether they understand it or not, it is the job of the Christian community to love everyone as God loves us.

Evolution

Standing somewhat opposed to traditional morality is another form of religion, although its believers would never admit it. This religious belief is the theory of evolution. In this belief system, only the strong survive and there are no moral implica-

tions associated with the actions necessary to survive and thrive. As I have stated and written publicly, it might be more difficult for evolutionists to describe the basis of morality than it would be for a creationist.

This is not to say that those who believe in evolution have no morals, but I was attacked by some biology professors at Emory University in Atlanta for allegedly saying that evolutionists were unethical. I suspected that their real objective was to drum up support for their opposition to my being invited as the commencement speaker at Emory, since I was a creationist and they didn't think that such people had the right to be honored at an institution of higher learning. They started a petition and received many signatures, but a counterpetition received more than four times as many signatures.

I did speak at the commencement and was received very warmly, probably to the chagrin of the intolerant instigators, one of whom subsequently sent me a note of apology stating that they had misinterpreted what I said. Obviously I was not attacking the character of evolutionists, but as is so often the case, many people who disagree with your beliefs find it more convenient to distort them than to refute them, so they can proclaim you to be an idiot.

It is amusing to me that many in the "intellectual community" suggest that those with deeply held religious beliefs are antiscience. Many times I have heard it said of me that my opinions should not be held in high regard, because I believe that God created the earth six thousand years ago. How can anyone, they argue, with such beliefs understand anything about science and medicine, which is based on science.

I can unequivocally state that I love science and understand

and accept its basic laws. I do not know whether the earth is six thousand years old or not, and I'm not sure that such knowledge is important. The Bible says "In the beginning, God created the heavens and the earth." It then goes on to describe the creation week without in any way indicating what the period of time was that elapsed between the first verse of the Bible and the start of creation week. It could have been billions of years, or it could have been less than one day. That means the earth could be billions of years old, or it could have been created in an already mature state by God six thousand years ago.

To say that anyone believing this is stupid and nonscientific is pure demagoguery and bigotry, and certainly is uncharacteristic of a true scientist. The fact that I and millions of others believe that God created the earth and everything on it in an orderly fashion is no more antiscience than believing that something came from nothing, exploded and formed a perfectly organized solar system and universe, particularly in light of the second law of thermodynamics, which states that things tend to move toward a state of disorder. Both beliefs require faith in things that have not been proven and neither has the right to proclaim the other as foolish.

As a doctor, I have to say that it also requires a great deal of faith to believe that an organ system as complex as the kidney or the eye formed through the process of natural selection, which states that things that are not useful to an organ simply disappear, whereas things that are useful are genetically passed on to the next generation. There are many components to organs like the kidney or the eye that are useless without all the other components and, therefore, according to the theory of evolution, should not be passed on to the next generation. In

fact, according to the theory of evolution, without invoking all kinds of convolutions to the theory, it is impossible for any complex organ system to exist unless it just spontaneously formed overnight. That sounds crazy to me, but then again, if you believe that matter can form from nonmatter, I guess you can believe an eyeball can form overnight.

My understanding of science has not precluded my pursuit of a career as a successful neurosurgeon. The claims of some in the scientific community that belief in the theory of evolution is the foundation of all science is pure and unadulterated fantasy. Belief in evolution is just as much associated with religion as belief in creation. They both require faith, either in God or in man.

Unlike godly principles that are uniting in nature, many who believe in the evolutionary approach drive wedges between people by insisting that all intelligent people believe as they do and that anyone with a different belief leaves something to be desired intellectually.

An interesting question that frequently arises during these kinds of discussions is whether or not animals are capable of distinguishing right from wrong. Is it wrong for a lion to kill an innocent lamb or even to kill a human being when it is hungry or even when it is just being a vicious killer? If evolutionary theory is true, nothing should separate humans from animals.

Yet, surprisingly, these kinds of questions are much easier to answer when we are dealing with people as opposed to animals. Unlike animals, we have gigantic frontal lobes in our brains that allow us to extract information from the past and the present, and then formulate a plan that can be projected into the future

to guide our actions. We do not simply have to react to the environment, but can actually alter the environment to satisfy our needs. We have reasoning abilities that far exceed those of animals and our behavior, once we mature, is generally based on choices. Some may say that this impressive ability evolved, but I prefer to think we were given it on purpose. Either way, human beings have a sense of morality that does not jibe with evolutionary theory. It is legitimate to ask the question, "Where did our sense of morality come from?" Even if you enter the deepest, darkest jungles of Borneo, you will find that a thief tends to ply his trade in the darkness, when there is no one around to see him. This is even the case when there have been no missionaries in the area and no Bible to read. All people inherently seem to understand some basic principles of right and wrong. It is much easier to see such morality as God given than trying to explain how it evolved. But everyone is entitled to their beliefs.

Have you ever noticed how difficult it is to sit by and watch someone suffer? Almost everyone will try to help someone who is drowning. That might mean jumping into the water to save her, throwing her a lifesaver, trying to reach her with a pole, or calling for help. As a human being, this is your duty, because you certainly would want someone to do that for you. As an evolutionist who is also an atheist, your "survival-of-the-fittest" mentality should lead you to just walk on by, but of course your deep-seated humanity would not allow such callous behavior in most cases.

So where does that deep-seated humanity come from? Where did my conviction that wantonly killing an innocent bird was wrong come from? Has it evolved, or is it possible that if we

are made in the image of God, there is an innate sense of right and wrong that we all share as human beings? I believe there is good evidence for the latter.

There are no people anywhere that I know of who don't have a sense of right and wrong. Even a cursory reading of the Bible demonstrates that people certainly knew the difference between right and wrong before the time of the Ten Commandments. It was the outrageous behavior of the Israelites that necessitated the physical writing out of a behavioral code, despite the powerful evidences of God in their lives.

I do not believe it to be necessary for us to all agree on the source of morality as long as we agree on the basic principles of what is right and what is wrong. I believe there is general agreement that lying, stealing, and murdering are wrong. There is probably less agreement about what constitutes adultery and whether it is wrong, especially in the nonchurch community. Nevertheless, our guiding principle should be to help rather than harm our fellow man. Doing so earns God's blessing.

Are We "Under God"?

In America we claim to believe in God and in fact proclaim our trust in Him on every piece of our money. Many of our laws are based on the Ten Commandments, and in the bas relief crown molding that adorns the principal chamber of the U.S. Supreme Court, Moses and the tablets containing the Ten Commandments are depicted. Yet we take great pains to delete references to God and the Bible from all public spaces, especially our schools and municipal buildings. We seem to be having a difficult time determining whether we actually believe in

God or whether it is something that we have gotten used to saying in a pro forma manner without actually thinking about our words.

The words *under God* were not in the original version of the Pledge of Allegiance. They were subsequently added to signify the importance of God in every aspect of our lives. Admittedly, the acknowledgment of God in virtually everything we do does not show a great deal of respect for atheists and others who do not harbor traditional views of God, but as the Bible says, you cannot serve both God and man. This does not mean we must force others to believe what we do, but it does mean we have to make a choice as to what we believe and form our societal values around that choice.

In no way does choosing God mean that we need to be unkind to nonbelievers. It is contrary to the American way to force our beliefs on anyone else. By the same token, it is most unreasonable for atheists to make attempts to legally force Christians and their beliefs underground. The persistent attempts by some atheist groups to have the words *under God* removed from our pledge or the phrase "In God we trust" removed from our money should be tolerated because we believe in being fair to everyone, but it is the height of absurdity to seriously consider such challenges in a country where religious freedom and freedom of worship are guaranteed.

Interestingly enough, we in the United States have had many manifestations of God's mercy and favor throughout history. In August of 1776, General George Washington and eight thousand troops were trapped on Long Island with British General Howe preparing to crush them the next morning. The island was surrounded by the British armada. Desperately, Washington

drafted every local seaworthy vessel available, from fishing boats to rowboats, in an attempt to ferry his army across the East River all through the night. At dawn, many of his troops were still in grave danger by their exposure to the huge British fleet. However, most curiously, the fog that usually would rise from the river once the sun rose, did not move. It remained dense long enough for all of Washington's men to escape to safety. This had been the British's best opportunity to clinch the victory over the Americans. Major Ben Tallmadge, who was Washington's chief of intelligence, wrote of that morning:

> As the dawn of the next day approached, those of us who remained in the trenches became very anxious for our own safety, and when the dawn appeared there were several regiments still on duty. At this time a very dense fog began to rise [out of the ground and off the river], and it seemed to settle in a peculiar manner over both encampments. I recollect this peculiar providential occurrence perfectly well, and so very dense was the atmosphere that I could scarcely discern a man at six yards distance . . . we tarried until the sun had risen, but the fog remained as dense as ever.

Like the Israelites in the Bible, we have wandered away from our strong belief in God and many of us now don't seem to know what we believe. Church attendance is steadily declining, especially among the millennials; traditional families are rapidly becoming a rarity; and many of the things forbidden by God are spreading like wildfire. Traditionally, once a nation starts down the path of lack of identity and vision for the future, it is de-

stroyed, or deteriorates from within, losing most or all of its relevance to the world.

Although we appear to be sliding downward, it is possible for us to reverse the trend, even though we are composed of many people with lots of different ideas about morality. It may be hard to agree on the origin of morality but it should not be hard to agree that that sense of morality, should guide our decision making and determine what kind of society we have. As human beings we have a strong sense of right and wrong. As Americans, we have a heritage of Judeo-Christian morality. Let's remember who we are and unite around the vision dictated by our identity.

Action Steps

1. Ask your associates whether they believe absolute right or wrong exists.
2. Ask your friends whether they would be okay with polygamy if most people said it was okay with them.
3. Determine the basis for your moral code. Ask your friends how they have determined theirs.
4. If you believe God to be the author of morality, consider how you can better cultivate a relationship with Him.

17

TAKE COURAGE

Those who fear the Lord are secure; He will be a place of refuge for their children.

PROVERBS 14:26

The power of a determined human being who is not willing to give up is truly inspirational. I have been inspired over the years by many of my patients who have had absolutely devastating diseases. One young lady has endured over one hundred operations and was near death on many occasions, but persevered and graduated from high school in June 2013. Another patient, Mandy, who is well into adulthood now, has faced death on numerous occasions while remaining cheerful, upbeat, and unafraid. She is wheelchair bound and has significant weakness of the upper extremities along with other serious issues, but she will never give up, and even completed a college degree.

The question is do the people of this nation have the determination, drive, and willpower to seize the reins of power and return the country to its place as a beacon of light and inspiration for the world? A nation that is powerful, yet benign? Do

we have the courage to stand up for what we believe or will we continue to cower in the corner and hope no one sees us?

One way to develop courage is to consider what will happen if we fail to act. When considering action, I always do a best/worst analysis. I ask the following four questions about the prospective action:

1. What's the best thing that happens if I do it?
2. What's the worst thing that happens if I do it?
3. What's the best thing that happens if I don't do it?
4. What's the worst thing that happens if I don't do it?

Let's consider these questions with respect to being courageous enough to go against the flow of political correctness and demand your constitutional rights. What is the best thing that happens if we refuse to abide by the dictates of political correctness? I believe that we could return to a nation that truly cherishes freedom of speech and freedom of expression. A nation where people are unafraid to express their opinions and beliefs and are eager to engage in intelligent and constructive conversations about their differences. A nation where we value even those with whom we disagree and work together to accomplish common goals.

What is the worst thing that happens if we oppose political correctness? I believe that every attempt would be made to silence those who oppose political correctness and to make examples of them to discourage others. World history demonstrates that it is very difficult to eradicate every single fighter for freedom.

What is the best thing that happens if we don't oppose po-

litical correctness? I believe we would achieve a very homogeneous society with little original thought but complete harmony. What is the worst thing that happens if we don't oppose political correctness? I believe we could see a dictatorship with brutal domination of any individual or group that opposes the leadership. The worst things that can happen if we don't take action are considerably worse than the worst things that can happen if we do take action. Therefore, we must take action.

This exercise guided me as I considered topics for the National Prayer Breakfast. As it turns out, one of the better outcomes was achieved, because I have encountered thousands of Americans who had given up on our country, and now are reinvigorated and ready to stand up for the freedoms that are guaranteed in our Constitution.

There is no freedom without bravery. As a society, are we free if we tolerate intimidation by government agencies like the IRS? Are we free if we allow the NSA to illegally search and seize our private documents without cause? Are we free if we allow the purveyors of political correctness to muzzle our thoughts and our speech? Are we free if we allow ourselves to be forcibly placed into an ill-conceived health care system that controls the most important thing we have: our lives? Are we free when our government controls every aspect of the business community and stifles the entrepreneurial spirit that built America? We are in the process of relinquishing the freedom that is America. Are we really brave if we allow all these things to occur and keep silent because we're afraid that someone will call us a name?

Freedom is not reserved for those unwilling to fight for it. When you see the American flag, think about George Washing-

ton, who fought alongside his men and led a ragtag bunch of militiamen to a victory over what was then the most powerful empire in the world. Remember Alexander Hamilton, who used his financial wizardry to establish a viable financial structure for a fledgling nation. Consider John Adams and Sam Adams, who were willing to give not only of their resources but also tirelessly of their efforts to establish an understandable legal foundation for our nation. Honor the millions of soldiers who fought and died to preserve our freedom when the world was threatened by tyranny. Revere Dr. Martin Luther King Jr. and his dream of a nation where people were judged by the content of their character and not by the color of their skin. Imitate Henry Ford and Andrew Carnegie, who used their entrepreneurial talents not only to enrich themselves but to provide a mechanism to proliferate and empower the middle class in America.

Why did all of these people toil so relentlessly for an idea? It is because they had a dream of a nation that was different from any other; a nation where people could determine their own destiny and choose their lifestyle based on their own endeavors; a nation where people could choose how to disperse their own wealth after contributing a small, but reasonable amount of their resources to conduct the affairs of government. Through complacency, are we ready to throw away their ideas and the results of their labors?

Our nation was formed by men and women of tremendous courage. If we think about it, I'm sure that each of us can remember numerous brave individuals whom we have encountered throughout life. I am aware of a multitude of my physician colleagues who have stood on principle and faced expensive and embarrassing public malpractice suits when they could have

simply settled the case in secret. These courageous individuals refused to be blamed for bad outcomes when they not only did nothing wrong but had gone the extra mile to try to ensure the patient's well-being. Each such fight will get us closer to badly needed tort reform in our country.

When I was in high school, it was not uncommon for some of the tougher boys to intimidate and control many of the teachers. I was in the marching band and the concert band led by Mr. Dee. He was a short but stocky young man who refused to yield to intimidation. One of the boys who was particularly brutal repeatedly challenged Mr. Dee's leadership and many verbal confrontations ensued. One day after a practice session, Mr. Dee publicly challenged the belligerent young man to back up his verbosity. The two of them remained in the band room after everyone had left and I never knew what actually happened, but I did notice that the troublemaker never challenged Mr. Dee again. This example of courage was not lost on all the other students and demonstrates how teachers can be an important influence on students even outside of their area of expertise.

I have seen numerous examples of courageous patients and families throughout my career. In one case a young family from the western half of our nation had been told that their infant boy had only six months to live after a biopsy at the university hospital proved consistent with a malignant brain stem tumor. With help they made their way to Johns Hopkins Hospital where I performed a series of operations that would have been considered futile by many. The family never lost faith and endured many hardships, but had the courage and fortitude to persist in their efforts to save their child. A few years ago I was

giving a lecture at the university in the home state of that patient and I was approached after the lecture by a young man and his family. It turned out to be the same young man on whom I had operated when he was an infant and he was now a junior at the university and had no neurological deficits. I feel confident in saying that he would not have been alive without the courage and persistence of his family. There are plenty of courageous people out there who can inspire all of us to undertake difficult tasks in order to achieve a better future.

The next time you hear the national anthem, think about what it means: "Oh, say does that star-spangled banner yet wave / O'er the land of the free and the home of the brave?" We are still the home of the brave, and it is time for us to stand up and preserve our flag and our freedoms.

EPILOGUE

We all have a tendency to assume that our day-to-day routines will continue as usual without catastrophes. I certainly made that assumption on March 20, 2012.

I was driving to work and was one block away from the hospital, entering an intersection with the green light in my favor. Another driver ran the red light on the perpendicular street going sixty miles per hour. Our cars met in the intersection and the next thing I knew there were flashing lights, police, and medics all around. My air bags had deployed and my car was completely destroyed.

I was relieved as I examined myself and found only a few minor scrapes and abrasions, as well as some chest discomfort from the explosive force of the steering air bag. My cell phone was broken, but an officer lent me his phone so I could call my wife. I also called the operating room to let them know that I would be slightly delayed, but intended to get there in time to

complete the operations that were scheduled that morning. I convinced the officials that I was okay, and one of the police officers pried open the trunk to retrieve my briefcase. He then drove me the rest of the way to the hospital, where I completed three operations without incident.

Since that experience, I have frequently thought about how lucky I was to have not been killed or seriously injured that day. I keep a picture of the mangled mass that used to be my car on my phone to remind me of how fleeting life can be. Tomorrow is not guaranteed to any of us, and if something needs to be done, it is usually best to just go ahead and do it, rather than engage in endless cogitation with no action.

If we are not an exceptional nation, we can quietly continue our slide into insignificance, but if this is the America of Washington, Franklin, Lincoln, Kennedy, Edison, Ford, King, and the millions who gave their lives for our freedom, then we must shake off the indifference that has gradually stolen our pride and our freedom and threatens the future of our children. We must exercise our duty as responsible and informed citizens and actively shape the nation we desire by investing time, resources, and energy into choosing appropriate leaders who share our vision. In some cases, we may even need to offer ourselves as candidates for public office.

Who knows what tomorrow holds for each of us and for our nation? We have no time to waste. Today is the day to act. Resolve to take one step toward helping our nation return to greatness. If we all do so, we cannot fail to remain "one nation, under God, indivisible, with liberty and justice for all."

The New Beginning

ACKNOWLEDGMENTS

Many thanks to those who made this book possible, including Sealy Yates, Adrian Zackheim, Bria Sandford, Will Weisser, Washington Speakers Bureau, Audrey Jones, Stephanie Marshall, my many medical colleagues and patients, Armstrong Williams, and Xavier Underwood.

INDEX

"I wrote this book to encourage every citizen to think about the Constitution and to help defend it from those who misinterpret and undermine it. In our age of political correctness, it's especially important to defend the Bill of Rights, which guarantees our freedom to speak, bear arms, practice our religion, and much more." —DR. BEN CARSON

COMING ON OCTOBER 6—ORDER NOW FROM YOUR FAVORITE BOOKSELLER

For more information, visit www.bencarsonbook.com.